£2.99

C000148089

ANTHONY LE MOIGNAN

IN ANOTHER LIFETIME

First published in Great Britain 2020

Copyright © 2020 by Anthony Le Moignan
All rights reserved

The moral right of the author has been asserted

No part of this book may be used or reproduced in any manner whatsoever without permission in writing from the author, except in the case of brief quotations embodied by critical articles or reviews

Anthony Le Moignan
www.anthonylemoignan.com

Author photograph by Dan White

Printed and bound in Great Britain by Biddles Ltd, King's Lynn

First Printing: April 2020

Paperback ISBN: 978-1-9995902-3-9

Preface

IT'S NOW 36 hours since it happened.

I was counting in minutes until a whole day had passed; that's 1,440 minutes in case you're curious. I'm writing this down because if I don't, I won't believe what I've experienced—won't believe what's happened to me.

Dawn was half-an-hour ago, and I know that if I look out of my bedroom window, the people of Cambridge will be starting to populate the street outside my parents' home. They'll be walking along the pavement, greeting each other with a brief smile, or a nod, or maybe both, as is common across the world in the Very Early Morning club.

This cheerfulness is deeply painful to observe. It's as if they don't realise the world as we once knew it has ended, and I resent them, all of them, for their happy, blissful ignorance. The heavy crimson curtains I was so proud of in my teenage, gothic years remain tight-drawn, untidily and frantically overlapped for fear of intrusion.

My friends (and I don't have that many) appear to be in a form of social limbo towards me. They desperately want to make contact, to find out all the gory details, to discover what it feels like, but nobody's actually called me.

Sure, there have been emails, texts, and messages on WhatsApp, but that doesn't count; not to me at any rate. I think I'm very easy-going by nature, so I'm not entirely sure what they're worried about. I guess I'd be the same as them, though; wanting to know but not daring to ask.

I've gone through a plethora of emotions (or is it a *gamut*?—I'm not certain, and I don't think there's a collective noun for emotions). And, as you'll already have deduced, I'm at the point where I can't keep my mind from wandering. I think I may be dying from shock or from heartache. Maybe both?

I used to have a lot more friends, but once I moved in with Rick, they sort of fell away into the background. It was a very gradual and organic process, so I didn't really notice.

Looking back now, it seems that one day I was going to the bars and clubs and parties every weekend with my mates, then one day I was wondering how many months or even years it had been since I'd done that.

Rick, you see, wasn't very keen on that side of me. But don't get me wrong—it wasn't as if his preferences were against my will; far from it. It actually made me feel warm and wanted, knowing that his whole world was me.

I think there's a fine line between over-protective jealousy and an all-encompassing desire for someone—to want to spend every moment with them. I never felt the urge to curtail Rick's nights out with his friends (and there were many—nights out and friends), but he just preferred me to stay at home. Thinking back, it was never a demand, but more like a carefully applied preference—a soothing balm for a minor burn.

Initially, he was cool with me going to the cinema with a friend or two (girls only, obviously) but then there'd be the dilemma about contact. Rick liked to be able to call if he became *worried* (his word) about my *well-being* (ditto), and the necessity for phones to be switched off in a cinema was at odds with these requirements.

We found a temporary solution when I set the ringtone to vibrate only, but when he called (most times), I'd need to scurry past irritated people and run up the aisle whilst answering, and half the time I'd miss his call. When I phoned back a moment later from the foyer, it nearly always went to voicemail.

I even started sitting at the end of a row for easy access to the exit when he called, but then I'd start to feel self-conscious about this bizarre behaviour. None of my friends commented, but I could tell they thought it was a bit odd. No matter; I trained myself to believe it was their jealousy about the closeness of my relationship—the strength of Rick's love for me and mine for him.

When I think about that now, I feel deeply ashamed. I want to go and crawl back under my clumped and creased bed sheets, to a place where Mum's incessant door-knocking and never-ending questions are just a distant, indecipherable thrum.

Dad's voice is more than a thrum. However hard I wrap a pillow around my ears, his words come through loud and clear. His most consistent sentence is very short and very repetitive—*I told you.*

Right from the very start five years ago, he never liked Rick. I tried to remember some of the words Dad used, to see if it made more sense now—*Sulky; moody; sullen. Lippy* was a favourite, and usually followed close on the heels of a rare conversation between them.

Yet none of those descriptions rang any alarm bells for me. Apart from ...

3

A sinister chant rolls over and envelops me like a general anaesthetic seeping into the veins, cold and dangerous; *I don't trust the lad.*

With hindsight, *that* was an observation I couldn't fault. It was devastatingly accurate and took the breath out of me yet again, reducing me to a sobbing wreck—a huddled ball of salty dribble and snotty self-pity.

Everyone's witnessed this scene unfold on a television, at the cinema, or read with clammy, page-turning fingers. It's something we all know will never happen to us, but enthrals and appals us all in equal measure, like an atrocity on a far-away continent.

When you steal a look at your loved one and they're unaware—your partner for life—the one that makes everything so perfect that you genuinely feel sorry for everyone who doesn't have this magical connection —why is it that you sometimes dance with the devil and visualise this scene of ultimate destruction?

45 hours earlier

WE'D ARRANGED I'd get to my parents' house by eight a.m. Rick was never the best at time-keeping, and mornings weren't his strong suit either, so Mum had factored this into the itinerary—she knew her future-son-in-law's shortcomings, though there were few in her eyes.

A little after eight-fifteen and my dad is shifting inexorably from agitation to anger, fidgeting in the driver's seat of our family Volvo. Rick is loading my carry-on bag next to my mother's two large suitcases, in the necessarily cavernous boot.

He leans in the rear window and kisses me on the lips. It doesn't linger, not much more than a peck, and I choose to

4

believe this is shyness—he's framed squarely in the reflection of Dad's door mirror.

My boyfriend moves around the back of the car and hugs my mum, giving her a kiss on the cheek as they part. She giggles, I mutter, Dad revs the engine.

Rick stoops a little so his face is now exactly in line with Dad's passenger-door mirror, waves at him, winks and shouts *Laters*, a few decibels louder than the three or four thousand revs of mechanical thrash coming from under the Volvo's bonnet—no mean feat.

Then a moment I'll never forget and will probably spend the rest of my life trying to fathom out; he presses his opened palm on my window and gestures for me to do the same. Our hands pair either side of the slightly tinted glass, mimicking some high-security prison visiting-wing, and he mouths *'Penny for them, Tabby.'*

In the last few tortuous hours this image has returned to me in ultra-high definition, again and again and again. It's like a three-second GIF someone might place on their Twitter-feed—if you don't continue scrolling to the next Tweet, it loops over and over in the ether, taunting you to watch just one more time.

Why did you say that, Rick?

*

Mum and I were off to Santorini for a fortnight, and this would be the longest period of time that Rick and I had been apart in five years. Living together in a rented apartment for the last three, we nevertheless still had what most would consider a honeymoon-period relationship. I won't be drawn

5

into specifics or statistics, but I'm sure you know what I mean.

The last night had been no different. If anything, Rick was even more passionate than usual. I put it down to the time we'd be apart and the longing for each other in those two weeks.

The destination sounded far more exotic than the itinerary. I'm not suggesting it was a back-packing holiday, but the hotel wouldn't be sprouting from one of the blindingly white cliff-faces of the island. The flight to our destination involved little legroom, a seat-back void of any tilting movement, and an airport with a seriously tenuous relationship to London, whatever they chose to call it.

It was a holiday that Mum had been pestering my dad to go on for ages, but he loathed hot climates, and this was his compromise; he paid, and his wife and daughter went instead.

We arrived a good half-hour before the airline's suggested time, Dad putting it down to a highly unusual lack of traffic. Mum had congratulated him on his driving prowess and winked at me—the ETA was just about as she'd planned.

There was no real surprise when the flight wasn't running to schedule, such are the vagaries of low-cost air travel. However, as we approached the third hour of delays (the point at which compensation from this airline came into play), there was talk amongst the passengers of a cancellation.

Two large glasses of white wine later, up went the notice which everyone was by now expecting—the flight to Santorini had been put back to the same time on the following day.

An efficient coach service saved the necessity to call Dad out, and we eventually arrived back in Cambridge alongside the evening rush-hour traffic. Mum took a taxi home with her two maxed-out suitcases, while I chose to walk the short distance from the bus-stop to our apartment in Mill Road.

I'd tried a couple of times to call Rick during the day, but his phone went straight to voicemail, which wasn't a surprise as the battery was on its last legs. I left a brief message but didn't expect a call back—it was no problem anyway, as I had my own door key with me.

I was smiling as I unlocked the door—it was an unexpected extra night for us—perhaps we'd have a meal somewhere or a quiet night in. Whatever we did, I was reasonably confident how our night would finish. I was still smiling to myself as I walked into the bedroom.

I saw her back first.

I'd so like to report that it should more appropriately have been housed in the desperately sad embers of the Cathédrale Notre-Dame, but …

Young—so young; perfectly bronzed, slim, yet muscular. Above all, swaying—slowly gyrating, snake-like goddess, not of my world.

Be gone—be in that cathedral as it burns—leave my sight now—leave us now.

Then Rick's sweat-sheened face, mystically rising and sinking above her left shoulder-blade, in the dimmed lighting of my, yes, *MY*, fake Tiffany lamp.

Eye contact. Game over. End of world.

Please let me die or wake; either, but hurry.

There are three words which bond a relationship.
There are six which tear it to shreds.

'It's not what it looks like.'

Penny for them, Rick.

1

CHAT ROOM Terms of Engagement – Click one of the 2 options below after reading our rules:
1) Treat people as you would in real life – be courteous and respectful
2) Do NOT annoy anyone or cause them distress
3) Do NOT swear. The C word will get you <u>an immediate lifetime ban</u>. The F word will be frowned upon and <u>may get you banned</u>. Even the S word could be a problem.

Spitfire Chat is for members with a common interest in the Triumph Spitfire sports car (all models built from 1962 to 1980).

I ACCEPT THE RULES AND WISH TO ENTER SPITFIRE CHAT

I DO NOT ACCEPT THE RULES (YOU WILL BE REDIRECTED FROM THIS PAGE)

SPITFIRECHAT.COM - August 02 2018—(local time / Sydney, Aus : 02.26)
GrantyBoyMkIII ::

GD3: It's not a problem Tabby, he died happily! And just where he'd have chosen! LOL!

TABS: God I'm so sorry Grant. I had no idea! Would never have asked you - feel awful now. ☹

GD3: Hey, no sweat. REALLY! Gramp Albi was V V eccentric! He bought the car new in 1967 and drove it until they took his licence away when he was 94. So that would have been ermmmmmmm about 2002. He stuck the car in a wooden shed in his garden and just used to sit in it. He was a bit bonkers if I'm honest.

TABS: Poor Albi, that's terrible. And did you, you know, find him? Like ... in the car?

GD3: Nahhhh my dad did. We hadn't seen or heard from him in a couple of days, so Dad went round to Gramp's place. It was a really cold winter so we checked on him regularly. That was a blessing really. No messy stuff. What I mean is, he was really cold and not ... yukky.

TABS: Oh bloody hell! That's terrible - urrgh. But you said he lived to 100? That's awesome!

GD3: 101 just. He got a birthday message from the Queen – he was so proud of that. Had it framed and put on his mantelpiece next to Nan's ashes. They were in a box, obvs.

TABS: Obvs! LOL! So did he love the royal family then? It's gone mad over here since Harry and Meghan got hitched and the baby and the blah etc.

GD3: Oh yeah, he was nuts on the Queen! While I was busy being born we had this prime minister over here – Paul Keating. Bloody hell, Gramp HATED him! He actually touched the queen when she toured Aus which apparently is a big NO-NO, and he wanted your bit of brit flag removed from our Aussie one. My total fave part of Gramp was the joke he used to tell at parties. Sooooooo funny! Even after hearing it forever. LOL!

TABS: Nearly as funny on here, or do I have to hear it for maximum effect?

GD3: Dunno – here we go. The Queen and Prince Philip and Paul Keating are on a stage in front of thousands of people, and before Keating starts his speech he turns to the Queen and says 'I've decided we're going to become the Kingdom of Australia.' So the Queen quietly informs him that he won't be doing that because he isn't a king. All good so far?

TABS: Yep ☺

GBP3: So Keating says fair enough, but in that case it's going to be the Principality of Australia. And the Queen says again, with respect, that won't be happening either because he isn't a prince. At which point Prince Philip leans forward and suggests to Mr. Keating that he should stick to being a country.

TABS: Ummmmmm ... I don't get it. ☹
TABS: OH HAH! Hahahahahahahahaha!! ☺☺☺ BRILLIANT!!! ☺

GD3: Yeah, I'm howling now and I knew the punchline! I wonder if I'll get an immediate lifetime ban? Chat Room rules and all that...

TABS: Oh God, that is soooooo funny!!! I'd love to have met Gramp.

GD3: I might have been a lot more normal if it wasn't for Gramp. Still, at least I got to drive around in my, sorry OUR dream car. Pity you're the other side of the world or I'd ask you out for a spin.

TABS: I'd really like that. I can't believe you managed to build it back to brand new condition again. I'd love to be able to do that but I don't have a clue. I'm not sure I could even change the spark plugs. I'd love to try one day tho.

GD3: Well if your dad owned a garage and you started working in it as an apprentice mechanic, you'd be just the same as me. It's actually a hell of a lot easier than you think. Welllll, as long as you don't mind the occasional bit of oil on your hands and face and a few cuts and bruises?

TABS: Not at all! Especially if I was working on my own Spitty. Do you think I could ever find that one in the photograph when I was a kid?

GD3: Doubt it. ☹ If you knew who'd owned it that would be a good start, but standing next to one in the street 25 years ago makes things pretty much impossible. A lot of them are in the great scrapheap in the sky now. But you'll find the same model – if you're really lucky you might even get the same colour. I'd help you but being the other side of the world makes it a bit tricky. But... you never know...

TABS: That's a lovely thought. ☺ Hey, I have to go have dinner and you need to go to bed. It must be nearly 4am now?! How will you get up for work?!

GD3: No sweat - I had a zizz earlier this evening.

TABS: Sorry again. I always seem to be keeping you up – it's not fair on you. ☹

13

GD3: Honestly it's no prob. I really like chatting with you. A lot.

TABS: Me too. I'd better go now. How about I log on during lunch tomorrow?

GD3: Sure, I'll be here. Big hug from me until then. XX *gone*

TABS: And you. Hey and thanks—you make me smile ☺ XX *gone too*

CHAT ENDED

*

Grant looked again at the profile photo of Tabatha. A small child grinning straight into the centre of her dad's camera lens, an arm resting on the front wing of a bright red Triumph Spitfire. For the umpteenth time he tried to imagine what she'd look like now, but it wasn't really possible.

When you knew what the grown-up looked like and they showed you a picture of themselves when very young, it was easy to make the connection, but the other way around was impossible for him.

They'd first connected last month, and he'd suggested a chat on WhatsApp or FaceTime, but she wasn't keen on giving out her number. She'd apologised for being hesitant and wary, but the last thing she wanted was to give him the wrong impression; she'd recently come out of a very messy split with a guy, and just wanted the anonymity of a chatroom for now.

He'd hung onto those last two words. Like most Aussies, he was positive by nature—she'd change her mind one day. At the moment, their mutual admiration of a little old British sports car would have to suffice. Almost insignificant, really, but without that in common, they'd never have met in the first place.

He knew what it was like to go through a rough time at the end of a relationship. Grant had only ever been out with one girl, meeting Kimberley at a youth club when he was seventeen. They'd travelled extensively on Inter-State table tennis championships, both of them junior singles champions of New South Wales.

He'd been with her for six years, but then the subtle little signs crept up—all was not right. The extended periods of radio silence and unanswered messages. The looks from team-mates who all seemed to know more than he did.

He eventually discovered it was his best friend—a guy he practiced and played doubles with—someone who always hung out with the two of them.

After that, it was a rough couple of years, and a period that he'd managed to come through only by burying himself in the restoration of his grandfather's car.

Sure, he'd made out to Tabby that he'd been working on it for years and years, but the truth would have to wait a while. However bizarre it felt and sounded, this woman he'd known for only a month, a woman whose voice he'd never heard and face he'd never seen, had become the focal point of his life.

*

'No, I don't know what he looks like, but why should that matter?'

Tabatha's mum remained unconvinced.

'Doesn't it tell you something when he's staying up into the middle of his night just to chat with you? Don't you want to know what he looks like? I certainly would.'

'Well that's you, but I really don't have any interest. I know he's five years younger than me, I know we like the same music, and I know we like the same car. That's plenty.'

Tabatha folded her arms.

'Plenty for now, but it's six months since Rick. I hate to see you moping about on your own, sweetie.'

Tracey put the somewhat dried-out chicken breast on the table in front of her daughter, sliding the salad bowl towards her.

'And that's been simmering in the oven for an extra twenty minutes. I do wish you'd tell me when you want to eat.'

Tabatha sighed inwardly and thought about leaving home yet again. As her mum said, it had been about six months since the world had blown up in her face.

She could still hear Rick pleading that it was all a complete misunderstanding.

Well, that part, at least, was true.

She landed on her parents' doorstep an hour later, the taxi driver helping her with the suitcases, filled with the last three years of her life.

In the months that followed, relationships with her mum and dad had become strained. They were great—both wonderful parents in their own right—but she was a 30-year-old woman, not a teenage daughter.

Grant was the best thing that had happened to her in a long while. He made her happy, he made her smile, but above all, he made her laugh. As the days went by, she found herself torn between desperately wanting to hear his voice and see his face, but not wanting to know anything more about him than she did already.

At the moment, everything was almost perfect except for the stumbling block of a nine-hour time difference, and that was a tricky one to fix. Her parents had heard her howling with laughter on many occasions, even though in the locked privacy of her bedroom. Grant managed to say things in his typed words which really did make her Laugh-Out-Loud.

Once or twice, Tabatha had made up her mind she would ping him a photo if he asked for one, but when she was braced, the occasion didn't arise. Then, when he eventually suggested exchanging pictures, she wasn't mentally prepared for it, making some hopeless excuse.

She knew this couldn't go on; she'd already taken dozens of selfies to get the image she thought best reflected her personality, then deleted nearly all of them for portraying her as a total gork.

It was just the same when she first met Rick—the pathetic indecisiveness—never knowing what to wear and what to say when they went out together.

Something had to change though, because she feared the mental-image she was building of Grant would be wildly inaccurate.

Even worse, the opposite might be happening. Grant may at this very moment be imagining her to be some goddess with long blonde hair and an impossibly-perfect figure, all wrapped up in flawless, tanned skin. Well, she had blonde hair—sort of. It sure wasn't long, though, and as for the tan, she really didn't like the sun that much at all. Figure-wise, she could probably do with putting *on* a few pounds, if anything, which meant he was bound to crave a voluptuous figure.

She'd told him her height. He was talking about how some people can feel cramped in the tiny interior of a Triumph Spitfire, and he'd said that anyone over six foot might need to order a seat-rail extender kit. It was fine, she'd told him; there'd be no need for the extra expense as she was '*less than that.*'

His interest had been piqued; it must have been, because he'd broken an unwritten rule and asked her a directly personal question.

'*Okay great. So how tall are you, then? Oh, I mean just approximately—from a car situ, so to speak? I'm five foot ten, maybe a tiny bit more—not that you asked or need to know.*'

She'd laughed and couldn't type for a moment. Then when she could, her fingers hovered after she'd pressed the *5* key. This was absurd; she was five-foot-five. She'd Googled it, and that was exactly the average height for a woman in the UK.

Tabatha had no idea why she was pausing or what all the fuss was about. Reassured, she typed '*It's okay, silly—I'm 5'6, maybe a tiny bit more.*"

She made a mental note to explore shoe shops for slightly higher heels than her norm. Thankfully, Cambridge had an abundance of good shoe shops. Students, traffic, and shoe shops.

*

Grant couldn't help it—he visualised holding his ex, Becky, in his arms; he just couldn't help it. She was 5'6" and it felt so right. It was a small pang, but a pang nonetheless—that little bit of breathlessness as he thought of her with his best-now-worst mate. Then the present interrupted his dark thoughts.

'*That's a great height. You'll fit perfectly—nice and snug. Behind the steering wheel. Like in the driving seat, I mean.*'

'*Well, not perfect by any means, but average. Just average.*'

Tabatha was whispering '*Shoe shops*' to herself in a mantra-like state as they signed off.

Grant went to bed at 3.45 a.m., as was now becoming the norm. Sleep escaped him, though; why on earth hadn't he told her he was 5'9"? Was he stupid or something? And what was that '*maybe a little more*' rubbish he'd added? He'd need to get some new shoes—maybe the ones with a disguised inner-sole, to give an extra inch or so …

2

A WEEK later, Tabatha was being kept awake by the raised voices of her mother and father. The words were indecipherable, but the tone and rhythm were unmistakable. It was an argument of sorts, which was a rare occurrence.

David Mercer had taken retirement recently. A career in banking which culminated as manager in the local high street branch had given his wife and daughter a comfortable lifestyle.

The lack of a regular income was buoyed by his retirement package, shares in the bank, and an apartment he'd recently purchased near Cambridge Station. Home was a fairly large terraced property in Brookside, less than a mile from the station.

Tabatha had no brothers or sisters, living the life that always seems the sole preserve of an only child. Refreshingly, she had shunned a lot of the trappings and worked hard during school holidays to eventually almost self-fund her university years. Admittedly, fees at St Catharine's College were substantially less than for most, as her accommodation involved little more than a ten-minute walk to and from home each day.

She somewhat envied the first real escapism her peers were experiencing and regularly stayed with friends in their dorms over weekends. Nevertheless, she was secretly happy to know she'd not be strapped with a heavy student loan for the first years of her working life.

As her parents and tutors had expected, she attained a First-Class Honours Degree in English Literature, then followed a path, initially as an events-organiser at a local bookstore, before starting her own small PR and Promotions online-company from home.

It was a career-move which shocked and worried her father—self-employment was something completely alien to him—there was nothing as safe as a regular monthly wage.

In the beginning, her dad had certainly been right. The main contract she'd been relying upon when quitting the bookstore—the one her manager had promised as a close friend—failed to come to fruition. It was a new independent book publisher based in Bury St Edmunds. Everything was in place to take the publishing world by storm. Everything, that is, except the finances.

Tabatha had been putting in 70-hour weeks in tandem with a local website designer, but neither was getting paid bar the first small retainer. It certainly wasn't the intention of their young client, who had a clear vision of taking on the major publishing houses at their own game, but she was forced to pull the plug on the venture after nearly ten months.

'*A year's free work*,' as Dad was inclined to remind her on an irritatingly regular basis.

During this time, she'd worked closely with Rick, the owner of the website design company. The common bond of their spiralling debts brought them together for drinks of solace at various pubs around the Colleges of Cambridge.

It seemed only natural to meet up physically after working remote ten-hour days in their respective homes, constantly online to each other, attempting to solve the myriad problems a start-up business throws up.

Rick was a charmer, though she certainly wasn't conscious of that fact at the time. *Subliminally mindful* would have been a fairer assessment.

He could almost have been a very good spy, such was the ordinariness and averageness of his appearance. His hair, or lack of it, was the one feature of note. Suffering from hereditary early hair loss (he claimed he was nicknamed '*Slaphead*' at school, and who would lie about that), Rick had taken the decision many men believed was the only solution—he'd shaved his head. Aside from that one quirk, he was the definitive Joe Average.

Average, that is, until talking to an attractive woman. Even the *attractive* part wasn't essential. Conversely, he would border on rudeness when introduced to men. But, with women, he would flirt, flatter and charm at random, and with no small amount of finesse.

Naturally, Tabatha was the last person to learn of this, having already been anaesthetised by his predominant skill-set. On the few occasions Rick visited Tabatha's house during their relationship, David Mercer would implore his daughter to come to her senses; to '*see the lad for what he is*'.

Unsurprisingly, Tracey Mercer thought Rick was delightful. She would have had him as her son-in-law in a heartbeat.

*

Post-bombshell, life for Tabatha revolved around waking up late, little or no lunch, then replaying the last few years of her life in a continual loop of ever-spiralling desolation.

Stomach problems led to tests and a diagnosis of gluten intolerance. Not on a celiac level as some poor souls suffered, but enough that the gluten-free food she now consumed had caused a loss of weight. For some people, a joy, but Tabatha was now on the very slim side.

She ventured into the attic one day through sheer boredom, coming across a cardboard box filled with family photographs. For some reason, she particularly remembered the one beside a little red sports car. Even now, she could hear her father; '*Say cheese, Tabby.*'

Through the randomness of chance and the vagaries of the internet, she now exchanged voiceless words with someone who proved her heart was still beating. The wall she'd built around it in the past few months was beginning to crumble, loth as she was to admit that to herself.

*

Tabby saw Grant first in a dream.

She was expecting him and waited outside her house. Brilliant sunshine reflected off the chrome bumpers of the little sports car—the one in the photo. He'd restored it for her, and it was now better than new. From a distance, she could see the top was down, the interior hazy in the sticky heat of the day.

He wore a red and white baseball cap backwards, but she could still make out dark hair underneath. And the tan—not a colour that anyone in the UK could achieve, no matter how much they diced with future melanomas.

The smile exposed the teeth, the whiteness emphasised by the contrasting tan. And he was looking directly at her; even from this distance, she could see him staring at her, smiling.

Then her eyes were drawn to the passenger seat. The car carried two people, not one. There would be no room for her in this car, because another person, another man, sat in the passenger seat.

Rick was sitting next to Grant.

She heard her cry before consciousness surfaced. Sweat trickled as she grabbed her phone to see the time—*04.06*. As had become a habit in the past few weeks, she added nine hours to calculate where Grant would be at this moment— probably on a lunch break at his dad's garage. If she'd had the number, Tabatha would have called him this very moment, but she didn't.

Scrolling through the apps on her phone, she brought up the chatroom and checked his status. He was offline— obviously. There was a facility to leave a message; she thought carefully before committing to any note.

Perhaps that unique middle-of-the-night atmosphere compelled her, or perhaps it was the dream. No matter, the words which followed ramped up their current friendship, and she now felt comfortable with this.

I've just woken up at 4 in the morning after a weird dream. I would have called you but don't have your number. Here's mine: +44 (obvs! ☺) 7797 658492. Goodnight. Or Gnight as you'd say. Xx

Tabatha was about to press *Send* when she held back and pondered. Looking through her photo library, she found the selfie she least disliked and attached it to the message.

ps You already have one piccy of me—here's another taken 23 years later. x

And then she took a deep breath and pressed *Send*.

*

Grant felt and heard a *brrrr-ting* in his overalls pocket. Although offline in the Spitfire chatroom, he'd set things up so any direct messages would still come through immediately. Under an elderly Australian Holden at the time, he pushed the wheeled-trolley he was laying on and temporarily flinched as his head appeared from under the car and into the blinding Sydney winter sun.

Tabatha was even more stunning than he'd imagined, and he'd visualised her as being beautiful. He had three almost simultaneous thoughts:

How would his dad react to the request for an extended holiday?

How quickly could he get to England?

Should he send one of the many selfies he'd taken specifically for this occasion, or should he take a fresh one now?

On a whim, he lay back down on the mechanic's trolley, held the phone at arm's length directly above him, and looked at the image on the screen.

Two days of beard bristle—a result of middle-of-the-night chats and close-to-the-wire morning alarms.

Oil on the forehead and on one side of his face.

Hair wasn't an issue—always cut short enough to always look the same—whatever he did and wherever he was.

Conveniently, it was also very dark hair, so any motor oil wouldn't be too noticeable.

He took three shots in quick succession, just to make sure his eyes were open in at least one. As satisfied as he could be, he added a caption to what he thought was the least worst one.

And here's another taken 23 seconds later. x

He pressed *Send.*

Grant rolled himself back under the Holden and resumed work on a stubborn rusted exhaust bracket, but his mind was now on the other side of the world.

*

'It's good to see you eating some breakfast, however late it is. You look a little perkier too—some good news?'

Tracey was keenly attuned to her daughter's every mood, however irritating that might sometimes be for Tabatha.

'Yeah, I'm okay. I woke up in the middle of the night; a really bad dream I can't remember now.'

Tabatha had two fingers on the screen of her phone, enlarging the image of Rick's face. She was about to screen capture the new image when she noticed her mum peering from the other side of the table.

'Now *he's* a good-looking boy; *very* good-looking. Is that your lad Down Under? I thought you didn't have a picture of him?'

'Oh Mum.'

Tabatha quickly saved the enhanced image and turned her phone face-down.

'I couldn't get back to sleep after that nightmare, so I sent him a quick message and a photo. He sent one back—no big deal.'

She was tempted to turn the phone over again for another quick glimpse, but made do with a forkful of scrambled egg instead.

Her mum was now smiling in a knowing way, which was sweet, annoying, and slightly embarrassing, all at the same time. Tabatha felt about fourteen.

'Well all I can say is, it's a shame he doesn't live in Cambridge. He looks a nice boy, though I guess that's not very complimentary nowadays. Is *hot* the right word? He's definitely that, and I've only seen him upside down. Is it a bad photo or is he really that tanned?'

Her mum's food was delicious as always (as was nearly everything Mum cooked), but Tabatha was sorely tempted to jump ship and run upstairs for some peace. She needed to focus on a balanced reply to Grant, who would by now have finished his dinner and be watching a vitally important game for his Sydney Swans.

He was crazy on Australian Rules Football, a game she'd checked out on YouTube and found completely bizarre, though she hadn't shared this opinion with him. The Swans were apparently in a very good position to win the league.

From Tabatha's perspective, there was just one problem with Grant's looks—it made her wonder if he'd behave in the same way as Rick. Neurons zapped together, and she recalled the dream, surprised at the similarity of her image and his photo.

Grant would be very different from Rick—he had to be. She so wanted to believe this, that she accepted her judgement could be skewed.

The next step was obvious; talk with him on the phone, then progress to FaceTime. Maybe this would tell her all she needed to know.

Up in the privacy of her bedroom, she stared at his picture on her laptop. The bigger the image, the stronger the spell.

She sent another message attempting as cool a response as she could manage, though her feelings were anything but that. If he had a few minutes at half-time, then perhaps he'd like to phone for a quick chat? ...

*

'You sound soooo British. Lovely, though. Kind of exactly how I imagined. It's great to talk at last, Tabby—thanks for your number.'

'And you sound soooo Aussie. Hey, am I interrupting your footie? How's it going?'

'Ah, shithouse. No problems though—we have twenty-minute breaks at halftime. We're seventeen points down at the mo against the Magpies—that's Collingwood in case you didn't know—but I have a funny feeling we'll turn it around. Never mind about my footy, though, what are *you* up to?'

'Oh, just chilling in my room. Was that oil on your face, by the way? I wondered if you'd put it on just for me?'

Tabatha surprised herself by teasing him, but it felt very natural.

'I did, actually. I wanted to underline that when you work on your own Spitty, you're in for some serious mess. It served a purpose as well, 'cos my natural hair colour is grey. I went that colour before I was twenty, so I just used some engine oil for effect.'

'What? Really? Well, okay, that's cool. Yeah, that's fine—no probs. Hey wait a minute, you ...'

Tabatha could hear stifled laughing in her ear.

'You louse! Pants on fire! My mum warned me about Aussie guys – *'bunch of liars'*, she said.'

'Ouch, honestly? Bet she didn't; bunch of convicts, maybe.'

It felt as if she could hear his smile.

Tabatha would have been quite happy to stay on the phone with Grant all night.

'I'll be honest, unlike you—Mum was slightly more complimentary, actually. I can't believe I'm going to tell you this, but she caught sight of the photo and said you were *'hot'*. That's when I, like, ran up to my room and locked the door.'

She was grateful that blushes couldn't be heard.

'Wow. Well you can pass on a message to Mum; please tell her I'm over the moon about the compliment, and can she send me a photo of her guide-dog one day—I love Labs. You, on the other hand, are something else.'

Her face was pretty much on fire, now. Stuck for something to say that wouldn't sound moronic, Tabatha said the last thing she wanted.

'I'm going to be encroaching on the second-half. Get back to your footy and let me know how your team got on, eh? I'd better go now.'

Grant was disappointed but had a moment of inspiration:

'Oh okay, but tell you what—how about chatting on FaceTime tonight instead of in the chatroom? I mean, we know what each other looks like now—well, apart from my grey hair, obviously. Are you alright with that? I won't take no for an answer, so if you don't fancy answering when I call later, don't pick up. Fair enough?'

Short of a lost Wi-Fi connection or death, Tabatha was going to be taking his call.

She was already planning make-up, hairstyle, and perfume as she said goodbye, though the latter might not work its spell on this occasion.

3

RICK HAD never been the same after Tabatha. It wasn't so much that he'd been caught *in flagrante delicto*, though that would have been an indescribable horror of horrors for her. No, it was *why* it had happened that killed him.

It was said that once was a mistake and twice was a choice, and he would never, *ever* choose that course of action again. There was never a clearer case of *Needs Must*.

His older brother, happily married with three kids, a dog, a mortgage, and a set of golf clubs, was staggeringly unsympathetic towards his only sibling and didn't want to hear any of the '*tragic excuses*'.

His theory was that Rick not only invited this cataclysmic *faux pas* by his actions, but positively revelled in the potential for their disastrous and total finality.

Rick never owned a property, always happy to rent until the current relationship exploded, then ran to his brother's house and the small games-room, which seemed to constantly double as his single-status digs. It contained a battered ex-pub pool table with torn baize, a plastic foosball table, and a darts board, plus a single put-you-up bed. All of this was contained at the end of the garden, in what most people would have fairly described as a garden chalet.

But Tabby was different.

In the aftermath, the apartment they'd rented for three years had lay unoccupied for months, but still he persisted in paying the rent.

This was the result of two developments: he'd bagged a lucrative contract with the local Cambridge telecoms company for a flashy new website with all the bells, whistles, and ringtones, right from under the noses of some heavyweight web-design companies. This afforded him the ability to keep the rent going with hardly a thought to the extra cost.

The other reason was due to his complete inability to confront the memory of Tabby—or go back to where it had all gone so drastically wrong.

He still missed her on a debilitating scale, and although something prevented him from directly contacting her, it was Tracey, her mother, who took the brunt of his despair. Rick would regularly message Tracey on WhatsApp, hoping she'd pass on the info, if not in full, then perhaps in part, and hopefully the part that mattered.

From her mum, he learned there was still no Significant Other in Tabby's life. Better still, Tracey was open enough in her replies to give him more than a hint that there wasn't likely to be any blossoming relationships for her daughter in the immediate future.

Rick also had an ace now, literally up his sleeve. He'd nearly taken a photo of it and sent it to Tracey, but he didn't think it would have maximum impact via that method. He was also nervous that David, Tabby's pain-in-the-butt father, would see the photo, pour scorn over it, and promptly delete it from his wife's phone.

This was why he now sat in his favourite coffee shop in Cambridge, nervously waiting for Tracey to walk across the road from the family home and join him.

*

'Hello, Mrs. Mercer; thanks so much for seeing me—really appreciated. Here, come and sit down next to me—the benches are much comfier than the chairs.'

'Thank you, Rick, and for goodness sake, don't call me *Mrs. Mercer*. It's always been *Tracey*—you know that.'

It was many months since he'd last seen her, but Mrs. Mercer looked younger. Actually, a *lot* younger. Rick had spent his adult life studying women, often from very close quarters, so he was quick to notice that Tracey's make-up was much more vivid and heavier.

It certainly worked, though. And her hair was shorter and in a very now-ish style—it sure hadn't been blonde before, either.

'Rick? Calling Rick Harrison; respond if you're still on planet Earth?'

'Uhhh? Oh! Sorry, Mrs Merc ... Tracey—just drifted off there for a second.'

'As was your habit now and then in the past if memory serves me correctly? So, what's on your mind? It's bound to be Tabby, I guess?'

'Ummm, yeah. Tabby, of course.'

The smile wasn't totally convincing, but it gave Rick time to re-gather his thoughts.

'I wanted to talk with you about something I've done very recently.'

Tracey was intrigued, not only with what Rick might have to say but also the strange way he'd been looking at her—she couldn't put her finger on it.

'It's a little bit humid in here all of a sudden, don't you find? Let's sit outside, shall we?'

They moved onto one of the two available pavement tables, and Rick proceeded to roll up a sleeve of his shirt.

'This is something I could have photographed and sent you, but I wanted to explain my reason behind it at the same time. It's a lemniscate.'

He grinned proudly as he held up his forearm to her face.

Tracey was of an age where optimum focal points had considerably lengthened, though she'd been assured by her optician that she was a decade ahead of the game—the average age for the start of presbyopia was early-forties.

She'd need reading glasses soon, though; that or arm extensions. Holding the muscular forearm in both hands at arms-length and trying not to squint, she remained confused.

'I don't get the lemon reference—isn't this an infinity symbol?'

'A lemniscate and an infinity symbol are one and the same, but that's not the big deal—look in the two loops.'

Rick was grinning quite proudly.

Tracey drew the arm closer to her face, then realised the error of her ways and pushed it as far away as possible. It was a bit like focussing a camera—out, in, out, in, bingo. Squinting was now unavoidable.

'An 'R' and a 'T'?'

'Just a token gesture to symbolise my feelings towards your daughter.'

Rick had composed these words yesterday and practised them at length.

'And it's there for life,' he added proudly.

He put his hands over Tracey's, moved closer, stared into her eyes.

'Tracey, would you do something for me? It would mean the world.'

Time stood still, and the traffic along Trumpington Street seemed muted. Had it been a scene in a film, the camera lens would have zoomed into the two faces, blurring everything else within the frame.

In this unfortunate case, the camera lens was replaced by the bespectacled eyes of David Mercer, carefully cycling home from a regular visit to his beloved Fitzwilliam Museum, of which he had been an annually paid-up 'Friend' for decades.

Normally an extremely cautious cyclist, Mr. Mercer had been negotiating the roads of Cambridge for nearly 50 years and had yet to experience even a minor altercation with a car or pedestrian. Although no official statistics existed, this unblemished bikesmanship was almost unique in the history of the city.

Neither had he and his bicycle ever come close to jumping a red light, ridden on the pavement, nor gone up a one-way road in the wrong direction.

This accomplishment was *completely* unique.

Until now.

The noise of the bike clipping the curb and sliding across the pavement into a nearby post-office store had broken the spell; Rick and Tracey's heads pivoted in unison, to the noise of the carnage.

The strangled cry of anxiety lasted only until the crumpled heap fell, unconscious.

The metal chair clattered to the pavement as Tracey rushed to her husband's aid, while Rick hit 999 on his phone and summoned an ambulance. He calmly finished his coffee—the one-time future father-in-law had never liked him.

And besides, a crowd was already gathering, and he wanted to give Mr. Mercer as much breathing-room as possible ...

*

Rick had attempted to remain in the background, but Tracey insisted he come along in the ambulance to Addenbrooke's Hospital. They now sat either side of her husband in an A&E department bed.

Mr. Mercer had angry grazes to an arm and both palms, and an unsightly cut to his face. He'd drifted in and out on the journey to hospital, but x-rays showed nothing was broken.

Although he'd be in the ward for another seven hours, as protocol dictated when someone loses consciousness, he was now resting comfortably, trying to untangle the confusing memories before his world descended to blackness.

However unlikely it seemed, could his wife *really* have been with that character, Rick? Surely, he'd seen the last of that lothario a few months ago?

A vision swam in his memory; a still image of his wife's face, intimately close to the bald-headed thug.

Then their voices above the bed, invading his confusion, bringing an awful clarity to the nightmare. The last thing he wanted was to open his eyes, so he was forced to listen instead. Some rubbish about *a tattoo* and *a sweet gesture*. Then drivel about *initials* and *undying love*.

Absolute tosh. Complete gibberish.

He turned on his side and surreptitiously opened the eye nearest to the pillow.

A fist came into view, the knuckles pointed towards him, the hand wrapped around the bed's grey metal sidebars. It was too near to see clearly, and his eye rotated upwards as he took in the hairy arm. There was a raised, vivid blue symbol on the forearm.

Mr. Mercer had no knowledge of tattoos and found them rather vulgar and intimidating. During his working life, it was rare he'd grant a loan, however safe the risk, if the client was sporting scribble all over his (and with a depressing increase, *her*) body.

He could hear his beloved wife's voice again.

'It's beautiful, Rick; very special and rather fetching, if you don't mind an older woman's opinion?'

Then a little giggle from her—so familiar—a sound he so cherished.

Mr. Mercer stared at the tattoo—a figure '*8*' lying on its side.

He saw the initials in the two loops—'*R*'—'*T*'.

Rick.

Tracey.

He passed out again.

4

THE FACETIME sessions had proved a big success, though the sleep patterns of both Grant and Tabby had been severely affected. This wasn't a problem for Tabatha, who was yet to find a job, but Grant's father was cranking up the pressure.

Grant was never late to the garage, and lateness wasn't in his makeup, but his productiveness was way below par, and he couldn't dedicate enough extra hours to catch up. His father had raised the subject gently over dinner a couple of times, but things were inevitably going to come to a head.

It was hardly the best circumstances in which to mention his plans, but Grant had already decided what he was going to do, and he had the savings to carry out these plans.

'I can't put it into words, Dad, but I know in my heart what I want, and I just have to follow that path. The last thing I'd do is let you down; you know that. I'm not quitting on you, but I just need a break; I need some time.'

Paul Davis stared at his son across the dinner table. A parent should never have a favourite child, and by God, he'd protect either son with his life, but he saw Ashleigh so rarely now … It was difficult not to feel a special affection for Grant.

Ashleigh hadn't lived at home since he was eighteen. He had his mother's head for numbers and wanted to be an accountant like her. Gaining a place at the University of New South Wales was a big hurdle, and he never looked back after that.

With a degree in business management, he qualified with relative ease as a Chartered Accountant, and at the age of 28 was a senior manager in one of Singapore's main accountancy firms. He adored the country, and a partnership beckoned in the not too distant future. By now, he wasn't coming home for much more than the Christmas holiday, and he'd even missed that last year.

It had been a traumatic upbringing for both boys. Their lives had been ripped from under them when their mother had succumbed to cancer after a short and devastating illness. Ashleigh was only sixteen at the time, and Grant, just thirteen.

With a fledging business to run and now two kids to look after, Paul Davis had come close to a nervous breakdown at times. Without the help of his elder sister, he'd never have kept going. On the rare occasions when he had some time to himself, he'd contemplate the possibility of another relationship, another woman. As soon as the thought came into his head he quietly wept in the privacy of his bedroom—he was a one-woman man; for life.

He watched with a heavy heart as his youngest son had been unceremoniously dumped. He'd never have believed it unless he'd witnessed the destruction of the relationship with his own eyes. He was sure the girl would be his future daughter-in-law and had treated her accordingly for years. And then the deceit and the lies, learning that not only had Grant lost the love of his life, but been betrayed by the boy's best friend. It was difficult not to feel bitter.

39

Paul wasn't stupid—far from it; he'd seen the way this woman from England had reignited a spark in his son's life. He couldn't begin to comprehend how a relationship could blossom in a few weeks at the end of a phone-line, but he was willing to accept that he was a dinosaur where technology was concerned.

All that mattered was the happiness Grant was now displaying, and Paul Davis silently prayed to a God he hadn't believed in since losing his wife, that this woman on the other side of the world was everything his son believed she was.

*

'So Dad was as good as gold. I'd been dreading the conversation, but it was as if he knew what I was going to say. You look gorgeous by the way, even though the picture keeps freezing. When the signal drops mid-blink, it looks like you've gone to sleep on me.'

'Thanks, you don't look so bad yourself. Your dad sounds very special—has he really not asked how long you'll be away? Surely he'll need to get someone to cover for you at the garage?'

'He's got so much work on at the moment that he was thinking of getting another part-time mechanic to help out anyway. He said he'll just advertise for a full-time position instead. I wanted to give him some sort of time-frame, but I really don't have a clue. I reckon I have enough savings to last me a few months, and my visa's good for a year. Maybe I'll look for a job as soon as I get to Cambridge—see how it pans out, I guess.'

'I'm sure you'll get a job soon enough, but accommodation is quite expensive here, and everything gets snapped up really quickly by the students. Hey, are you excited about coming over?'

It wasn't meant as a loaded question, but Tabatha wished she hadn't asked—it sounded like she was grovelling for a compliment.

'Never been more excited about anything in my life. I've kind of wanted to go to England since I was a kid. There are so many Brits here in Sydney, but I know there's a load of us Aussies in the UK too.'

'Not so many in Cambridge but a whole heap down the road in London. Earl's Court is like a mini-Australia, apparently.'

'If I said I could be in Cambridge this time next month, would that be too soon for you?'

Tabatha wasn't sure what she thought about that. She knew Grant wanted to come over, and the thought thrilled her, but now there was a time frame, she suddenly felt clammy and nervous.

'Yeah, sure. I mean, whatever works for you.'

It was a feeble reply, and she knew it. Grant probably thought the same, and she braced herself for his reply. For some inexplicable reason, Rick had floated, uninvited, into her mind.

'Are you okay, Tabby. Hey, if it's too soon, I can make it later; I haven't booked flights yet. Is it too soon?'

Grant cursed himself—he hadn't been able to hide the disappointment in his expression. The screen froze again, and he stared at a static image of the girl he'd fallen in love with over the past weeks. She looked to be far away, in a world of her own. Maybe he was being over-sensitive, but she also looked troubled.

'It's fine, Grant, whatever works for you. I have to go now—Mum's shouting at me for dinner. I'll speak with you again tomorrow, eh?'

The photo was still frozen, but there hadn't been a problem with sound. He'd heard Tabby's constantly miaowing cat in the background a few times, so he knew he'd have heard her mum's voice too.

He was pushing things too fast, escalating their situation when it wasn't necessary. He was hopeless at patience and hated himself for it. If he wasn't careful, he'd blow everything out of the water, and he couldn't bear the thought of that—of losing her. Not that she was his to lose.

Not yet, and not by a long way.

'Of course. Hey, have a nice meal and don't forget to feed Cleo—he sounds hungry. Speak tomorrow and a big hug and a kiss from me.'

'Thanks. It's Chloe by the way, and he's a she. Bye.'

'Oh, and hope your dad's head is feeling bett ...'

But Tabatha was no longer on the line.

*

An awkward silence hung above the family at dinner. The interactions of cutlery and plates felt unskilfully child-like and rudely intrusive. Tabatha scanned her dad's injured face, focussing on the angriest of his lacerations. A fairly deep cut starting in the middle of his right cheek, angling up in a straight line towards the bridge of his nose. Nasty, but apparently not deep enough to warrant stitches.

It reminded her of something, but she couldn't retrieve the long-buried memory.

He was holding his knife and fork between thumbs and forefingers in a dainty and almost effeminate way, the white bandaging around both hands forcing his remaining fingers into an elaborate yet satisfyingly symmetrical pattern. It served as a parody for the awkward atmosphere hanging over the spacious dining-room.

She picked up her utensils and in a genuinely innocent manner, mirrored her father's manoeuvres, just to see what it felt like. The broccoli, carrots, and new potatoes were manageable, and the spinach was a doddle, but steak would have been a major challenge.

Fortunately, Mum had served cod off the bone with some sort of grilled cheese topping; this was probably a very sweet gesture and a nod to her husband's current dexterity issues, as today was nearly always roast beef—a family favourite.

Tabatha continued her new style of eating (it was actually better for removing the odd, random bone from a chunky shard of fish, and considerably easier to adapt to than, for instance, chopsticks) until she became aware that her own personal overture of blade-and-tines-on-china was no longer accompanied. She looked up from her plate.

'What?'

Dad was wiping his mouth with a napkin, careful to keep the starched cotton out of contact with the graze on his chin.

'Daddy can't help the way he has to eat, Dear—I don't think that behaviour's very kind. The hospital said he has a moderate concussion, and we have to monitor him closely for the next forty-eight hours—not imitate him.'

Tabatha felt this was unjustly harsh.

'Well, I *was* monitoring him. For God's sake, Mum, it wasn't my fault he fell off his bike.'

Since retiring, David Mercer had found life very different. If he were honest, he'd found it a little difficult. He'd popped into his bank a couple of times, well, a few times in truth, ostensibly to see his old work colleagues. Perhaps more accurately, it was to see how the business was managing without him.

Regrettably, it was patently obvious that the bank was doing just fine without him. He found the staff talking to each other as if he wasn't there. A little like now, really.

'It's fine, Tabatha—please carry on eating any which way you like. I'm just finding it a little painful if anything presses on my palms at the moment; the doctor apparently took a fair portion of Trumpington Street out of the flesh. I'll be fine in a couple of days.'

In a few seconds, Dad had managed to disarm the situation. It seemed that every occasion with even the slightest friction in her life had been diffused by her father. In equal measures, she both loved him and found him exasperating.

'Sorry, Dad, are you feeling any better? I still can't believe you fell off your bike. It was obviously someone else's fault, right? I mean, you're the world's safest cyclist—end of.'

'Well thank you, dear. I'll take that as a compliment—I think. We needn't go into details, but let's say I was just momentarily shocked—took my mind right off the Highway Code and all that jazz.'

Tabatha sat up straighter—this was almost interesting. Her mum seemed less interested and was already clattering plates together.

'So, who's for dessert, then? I still have a nice selection of cheeses from the weekend, and I bought some meringues to go with vanilla ice-cream. I didn't have time to make them today, what with your father's, you know ... *problems*.'

44

Tracy had a very good set of teeth when she chose to show them, and now was one of those occasions.

'Go on, Dad—what shocked you?'

'And some double cream to drizzle over the meringue. David? Tabatha? Yes?'

Tracey looked pleadingly at them both, morphing into a front-row spectator at Wimbledon's Centre Court.

The room held its breath, but there was an air of inevitability within the stillness.

'I'll put the plates in the dishwasher, then.'

Laden with crockery, Tracey slithered to the kitchen, all semblance of her excellent natural posture eluding her.

'Errr, is Mum okay?'

'Sort of; we had words last night.'

Tabatha was well aware that this seemingly innocuous statement was anything but—her mum and *dad* having *words* was the equivalent to her kneeing Rick in the groin.

'I heard raised voices but thought you must be reliving your crash. It had to be the other person's fault, right?'

David Mercer sighed in slow motion, closed his eyes, and put a hand through his thinning hair. Wincing at the pain, he placed the hand tenderly back on his lap again.

'I'm afraid I'm deeply upset, Tabatha; with your mum, that is. Well, not just her, but that louse you used to hang out with all the time. The blame for my accident lies equally and entirely with them both.'

Tabatha couldn't be certain, but it looked as if her dad was welling up. This was unique, unchartered territory and needed to be handled *very* carefully.

'You've lost me, Dad. I've never really hung out with anybody since I started seeing Rick. And I certainly can't think of anyone since him. Are you sure you're not a bit mixed up? Maybe that bang on the head, perhaps?'

As he was about to reply to his daughter, the kitchen door slowly clicked shut.

'The two of them—they were … well they were … *together* ... I caught it in my peripheral vision, turned my head to look directly, and there they were. The two of them—inches apart. They were … t*ogether.*'

David Mercer put a bandaged hand over his face and winced again.

'I don't get this; you're making no sense. Mum and *who*? A woman or a man?'

She was fairly sure of the gender but didn't want to be presumptuous. This conversation was going way off the scale; neither of her parents was capable of looking at another person, much less have an affair.

A silence crawled over the dining room as Mr. Mercer attempted to dab the corner of his eye with a part of the gauze untainted by rusty-dry blood.

Tabatha went through her hopelessly small list of post-Rick former male friends in her head. Though the silence was absolute, they could both hear Mrs. Mercer listening; could the act of holding breath be audible?

'Try one more time, Dad—I honestly don't know who you're talking about. Mum was inches next to *who*? The only person I ever used to *'hang out with all the time'* as you put it, was Rick.'

If ever there was an occasion when silence appeared to grow louder, here was that very moment in time.

And entangled within the quiet, a shiver of dawning knowledge.

Modern English language, with its ever-populating list of acronyms, may suggest this to be an OMG moment or a WTAF scenario; Tabatha, however, the product of a more traditional upbringing and a degree in literature, deduced it to be one of just two things:

A dreadful misunderstanding or the end of life (the sequel).

The kitchen door interrupted again, though this time, more obtrusively.

'Right, I've had just about as much of this rubbish as I can take. Rick invited me to a coffee shop to show me something.'

Tabatha's jaw began to slowly drop, but her father was less passive.

'I bet he did!'

Tracey was just as efficient at interjecting.

'To show me his new tattoo!'

'Oh my God!' cried Tabatha, who could feel an out-of-body moment coming on.

'Yeah,' sneered Mr. Mercer, who had never said *Yeah* or sneered in his life, to the best of either woman's knowledge.

Nor was he finished …

'And the bald bastard had the temerity to put my wife's and his initials on the sodding thing!'

'Oh, for fuck's sake, David, the *T* was for Tabatha! It was Rick and *TABATHA*!'

Watching her dad's facial turmoil and his livid cut start to darken, it came to her.

'Action Man!'

Despite the worst argument in the family's history, Tabatha felt quite chuffed. She'd had Barbie, Sindy, and Action Man as a child, but always favoured the man-doll.

'That gash on your cheek? It's *exactly* like my old Action Man.'

*

Much later that night, Tabatha could again hear her parents
talking in their bedroom. The tattoo story had now sunk in,
and she couldn't deny that she'd pondered the matter with
not only amazement but a little pride as well. It was a
pathetic state to be in, she knew, but it wasn't every day that
someone had your initial indelibly engraved on their body.

As her head sank peacefully into the pillow, Tabatha was
idly curling a strand of dark blonde hair around a finger as
her mind skated through a myriad of special times with her
old boyfriend. The last moment was conveniently missing
from this collection of memories.

She was drifting off as her phone chimed, the ringtone
signifying a FaceTime call. It had been a long day, and she
was tired—so very tired. The ringing stopped, then started
again a minute later. Then the same thing again, a call of love
from the bottom of the world.

Silence at last. With guilty relief, she drifted into sleep.

*

'I still don't know why in God's name you didn't tell me,
Tracey.'

Both had their arms folded, the only illumination coming
from a flexible reading lamp on her side of the bed, pointed
down at the soft beige carpet, a remnant of the
incompatibility of her late-night reading habits and his early-
morning alarm for work.

The light had meaningful history, a car accessory which
David had bought when they were both in their teens. He'd
clamped it to the passenger-side dashboard of his overtly
flashy Ford Capri and named it a *'fanny light'*. Conveniently, it
could run off the car battery or the household type.

Those were the days—the days when David would come out with something like that. Tracey thought that might be about a century or so ago.

'Because of the way you'd react, David, which seems to have been rather justified on this occasion, don't you think?'

'He's got a bloody nerve if he thinks he can just waltz back into my daughter's life …'

'*Our* daughter's life.'

'*Our* daughter's life, and just sweep her off her feet again, as if nothing had happened. If he so much as lays a finger on her, I'll … I'll …'

'*If* they get back together again, I imagine he'll lay a lot more than a finger on her …' Tracey felt slightly guilty that she may be enjoying this a little bit.

'He'll do no such bloody thing! I'll call the bloody police! Or take matters into my own hands.'

David had begun to clench his bandaged hands. He tried to stifle the immediate whimpering by biting his lower lip, catching the graze just below instead.

Her husband's grimace now had Tracey's full attention; Tabatha was right, it really *was* like Action Man.

Wellll, the gash was. The hair was different; the face was very different, and as for the body …

She was sure Tabby used to have a bald Action Man, one where you could use different colour micro-wigs for when he went spying or out to a ball or something like that.

Now there was a thought—a bald Action Man. All that was missing was a cute little tattoo on the arm and voilà—a perfect miniature Rick.

'Tracey? *Tracey?* Are you listening to me? You've gone all glazed again—what on earth is the matter with you?'

'Oh, nothing Dear, just thinking … It may be that Tabatha still has a soft spot for Rick. We have to keep out of it—let nature take its course.'

There was a distant smile on her face.

'WHAT?! Are you *insane*, woman? He's cheated on her. *Cheated! In front of her!*'

In the shadowy light, it looked as if her husband's facial wound might be opening up, and the last thing she needed was blood on the white sheets. She leaned down and pulled the reading light back up, pointing it in his face.

'Ow! What the … are you trying to blind me?!'

'Oh, stop over-reacting. Your blood pressure's going to open that cut; just calm down, for goodness sake. Yes, Rick cheated on her, but he was backed into a corner. He was being manoeuvred by a very manipulative woman. He had no idea; he was just being used, poor kid.'

'What an absolute pile of bunkum. That so-called woman was a *girl*, for God's sake—Tabatha said she was fifteen years younger than him—at least! And besides, where the hell did you hear about this? You told me you were only talking to him for five minutes before I crashed in on your little party?'

'It *was* only five minutes. Ish.'

'That's not enough time to get all those gory details. R*ubbish* details, I should add. A pack of lies, clearly.'

'On WhatsApp.'

Tracey swiftly yanked the interrogation light back towards the carpet and bit her tongue.

'On WhatsWhat? That social media nonsense the kids are using? You're chatting with Rick on WhatsThingy? You told me you hadn't heard from him since, you know, since …'

'Well I hadn't! Not to speak to. He'd just send me a message every now and then to keep me up to speed on things. News ~that sort of thing.'

'*News*? From *him*?! Nothing is ever '*new*' about him. He's a damn Casanova who can't keep his thingy in his underpants! He's always been like that, and he always *will* be like that. Bloody Warren Beatty, he is; it's disgusting. So what else do you know about him, eh? During your *secret* chats?'

'I know that he and Tabatha would make a beautiful couple if they could work things out. And beautiful kids too, if they had any—and they would.'

Tracey turned away, though she could still see her husband's face through the corner of her eye. It seemed to be turning into a scowling orangey-red emoji face you could find on WhatsApp—strangely, the one Rick used when referring to *Mr. Mercer.*

She grinned to herself, and a slight giggle escaped, which she attempted to disguise as a sniff. Putting a tissue to her nose, she turned around and looked at her husband.

'You're bleeding, Dear. Here, take this and go and mop up in the bathroom.'

She turned on her side and flicked the reading-lamp off, trying to ignore his pained groans.

'Oh, and I think you'll find Warren Beatty's in his eighties; Rick's only thirty-four.'

5

IT SEEMED to Tabatha as if there was a direct correlation between the amount of time spent looking at classic car websites, and her dwindling ability to afford even the rustiest wreck of a Triumph Spitfire. What a bitter irony that was, or, as Rick used to say when suffering a rare bout of negativity, *'life's a bitch, and then you die'*. The bouts used to occur soon after a late-tax demand letter in the post.

How strange it was that Rick was now relatively well-off. She'd intermittently peep at the local telecom website, and it was an impressive thing to behold. More importantly from Rick's point of view, it was constantly being updated and improved. Some rough calculations in her head, if even vaguely accurate, told her Rick's constant poverty was long gone.

Good for him, but she couldn't even dream about that type of financial freedom. Tabatha clicked off the website and closed her laptop. Lucky old Rick …

Although he could now buy plenty, there wasn't much which Rick was really enthusiastic about. He didn't buy designer clothes or wear an expensive watch. They'd hardly ever been out to an expensive restaurant, though they did dine out once a week at a pub, and maybe take in a film at the cinema. He certainly wasn't a big drinker, either.

It was the amount of time they'd been a couple which had made her forget about this part of him. They were positive attributes, really, and she'd never thought of them like that. His monthly gym membership was probably the most extravagant expenditure, and there were definitely positive benefits to that. And, of course, there was another thing he was always extremely enthusiastic about …

Though on her own in the kitchen, Tabatha felt her cheeks redden.

Not only enthusiastic, but good – *very* good, in fact. Very good and remarkably unselfish and giving …

Just as her mind began to select specific memories of many moons previous, the one fly in the ointment buzzed around her face. The reality was that anyone who practised something a lot became good at it. And the horrible truth was that he'd obviously been practising more than she had; probably a hell of a lot more than her.

She hated and loathed him instantly, both fists thumping down on the table as she ground her teeth together.

Why? Why did he do it? What did she do that was so wrong; what could she have done differently?

Could it really be her fault?

Her mouth relaxed, and she unclenched both fists. What if the only time he'd ever been unfaithful was when she came back so unexpectedly? She'd refused to listen to any explanation at the time and not spoken to him since, so wouldn't know.

If that were true, it would explain why he'd tried so many times to call her that first month. The bouquets of flowers she'd insisted be left in the garden, sitting in vases her mum had put them in. How childish she must have appeared, yet her mother had never questioned the behaviour.

And the tattoo.

Would someone go to those lengths if they didn't truly love the person?

Why did you do it, Rick?

Her phone beeped; a WhatsApp message.

Hey Tabs, Sorry to bother you. Just wondered how you were – haven't heard from you for a couple of days. Is everything ok? I keep hoping it isn't something I've said or done. ☹
Call me if you can, so we can talk about flights and dates and things. Miss you and big hugs. Grant xx Oh, and I'm going out for a drive in the Spitty now – wish you were here. XX Bye

Tabatha placed the phone on top of her laptop and stared at the bright screen until it faded to black.

How had this all happened?

If she had three magical buttons in front of her now, one saying '*Rick*', one saying '*Grant*', one saying '*Neither*', which one would she press?

'*Neither*' looked like a clear winner—her cheeks puffed out as she sighed.

Grant needed a reply; no, he *deserved* a reply. What had he done for her to treat him like this?

But what would she write?

Tabatha lined up the magic buttons again—*Stay*—*Come*—*Neither.*

This was too much pressure for her; way too much pressure. She couldn't make a decision and didn't want to.

Then the answer came to her. She'd pick up her phone and look at the time; if the last digit was odd, she'd tell Grant he needed to forget about her; a 2, a 4, a 6 or an 8, and she'd invite him to come as soon as he wanted.

She picked the phone up.

15.20

Tabatha put her elbows on the table and her head in her hands.

'Neither' was the answer—leave it all to fate.

Hi Grant, Sorry about this but I just need a little time – I'm not feeling that great at the moment. X

*

Tabatha needed a heart-to-heart with her mother. An opportunity arose later that week when her dad had gone to his *Tai Chi* class.

Unable to cycle because of continued discomfort with his hands, David Mercer had set off much earlier than normal, in order to walk to Grantchester.

The elderly Chinese instructor who conducted these sessions would not accept lateness and had been known to turn people away for such a transgression. Unsurprisingly, David was an enthusiastic supporter of this somewhat draconian discipline.

Mr. Wong had a small band of followers who could more accurately be described as semi-worshippers. Many had benefitted from almost miraculous cures from various mobility problems through these classes, and his considerably more expensive acupuncture treatments.

David had yet to go under the needles but had seriously contemplated it. Not for any medical problem as such, but he suspected an inner-clique existed within the class, with acupuncture representing the common denominator.

Illogically, he often found himself yearning to be in Mr. Wong's favour, receiving the occasional compliment about his technique and general progress within the class.

With a brisk 45-minute walk ahead, he left the moody atmosphere of his home and began to contemplate the reactions of his fellow students as they took note of his battle scars.

Perhaps even Mr. Wong would pay him some sliver of respect in front of the others?

His mood brightened at the thought.

Loch Fyne was always busy, and a Friday lunchtime in Cambridge was no exception; they'd been lucky to get a table at such short notice.

Tracey was certain this special treatment was reserved for the restaurant's more loyal patrons (or *'preferred clients'* as she'd put it), though Tabatha was inclined to believe there'd been a late cancellation.

They were studying the menu as they talked.

'Why do you think people make a big deal about having fish on a Friday?'

'It's because of Jesus, Dear.'

Tracey smiled benevolently at her daughter; like so many people, she loved it when someone asked a question she knew the answer to.

'What, you mean he started it off? Ohhhh, you mean with the loaves and fish miracle?'

'No, no, sweetie—when Jesus was crucified. It was a Friday, and it became the Christian practice to abstain from meat, or even fast on that day. *That's* how it started, and a lot of people still observe the tradition to this day. It's rather lovely, don't you think?'

'Yes, but what about people living on, like, the Cook Islands, or somewhere like that? Or Hawaii, maybe?'

Unbeknown to Tabatha, this was also a significant lunch for Tracey. She knew her daughter was at a personal crossroads and looking for guidance; why else would she want a private meal with her mother?

She prided herself on keeping up with the times. Whilst her husband languished in an imaginary world set somewhere in the late 1950s, where people looked up to a bank manager as a pillar of society and listened to the World Service on the radio, Tracey kept abreast of the latest fashions, used social media regularly, and listened to her continually updated playlist via airpods (though her ears were still acclimatising to that).

That said, Tracey was still occasionally flummoxed by the unfathomable enigma which was her daughter.

'I'm not sure I quite under …'

Tracey wore half a smile, but the fuzzy warmth she'd gained via her fish-on-Friday knowledge was already wilting.

'Hawaii has to be a good twelve hours behind Jerusalem, right? So that means it could have been a Thursday or a Saturday for them when Jesus was crucified, surely?'

A timely waitress came to the assistance of Tracey's mind-numbing perplexity.

'Are we ready to order, ladies? Chef is saying the halibut *bonne femme* is legendary today.'

Tracey's phone, placed upside down next to her side plate, vibrated briefly. She'd feared this might occur but was nowadays finding it difficult to be apart from her phone for very long.

Whilst her husband was pre-occupied with some pre-Kung Fu lesson stretches this morning, or whatever he called it, she'd taken advantage of the privacy to send Rick a message, letting him know of her imminent lunch with Tabatha.

'That sounds fine, but no wine for me—just tap-water, please. What about you?'

Tabatha could have done with something stronger, but it was no fun drinking alone.

'I guess the same. I was going for *foie gras* followed by calves' liver, but I feel a bit guilty now.'

She winked at her mum.

'I'll have the fish and chips, please. Happy now?'

It was only a brief time before they broached the subject hanging above the table.

'You don't seem to be talking with Grant so often. Have you had an argument?'

'No, of course not, he's being very sweet; too sweet, if anything. He's so keen to come over that it makes me feel—I don't know—kind of responsible for him. As if we're already in a relationship?'

'Well, aren't you? I can't imagine how this type of thing works from such a distance, but don't you feel as if you and Grant are already an item?'

'I do, sort of. I'm just worried that I've built him up to be something that's impossible to live up to, and then I'll feel let down?'

'Maybe he's done the same with you? Perhaps you'll gradually see each other's faults when he's here, and then it'll all work out? Or maybe it's safer to be with someone who's already let you down?'

Tracey avoided eye contact and peeped at her phone. As she'd guessed—a message from Rick, but with a picture attached

'Grant may think he loves you, but I don't think he's the only one.'

She passed the phone over, so her daughter could see the photo of Rick's arm.

The image hit home.

'Oh … an infinity symbol.'

She touched the screen with a finger.

'It's lovely,' she whispered, almost to herself.

The message appeared:

'Please tell Tabby I still love her so much. I wish we could be together again.'

Passing the phone back, Tabatha stood up and hurried to the solitude of the Ladies.

*

Grant wasn't a stranger to these feelings of confusion and helplessness. Although with limited experience, the rejection he was suffering felt painfully familiar.

Of course, Tabby wasn't his girlfriend; he had to keep reminding himself of this. However much he felt for her, he wondered if it counted for anything. Perhaps she was already in a relationship and had lied to him?

It was hard to imagine, but that was what it felt like.

Although she'd skirted over the details of a long-term boyfriend, perhaps there was someone new?

Grant's stomach lurched, and nausea gripped him.

Why was she so offhand with him now? What had he done?

Something had changed, but there was no way he could ask her directly; it just wasn't how they spoke.

So much chat about anything and everything, but with the one unwritten rule—nothing too personal—nothing too emotional.

He longed to know more about the real woman behind the type-written words, the voice, the images.

And what of her ex? She'd shown no desire to learn of Hayley, so he could hardly push for details of her previous boyfriend.

It was '*Rick*'—he knew that much. She'd mentioned the name when talking about her failed business venture.

Grant wondered where the guy was now. Did he still live locally? And what did this Rick look like—how old was he?

Maybe it was best if he didn't contact her for a while. It would be tough, but he hated the idea of pestering Tabby, for that's what he felt he was doing at the moment.

It was a depressing thought, because he really, *really*, liked her. More than that, he dared not admit to himself at the moment—maybe not ever.

And then from the fog of depression, a bolt of clarity:

Hey Tabby, A quick text - no need to reply. Just letting you know I'll be in England in a few weeks – maybe mid-October. I'd like to base myself in Cambridge but am happy to stay in London if it's a problem. Hope to see you – will send another message when I arrive.

Hugs, Grant x

PS - may have a little surprise for you…

*

That week, David's *Tai Chi* class was even more of a tonic than usual.

Mr. Wong was definitely more receptive to him, and a couple of the fellow students had been very kind. One of the ladies had been so sympathetic he'd felt obliged to tell her the whole story.

Her fascination had encouraged him to divulge his fears—he honestly couldn't remember if he'd ever discussed personal matters like this before.

Still, it felt right, and when he'd reached the part about Tracey's unhealthy interest in a lad nearly twenty years younger, she'd gasped with shock and squeezed his shoulder (which still boasted a nasty graze and bruising, but he didn't flinch).

On a roll and succumbing to that most human of instincts—a subconscious craving for a kind ear doused with sympathy—he'd let slip that not only was the boy a rampant gigolo but the ex-boyfriend of his only daughter, no less!

At this point, Mrs Blake (who insisted it was *Ms* Blake initially, then *Jane* soon afterwards) had put both arms around him and held him very tightly, while patting his back gently (another sore area, but bearable).

He'd have sworn this could only lead to feelings of extreme embarrassment, but it was oddly comforting.

He stifled the urge to burp, presumably the bi-product of rhythmic back-patting, and when he began to wonder what he should do next, Jane took a step back, smiled quite wonderfully, then kissed him on the side of the face.

'If you ever need a sympathetic ear, David, you can count on me.'

At a loss for words, he'd fallen back on a lifetime of bank-talk and immediately cursed himself.

'Absolutely. We'll be in contact in due course. I'll be in contact, I mean. And not in due course. Obviously.'

Jane put a hand on his face, curing his social ineptitude swiftly.

'Fan-TAS-tic. See you on Tuesday, David. Hey, and have a simply *wonderful* weekend.'

David was practically floating on air as he walked back from Granchester.

*

They appeared at each end of Brookside, fifty metres apart; Tracey and her daughter laden with boutique and shoe-shop bags; David sporting a tracksuit, bandages, and an uncharacteristic grin.

The painful sight of blatant, out-of-control consumerism would normally have disappointed him. After 34 years of marriage, he was still under the hopelessly misguided impression that there was a finite amount of clothes and shoes a woman could buy.

On this occasion, though, it went unnoticed.

Tracey cursed the unfortunate timing; two minutes earlier, and the excessive stash would have been in the house and out of sight.

'I know what you're going to say, darling, and I realise the old bank manager in you might not quite see the logic, but you can't imagine how much money we've saved.'

Not waiting for an answer, Tracey was already putting her key in the lock of the front door; she'd heard every version of her husband's replies over the decades, all of which centred on the same terse theme.

'Excellent news – I'm sure you've almost driven the shops out of business.'

Sarcasm wasn't something he used often, and this was enough to grab Tracey's attention. She turned to face her husband, anticipating his exasperated scowl. Instead, David appeared genuinely cheerful.

'Oh. Are you alright? You haven't been taking too many of those painkillers, have you?'

He held his hands in the air.

'Far from it—I'm feeling much better. Think I'll take the bandaging off when I get inside.'

It was a genuine smile, full of warmth. Her husband hadn't even asked how much she'd spent (Tracey had decided to quote a figure of £480, which was only about £170 from being accurate. However, this omitted the amount she'd spent on Tabatha, which was slightly more than herself.).

'And you say you're fine? No headaches or dizziness? Any nausea?'

David chuckled as he pushed open the door for his family. 'Never better, honestly. You must both show me what you bought—hold tight while I put the kettle on.'

Tabatha looked at her mum, both women gaping at each other.

'Why don't I make the tea, Dad. You go and put your feet up in the lounge. What was your session like today?'

For eight-hundred pounds of new gear, Tabby was more than capable of kindness and feigned-interest in her dad's activities.

'Funny you should ask because it was fan-TAS-tic,' he said beaming.

Tabatha's eyes narrowed as she studied her father—this was moving from spooky to concerning.

'Has something happened? You seem … a little strange? Happy and strange?'

He chuckled. 'All is good with the world, my dear. Now go with your mum, and I'll make the tea. You too, Mrs M—I think I'll cook dinner tonight. Bottle of nice red with a steak, shall we?'

Tabatha wandered up the stairs to her bedroom, carrying the bags of clothes she suspected were chosen more for Rick's benefit than her own.

'You haven't had one of that Chinese man's acupuncture sessions, have you? I do worry you place too much trust in that Mr. Kong; is he fully qualified? I mean, has he been doing that for long?'

Tracey was a little concerned; perhaps her husband had started drinking during the afternoons?

'It's Wong, darling, and he's been practising acupuncture for longer than you've been alive. For all I know, his family has probably been acupuncturing for a thousand years. Not that it's relevant, as I haven't been receiving any treatment from him. I'm simply enjoying the class; they're a lovely bunch of people.'

David was about to expand and divulge his new favourite person in the group, stopping short as a pang of pure terror hit him squarely in the lower stomach.

A sheen of sweat appeared on his face as a dull thump reverberated in the back of his neck. He could hear his heart beating, and feel his armpits start to dampen.

'David? Good grief, are you having a seizure on me? It's those bloody painkillers, isn't it? I knew you'd taken too many.'

Tracey took his arm and led him to a sofa in the lounge.

'Put your feet up. Shall I call the doctor?'

'I'm fine now—really. Maybe I overdid it at classes today.'

'But I thought it was all about slow-motion movements and postures? How can you overdo that?'

'Well, it's not quite that simple.'

And David, with unknown emotions flooding his brain, began to realise it was going to be anything but simple.

The women's voices were low enough to be inaudible from the kitchen.

'I don't think I've ever seen your dad have a turn like that. Did you see the colour of his face?'

Tracey was absentmindedly stirring her tea, still a habit, though she'd last had sugar in the early-80s. Her husband's cup was still sitting on the sideboard, long past drinkable.

'I think he looked embarrassed rather than ill. Like he was hiding something.'

Tabatha had identified with the expression and was trying to remember where she'd seen it before. What had her father been talking about just prior to his instant suntan?

But Tracey was having none of it.

'Don't be ridiculous. What would he have to be embarrassed about? The last time he had a flush like that was at the altar. Oh, and on your eighteenth birthday when you projectile-vomited at that really expensive restaurant.'

Tabatha rolled her eyes—it was a rarely-mentioned incident but appeared to have life-long usage.

'And probably just before he rode his bike into the post office door, though you wouldn't have seen his face with a helmet on. And you weren't looking his way either, I guess.'

It was an unnecessarily barbed comment, and Tabatha wasn't sure where it had come from, or why she'd spoken to her mother in that way.

'I'll go and thank Dad for the clothes.'

She stood up and walked out of the kitchen, leaving her mum in a bewildered and slightly guilt-ridden state; kids could do that, however much you loved them.

6

'YOU'RE HEALING up nicely, David—there'll be no scars on that rugged face of yours. How was your weekend?'

For David, the weekend had been spent in his garden and garden shed. Ostensibly gardening as he did on many days, it also gave him the privacy he required to try and come to terms with things; to methodically piece together what had happened to him in the last few days.

He tried to compartmentalise this under an educated title, but *'Stuff'* described his anxiety and excitement most accurately.

Guilt was in the box too, and this was where he really struggled. Listening to two opposing voices of reason perched on his shoulders left him with a drastically reduced ability to carry out what were essentially very basic gardening tasks.

When he noticed his wife looking at him from a window, he felt certain she must know what he was thinking about. Then the other voice would pipe up—*'Rubbish; if she did, she wouldn't be in the house behind a window, would she? She'd be in your face with a hand extended, demanding you hand over the keys to your house. Her house now.*

This was absurd. He'd done absolutely nothing wrong. *Nothing!*

He smiled (which never came naturally), and the gesture was returned.

He felt his voice falter.

'Fine, thank you, Jane. Yes, quite fine. I spent a lot of time in the garden, actually.'

'Well never let anything come between a man and his garden, that's what I say. Mine's only small, but it used to look beautiful. Then Rupert passed away—that's my husband, *was* my husband—and I'm afraid it's gone to rack and ruin. Upsets me to see it, but with my back problems, there's not a lot I can do. That's why I do these classes—it seems to help a little.'

She continued to smile, making it very clear she was after absolutely no sympathy. David's chest felt strange, and his mouth lost all moisture. He filled the increasingly awkward pause with a slight cough—he had no clue what he was going to say but knew it was his turn to speak.

'I could do it for you. I'd be happy to help.'

His flushed grin prompted Jane to touch his face.

'How sweet of you, but are you sure you have the spare time? And what about your wife?' Her eyes moved briefly to his left hand. 'Wouldn't she have something to say about that?'

David felt emboldened—yet another alien emotion.

'Not at all—I *insist*. Oh, as long as I'm not intruding, of course? Perhaps I could come around and have a look one day?'

'Well yes, lovely, but only if you're sure. I'd hate to cause you a … well, *a problem*.'

Mr. Wong and the rest of the class were looking their way. Like errant children, they took up their normal places in the group.

'So, will you let me know your address or, errr, can I phone you and arrange to meet up? Once I see the garden, I can tell you what I may be able to help with.'

David could no longer hold eye contact and was studying the black tick-style motif on Jane's unmarked white trainers.

It seemed familiar, though goodness knows how that could be possible. He certainly wasn't a follower of fashion and product branding, so perhaps it was a form of immersive, subliminal advertising? The world seemed full of adverts nowadays.

'Well, I'd suggest you come and have a coffee or cold drink at my place now—it's only a five-minute walk away—but I'd hate to appear too forward.'

As sometimes occurs when staring into an open fire, David's eyes had become glazed whilst looking at Jane's shoes.

Something was at the back of his mind, and he hadn't been giving the conversation his full attention. Then the light dawned, the recall filtered through, and he grinned in triumph.

Still looking at the shoes, he mumbled, '*Just do it!*'

'Oh, David. I like a decisive man who speaks his mind—shall we go, then?'

*

The garden was in a worse state than he'd anticipated, but thankfully smaller as well.

David deduced that Mr Blake must have either died quite some time ago or not had much of an interest in gardening.

They were both sipping icy-chilled Prosecco from flutes with absurdly long, coloured stems and no base. His stem

69

was blue, and hers, pink, the glasses tailing off into blunt points.

He had a distant memory of Tracey buying a set many years ago as a Christmas novelty. The six glasses were propped in a type of flower vase, sitting on the dining-room sideboard for the duration of the festive week.

They were the type of item that was deemed to be '*oh, how clever*', and used two or three times in quick succession to some amusement, before gathering dust, eventually to be temporarily placed in a rarely-opened cupboard. Only when the occupants moved house, would the glasses see the light of day once more.

David's mind conjured up the images of similar fleetingly-essential items:

A vinyl LP called '*Tubular Bells*'.

A fantastically infuriating *Rubik's Cube*.

A *Slinky* you could witness *walking* down the stairs (those in bungalows had to make do with a form of static juggling).

A *Soda Stream,* to make your very own sparkling water or even Coke at a fraction of the retail cost, courtesy of an additional syrupy potion—epically disgusting and only palatable with a hefty shot of spirit.

And a cuddly toy—don't forget the cuddly toy.

A lump was developing in David's throat as his glass came back into focus. He visualised his wife in her Christmas apron, passing these absurd glasses to bemused family members.

'A top-up? I'm a bit partial to a drop of fizz; did you know you can buy three bottles of Prossy for the price of a reasonable bottle of shampoo. No prizes for guessing which I prefer, mind.'

Jane giggled, and David noticed her glass was empty; his remained untouched.

'If it's all the same to you, I think I should be making tracks.'

The enormity of the situation had found its way behind his eyeballs—an ominous sign for the impending agony of a 48-hour migraine.

He looked up and attempted a smile, wondering where and how to leave his full glass.

'Yes, right, of course. I wasn't sure it was the right thing to suggest, but you seemed to jump at the idea, so I ... '

Normally so sure of herself, Jane was now at a loss; things had been going so swimmingly until a glazed look had flashed across his face.

She felt foolish for offering the alcohol and extended a hand to take David's drink, but he'd already turned towards the house.

He stooped down, deftly planting the long stem deeply into an exposed mound of soil, the glass now hidden amongst the weeds and brambles.

'I'll see myself out—sorry about this.'

'Not at all—I'll see you on Friday, then?'

But he was already beyond earshot, closing the back door quietly behind him.

*

Grant had spent the last few days getting quotes. The best deal was 3,000 dollars, give or take a few bucks, and that included all the extras he'd requested.

He went for the deal and paid the guy, relieved that he now knew when he had to be in England. The flight he booked had a changeable return, for he genuinely had no idea when he'd be coming back home.

He studied living costs in Cambridge, calculating that he'd have around seven weeks in which to find a job—if he wasn't employed by then, he'd be on the coach back to Heathrow.

With everything settled, he decided there'd be no harm in sending Tabatha a message with his arrival date. It wasn't quite in keeping with his last message to her, but at least she'd know of his plans.

Hi Tabby, Hope I'm not bothering you. I've booked my flights— arriving London on 30ᵗʰ September. I have something to sort out which might take a couple of days, but I'm going to visit Cambridge soon after that. BIG Hugs, Grant x

*

Rick had always loved Gothic culture, and this first attracted him to Tabatha.

She'd been goth-like since her mid-teens, always favouring black clothes and black and white make-up.

Her skin was naturally pale, which also helped with the look, though she sometimes wondered if her ability to burn in the tamest sunlight might also be a factor in this lifestyle choice.

She'd have sensed if Rick was just going along with this fashion preference to please her, but she knew he found it sexy. She knew it in her bones.

Dad had never liked her '*lack of feminine colours*', and it made matters worse when Rick wholeheartedly approved of her tastes. He'd rant on about how Rick had steered her towards these tastes, conveniently forgetting the timeline involved.

But it was for this reason that she could never have shown off the latest selection of clothes which Mum had bought her with Dad's credit card, even when he'd bizarrely asked her to do just that the other day.

In the full-length mirror in her bedroom, Tabby studied herself with a critical eye. She liked what she saw but couldn't help wondering what Rick would think.

Her mum had given unanimous smiles of approval in the shops; she sensed who her daughter was dressing for, and it met with Tracey's wholehearted approval.

As she was wiggling out of a challengingly-tight pair of black leather trousers, Tabatha's phone chimed with the promise of an incoming text.

It was madness to think it might be from Rick, but she was in a sentimental frame of mind at this moment. With a nervous yet slightly pleasurable feeling in her tummy, she picked the phone up from her bed.

Tabatha hated to admit it, but it was almost a disappointment.

She started to compose a reply in her head. Could she ask if the ticket was refundable? No, of course she couldn't.

Could Grant maybe change the dates and come after Christmas?

Again, how callous was that?

Tabatha sat down on the bed—she was ashamed of herself.

She tapped out '*Dear Grant*', but that looked awful as well. She deleted it and lay back on her pillows, staring at the ceiling. Remnants of Blu-Tack could still be seen, giving an accurate indication of the size of the pictures they once secured.

The putty-like substance had been there for nearly half her life. Tiny isosceles triangles of poster with one torn, jagged side, still attached to some of the little pale-blue blobs.

There had been posters and photos on the walls as well, but the important stuff was directly in front of her when she lay on and in her bed.

There were four posters in total, and though they'd been thrown away when Rick became the major part of her life, she could imagine them as clearly as if they were still there.

Initially, she'd made the mistake of trying to place them in a perfect rectangle, but her eyes were drawn to the thin magnolia-coloured cross of ceiling paint, formed by the space between the images. She could never get them perfectly straight, so instead, she moved them to carefully haphazard positions, so nothing had to line up with anything else.

She remembered her father peering into the room and muttering '*OCD*' and had looked the acronym up. Far from hurt, she felt quite proud of his observation.

It appeared to be an eclectic mix of pictures with no relationship, but the binding theme was always the colour.

Black dominated everything, with sections of red and white for contrast.

A poster for Jurassic Park sat next to the iconic image of Che Guevara, and the Rolling Stones *Sticky Fingers* album, with the massive red lips and tongue on a black background, nestled beside a poster advertising the film, *V for Vendetta*.

Tabatha had never felt so close to being seventeen again.

Grant's message stared back, pleading for a reply, but words eluded her.

Seeking inspiration in the emoji section of WhatsApp (there were over 1,500 images to choose from), she elected for a *thumb-up* symbol to denote far greater optimism than she felt. To lessen the abruptness, she followed the cheery little hand symbol with the letter X, changing from upper-case to lower-case in a last-second change-of-heart, then pressed *Send*.

It was woefully inadequate and bordered on rudeness, but she could fall upon the ubiquitous '*busy-busy*' if, by way of reply, a single, probing question-mark appeared a moment later, and who the hell could blame him?

Tabatha felt loathsome and felt an overpowering desire to rest her eyes.

*

With the messages of encouragement which Tracey had been sending him recently, Rick decided he could finally face moving back into the old apartment in Mill Road.

It was a relatively easy transition from his brother's garden chalet. He'd brought very little with him and had added next to nothing in the past few months, save for an updated games console and the latest games on the market—it was an obsession he found impossible to give up.

Girls had come and gone in the first couple of months after Tabby. Those words used to make him chuckle, but that was the past. Three months of serious retrospection had led him to the conclusion that Tabby was the most important person in his life.

With absolute conviction that she was the girl for him, for life, he'd made the short trip down to a tattoo parlour and indelibly pledged allegiance to this woman.

Now he rubbed the tattoo on his forearm, the two of them linked for eternity.

He'd spent many days researching the lemniscate symbol before coming to a decision he was happy with.

One of the few books he still owned and treasured was a collection of the art by M.C. Escher; the works astounded him. He found what he was looking for on page 186— Möbius Strip II—a picture of red ants walking around a never-ending band, the shape of a subtly twisted figure 8. Like most of Escher's work, it completely defied visual logic.

He took the book to the tattooist and earnestly pointed out what he'd like; it was to be precisely as it appeared in the book.

The heavily-inked, middle-aged man had looked at him as if he inhabited another planet; they settled on the symbol of eternity …

Rick smiled as he touched the *T*; when Tabby saw this for real, he'd point out that both their initials were in medieval gothic font. She'd love that, he was sure.

He was a determined man; whatever it took, *nothing* would get in the way of his dream.

7

IT WAS the first time David had contemplated missing his *Tai Chi* class.

He'd missed the occasional session through sickness, and one a couple of weeks ago after his bicycle incident, but never under these circumstances.

He'd made a complete idiot of himself by offering to sort out Jane's overgrown garden, and his face glowed as he remembered the brazenness of his actions. It was ludicrous actions like these that ruined perfectly good marriages.

Fortunately, florists and high-quality restaurants existed for exactly these situations, and Friday was as good a day as any.

'Off to Keep-Fit, Dear? No over-doing it today; you looked very peaky after Tuesday's session.'

David's heart had travelled up to his mouth again—just as unpleasant as the first time, but he was getting a little more used to it now.

'Did I? Well I've no idea why. There's absolutely no logical reason for it, I assure you.'

Tracey was looking at him in a very strange way; in his current mental state, it felt almost intimidating.

'What? What's the matter? Did I say something wrong? I've told you—I feel fine—never better. Actually, I'm astonished how good I'm feeling at …'

'David, what's the matter? I mean, *really*—what's the matter?'

It seemed impossible, but it must be true. He'd heard of female intuition but disregarded it as pure myth. Yet here it was, in all its glory, toying with him, terrorising him. It was like his thoughts and fears were tumbling out of his ears in the form of Scrabble words, for his wife to read at her leisure.

All seven letters and a triple-word score—you're out, David,— you're fucked.

Perhaps he should just confess? Get it all off his chest and accept that a life of solitude and abject misery was just around the corner. Tracey knew him so well that not even his thoughts were private.

David smiled to himself; how ironic—if only Tabatha had been blessed with the same gift, she could have predicted how it would end up with that Rick Harrison.

But maybe not; you didn't need to be a clairvoyant to know what the future held for anyone unfortunate enough to be involved with Tricky Ricky.

He didn't know what he'd do if that smarmy little shit ended up crawling his way back into their lives. Shuddering, he visualised the four of them at a restaurant, paid for by yours truly, obviously. The image of Tabatha and Tracey openly fawning and flirting, pawing his damn tattoo.

David began to feel sick. There was a high-pitched whining in the distant background, repetitive and consistent, vying for his attention.

'I'm calling a doctor. Where are those painkillers—I suppose you've finished the lot, have you? Oh, for God's sake, David, can't I trust you with *anything*?'

He could definitely taste lunch in his mouth. Smoked trout was always a bad one for repeating, but even so …

It was Tracey's voice, alright, and she didn't trust him—she was angry.

Jesus—really, REALLY, strong, trouty-taste.

The toilet was too far away.
Oh hell …
Oh well …
Oh dear …

'*DAVID!*'

*

Even with the bedroom door closed and locked (as it nearly always was), Tabatha could hear the unmistakeable sound of someone being sick.

Having had her fair share of binge-drinking before Rick came along, she'd taken part in the occasional throw-up, both as a spectator and a participant.

It was strange that you could never tell the gender of a person by the sound of them being sick. It was much like yawning, too—as soon as you saw or heard someone, it was kind of contagious.

This was the last thing Tabby needed at this moment, dressed in her new goth gear, with matching full-face black and white make-up. The facial piercings had been stubborn at first (it had been a while since she'd last worn studs in her lower lip, nostril, and eyebrow), and the top of the ear had pinched a bit, but the ear-lobe was fine as she hadn't stopped wearing earrings.

'*Tabatha*?! Get down here at once, please? I need a hand—*now*. I'm afraid your father has disgraced himself.'

This was a disaster. She so didn't need her parents to see her like this—Tabatha currently made Amy Winehouse look like a cherubic angel.

'*TABATHA! NOW, PLEASE!*'

'I'm in the loo—I'll be a few minutes.'

'*NO YOU'RE NOT! YOU'RE TALKING FROM JUST BEHIND YOUR BEDROOM DOOR!*'

Tabatha sighed and unlocked the door; why bother to reminisce about one's teenage years?—just stay at home with the parents and relive them for real.

She spotted her dad lying at the bottom of the stairs; he appeared to be eating his own vomit.

'*What the fu …*'

Tracey looked up and saw Siouxsie *sans* her Banshees sashaying down the stairs.

'*What the fu …*'

David, regaining semi-consciousness, revolved his face in the warm stew to take in Miss Dracula standing next to him.

'*What the fu …*'

*

Much showering later (all three of them—Tracey had fallen foul of collateral diced-carrot strafe damage, and David refused to apologise to his daughter for the glop on her precious new shoes, whilst she appeared to be attending an

Addams Family convention), they were sat around a very sullen kitchen table.

Tabatha was determined to remain in listen-only mode, slowly turning a rebellious gold ring in her left nostril. The fact she'd had to pluck up the courage to wear this, to even consider it to be an act of defiance, made her want to weep.

She wanted to leave home before dinner—even before finishing the mug of tea in front of her, but the small matter of finances made that impossible. Well, not impossible; not if Rick was added to the equation.

It was probably only one tantalising text away—freedom.

As her parents chuntered on, Tabatha tried to imagine the words she'd need to compose to have Rick running from his brother's house to her.

It wouldn't even require any real finesse, which was weirdly disappointing. *'Come and get me'* would have brought him to the front door within the hour.

This was confusing. Why was Rick less appealing because she knew how much he wanted her? Had she desired him more when she knew he was off-limits?

And why was she even *thinking* about getting back with someone who'd hurt her so much that she wished he was dead?

How could life pan out like that? How could she have chosen those new clothes with only Rick in mind—wanting to please him, even though she wasn't with him and he'd ruined her life?

She visualised walking into their apartment again unexpectedly, shuddering as the images played once more in her mind. Unbearable pain; why did she do this, over and over again?

The swaying, grinding, agonising seconds before Rick saw her, his face hot with colour and sweat. Then the final second as he jumped away—away and *out* from that girl.

Tears flowed down her cheeks. There was no urge to howl or even whimper—just burning behind the eyes and a tickle on the face as the liquid found a path to her lap.

The nightmare had temporarily dialled out her parents' incessant bickering, but she gradually became aware they'd stopped talking.

Tracey put a hand towards her daughter's face, but Tabatha recoiled.

Abruptly, she stood up. The chair legs screeched loudly on the tiles. (When sticky-backed felt pads had failed to work years ago on the newly-laid travertine floor, David had fitted 24 punctured luminous-green tennis balls to the chair legs. His wife declared him clinically insane, before throwing them all in a bin.)

'Just leave me alone. Leave me the fuck alone!'

Tabatha ran to the kitchen door and slammed it behind her, the house-shuddering explosion of the front door following close behind.

Tracey was walking to the door before David put a hand firmly on her wrist.

'Best let her go. She won't listen to either of us, and why should she? She's in her thirties, for God's sake.'

Tracey stared at David's hand around her wrist; this could soon spiral into uncharted territory for them both. She looked into his face, and he reluctantly released his hand.

'What's happening to us, David? How have we got to this stage? Everything was so perfect, and then …'

'And then Rick shattered our daughter's life. Then he was gone, and everything started to heal, but now you're helping to bring him back into her life—our lives, once again.'

The kitchen door made an even louder noise, followed by the rhythmic thumps of Tracey ascending the stairs.

David covered his face with both hands and began to quietly repeat Taoist *Tai Chi* chants.

*

It was always a bustling road, full of cosmopolitan diversity and ceaseless commerce. One either loved it or avoided it, much like motorbikes, fitness-gyms, and Marmite.

Tabatha adored Mill Road. This was where she thought her world had ended, yet the place still called to her. London had bohemian streets like this, but only for so long, then high earners and designer labels and coffee houses moved in (though nobody had yet discovered which occurred first), and property prices soared.

And then it was never the same street again.

Mill Road had always been and would always be, well, Mill Road.

An empty mug of coffee sat on a pavement table in front of her as she stared at the little terraced-house on the opposite side of the road. The two upstairs windows held all of her attention. The curtains were drawn open, but with no lights on the room was dark, no interior details to be seen within.

Tabatha didn't need illumination. She could see the room now and everything in it, including Rick and the trollop.

That wasn't really fair. Whatever story Rick had fed her mum, the girl could easily have been an innocent victim of his seduction techniques. The most galling thing was that she'd been so much younger. True, she was slim and pretty as well, but Tabatha had spent enough time analysing this to deduce that the opposite would probably have been even more painful.

Short of confronting Rick and asking him, it was all pure conjecture.

She played out a scenario where she was only allowed to ask him one question; if so, what would she choose to ask?

'*Why?*' was a bit simplistic and all-encompassing—a cop-out.

'*What did I do wrong?*' fell into a similar category—bleating like a martyr and too generalised.

No, after much deliberation, what she'd really like to ask Rick was, '*How long has this been going on?*'

Oh, and if she were allowed a Part B to the question, then, '*And how many others have there been?*'

It took her some time to conclude that these were the answers she wanted more than anything else. Yet, once she'd reached that decision, it seemed the most obvious thing in the world. Wouldn't *everyone* want to know that before anything else?

This would be her second question to him, then. If and when she saw him again, and with pleasantries out of the way, this was what Rick Harrison would hear from her lips.

There was just one problem with her theory. Rick would lie—probably. Well, he'd lie if he thought the truth would be something she didn't want to hear.

So, what *did* she want to hear? Well, she wanted the truth above all else. That was what she craved more than anything and everything.

As long as it was a palatable truth …

'*That night was the first time, and there have never been any others, I swear—nor will there be—ever.*'

84

That would have been the best answer. After seven months, she could just about handle that and, perhaps, learn to forgive. Possibly.

What if it was a complete lie? Did she have any way of proving it, short of hiring a private detective with money she didn't have?

And what of the worst reply?

'Sorry Tabs, that one's been going on about five years, and I guess about sixty or so women in total. Yeah, I guess about one a month on average. But I'll stop now, honest.'

At least she could be certain of the truth with that answer.

For the second time that day, she was going to cry.

It was the last thing she needed, especially on the pavement of a busy street, but it wasn't going to be possible to hold the floodgates back.

Why wasn't I enough for you, Rick?

Tabatha closed her eyes and felt the tears roll again. She'd only open them once she knew the crying had stopped.

'Penny for them, Tabs.'

She'd lost track of time, but it surely couldn't have been long? The words in her head were so clear—she could almost hear him for real—as if he was there in front of her. *'Penny for them?'*

Even clearer, if that was possible.

Something touched her arm.

'What the fuck?!'

She jerked back involuntarily and opened her eyes.

Rick was the other side of the small metal table, kneeling on the pavement with his bare arms folded, forearms resting inches away from her cup.

She took in the new tattoo before her eyes met his.

'What the hell are you doing here?'

'Hey, calm down, I live here; I came over the road for a coffee. What are *you* doing here?'

He smiled into her eyes as he rubbed the tattoo self-consciously, then he took in the sight of her whole face.

Tabatha put both hands under her eyes and rubbed the skin furiously. Dampness and dark make-up smeared the sides of her index fingers. Infuriatingly, Rick was already offering a café-branded napkin.

She snatched it and buried her face in the scratchy paper. Tabatha badly needed to blow her nose but knew it would sound disgusting. As she was coming to terms with this mini-disaster, Rick saved her by offering to get a refill. Without waiting for a reply, he disappeared inside.

'When did you move back here? I thought you were at your brother's place?'

Tabatha guessed she probably looked like a Panda, but at least her face and nose were dry.

When she'd stormed out of her home, she was armed only with a ten-pound note and some loose change in the tiny single pocket of her black leather trousers. A make-up emergency trip to the Ladies was therefore not an option.

However, even if the choice had been available to her, it would have sent out the wrong signal, and Tabatha had no intention of losing face to gain a face.

'I only recently moved back. It's taken me this long to come to terms with, you know ...'

'With how you fucked up?'

The remnants of her recent explosion were bubbling again.

'Oh, come on, Tabby, you never gave me a chance to explain. I tried so hard to contact you, but you just didn't want to listen.'

'A chance?! And what *chance* did you give me when I walked into our bedroom—*our* bedroom. What fucking chance did you give me?!'

For the second time that afternoon, a chair slid violently back as she stood. This time, the table in front of her wasn't an 8-seater made of solid mahogany, but a 2-seater built from the flimsiest alloy-metal.

The table and its contents landed briefly in Rick's lap before he stood even more abruptly than his ex. The black Americano was having a more immediate effect than her milky Cappuccino.

'*Shit*, you've burnt me! What the hell?! Christ, I need a bucket of iced-water—*QUICK!*'

'Damn, I should've thought of just that when I walked in on you—that's *exactly* what you needed.'

'*QUICK! It's agony!*'

'You're not wrong. It was, as you rightly say, agony.'

'*Tabby! HELP!*'

'Dad was right; it probably *is* Mum's initial that's on your tattoo.'

'*What? Hey, wait!*'

Tabatha ran blindly across the road, narrowly avoiding contact with a stunned and instantly-furious taxi-driver.

She could hear Rick calling out her name as she continued to blindly run, having no idea where she was heading.

Nearly out of earshot, she heard him shout across the traffic. The words tore through her;

'*It's not what it looks like.*'

Tabatha turned and looked back at the café; Rick was limping towards her.

'Please wait, Tabby. Please?'

8

SHE HADN'T known about his car.

It was chocolate-coloured, a Mercedes convertible, old enough to have become desirable and more valuable again, not that she was aware of this.

The tan-leather upholstery was warm to the touch in the September sun.

Typically, he'd left the hood down, even though left in the train station car park. Rick had never been too fussed with security; plenty of times in the past she'd return to their home, only to find the door unlocked.

'Aren't you worried about someone stealing it, or taking what's in the car?'

'There's nothing to take unless you count the odd spanner or spare fuse. Besides, I've over-insured it anyway; if somebody wanted to nick it, I'd make a decent profit.'

'Typical. Business must be going well, then?'

'The telecom contract was really good news, but don't let that Mercedes badge fool you. I bought it at an auction in Duxford a couple of months ago. It didn't sell in the official sale, but I was looking at it when the owner jumped in to drive it back home to London. We had a chat, and it was obvious the drive back wasn't very appealing ...'

He smiled.

It reminded her of good times; very good times, but from another life.

'Pop your seat belt on, and I'll take you for a spin. It's hardly luxurious, but a definite improvement on Rusty.'

It was difficult for Tabatha not to smile back. The memory of *Rusty*, a decrepit old Fiat Rick had owned when they first met, was surprisingly vivid.

A shade of burgundy when new, now more accurately described by its adopted name, they'd foolishly headed down to the South of France in *Rusty*. They'd paid their last respects to the car (and a hefty dumping-charge) just outside Lyon. Her dad had paid for their trains and flights back home.

'Not a long spin, though.'

'Absolutely not; I'll make sure you're safely back with Mum and Dad long before dusk, scout's honour.'

'We're coming up to rush hour—will it blow up like Rusty if we sit in traffic for long?'

'If I knew where Eva's ears were, I'd put my hands over them.'

'Eva?'

'Well, what with her being German and brown, yeah?'

His impish expression was incredibly familiar.

'You're mental.'

'Thank you.'

The car started with a bassy-thrumming purr, which told her it was a V8 engine. It wasn't that she was an expert, but a V8 was the easiest engine to identify of them all.

'So how many gallons to the mile does Eva do, then?'

'Tabby! How can you be so rude? She's no more of a drinker than you are.'

He stroked the steering wheel lovingly.

'Ignore her, Eva—she's only teasing.'

The traffic was better than Rick had feared (he'd specifically avoided rush-hour driving in this car for fear of blowing a head gasket or worse), and they made their way slowly but steadily along Trumpington Road.

She'd been invited to choose one of the tapes that lay huddled in the glove-box—the 40-year-old cassette player was still in situ and working.

'I emailed the old owner to see if he wanted them back, but he doesn't have anything to play them on now.'

'I'm not surprised. How old is this car? It's very comfy and all that; like sitting in an old armchair, but it's kind of … worn … ish?'

'Oh, you mean the patina? You have to pay extra for that, you know—provenance. All the marks confirm how genuine she is and back up the mileage.'

Rick put a hand through the hair he used to have fifteen years ago—a habit Tabatha had always found fascinating.

The clouds were forming, and the temperature had started to drop, as so often seemed the case in the UK, when people drove around with the roof down.

She leaned his way and glanced at the speedometer.

'Fifty-eight thousand miles? Doesn't that seem a bit low for all of this … *patina*? Are you sure the speedo hasn't been clocked?'

'I'm very sure. It's been back to zero a couple of times, but that was while on its way to what you see now—two-hundred and fifty-eight thousand miles.'

'Oh my God—a quarter of a million miles? That's further than the moon!'

'Yup. Eva and I are currently on our way to Venus, aren't we, old girl?'

He patted the top of the sun-damaged dashboard.

'You're welcome to join us.'

Rick turned to Tabatha, but she avoided his stare, sensing the loaded question.

'*In Flight* by George Benson—is that okay? Seems to be a similar vintage to the car … I mean *Eva*. Do I just slot it in?'

'Yup, but turn it on first. Twist the button on the left—that's the volume too. All mod cons and no expense spared.'

His mood was infectious, and she was fighting it. Tabatha followed the instructions, and an aerial rose jerkily from the front wing.

'Oh, you have got to be *kidding*!'

Tabatha couldn't contain a giggle.

'I haven't seen one of those in *years*.'

'My absolute fave bit of Eva. Took me two hours and half a can of lubricant, but voila—the electric workal is aerialing. Apparently, I used to say that when I was a kid. I couldn't stop making the damn thing go up and down in Dad's car. He used to get so mad, telling me I'd break it. Then it broke …'

Rick put on a sad-clown face and looked at her again.

'You're a nutter.'

'You said I was '*mental*' earlier; is that a slight improvement?'

She punched him on the forearm.

'Ow! My tattoo! And you could have killed us—can't you see I'm driving?!'

'The tattoo's on your other arm, Rick, and we're doing three miles-an-hour—not even *you* could get whiplash-injury compensation if we crashed now.'

The sad clown expression remained as he leaned to his left and bumped her shoulder with the side of his head.

Tabatha found the music of Mr. Benson to be amazingly good.

They were free from the worst of the snarl-up and heading towards the M11 exit, which he ignored. From that point, she knew exactly where they were going.

'Are all the tapes as good as this? The old owner has good taste—how old was he?'

'She.'

'Figures.'

'Tabbbbyyy … She was in her sixties, maybe seventy.

'Forties, maybe thirty?'

He didn't take the bait.

'She'd owned the car from new—hubby bought it as a birthday present.'

'Nice pressie—true love, eh?'

Breathe … and continue.

They had places in Cannes and Lake Como, and they always drove—you can see where the quarter-million miles came from.'

'So why sell it?'

'Her husband died a few months ago. She couldn't handle seeing the car in the garage anymore—I guess the memories were too painful.'

He bit his lip, cursed himself, waited for the reply he knew was coming.

Silence save for George Benson.

They arrived at their destination—a quiet country pub they'd been coming to for years. He parked up, and they sat there, lost in their own private thoughts.

It was chilly sitting here with the roof down, the daylight sky bleeding towards a moody autumn dusk.

He put a hand on top of hers and looked into the part of a person's eyes which, every once in a while, exposes a fleeting glimpse into the soul.

'Can we listen to this track before we go in?'

And the words of '*Everything must Change*' were crystal clear.

With last orders being called, Tabatha realised she hadn't contacted her parents.

She felt bad; they'd be worried by now, but the evening with Rick had been special. She hadn't given it a thought.

Rick was peering out of the pub door.

'Oh bollocks!'

'What now?'

'It's pouring with rain!'

'That often occurs after thunder and lightning.'

'Tabby, my car's drowning!'

Oh, for Christ's sake, don't be so precious—at worst, she's getting a wash. What's the grief?'

'I left the top down!'

'Ah … that may be a problem.'

Tabatha peered out of a window and into the car park. As dark as it was on a sliver-mooned night, an ancient sodium light picked up the pitiful sight.

'Whoopsie.'

'*Fuuuuuuuck*.'

Rick sprinted into the car park. Dancing around the car, he appeared to be attempting to deflect the rain from entering the cabin by frantically waving his arms and hunching his back over the seats.

From the comfort of the bar, Tabatha was doing her best not to play a supportive role, but a gathering of cheering locals next to her was making this difficult.

The laughter curled its way outside to Rick.

Initially, he seemed unamused, turning towards the glow of the window and the small party of spectators. Even a novice lip-reader would have picked up the gist of his thoughts.

Then he slowed down, walked towards the darkness of a nearby shed, and came back holding a bamboo stick.

The dance movements were a little wayward, but the off-key chanting of *'I'm Singing in the Rain'* was met with unanimous and raucous approval by the entire pub.

The soft-top roof was eventually erected, turning the interior of the car into an indoor paddling pool.

Miraculously, Eva had started without complaint, but although it was impossible for Rick to get any wetter, the ride home for Tabatha was a very unappealing proposition.

With a promise from her that they'd meet up for dinner very soon, Rick called and paid for a taxi, then pointed the pseudo-amphibious vehicle towards his brother's house.

It would require a good two days' use of his sibling's single garage, the rental of an industrial-grade de-humidifier, and every towel in the house, but Eva wasn't catching pneumonia on his watch.

*

'How *could* you be so selfish? We've been worried sick about you! It was all I could do to stop your mother from calling the police. You realise it's after midnight?'

For a mild-mannered man, it was an outburst of rare severity.

'Oh, for God's sake, Dad, I'm in my *thirties*. What was she going to say; *'There's an adult who's temporarily living here, and she's been gone from the house for nearly half the day!'* Do you think that would have raised a SWAT team and helicopters?'

'There's no need for that type of attitude. You're only thirty …'

'Which I think you'll find is *in the thirties* …'

'And living somewhere for seven months is hardly temporar …'

'Well if you'd told me you were counting the hours …'

'I didn't mean that, and you know it, Tabatha. You left in such a storm today—such a mental state …'

'Oh, right—and you were in a perfectly normal frame of mind at the time, were you?'

'Not entirely, no, but I didn't run off into the wilderness …'

'*The wilderness* of … what? … Cambridge?' She wanted to laugh for effect, but her mood was too dark.

'You're a vulnerable single girl, and you're our daughter. We were both very worried …'

'And what makes you assume I'm *single*, hmmm?' Tabatha enjoyed a glow of smugness, which felt way better than any brief snort of derision.

'Well, I … I mean … Surely that's why you're living with us? Isn't it? Unless you mean that Aussie chap you've never met?'

'Much nearer to home than that, Dad. Pretty much in *the wilderness of Cambridge*, actually.'

96

She wanted to bite her tongue, but spite was a drug, and shock, its favoured poison.

David Mercer was at a loss. His wife was adamant that there had been no other boyfriends since the catastrophic debacle that was Rick Harrison.

Mental cogs more accustomed to the sweaty pressure of face-to-face personal bank loan applications were being frantically deployed, as he struggled in vain to fathom out the bewildering enigma that was Tabatha Mercer—his beautiful and priceless daughter.

And then it dawned.

'No … Ohhhhh, no.'

Blood was draining from his face at an alarming rate.

'I … I couldn't allow that to happen. *No.*'

'Oh, couldn't you now?'

Tabatha tightly folded her arms, very much in harmony with her mood.

'I didn't mean it like that, Tabby. You know wha …'

'*Tabby?*—I'm not sure you've ever called me that before, *Daddy.* As far as I recall, only Rick calls me that. You remember Rick?'

Crestfallen, David lowered his head.

'Surely you can't be serious? Even contemplating contact with him again would be insanity. He'd just walk all ov …'

'*Contemplating?* You need to keep up with the times, Dad—Rick and I are going out for dinner tomorrow night.'

Tabatha cursed under her breath—this wasn't entirely factual. A technicality, of course; she'd promised to go out with Rick *very soon*. Still, she couldn't back down now.

'And to save you or Mum calling out Special Forces and the National Guard, I very much doubt I'll be back tomorrow night. As in, not until the next morning, or afternoon, or whatever.'

This was odd; she'd smashed her dad to pieces, but the victory felt hollow. If she remained in his presence a moment longer, there was the very real risk of hugging him.

Tabatha walked briskly out of the room, but this time the door was shut gently.

*

There was a major glitch in the lie about tomorrow's date with Rick; what if he didn't call for a couple of days?

Tabatha was sure he'd eventually call, probably suggesting a meal on the weekend, but Thursday night? Unlikely.

She couldn't call him—that was sending out all the wrong vibes. She needed to be chased and wooed and, well, worshiped would be great, but spoilt rotten was sufficient.

No flowers, though. Absolutely *no* flowers at all.

Tabatha winced and started nibbling the side of a thumbnail. Any telepathy she shared with Rick was long gone; he wasn't going to call because she wanted him to.

Then it came to her—a text. More formal than WhatsApp—a little less *'I'm contemplating slightly forgiving you'*.

'Hi Rick, I don't want to break my promise, but I'm busy this weekend and most of next week. If you want to see me soon it will have to be tomorrow. I'm out for lunch with Mum' ...

She stopped tapping keys and stared at the words.

... 'I'm out for lunch with friends but could make it for dinner tomorrow night ...

Too needy—hmmm …

' *… but might be able to make it for a quick bite to eat tomorrow evening. Let me know, Tabs.'*
Nearly.
'Let me know, Tabby.'
Nope.
'Let me know, Tabatha.'
Hmmm.
'Tabatha X.'
Yes … no.
'Tabatha x.'
Send.

'Yeah, no probs. Pick you up from your place at 7? *kisses*

'Yes ok. Do I need to wear a dress or will jeans do?'

'You suggested a 'quick bite' - I wasn't planning on anywhere too posh?'

Shite—rule number one when lying—remember one's lies …
Tabatha nibbled some more as she typed one-handed.

'I meant the style of the place. It doesn't have to be a 12-course tasting menu to wear a dress!'
She pressed '*Send,*' and the gnawed skin came to the end of its tether, painfully nipping the side of her thumb in protest. A *whoosh* sound and a new blue box appeared on the screen. '*Delivered*' helpfully appeared below the box, much to her despair (WhatsApp offered the facility to delete a message just sent—plain old text messages did not).

'Bollocks,' thought Tabatha.
'*Delivered*' changed to '*Read*'.
'Bollocks,' said Tabatha.

'*Ok OK - Sorry! Jeans will be fine.* :-D'

His exclamation mark was a mixture of martyrdom, humour (at her expense), and patronisation. How the hell was that even possible?

Tabatha sighed and started on the other side of the throbbing thumbnail.

The big 'D' smile was more of the same.

She spat out a thread of skin and scrutinised the blossoming dot of blood on the quick.

'*Jeans it is then!!* :D :D *See you tomoz at 7.*'

Such were the vagaries of lying. She turned the phone off for fear of sending any more incriminating rubbish, then stared absentmindedly at her large clothes cupboard.

There were a dozen or more pairs of jeans in a variety of shades, ranging from summer white to winter black.

From brand new and never worn to more holes than denim (also unworn and mostly more expensive, in a blatant piss-take to the consumer aka mug).

She browsed possible tops to wear, then dragged everything out and put the lot on her bed. With shoes and a scarf to add to this unfathomable puzzle, it would take a couple of hours to create a look that appeared to have been conjured up in an idle couple of minutes.

*

'Very smart. Don't you think you'll be a little chilly, though? The evenings are drawing in now; it can get really nippy.'

Tabatha eyed her mother, just about managing to avoid putting hands on hips and sighing.

'I'm not going to hang out in the park all evening with my friends and a few cans of fruit cider, Mum—I'm not fourteen. I'm going for a real meal. In a restaurant. Indoors.'

Tabatha looked down and wondered how her hands had reached her hips and her voice had mutated to that of a fourteen-year-old.

She sighed.

'Well, I'm sure you know best, sweetie. You look lovely; a little birdie told me you're out with Rick tonight?'

'Since when did Dad morph into *a little birdie*? I don't imagine he told you, either; more like a spittle-fuelled rant, was it?'

'You know I'm on your side, dear. Have a lovely time, and we'll see you … when …?'

'When you see me … If that's alright with you? I mean, as long as I have your consent?' She could feel the fingers digging into her hips, the defiance of a young teenager oozing from every pore.

Tracey thought to touch her daughter gently on the face and calm the child, but wisdom stopped her just in time.

'Have a lovely time. Take a key with you—we won't wait up.'

'I wasn't planning on taking one; someone's bound to be here around lunchtime, surely?' Tabatha's heels squeaked on the tiles as she swivelled 180-degrees, some errant midnight-blue shoe polish grinding into the floor.

Tracey dampened a scouring pad as she listened to yet another stairs stomp.

The knock at the front door announced Rick.

As far back as Tabatha could remember, he was the only person who didn't use the doorbell.

With a final pre-flight smile and a pout in the hall mirror, she opened the door.

His eyes lit up.

'Very smart, Tabs.'

'Thanks; that's exactly what my mum said.'

'Ah, well that has to be a good thing, right?'

Rick's smile instantly disarmed what could have been a poor start.

'And *hello*, Tracey; lovely to see you.'

Tracey slunk out of the almost-closed dining room door she'd assumed would render her invisible.

'Hello Rick—what a surprise!'

She patted the back of her hair as the world went still.

Tabatha's eyes rolled.

'Shall we go, then?'

Tabatha's once-over of Rick whilst her mother fawned had noted identical clothing to the pub, save for a different shirt. At most, he'd spent a couple of minutes getting ready. It was still a man's world, whatever the feminists liked to think.

'I'm sure you'll take good care of her. Will you be back … late?'

'*Muu-UMM*! What the actual fu …'

Rick's timely interruption drowned further awkwardness.

'She'll be back well before tomorrow, Mrs. M.—trust me on that. I mean, what's there to do after midnight on a school-night in Cambridge, eh?'

Tabatha pushed past him and towards the brown Mercedes in the road. If the seat was still a puddle, so be it— she couldn't stay in her parents' house a moment longer.

Impressively, the car was not only bone dry but pleasantly warm. She watched Rick kiss her mum on the cheek, then a hug, obviously, and walk down the path.

As Tabatha watched her resume the hair fluffing, the women locked eyes, and the front door closed.

A floor above, her dad was staring down, a mix of dismay and confusion etched on his face.

*

Coffee had followed a pleasant, if slightly spicy meal, at one of the city's more intimate bistros—this one with a Mexican theme.

It would surely get busier at the weekend, or the restaurant was doomed. Small talk with an ex-lover in this environment was an easy enough game to play, as long as it remained small.

Tabatha had thought long and hard about how to steer the conversation towards what she really wanted to talk about. As with seemingly everything involving relationships, the plan was doomed from the start when Rick asked her the very thing she'd been plucking up the courage to raise.

'So, any significant others in the past few months?'

It was delivered with so much calm. Why did he never display or suffer stress?

Maybe he wasn't stressed or jealous? Maybe he was genuinely interested in her love life post-apocalypse, and didn't give a shit what the answer was?

Maybe he didn't even believe an apocalypse had occurred?

Maybe …

'Tabby? Oh, you're tallying up?'

Rick chuckled as she jolted to the present. He really *didn't* give a shit. An all-new Rick, void of all jealousy.

Tabatha swallowed the simmering rage.

'There's been nobody, and there is currently nobody. I'd hardly be sitting opposite you now if there was, would I?'

Rick's face was unreadable—a pleasant, static smile.

She couldn't bear the nothingness, the silence, even as the distant memory of a school psychology lesson churned away. *Here's your hole in the ground, Miss Mercer, and here's the JCB you'll be using to drastically enlarge it—don't forget the seatbelt.*

'To answer my own question, no, I wouldn't be with you now if I was seeing someone else. I suppose you've been fighting them off for the past few months?'

In a fair world, the question would have been delivered via WhatsApp, so she could immediately delete it and try again.

'What about the Aussie lad? The one you're apparently besotted over; doesn't he count?'

She hadn't thought about Grant since forever.

Well, weeks perhaps—definitely a couple.

'*Besotted*—really? She'd never even met the guy, so how did that work?

She wouldn't be here now if she were *besotted* with someone else.

Besides, what was she worrying about? The man across the table had cheated on her. Cheated in front of her. *IN FUCKING FRONT OF HER!*

Tabatha began to hyperventilate, but if anything, it seemed to help. Just as she sensed Rick's concern, she looked up and stared at him.

'Actually, he *doesn't* count. I haven't touched him, dated him, or even kissed him. And, more importantly, *much* more importantly, I haven't gone to bed with him.'

Deafening silence.

'What's your take on that, Rick?'

This was so *not* how Tabatha had planned it. She was sweating and wincing, still unable to read anything in his body language.

'I've been waiting to tell you this for months.'

'Plenty of time to come up with your best ever story then, hmmm?'

She tasted salt on her tongue and stifled a yelp of pain.

For once in my life, can't I just shut the fuck up?

'I'm not like you, Tabs. I don't have the life you've had—the privileged background and all the goodies that go with that.'

'And that's the best you can come up with?'

No, I can't—of course I can't.

He showed no sign of impatience or exasperation; quite the opposite.

'Tabby, when I finish this glass of wine in front of me, I've finished my story. Then I'll answer any and every question you have, I promise.'

She'd drunk more than him, as always, her glass long empty. She reached for his, sipping the velvet-coloured burgundy, leaving him a quarter of the contents.

It also served to coat the taste of blood in her mouth.

'Keep going, I'm all ears.'

It was a doleful smile. His hand moved across the table to make contact with hers, but she was having none of it. Tabatha crossed her arms.

'Whenever we've had money problems, they've never been problems for you—not really. You'd stress when big bills came in and we didn't have the funds to pay for them, but ultimately, you knew Mum or Dad would bail you out.

You never rubbed my nose in it, and I'm eternally grateful for that, but ...'

'Oh Rick. You know I'd never ...'

'Let me finish, sweetheart.'

There was a gloss of perspiration on his freshly shaved head; he took the glass and finished the wine in one mouthful.

Like someone putting on their best clothes, Tabatha knew Rick would always shave his head before a special occasion. He never let it grow beyond a stubble, but this habit was one of his quirks. Ridiculously, she felt smug that he'd considered this to be just such an occasion.

'I have to get this out. Let me—please?'

Tabatha nodded, looking for more wine. She was close to signalling their waiter, but now was not the time.

'You never spoke about the money; never, ever spoke about it. The money—the fucking money.'

Rick wiped the back of his hand roughly against the corner of an eye, and this took her breath away; five years and she'd never seen him cry.

'Don't you see that's what this is all about? It was the money, not the sex. *Always* the money. I never had a fall-back. When I was short on covering the bills, I was short. Nowhere to turn, not even my brother; not after the first couple of years, at any rate.'

This was a Rick she didn't remotely recognise.

'I started on the credit cards at first, promising myself I'd settle up when the bill came in.' He chuckled darkly and stared across the room; the last table of diners was leaving, and the staff had evaporated.

'I maxed out the credit card, then applied for another one with a bigger limit, and stuck the lot on that one. When work came in, I'd pay as much as I could, but I was only scratching the surface. Most months, I was barely covering the interest payments.'

Tabatha's mouth was falling open.

'But what about all the websites you were designing? You were always working. *Always.*'

'Working on trying to secure a decent contract, or maybe on one that paid peanuts. Until this telecoms contract, I was only ever breaking even.'

'Why didn't you te …'

'Why didn't I tell you? Isn't it obvious? Your dad was always looking down his nose at me. How many times do you think I heard him tell you what a huge mistake you'd made by ending up with me? And not just telling you. Didn't you ever wonder why I did everything to avoid going to your place? What do you think it was like to have your father grill me about the money he gave you every couple of months to keep you afloat—*us* afloat?'

Her mouth was very slowly opening and closing, her eyes beginning to sting. Tabatha knew she could only listen; there were no words to offer.

'It got to the point where I couldn't get any more credit cards. I'd started to default on the minimum payments, and my credit ratings went to shit. Then I got lured in by a loan shark—*"Reduce all those bills to just one easy payment every month"*, or some crap like that. I knew the interest rates were insane, but I was going out of my mind with all the bills and phone calls. I couldn't take it anymore, Tabby.'

As he looked at her, the defeat turned to defiance; nostrils flared, and his eyes glared aggressively.

'But Dad could have … I mean, I could have hel …'

'You see? You *see?!* I never told you because you'd have never understood. It's impossible for you to understand.'

He called out loud, and a waiter came scampering.

'Two large glasses of red—whatever the nearest bottle is to hand—I don't care.'

The man was apologetic and attempted to point out that the restaurant was closing, but this wasn't his lucky night.

'I'm sure it'll be closing soon—probably this month—but for now, stick them on the bill and bring that along with the drinks. Thanks.'

Rick's expression didn't bode well for a refusal. The waiter scurried away and returned quickly.

Handing a credit card over, he turned to Tabatha.

'Don't worry—this one will do nicely. I've paid all the others off and ditched them.'

He told the employee to add ten percent and punched his number in.

'Can we at least go halves?'

The glare answered her question.

He raised his glass.

'So, before I was rudely interrupted—ready?'

Tabatha nodded, and glasses made contact.

'Please don't believe I'm trying to put the blame on others, but this has an awful lot to do with Granger.'

Granger. Alpert Box-Granger to be precise—the pain of Tabatha's existence with Rick.

He was the point of an entirely unnecessary and unwelcome triangle, vying for Rick's attention at all times. It was classic best-mate's syndrome and a potent opponent to any couple.

Alpert (she refused to call him by the tail of his ludicrous, double-barrelled surname, like some sort of public prep-school religion) and his mother were the living proof of the axiom, '*From riches to rags in three generations.*'

Nearly a hundred years ago, the Box-Granger family had a formidable chain of bakeries, their more fanciful products being enjoyed by no less than Georges V and VI. The royal seal of approval on the sides of their dainty pastry boxes was a licence to print money.

For Alpert's grandfather, the only child of the original founder, it was also a licence to sell said company when the old man popped his clogs. Considerable funds and efforts were spent becoming a second-string racing driver before falling upon the much costlier option of running his own racing team.

He perished on his yacht along with all the crew, sailing from their base in Monaco to his home on West Palm Beach.

Alpert's father, having known nothing but the most privileged of backgrounds, was ill-equipped to halt the family's declining fortunes. He had the sense to sell the remaining homes and cars and yachts, placing all the money in a bank close to their one remaining, but suitably lavish, property in London.

All would have been well, save for the lure of Mayfair's nightlife and, more significantly, the nearby casinos.

Father had died from sclerosis of the liver in his late-40s, the bank balance and heavily-mortgaged property in a similar state of decay. Alpert and his mother had moved up to Cambridge and purchased a small townhouse with much of the remaining money.

The boy had never worked a day in his life, which initially led to swift expulsion from his local school, where he'd first met Rick. His mum continued to drink the final thousands left, whilst Alpert claimed benefits and went to the Job Centre every week to prove he was completely unemployable.

He hung around continually with Rick, becoming extremely adept at completing all manner of PlayStation and Nintendo games.

Tabatha had heard this seemingly Walter Mitty history of the Box-Granger family more than once from Rick. The more she heard it, the less plausible it felt. He gave her the creeps, and she'd always kept a wide berth of him when possible.

'Why does that not surprise me?'

'As I said, this is all about money, and Granger had found a way to elevate himself from the breadline. He knew I was in a desperate situation with this loan company, so he told me how I could bale myself out. Just a temporary measure.'

Rick took a large gulp of courage.

'Oh, my God! You were selling drugs?! Oh Jesus!'

'No! Nothing like that—it wasn't illegal at all. Immoral, maybe. Yeah, definitely immoral.'

It was a shock, but nothing was going to surprise her about Alpert, though this was hardly enough of an explanation for what had torn her life apart.

'So, he's turned his hand to pimping?'

'No. Again, no, nothing like that. Well, when I say *nothing* like that, I mean ...'

Rick was sweating profusely.

'What I mean is, Granger had found a way of getting an income—quite a lot of money, by, well ... Look, he found this website where men could become errr ... like, escorts.'

She looked down at the detritus-stained white tablecloth and felt herself shaking.

'Escorts? *Escorts?* As in ... prostitute escorts? Hookers?'
'Well kind of, I guess ...'

'You're saying that Alpert is a prostitute?'

'Well an escort, really. More than a prosti ...'

'So Alpert's a hooker. Okay. Okaaay ... But disgusting as that is, what the hell has it got to do with you? Can we stop beating around the bush, here? How about you tell me why I came back home and caught you fucking a girl I've never seen before? How about doing that, Rick?'

His face was moving from tanned-sheen to a colour not dissimilar to the wine they were enduring.

'I just have. He was earning a hundred quid an hour, Tabby. With you being away for a couple of weeks, I'd done the sums—I could get myself back on my feet—get everything back to normal again.'

The restaurant's background music had been turned off some time ago. With only cyclists allowed to ride down Trinity Street, a heavy, sweat-filled silence had fallen from the low ceiling.

The only other person in the restaurant, their waiter, cleared his throat and moved back to the bar near the main door. He'd been preparing tables quite close to them, and Tabatha assumed his timely exit signified he'd heard everything.

'Perhaps you should give the waiter your number? You know, in case his girlfriend or wife needs a little extra something on the side when he's at work?'

'Tabs! Do you know how hard it's been for me to tell you all this?'

'Hmmm, about a tenth of one percent as hard as having to witness it in the flesh?'

'Look, babes, I did it because of the money – to get myself back on my feet and …'

It was an unfortunate choice of metaphor and irresistible for Tabatha:

'Or back *off* your feet in this case.'

Rick sighed deeply, shook his head, and downed the rest of his wine.

111

'I knew there was no way of describing this that could avoid upsetting you.'

'How astonishingly telepathic of you.'

Now there was no wine in either glass.

'Shall we go, Rick? Don't forget to hand the man your business card on the way out.'

They were walking across town, ostensibly to get to his car, but it was also the quickest route home for Tabatha.

This bombshell from Rick had left her reeling. It had also caused a major setback to her plans for the night. She'd assumed he'd be more than keen to take her back to his place, and the excitement of that, plus the statement of independence to her parents, was an intoxicating blend.

She couldn't go back home tonight—it simply wasn't an option.

But she couldn't go back with Rick, either—that was even less of an option. Apart from anything else, she wouldn't have been able to resist asking him how much he was going to charge her, and if she might be able to get a mate's rates discount.

'At least let me give you a lift home?'

She stopped walking and faced him, her arms still rigidly folded.

'What part of *fuck* and *off*, don't you understand?'

They continued their walk up Trumpington Street, a good metre of distance between them. There were a few random students wandering or staggering, clearly a lot the worse for wear than either of them. They all laughed and cackled with the abandon of those who possess no responsibilities or worries. She envied and despised them all in equal measures.

'I don't understand either word. Can't you understand I made a terrible mistake, caused by being backed into a corner with nowhere to turn?'

'I'm *certain* you understand the first word.'

It would have been impossible to detect, but even as she continued to attack him with everything she possessed, she was desperately trying to process his situation—their situation. Trying to justify his actions to herself, however abhorrent. She began to feel nauseous as she felt his hand on her arm.

'I should give up, shouldn't I? Forget you forever and disappear—get out of your life, once and for all. But I can't forget you—that's impossible. Whatever happens, I can never forget you.'

'Can you give me some space, please? Like, now.'

'Is there nothing I can say or do, Tabby? Anything? I'll do anything, darling. Please?'

'Space. Give me space. Absolutely, like, *NOW!*

He bowed his head in pure misery and stepped back.

This was the best move Rick had made all evening. The entire contents of an average-at-best Mexican meal and red wine combo ejected violently onto the pavement, exactly where he'd been standing a split-second before.

There was a cheer from a small group of revellers on the other side of the road. Rick instinctively jumped further back, stumbling in an ancient storm drain at the side of the road, so prevalent in this particular street.

Tabatha dropped to her hands and knees, vainly looking for anything to wipe her mouth with—a sleeve in this case.

*

A Double-Tree Hilton hotel was the nearest place they could find, and only a very sympathetic night-porter had saved the day.

Having vaguely tidied up in the Ladies, Tabatha was keen for a large bottle of spring water from the bar, convinced her earlier gastric outburst was more to do with the food than the alcohol. She wasn't entirely sober, but it took an awful lot more than most of a bottle of wine to produce that kind of volcanic effect.

'The barman says he can only serve residents now. I guess I could ask our friendly porter for a jug of tap water and a couple of glasses?'

'Don't hassle him again; I'll go back to the loo and drink from the tap.'

'You don't have to do that. Let me run to a late-night store and buy some bottled water. Just sit here and hang on a few minutes.'

'We shouldn't hang around unless we're hotel guests, Rick, or at least friends of guests.'

'Okay, well let's do that, then. I'll check you in, and then I'll be your guest—sorted.'

Before she'd had time to object, Rick had sprung up from the leather sofa in reception and headed for the one remaining member of staff behind the desk.

'All sorted—here's your key. There's apparently a complimentary bottle of water in the room, or we can get one down here.'

'Are you crazy? How much did that cost?'

'It's no problem. It's not a suite or anything fancy—just a single-occupancy room. That's okay, right?'

'You're mad. You can't afford to do that—I'll pay you back tomorrow. Well, Dad will pay you back.'

'That will *not* be happening under any circumstances. It wasn't much, and I can afford it now. I told you, things are different for me since the telecom contract. Hey, I'm dying of thirst too—shall we go to the bar, or shall I get a couple of bottles and take them up to the room for you?'

Tabatha's mind was spinning, but it wasn't nausea this time—more like panic.

'Why don't you nip up to the room now and grab a shower? I'll buy the water—sparkling for you, isn't it? Then I'll give you a few minutes and bring it up. Oh, don't worry—I don't have a key—I'll knock on the door, and you can open it if you're ready … as in, *decent*, I mean … I'm sure they have dressing gowns …'

He rubbed the back of his neck with a hand. It whispered vulnerability, and although he didn't know it, there was nothing Rick could have done that would have warmed her to him more.

'Is fifteen minutes enough? Just ping me on WhatsApp when you want me to bring the water up.'

The hand went to the neck again as he smiled awkwardly, then his expression changed.

'Oh, unless I just leave you to it and get off home. Is that better for you?'

Moments earlier, not only would it have been better, it would have been the only option.

There was a knock on her door. As much as knocks on doors were decipherable, this could be described as an almost apologetic one. Shy and hesitant, it made the ensuing silence a little louder and almost tangible.

The timing was good—almost telepathic (she had the phone in her hand and was just about to send him a message).

She'd expected a wisecrack about room service—this would have been typical—but there was nothing.

'Hold on; I'm coming.'

In the past, there'd almost certainly have been a wisecrack about that comment as well, but again, just silence. Perhaps a trifle forward and cheeky at this early stage, even for Rick.

She opened the door and was greeted by the night porter, bearing a litre bottle of chilled Pellegrino water on a silver tray, alongside a tumbler containing ice and a slice of lemon. There was also a white envelope with the hotel's crest in one corner, her name written across the middle in Rick's distinctively scrawled handwriting.

'Your colleague asked me to bring this to you, madam.'

Hey Tabby,

Hope you get a good night's sleep. I'll call you tomorrow and see how you are.

Sleep tight.

Rick x

She read the note again in bed, wondering why fate had conspired to have her sleep in a luxury hotel on her own, less than a mile from her home.

A message buzzed on her phone. Not from Rick as she'd expected, but from her mum—how was she and where was she?

'*Fine thanks. At the Hilton for the night. Any other questions?*'

Tabatha smirked as she turned the light off; the truth was the best policy. Wasn't that what her parents had always preached?

9

IT HAD been a bad night for Tracey. Unable to sleep, she'd gone downstairs and made a mug of hot chocolate. Whenever sleep evaded her, this would normally sort things out, but not tonight.

It wasn't just the worry of Tabatha not being home. Her daughter had at least taken the trouble to respond, albeit in a terse manner. She couldn't blame the girl, though—chasing a 30-year-old woman to get her ETA back home after a date, could reasonably be described as a tad over-protective.

Tracey couldn't help it—Tabatha was the most important thing in her life. Probably just like every mother, but maybe even more so with an only child.

It was devastating when she'd come back home in February—a night which Tracey would never forget. As the days turned to weeks, the girl hardly set foot out of her room, and Tracey wondered if psychiatric help may be the only way forward. Tabatha had always been so positive and out-going, that the contrast was even more shocking.

But gradually, things had settled down. And the truth was, she secretly loved having her daughter back home again. David had been less sensitive, but this wasn't entirely a surprise. Ever the practical, he'd begun to question Tabatha about the future, what her plans were, and whether she intended to get a job.

There was no point in telling him that their daughter's presence at home was adding little to the weekly food bill—he'd just say it wasn't the money and that wasn't his point. However, it was true—she was eating next to nothing, and this was another cause for real anxiety. Tabatha was naturally a slim girl, and the last thing she needed was to lose weight.

As much as Tracey was enjoying her daughter's company again, it was taking its toll on her own health. So, perhaps with her own well-being in mind just for once, she'd welcomed the news of this Australian boy on the internet. Realistically, though, although Tabatha had temporarily cheered up and found a purpose in life again, how could this type of thing ever go any further?

Then, when she'd learned that Grant intended to travel all that way to see Tabatha, everything changed up a gear. Could this really be a new partner—perhaps even more than that?

And naturally, as soon as the friendship ramped up with Grant, along came Rick to proclaim undying love for '*his Tabby*'.

Not directly, of course, but with her as a conduit. Give the lad his due; Rick was right on the money in assuming he had no chance with a direct approach.

It was typical of Rick; he was nobody's fool. He knew she'd convey his feelings to Tabatha—his best and only shot.

She knew Rick had a reputation as a lady's man, but in her limited experience prior to David, Tracey didn't think this was the whole story.

There were men that loved to flirt with women, but they'd never dream of straying from their relationship. She genuinely had Rick down as exactly this type of man. When she'd learned of the disaster, she was just as surprised and nearly as shocked as her daughter.

Rick hadn't gone into the gory details when they'd met for coffee, but when he told her it just wasn't as it seemed, she believed him. Quite how someone could be found in bed with another woman and still protest his innocence was, she had to admit, a tall order. However, for reasons she couldn't grasp yet, Tracey believed this to be true.

Whether Tabatha would eventually share that information with her was another matter, but Tracey had a strong feeling that Rick had bared his soul last night. The fact she wasn't back last night suggested that Tabatha had forgiven Rick in the ultimate way.

Perhaps it was a cause for celebration, but she couldn't help but feel a lot of sympathy for Grant.

Tracey was still in her dressing gown as she sat down at the kitchen table, a mug of tea having now replaced the hot chocolate.

Light was beginning to filter through the blinds—still a good half-hour before David came downstairs. Hopefully, he wouldn't have noticed her absence from their bed since the middle of the night.

Dressing gowns were double-edged swords; they gave the comfort that no other clothing could offer, yet there was always a hint of sickness attached to them. This seemed entirely appropriate, as she lifted her left arm up yet again, putting a hand gently on her armpit, then sliding it down across the side of her breast.

It wasn't her imagination now, and it hadn't been last month, nor every day in between. She couldn't describe it as pain, and it hardly registered as discomfort—a tenderness was more accurate.

She closed her eyes tightly to strangle the tingling—self-pity repulsed her.

Resting her elbows on the table, she put both hands over her face and curtained the growing light from her eyes. In the dim redness, fatigue was finally beginning to take hold and envelope her.

Tracey was a practical woman—she could see no reason for sharing her problem. For as long as it was humanly possible, David mustn't know, and Tabatha couldn't know.

There was a reason she hadn't taken action immediately she discovered the little, irregular-shaped lumps. She didn't need any professional diagnosis to tell her what was happening—history had done that a long time ago.

It had never been a question of *if*, but *when*.

The fact it was within a year of her mother's age was no surprise either—since her early 40s and even younger, Tracey had looked upon her 53rd birthday as a kind of D-Day. Any time she had after that without the inevitable invasion of death-cells would be a bonus.

Her grandmother had lived to 58. She'd never met the woman—only knew what she died from. There was no desire to go back any further—a wish her husband had never understood but begrudgingly accepted. He'd have taken her place if he could, died for her, willingly.

She'd been offered genetic testing when Tabatha was just moving up to senior school but turned it down. There was so much going on in their little world, that Tracey had no time and saw no point. This was something she'd prepared for throughout life, and couldn't handle the prospect of having her hopes raised, only to be crushed in misery and finality.

She trusted to fate. If the gene was present, then so be it, though Tracey profoundly *sensed* she was doomed—the BRCA gene test would only confirm what she already felt in her heart and soul.

And what was the point of having that information? She wasn't going to go through with a preventative mastectomy—never would she allow that. So, what was the point?

Ultimately, how many people would want to know when their time was up?

Not that many, Tracey was certain.

'How long have you been up?'

She woke with a start.

'Oh, a little while. I couldn't get back to sleep and didn't want to wake you. Tea and toast?'

'No, it's fine, I'll get it. You look exhausted—everything alright?'

She wondered if her face was streaked with tears but thought she'd managed to hold back. She wiped both sides of her face with the arm of her dressing gown.

'You've had trouble sleeping for a little while—do you think it's worth booking an appointment with the doctor? Oh, and any news from Tabatha? Her door was open, and I could see she wasn't in bed.'

'She sent me a message; she's at a hotel. I'm sure she'll be back later today.'

'Pretty much how she's treating this place, except *this* hotel's a lot cheaper. I just *cannot* believe how she's giving Rick the time of day, let alone anything else.'

Tracey put fingers to both temples. She could feel a headache building—all she wanted to do was sleep.

'I can't do this now, David; please can we drop it? I'm just so tired of it all.'

She turned away and snatched a tissue from the box, ostensibly to blow her nose. David knew his wife was crying as she left the kitchen.

*

Tabatha looked at her watch. She had nothing clean to change into, but at least her clothes were only an evening old. Despite the messy episode on the street, she'd somehow managed to avoid any direct contact.

A call to reception had confirmed that breakfast was included with her room—a kind gesture by Rick—and that she had less than an hour before last orders. She requested a toothbrush and toothpaste to be brought up and soaked in a bath for a few minutes, contemplating, yet again, why Rick would have left last night.

It was confusing; so disappointing when the night porter delivered her water, yet the whole episode was now making her smile. One day, hopefully sooner than later, she would have to ask Rick why he'd decided to do that.

She walked through reception and gave her room number to the girl at the dining room entrance, and was led to a table by the window, affording a very pleasant close view of the river.

Not only that, but an even closer view of Rick—he was sitting at her table, a pot of coffee in front of him.

Tabatha feigned disappointment.

'Oh, I thought you were Luke.'

'Well good morning to you, too. Luke?'

'Yes, the lovely man who came up to my room last night after you'd gone. Anyhow, never mind. May I sit down?'

'Errr, yeah … I guess so. Looks like she won't be turning up now, anyway. Still, at least I've been paid the money in advance.'

Their waitress, who'd been hovering a couple of metres behind Tabatha, politely cleared her throat. It was just a feeling, but she suspected the jovial small talk had run its course.

They turned in unison to look at the girl, and she promptly scurried away to a more manageable table.

'Sorry, not called for; I'm a bit out of practice with banter.'

'I should hope so. And your reason for disappearing so unexpectedly last night? Out of practice in other departments, too?'

'Look, I'm sorry if I upset you by going, Tabs. I was under no illusions with our date last night. I knew it was just a chance for us to have a quiet evening out and, well, you know, for me to try and explain the whole shitty situation.'

'Indeed.'

Remarkably, Rick's oafish attempt to humourise his behaviour had only upset her briefly.

'And when you paid for my room, you had no intention of coming up to, how shall I say this, *join* me?'

'I was going to come up and join you, absolutely—I said I would—but then it occurred to me that you'd get the wrong impression. Look, I just imagined it would be really awkward for both of us when I said goodnight.'

Tabatha's curiosity was being diluted by another emotion, and she couldn't deny it might be indignation.

'Let me get this straight; so you're saying you had no intention of trying to stay the night with me?'

The indignation was infectious.

'Of course not! I told you, I just thought we'd have a nice meal and ...'

'Even after you paid for my room?'

'Damn right. What's paying for your room got to do with it?'

The half-chuckle in his voice was almost painful for her, and he wasn't finished.

'If you hadn't been ill in the street, I was just going to drive you home—or walk you home if you preferred. Whatever the method, I was making sure you were safely home at a reasonable hour.'

This offered her something to grab at.

'Ahhhh, so this was all down to that promise you made Mum, then? You were actually *serious* about getting me back early?'

That felt much better—how stupid of her not to realise that, as per bloody always, her mum had poked her nose in and ruined things.

'Well no, not really—it was just a social gesture. I mean, I assumed I'd get you back well before midnight, so it was hardly a big deal to tell your mum that.'

'Before midnight? Oh I *seeee*—so my ball-gown wouldn't turn to rags? Well, as you can see, I'm not far off the rags-look now.'

They coloured simultaneously, both choosing to look out at the tourists in their punts on the river.

Unable to bear the silence any longer, Tabatha wandered over to the buffet, much less nonchalantly than she'd hoped.

Rick looked around the dining room.

'We're the last ones in the place again—it seems we're making a habit of this.'

'We probably have the most issues to work through.'

The arms were folded again.

'Well that's a positive sign then, isn't it?'

She studied his smile. Maybe this was the expression with which he greeted what had turned out to be his client—his *sexual* client.

Surely his story was the truth? Anything else he'd said couldn't have been worse than this, could it?

His smile was warm and genuine and disarming.

I could look into your eyes all day, Rick Harrison, and you won't turn away, will you—you never looked away first, did you ...

She lost again, as always.

'How do you manage to spin negative into positive?'

'Well, you just said we're working through the issues, and that's more than I could have hoped. You have no idea what a relief it was to finally tell you what really happened.'

His hand had encroached onto her side of the table as he'd been talking. Now it turned, palm open, hoping for contact.

It was close, but it wasn't quite enough—not yet.

'I may now know the context and the reason, but it doesn't change what you were doing—what I *saw* you doing. Tell me, what if it was the other way around? What if you'd come back to the flat and seen me under a young guy you'd never seen before? Then, much later, I tell you not to worry—*it's not what it looks like*—I'm short of cash and just doing a bit of part-time escorting. But it's okay because it's only for a couple of weeks.'

As she watched him contemplate this situation, the blood drained from his face.

It was a strange sight—he always seemed so permanently tanned—it looked as if he was dying.

His face was expressionless as he turned away from her. The hand he'd held out, no longer there.

Tabatha didn't know why, but she felt guilty. How could that be? She'd turned the tables on him, yet something nagged at her. She was just about to speak again when he slowly stood up.

Folding his napkin and placing it neatly on the table, he walked past her. Stopping briefly, he put a hand on her shoulder and squeezed gently.

'Silly me.'

And then he walked away.

*

'Where's Mum?'

'And hello to you too. Have a nice evening? Well, evening and night. Oh, and morning. Actually, just the evening will suffice—how was your evening?'

'Rick stood me up, so I went to the restaurant on my own. The food was crap, and I was ill, so crashed out at a hotel nearby. Then I had breakfast and walked home.'

David removed his glasses and put them on the kitchen table.

'Really? Are you being serious? If so, I apologise— wholeheartedly.'

Tabatha hung her coat on the back of a chair and flicked the kettle on.

'Deadly serious. Well, apart from one part, where I lied.'

'I thought as much. And which part was that?'

'The walking home part—I got a taxi. Can you go and pay the guy, please, I need to go upstairs.'

He put his glasses back on; when did being a father get better? Perhaps a son would have been easier? Still, at least

Rick bloody Harrison wasn't back in her life—back in *their* lives.

Tabatha quietly tapped on her parents' bedroom door, but there was no reply; she walked in quietly.

The curtains were still drawn, and the adjoining bathroom door closed, creating a darkness at odds with the late summer mid-morning light.

Tracey was still in bed, lying on her stomach with her face buried in a pillow, her body rocking gently as she inhaled raggedly. She was sobbing uncontrollably.

'Mum?'

Not nearly loud enough.

'*Mum?*'

Tracey swivelled round, her swollen eyes meeting her daughter's.

'Oh. I'm sorry dear, I didn't hear you. I wa …'

'You're crying, Mum—what is it?'

Tracey managed a stifled laugh of sorts, mid-sob.

'It's nothing, sweetie. Silly me; not such a good night's sleep. Tears of frustration at not being able to grab forty-winks now. Anyway, it's time I got up—what was I think …'

'This is all my fault, isn't it?'

She thought back to the last text she'd sent and hated herself.

'God, I am *so* sorry, Mum.'

Tracey was already out of bed and wiping her tear-drenched face, pulling tight on the cord of her dressing-gown.

'Don't be silly; it's nothing to do with you. Honestly.'

She vainly searched both pockets for a tissue, sniffing violently instead.

Tabatha stepped forward and hugged her tightly, burying the side of her face in the soft towelling. The action created an instant cry of anguish as Tracey staggered backwards.

'*What*? What's the matter?'

'It's nothing; really—nothing. Come here.'

Tracey moved forward to take hold of her daughter, but Tabatha held her hands up.

'Whoa, has Dad hurt you?'

Tabatha couldn't believe the words coming out of her mouth—she was boiling with fury.

'Tell me! Has Dad hurt you? What's happened? What's wrong?'

'Calm down—everything's fine—really.'

'Why are you holding your arms around your chest? Are you bruised, Mum? If he's done anything to hurt … I'm calling the police—now!'

Tracey moved forward quickly to grab her daughter's arm.

'*Please*, Tabatha, I've told you, nothing's wrong! How could you even dream that Dad would harm me? He'd *never* do anything like that, darling; your father's a *saint*.'

'Are you scared of him, Mum? Is that why you're protecting him? I've seen this sort of thing on documentaries; domestic violence—the woman so scared of her partner that she'll do anything to hide what's going on. You need to tell the police, Mum. I'll call for you.' Tabatha was trying to prise her arm free of the surprisingly firm grip.

Tracey was at the end of her tether. She hurt like hell, she was exhausted, and she was petrified—was this was what dying felt like?

She was an eloquent, well-educated, and *very* British woman. Melodramatics and excessive displays of emotion were right at the top of her Under-No-Circumstances list.

However, she was now at a complete loss.

'It's cancer. I have cancer. I'm so very sorry, Tabby.'

Tabatha heard clearly enough, but the words weren't processing.

Insanely, the biggest shock was Mum calling her *'Tabby'*—she'd never been called that by her mother before.

It came out as a whisper.

'When? Who told you this?'

Tracey's head drooped, tears dropping freely onto the carpet.

'A little while. No one told me; they didn't need to. I'm terribly sorry you had to hear it like this.'

The girl's eyes blazed. Agonising heartache was developing from deep within, fuelled by a burning denial.

'You're wrong. It's impossible, and you're *wrong*. You're just tired. Anyway, where is this … this cancer? Where's it supposed to be?'

Tracey raised her head and looked into her daughter's eyes. No words were spoken, and the gloomy darkness of the bedroom seemed tragically appropriate.

There was something about the older woman's posture.

The arms were folded, but not quite in the normal way. The palms of both hands were under the armpits, the thumbs pointing up and pressing into the shoulders.

It was more than a defensive pose. It was protective—overly protective.

And then Tabatha knew.

With no experience or knowledge, she knew.

In slow motion, she shook her head.

'No. Please tell me no? Mum?'

Her mother's mouth opened to reply, but no words followed.

Tabatha moved close to embrace her mother, then faltered, remembering the pain she'd caused a moment ago—a lifetime ago.

'I didn't think it was meant to be painful. I read that breast canc … a lump … I mean a *problem* … I read that it wasn't meant to be too painful?'

'They can be, dear. In my case, some of them are.'

Tracey let her arms move slowly down to her sides—no more protection was needed.

"*Some of them*? You mean more than …'

'Quite a lot, yes. '*Enough*' is probably the most accurate description. I believe—I mean I *know*—that it's quite advanced. '*Advanced*'—that always used to be such a positive word, didn't it? Isn't that a silly thought to have?'

Tears ran freely down her cheeks as she opened her arms to Tabatha.

'Why won't you go to the doctor, or to hospital? They can operate—sort it out—you'll be okay.'

'Sweetheart, I know I *won't* be okay. I tried to keep it from you and Dad because I knew how you'd both react. Now I have to ask that you don't tell your father.'

'But … but he *has* to know. You *have* to tell him. If you don't, I will!'

Tabatha backed away from her mum's embrace and stared at her defiantly, wiping away the tears.

'If you love him, you'll tell him!'

'I'll tell him soon, but he already knows; sort of.'

'What do you mean?'

'He knew about my mother and my grandmother—the family history. He knew there was every chance it would happen to me. It was just a matter of ti ...'

Shaking her head, she backed further away.

'No! You can't say that—you *can't NO!*'

Tabatha turned and ran out of the room, across the hall, landing and straight into her own room.

Tracey went to follow but heard the key turning in the lock.

She turned and lay back down on her bed in the darkened room. She'd had nearly 30 years to prepare for this, but nothing could have been worse than what had just happened.

*

'I've brought you a cup of tea. Do you want some lunch before I go to Tai Chi class? Bowl of soup, perhaps?'

David drew the curtains back, exposing the greying sky.

'Thank you, but I'm fine for now. Do you have time for a chat?'

'Is it urgent? I should be setting off in ten minutes; you know how awkward I find it if I'm late for Mr. Wong.'

Tracey sipped her tea before replying.

'Of course. Don't worry, dear, it was nothing urgent.'

'Okay, good. We can talk later over dinner, eh? I'd best be making tracks.'

He turned to his wife at the doorway.

'Hey, everything alright?'

'Yes, dear, never better.'

*

GD3: Hey Tabs, Sorry to bother you – noticed you were online and wondered how you were?

She wasn't sure why she'd gone onto the chat forum after such a long time. Maybe it was to try and escape reality.

TABS: Hi Grant. Yeah ok thanks – you? Up late as normal?

GD3: Yup, all good with me. Well excited about coming over – not so long to go now.

Really? She felt bad for not thinking more about him, but it had been a weird time. And now, with the bottom falling out of her world, she didn't know what to say, or think, or do.

TABS: I'm really sorry, but just not feeling well at the mo. Can we chat another time?

GD3: Sure, no sweat. And give me a ting if there's anything I can do. Sorry you don't feel so good – hope you feel much better soon Tabby.

TABS: Ok thanks. Bye.

GD3: Bye Bye Lovely Lady xx

She wanted to cry again. She was going to lose her mum, and it consumed her world—her entire existence.

But here was somebody who she knew was a friend—a special friend. Someone who'd never betrayed her.

God, did she need someone like that now.

TABS: Grant? Still there??

GD3: Nope – gone. Course I'm still here ☺

TABS: You're a great guy, Mr. Davis. You're very kind and I like you a lot. Bye

TABS: xx

GD3: Anytime! You still there??

'TABS' LEFT THE CHAT

10

ALL THINGS considered, and as always, it had been a very pleasant and relaxing session—just as Mr. Wong expected it to be.

He described his classes as '*Meditation in Motion*'—a perfect environment in which to gently exercise, release stress, and chill out.

Because everyone seemed hell-bent on keeping Mr. Wong happy, there was a whole heap of pressure on the students to let go of life's never-ending little pressures.

The class was performing their final routine, known as the *Closing Posture*; a simple enough manoeuvre involving cupped hands being brought slowly upwards while inhaling, then rotated and pushed downwards while exhaling. The Master required precisely fifteen of these, and it was an endless source of mystery why this should be the number, though it oddly matched the cost of the hourly session— fifteen pounds.

Not only that, but Mr. Wong insisted on receiving the exact amount from everyone. It was no good giving him a twenty-pound note and waiting for a fiver change—it wasn't going to happen.

Rumour had it that he frequented a local casino at night, only playing on the roulette wheel, and only placing bets on Black-15. Nobody had proof, though, and nobody was going to ask.

The louder than normal breathing during *Closing Posture* afforded those in the back row, should they so desire, a chance to exchange whispers. It was, quite literally, like being back at school.

The back row was also the most populated, but solely because the instructor insisted on '*harmony through symmetry*'— five in the back row, then four, then three, two, one. The front row or *point* position for these final exercises was awarded to the pupil who'd performed best that day—a slightly nerve-wracking and dubious honour, where relaxation became totally impossible.

David had never been on *point*, but he'd made a mental note of who had. In the twelve lessons so far (there were three to go, naturally), Jane had taken front-row duty on no less than six occasions, with six others sharing the remaining sessions.

It was beyond comprehension, but an outsider could almost have wondered if the teacher may have a favourite.

As luck would have it (and David, being a lifelong banker, didn't believe in this concept), Jane was standing next to him (his chance-theory therefore being justified yet again).

'I found a gardener,' the teacher's pet whispered from the corner of her mouth.

'To do what?'

'Keep facing the front, David. To garden; what do you think I had in mind for a gardener?'

'Oh, I see. Of course … well that's good. Isn't it?'

'Face the front! Yes, it's good—very good. He's asked me to go and choose some plants from the garden centre, but I have no idea—not a clue; Rupert used to do all that side of things.'

'Ah. Well I could always write a list for you? Definitely heather.'

He thought of his own garden and smiled to himself.

'You can have an abundance of colour with heather; explosions of pink and white and purple. Then there's quince – Japanese quin …'

A sharp clapping noise made him jump.

'David, *PLEASE*. A little less chatter and a little more concentration. Jane, I thought you'd know better. Annnnnnd, inhale and uuupppp. And holllllld. And exhale and dowwwwnnn.'

David's face glowed, not helped at all by the sound of Jane's stifled snigger. The three others in the back row were staring at them, but ahead, no one dared turn around, as much as they wanted to; it wasn't full-scale treason, but it was certainly an *episode*.

More sharp clapping.

'That'll do, everyone—I fear the atmosphere is lost. David? Jane? A quick word before you go?'

David was mortified, but Jane seemed only to find the escalating situation funnier, which made matters worse. It was now impossible not to feel a direct correlation between real life and school life.

'Jane, I'm surprised at you. You know how important concentration is to our combined relaxation as a group, never more so than during Closing Posture. And David, I'm nearly as disappointed with you.'

Mr. Wong's eyes were piercing.

It was all too much for David, who lowered his head in the most humbling of apologetic bows. Keen observers of Far Eastern etiquette would have been forgiven for deducing a massive caste imbalance.

Jane seemed less impressed. On the contrary, it had produced a fiery defiance which rarely saw the light of day.

'Do I detect a note of jealousy, Wang Yong? Is that what this is about?'

The upper half of David's body jerked up in shock and confusion. His hearing must surely be on the blink because he clearly hadn't heard what he thought he'd just heard.

The bewilderment centred on two points: How could Jane know Mr. Wong's first names, and how could his parents have been heartless enough to name him *Wang Yong*?

The former was way too much for David to take on board at the moment, the implications beyond his capacity.

'You most certainly do *not*, Mrs Blake. Oh, forgive me; should I say *Msss* Blake? Though really, I hardly feel your current behaviour leaves that particular nuance in much doubt.'

David made a mental note to book an urgent hearing test. He longed for the cocooned safety of an audiology department right now, many miles away from this unexploded social bomb.

He looked at Jane, who appeared disconcertingly calm and relaxed.

'I'm sorry your awkward and inappropriate advances gained you nothing, but it appears I have a lot more respect for Mrs Wong than you. Similarly, though I haven't had the pleasure of meeting Mrs Mercer, I have just the same amount of respect for her. So, Wang Yong, it would appear you may be *Wong* yet again.'

David hoped he'd remember to mention the letter R to the audiologist. He was definitely having difficulty with the letter R.

Mr. Wong took an almost ceremonial step backwards and placed his hands, very symmetrically, on his hips. David hadn't seen this movement in class before, but it looked easy enough. He wondered if enquiring about the name of the posture may break the rapidly forming ice age, but the decision was taken out of his hands.

'Ms Blake, I fear you have a vivid imagination, for I certainly don't know what you're talking about. Do you honestly expect me to believe that you and Mr Mercer were not blatantly flirting with each other, thus affecting the very harmonic soul of our group? For all I know, you may already be '*an item*'.'

David watched the Master raise both hands to his face before the last two words, the index and middle fingers wiggling in perfect unison. Again, he wondered if this movement might be covered in next term's syllabus; the symmetry was almost hypnotic.

'Quite an assumption when you take into account that I'm (and here, David noticed Jane performing the very same finger movement – she was patently a much more experienced practitioner of *Tai Chi* than she'd let on) '*gay*'.'

Mr. Wong's mouth opened to speak, but then it slowly closed. He attempted to straighten the knot of a tie he wasn't wearing, his virtually stubble-free jaw beginning to sag.

'This lesson is officially *over*.'

'That's for sure. Still, it's good when the teacher learns something as well, isn't it?'

The two of them stood, hands in tracksuit-trouser pockets, on the lovingly overly-varnished, elderly, oak floor, in the calmness of the empty recreation hall. The peace Mr. Wong constantly strived for in his class had returned, upon his and the rest of the group's departure.

Even with the windows open, the traffic noise in the centre of Grantchester was much less intrusive than Cambridge.

David, who had an almost pathological fear of longer-than-necessary periods of silence, felt the need to speak, though both were staring at different walls.

'I can smell autumn. It's definitely in the air; can you smell it, too?'

'I can smell the end of *Tai Chi* classes.'

'Yes, I suppose. That too.'

There was something he really wanted to ask her, but it wasn't the type of question he could put into words. Also, it was none of his business Also, what difference did it make? Also, why did he want to know?

Way too many '*Also's'* to possibly conjure up the right words to form a coherent question.

No, it was no good—he couldn't possibly ask—impossible.

'Errrr, you know when … you know … when you, errrr?'

'That's a difficult one to answer, David. I can't possibly imagine what you're about to ask me.'

'No, of course not. It was just that I wondered … well, I wondered … when you said … you know?'

'I'm not telepathic; how am I meant to realise you're trying to ask me if I'm gay?'

'Well, you're not. Oh. I see. Well yes, that's kind of what I wa …'

'No, you silly, dear man—of course I'm not *gay*.'

'But you told Mr. Wang, I mean Wong ...'

'Oh, the *Wang* bit was true—his first name really *is* Wang Yong. He's not from China, though—Hong Kong. I'll leave you to fathom that out, but I can tell you it really is the most fantastic homonym you've ever heard. Oh, and that's not a *'gay word'*, by the way.'

Though unable to conduct or take part in what his ex-work colleagues used to call *'banter'*, he wasn't immune to recognising it, particularly with Jane now grinning at him.

'I'm not quite up to speed, though. Why would you tell him you were ga ...'

'Golly, you're hard work, aren't you—have you never listened to someone apply for a loan, then tell you that, of course, they didn't really need the money because they were a multi-millionaire?'

'Well, of course I'm not at liberty to discuss individual cases or, indeed, any ca ...'

'*DAVID!* You're in the middle of an empty village hall, wearing tracksuit bottoms and a sweatshirt, with not a single loan application form in sight. I'm just trying to give you an analogy you might identify with, by way of an explanation for using the gay card. Come here, you old fart.'

She put an arm around his shoulders and pulled him close, his hair pressing against the side of her face.

'You really haven't got the hang of this retirement thing yet, have you? Seriously, you need to take the advice of Hong Kong's Wang Yong Wong—just relax and chill. Hey! How about we go back to my garden and share a bong?'

She held him at arm's length, beaming into his face.

'What's a bong?'

'That's the funniest thing I've ever experienced. Your nose really *did* look like an elephant's trunk—unbelievable! Oh … no offence intended.'

'And none taken. Did you know you laugh like Muttley?'

'Eh? Who's Muttley?'

'You've never heard of Dick Dastardly?'

'Sorry?'

'It doesn't matter. Go home, open a book, and press your lips against the edge of the pages; then blow a few times as quick as you can—that's what you sound like.'

'But I don't want to go home. Well … not yet, anyway. Hey, we didn't kiss, did we? I seem to think we might have. Oh, God, we di …'

'No, for the tenth time, we didn't. Because you don't smoke, I was breathing the inhaled fumes into your mouth to make it easier for you. That technique does admittedly require that the lips remain close, but no actual contact. As I told you—over, and over, and over, again.'

'You seem to be very experienced on these, errr, matters? How long have you, you know, been doing … *this*?'

He was pointing at an ornate and complicated-looking glass pipe.

'Wow, now you're asking. Three, maybe even four …'

'Years?'

'Decades, silly.'

'Oh, my godfathers! It's illegal! You'll go to prison! Oh, good grief—and I'll lose my job! This is a disaster. I'm fini …'

'You're retired, dear.'

'Don't say that. Please, anything but that.'

'Okaaaay. You're an emeritus bank manager—a man in his prime who's decided to …'

'No, *dear*. I mean, not '*No dear*', but the '*dear*' part. If you could refrain from calling me '*dear*?'

'Oh, I see. Sure, well how about '*Babes*'? Or '*Honey*'? '*Love*?'

'What I'm trying to say is that Tracey calls me '*Dear*'. It's a little ... confusing?'

It was as if an extractor-fan had been switched on, instantly sucking all trace of marijuana fumes from the lounge.

The room filled with a sterile void, brimming with formality.

'Shall I call you a taxi? It's getting on; it'll be dark soon.'

David jumped up from the sofa.

'Oh God—I've missed dinner. Oh God.'

'No, you haven't—I can put something on now, no problem. How about a fry ...'

'*No*! I mean I've missed *dinner*! *Real* dinner—at home.'

'I see. You seem to be making a habit of departing on a wave of guilt, David.'

'Yes, well, I'm very sorry, but I don't know what came over me.'

'Dope, perhaps?'

'Hmmph. I can't believe I did that. I just don't do that sort of thing—really—trust me.'

'No, of course not. Except you did. Perhaps you didn't inhale? If it's a good enough excuse for a President ...'

David made to object, but Jane had already started to sink to her knees in a fit of hysterics.

'You and Bill Clinton, both. Hey, you'd better go before I put on my Ms Lewinsky wig. Woo-hoo!'

She made a slow-motion mock grab for him, and David was briefly tempted to remain exactly where he stood—be grabbed, captured, and very possibly spend the rest of his natural life in this house of unimaginable temptations.

In a state of blissful happiness and unbridled terror, he uttered the only words he felt could suit this unique moment in his life:

'I'd best be going.'

'Awwww, pout. Spoilsport. Never mind—next time.'

'Yes, well, I'm not sure Mr. Wong will be inviting either of us back in a hurry, so that makes things a little difficult.'

'Au contraire, David. Methinks we *should* carry on; *absolutely* carry on. A couple of hours, twice a week; sounds perfect to me.'

'But he won't have us back—I'm sure of it.'

'Indeed.'

It was the longest time he'd stared into someone's eyes without blinking in an age.

'I'd best be going.'

'You best had. Have a lovely weekend, and I'll see you on Tuesday afternoon for another … *session*?'

She kissed her index finger and pressed it on his lips.

'*Our* little secret, Davey. Just ours …'

She turned and sashayed out of her lounge, leaving him on his own, floating on air and with the weight of the world upon his shoulders.

*

'I'm sorry, Mum—I'm terribly sorry.'

Tabatha had knocked lightly on her mother's door. With no answer, she'd let herself in and was leaning back against it when the latch clacked.

'Don't worry, darling; I was awake.'

144

'No, I meant sorry for being so angry. I didn't know what to say. I still don't.'

'You don't have to say anything. Come and sit on the bed.'

Tracey beckoned with her hands, her features becoming clearer as Tabatha's eyes again grew accustomed to the dimness of the bedroom. Her mother had been crying. But then, so had she.

'Is there anything Dad or I can say that will make you go to the doctor or to hospital?'

Anyone who didn't know Tracey well would have misinterpreted the smile—seen rays of hope where none existed. Tabatha cursed the momentary flutter of joy in her heart, even as she knew the answer would destroy her.

'It's too late, but it was already way too late, even before you were born. I'd made my mind up before I left school.'

'But why? Why couldn't you have done something if you knew it was going to happen?'

'Well, I didn't know—not for sure. I knew there was every chance, though. Once I knew I had this problem, then that was it—there was no going back. I saw my gran and my mother with this, sweetheart—I can't go through with it. I'm terribly sorry, Poppet. Beyond sorry. I ...'

Any other words were muffled by Tabatha's sweatshirt, hugging her mother as if life itself depended on it.

And, of course, it did.

*

David Mercer's powers of perception and empathy were, at best, a little below that of the average person.

His generosity to those he loved was indisputable, and his sense of fairness, unquestionable. But picking up the drift was not his forté.

However, to his credit, he possessed a natural kindness he often sought to hide.

Never one to seek or even peek the limelight, he nevertheless retained the subconscious nature of a philanthropist, and the shadows of anonymity they so often crave.

He entered the gloomy bedroom and took in the sight of his two loved ones, embraced in a slowly-rocking sadness.

And he knew.

He put his arms around both women. Three heads touched, and no words were needed.

It was the buzzing of Tabatha's always-silenced phone which broke the trance.

'I'll leave you two alone—I need to send a message. How about I cook the meal tonight?'

Her parents looked up, confusion on their faces. Tracey spoke for them both, which was nearly always the case.

'But you don't cook, sweetie; what had you got in mind?'

'Oh, well cooking was a loose term—I meant I'll order a takeaway. Indian? Chinese? Anything you want—I'm easy.'

The talk of food had brought her father round.

'I'm fine with anything, too. Actually, I'm famished.'

'That's not like you, David—is that Mr Bong working you too hard? I thought it was meant to be a relaxing session?'

David was about to correct the *Bong* reference, but a) he suspected his wife was being a trifle flippant, and b) she was, in fact, correct; it was undeniably the fault of the bong.

'You choose—give us a surprise. Here, let me give you some money.'

He went for his wallet, but Tabatha had already turned around.

'My treat for once—you've been getting them in for the last thirty years. Stay with Mum, eh?'

'How long? Why didn't you tell me? Oh, Tracey.'

He held her tightly in his arms, and she winced as her head rested on his shoulder. She refused to allow the sounds of pain to escape.

'Quite a while. I was going to tell you, very soon, I promise. I just feel so tired lately. I decided to tell you once I'd had enough rest and felt a bit livelier.'

'But that hasn't happened, has it?'

'Not yet, no. But perhaps ...'

'What if I called the doctor now? Get him here this evening—*now*—before dinner?'

'Then I'd refuse to see him, and you'd have to send him away. We'd both look stupid; allow me not to look stupid, David.'

'Christ Almighty, Tracey. Don't you realise you're sending out a message to Tabatha—to me—that you hate us? That you don't want to be with us?'

'No, I'm not.'

She touched his face and smiled, and the contact of her fingers caused him immediate grief, fury, tears—all so alien to him. Now he was thankful for the subdued light.

'Well you can't leave us—you fucking well *can't*—it's as simple as that.' He sniffed loudly and dragged an arm across his face. 'How could you do this to us? How *could* you?'

'Sweetheart, we both knew this was probably going to happen. You chose to blank it—to compartmentalise it in a

147

way that I couldn't. That's a luxury I'd have liked, but when I watched my grandmother taken from me, then my mother … I can't erase that—it's impossible.'

'Months ago, you started propping your pillows up before you went to sleep. You did it after I was asleep, but if I got up in the night, I'd see you sitting upright. I was going to ask you about it—*meant* to ask you about it. It was always the same book lying open on your lap. *Always* the same bloody book! *Why* didn't I ask you? For fuck's sake, *why*?'

He was distraught, but she couldn't hide a slight grin.

'That was silly of me, wasn't it? There's only so many times one can read The Thirty-Nine Steps. Don't get me wrong; I'm as big a fan of John Buchan as the next reader, but …'

'Stop it. For pity's sake, *stop!* Why are you trivialising this as if it's a fucking cold or a fever?'

'Now *YOU* stop it, David Mercer! I've never heard you swear so much in my …'

'*TRACEY!* I'm about to lose the person I love more than anything in the world. What do you *expect* me to fuc … to say? Shake your hand and tell you I'm very sorry to hear the sad news? For fuc …'

'Do you know, if I didn't know you better, I'd say you quite liked me.'

She bit her lip and smiled in a way that took him back to when he first met her—first laid eyes on her—wanted her more than life.

'I can't breathe. I can't go on without you—don't want to go on without you.'

The floodgates had opened, and he choked on tears.

'Hey, buster, I'm not dead yet. Don't you go spending no inheritance without me, you hear? Come and lay down and give me a hug. A gentle one, mind, and none of your mister octopussy hands all over me. Just relax, and I'll read you some thirty-nine steps—how's that?'

He was incapable of uttering a word. He took her outstretched hand, and they both lay, very gently, next to each other, staring up at the ceiling and their future.

It began to rain, lightly at first and then gradually heavier as the sound of water against the windows blended into the never-ending hum of traffic in the city of Cambridge.

Summer was coming to a close.

*

Tabatha had selected pizza; three American Hots now sat in their individual boxes on the kitchen table. Two remained sealed, and the third lay open, untouched, the scent wafting into her nostrils.

But Tabatha had lost her appetite. With two pizzas in her arms she'd got as far as raising a hand to knock on her parents' bedroom door. Instead, she brought them back downstairs and chose to send her mum a text. Twenty minutes later, and it still hadn't been read.

She knew the inherent risk of looking medical problems up on the internet—had made that very mistake when suffering a nagging pain in her stomach, self-diagnosing appendicitis.

When it worsened, she went to the A&E department and confidently informed the receptionist that it was an emergency—she had peritonitis. A little while later, a young doctor diagnosed colic and sent her away with a prescription for indigestion tablets.

But this time, it was very different. The grief was sinking in, like a viscous, cloying poison. It created a darkness of infinite depth—no tunnel, no end, no light.

As she scoured the websites, mostly American (lots of stethoscopes nestling on the crisply starched, bright white coats of studious, beautiful-looking doctors), she tried to imagine cancer.

It was grey-black, with the ever-changing, slithery appearance of oil globules in a lava lamp. But instead of relaxing and pretty, it was revolting and putrid. Unsuspecting eyes fixated hypnotically upon it, like moths to a streetlamp, the blurry vision of annihilation; prolonged, inevitable death to the cells of any living creature.

She focused on the ailments, the advice, the prognosis (so many conflicting opinions), the optimism (so little), the pessimism (too much).

Her posture was hunched, and she stood to stretch, noticing the dark night sky and teeming rain for the first time. The lingering smell of the now-cold pizza, so often the precursor to a ravenous and satisfying intake of junk food, now produced only nausea.

She squashed the box in half and stuffed it firmly into the kitchen bin. Gulping a glass of tepid water from the tap (for once, not concerned with letting it run cold), she sat back in front of the screen, knowing what she would look for next.

Hating herself for what she now sought to clarify.

The medical world had collectively conspired to anaesthetise the unimaginative, but accurate description, '*Breast Cancer*'.

Like so many institutions, it reverted to the ambiguous safety of the acronym. In this case, not one, but two, new sanitised 'words', safe for doctor-patient consumption.

'BRCA1'.

And 'BRCA2', for good measure.

Two genes—both accelerators of chance. Existing to skew Lady Luck and destroy countless-million lives, until science discovers the pathway to the little fuckers' destruction.

Hereditary mutated genes, flowing invisibly from one generation to the next. A cancer lottery where the bad guy always wins even when he doesn't, the decades of fear almost as bad as the potential outcome.

Tabatha pushed away from the table until her chair balanced on the two back legs. She was disgusted with herself; a couple of hours after learning of her mother's fate, she was more concerned for her own well-being.

She prodded her chest gingerly for tell-tale lumps but found nothing—yet.

Every site advised that the risks grew exponentially with age—on this topic, the opinion was unanimous. Her mind calculated the gap—she was 23 years younger than Mum.

But what if it happened earlier …

She carried BRCA.

She knew that—for certain.

Statistically, not a *certainty*, of course, but Tabatha *knew* it was her destiny.

She just did.

It was called '*prophylactic mastectomy*'.

According to the experts, it was by no means unusual to choose elective surgery. Indeed, even famous people had made the choice (she couldn't fathom why, but this celebrity endorsement seemed to make an important difference).

She rocked the chair forward and walked to the big mirror in the hall. Tilting her head, she appraised the reflection.

On the skinny side, she favoured clothes that were less than tight-fitting. Scrutinising the loose T-shirt, imminently destined for two seasons of rest, she could honestly have said that the lack of two breasts would have made absolutely no difference to the reflected black-cotton contours facing her now.

There was a time, from perhaps the age of fourteen until this afternoon, when this observation would have caused an instant depression. This was no longer the case.

She would book an appointment to go and see her doctor. Or maybe not—would it be best to see someone with no knowledge of her parents? Or should she tell her mother first?

Tabatha tried to imagine their chat.

It was a no-brainer; the last thing Mum needed was something else to worry about.

And it had to be a new doctor. He'd understand immediately and organise for the operation at Addenbrooke's Hospital.

Surely it had to be free—on the National Health? If not, she'd have to find the money somehow—it couldn't be that difficult to get a loan for this type of emergency. Surely?

Her mind was buzzing, crackling with the intense desire to remove the time-bomb from her body. In such a short space of time, the seed of an idea had developed into a full-blown life or death scenario.

She wanted a shower. Better still, a bath—a scalding one that took her breath away and turned her skin pink. She felt dirty as if days had passed since she'd last washed.

Tabatha ran up the stairs and nearly bumped into her father on the landing.

'Sorry—just need to get to my room. How's Mum?'

'She's fine … you know … Off out somewhere?'

'No, just wanted a bath.'

'I thought your generation only had showers—anything the matter?'

'Err … no … nothing; I just fancy a chill-out. Turn the lights out—light some candles—that sort of thing.'

'Do you have any candles? I assume they don't really work in the shower.'

'Umm, yeah, I've got one … I mean *some*. Rick gave it to me.'

'That was … nice of him. Can I smell pizza?'

'Oh, yeah, on the table—they might need heating up a bit. I'll see you and Mum in a few, okay?'

'Sure, that'll be good.'

Tabatha had reached the bedroom before her dad posed one further question;

'You have matches?'

'Sorry?'

'Or a lighter?'

Tabatha looked confused.

'For the candle? Or candles, was it?'

'Oh! Yes—thanks. I'll be down later.'

With the oven hot, David had placed both pizzas on shelves, though he suspected they'd get through less than one between them.

Placing the boxes in the bin, he noticed Tabatha's crumpled dinner, untouched. This was so unlike her that he made a mental note to ask Tracey if their daughter had been off her food lately.

Since her early teens, he'd been pestering his daughter to eat more, but Tracey would always come to the girl's defence. Apparently, it was better to be slim than overweight—healthier.

What did he know? He and his wife must have discussed the damn subject a hundred times over the years.

His throat constricted, and he sought the table with a hand to steady himself; there would be no opportunity for another hundred discussions with Tracey, on the diet of their daughter. It briefly consumed him—he'd have given his life for another hundred spats with his wife about Tabatha's eating habits.

He couldn't breathe for a moment, and that was a soul-destroying irony—Tracey had admitted her upright sleeping position was due to struggling for breath when lying down.

He clenched both fists tightly, and his shoulders dropped. This didn't happen to them – shouldn't and couldn't be happening to them.

Within weeks of first going out with Tracey, she'd made him aware of the possibility of hereditary breast cancer. She'd actually used '*probability*', but he'd chosen, over time, to downgrade and dilute that—*possibility* was much more palatable.

Now both words were redundant, replaced by the *C* word – *Certainty*.

He realised his tears were dropping onto one of the reheated pizzas. A hand squeezed his shoulder.

'Extra salt? That's not like you.'

He turned around, and there was no attempt to conceal the desolation this time.

'Are there any words I can use that would entice you to seek medical help? One single, magical sentence that would make you see sense?'

'I think you know there aren't, you dear, sweet man. But …'

'Yes? Anything—just name it—*anything*.'

He saw himself sinking to his knees in prayer.

'Can we carry on as we have been? Just, you know, like normal?'

The vision imploded.

'*What*? Are you serious? You expect me to just, what, pretend this *thing* doesn't exist between us? Are you mad, woman?'

'Not yet, but I will be if you don't hand me that pizza— and I'll have the less salty one, thanks very much.'

She kissed his drenched cheek and walked past him to the fridge.

'Now let's have a look. Oh, it's going to be a close call; do I toss a coin, or will you trust my judgement? I'd normally recommend the Pinot Grigio, but a 2017 is a trifle young, don't you think? Hmmmm … Oh hello—a Macon Lugny, no less. Hang on—it appears to be corked. Yup, it's corked alright, and the cork's made of grey rubber!'

She turned to look at him in feigned horror, but he wasn't joining in the game.

'Urrgghhhh, it's evaporated too—there's only half left! I knew this would happen when they did away with proper cork corks. AHA! Et voilà!'

She emerged triumphantly from their large, American-style fridge, a bottle held pretentiously in both hands, nudging the door shut with her hip.

'David, I'd like you to meet Monsieur Roger, but I'm sure you can call him Pol. Now I know you're a big fan of

Winston Churchill, dear, so you'll have plenty to talk about—
Pol, here, was intimate friends with the Prime Minister,
weren't you, Monsieur Roger?'

'Have you taken leave of your senses?'

'I might have guessed. I hope you're not going to spoil it
all and tell me champagne doesn't go with pizza?'

She placed the bottle on the table with exaggerated
deference and sat down. Running a finger across the
condensation along the neck, she glanced at her husband.

'I'm not too old to have a party with Pol on my own, you
know. Your choice—one glass or two glasses—hurry along
now.'

'You're bonkers.'

'Long may it last. Be sure to tell me if I stop, okay?

He pulled two glass flutes down from a shelf and turned
to his wife.

'Okay, I promise. But how long will it last, Tracey? How
long have we left? I so want and need to know, but then I
don't. I lov …'

She tapped the bottle with the nail of one hand, the
index-finger of the other moving to her lips—the globally-
accepted sign of silence.

She smiled provocatively.

'Pol and I are waiting …'

*

'Is that glass of fizz in the fridge for me?'

Her parents were sat together in their dressing-gowns on
the smaller of the two sofas. An episode of The Simpsons
was playing on the large television screen. Neither heard her
question, the volume set louder than normal.

She raised her voice and tried again.

'Okaaay, then. Since when did you become Simpsons fans?'

'Oh, hello, Sweetie. Well, I've liked the Simpsons since you first started watching it, soooo, maybe twenty years ago?'

'You're kidding me, right?'

'Not at all. Did you get your glass of champagne?'

'Yes thanks. There was a cherry in it.'

'Uhuh.'

'And an umbrella—a sort of paper and matchstick mini-umbrella?'

'Indeed. Nice, right?'

'Errrr … soooo … you're serious about The Simpsons?'

'Never more so.'

'Dad?'

'Oh, I'm a late starter. This is my first session—I'd know the music anywhere, though.'

'Riiight. Okay then—so Mum—any favourite characters?'

'Apart from Homer, Marge, Bart, and Lisa, you mean?'

'Umm, yeah—apart from them.'

'Well, it won't be a popular choice, but I can't help thinking of your dad when I watch Mr Burns.'

Tracey chuckled, and David looked at her over his glasses.

'Is that a good thing—a compliment?'

'Wellll, he's very good with money, dear. I think you'd get to like him. I'll point him out when he makes an appearance. Anyway, so there's him and obviously Moe, and Krusty, and Ned Flanders. Oh, do you remember that episode when Homer looks at Ned in his skin-tight skiing gear and says, "*Stoopid sexy Flaaanders*"? God, that was funny. And I know you'll think me weird, but I kind of like Snake—I can see his good side. And Barney—now *there's* a drinker for you.'

157

Tracey leaned back and laughed loudly and heartily, the noise coming to an abrupt end with a hacking cough.

David leapt out of the sofa.

'Christ, are you alright? Get her a drink of water, Tabatha—*quickly*!'

Tracey was waving her hands and managed to catch her breath.

'Don't be ridiculous, I'm fine. Stop it, you two. I'm just having a good time and laughing, okay?'

'Why didn't you tell me, Mum? Why?'

'Well … I guess I thought you'd be embarrassed.'

'What? *WHAT*?! Tell me you're joking, Mum?'

'No, truly, I did. Imagine any of your chums getting to hear about it – they'd ridicule you. Trust me, sweetie, you wouldn't have thanked me – not at all.'

'Am I in some sort of sick dream? This is the saddest shit I've ever heard in my life, Mum. For pity's sake …'

'If your school mates had discovered I was watching Homer and the gang, your life would have been a misery.'

'*I'M NOT TALKING ABOUT THE FUCKING SIMPSONS!*'

'Don't talk to your mother like that, Tabatha—you know she's not well. Here, give her this glass of water.'

She passed the glass and knelt on the carpet, resting her head on her mum's lap. The soft towelling of the dressing gown against her cheek took her back to the very earliest memories of her life. She felt a hand on her hair, and the illusion was breathtakingly real.

'You should have told me sooner, Mummy.'

'It would have hurt you for longer, child. Just relax and close your eyes a minute. Let it all go.'

David Mercer clicked the remote, and the silent grey screen returned. As he let himself silently out of the lounge, he wished the world would stop turning.

11

'HELLO RICK, *Any chance of a chat? I've had the worst weekend of my life and need an ear. I need to make a big decision and just need someone's thoughts. Are you free for an hour now? I guess you're working this afternoon – if not now, maybe this evening, early as poss/soon as poss? Thanks, Tabby (and sorry about the other morning)*

Hi Tabs, Didn't expect to hear from you but, hey, glad I did! What's up? I headed off to London for the weekend and still here. I'm going to see my telecom client at their main HQ here tomoz and head back home in the evening. Or maybe Weds morn if I'm taken out by them and have a heavy one. You know how rubbish I am with hangovers… What about lunch on Weds? See you, Me (and no sorry needed x)

Rick, I'll jump on a train to King's Cross now. Can be wherever you are in the Smog for late afternoon if you can make it? Sorry it sounds desperate, but it is. Where and when? I'd call but this isn't a facetime thing – need help. Thanks

No probs—kinda chuffed you'd think of me in this situ actually. Not trying to do myself out of a meet-up with you, but can't your mum help if it's desperate/urgent? Don't worry about getting to me—I'll meet you off the train. Just let me know ETA. X

Thanks a lot, will ping you arrival time when on the train – guessing around 5.30ish. Mum can't help with this – wish she could but she really can't. See you soon. x

'Can't Dad give you a lift to the station, at least? He'll be back in an hour or so.'

'It's fine, honestly—I need to go now. I've no luggage, and I'll be back later tonight. Now are you *sure* you're okay on your own?'

'Oh, for goodness sake, I'm fine—you don't need to be calling the funeral director yet.'

Tabatha closed her eyes and balled her fists, deciding to count to three, but only getting to one.

'Do you have to talk like that, Mum?'

'I fear I do, Sweetie—do you mind? I'll try and stop if it's *really* important to you.'

'I guess not. It's just that … I don't know … It's just that I love you so much.'

'Goodness gracious! Be off with you before I start blushing, young lady. Hey, and be careful down there— message me when you meet up with Rick?'

'Oh Muuuumm.'

'I'll worry until I hear from you.'

'Okay, then—I'll text you. Sorry.'

'Love is never having to say you're sorry.'

'Eh?'

'Never mind. Safe journey and love to Rick.'

The carriage was nearly full—the direct train from Cambridge to London King's Cross was never quiet.

Under normal circumstances, Tabatha would have been in the familiar crouched position, flicking through social media to see how many people had *loved* her posts, or had responded to her Instagram photos (nowadays, hardly ever). And just generally surfing, seeing how many other people were having a far better life than her (nearly everyone and sometimes everyone).

Today the phone remained in the pocket of her dark blue parka.

Within the constraints of a train and with nothing else to do, she scanned the carriage. Men's faces were more problematic to look at. If eye contact was made, it proved awkward. As she looked at the women's faces, she wondered how many had a parent, or child, or sibling, who was dying.

She wondered if anyone could guess the story she carried. Could they look at her face, her eyes, and see what was happening inside?

Across the aisle, a gorgeous French Bulldog was sitting on a woman's lap. Maybe it was a Pug—she wasn't sure what the difference was, but she loved both breeds—followed a few of them on Instagram and *loved* every photo.

The woman wasn't much older than her, but considerably more stylish and beautiful.

In a way that science has yet to definitively identify, the woman sensed someone staring at her.

She turned and met Tabatha's eyes. A fractional pause before the small percentage of a smile—the one where only muscles below the nose move—then a return to her original position.

Tabatha's focus lowered to the little dog. It was looking intently at her and appeared sad. The head cocked sideways, and she felt her soul being examined.

What do you see, little doggy? I've heard you guys can sense illness in humans—can you sense anything? Can you tell if there's something hiding in me? Is it something horrible? Something that has to be pulled out immediately?
What do you see, cute little doggy?

'Are you alright? Hello? Are you okay?'
Tabatha came out of her trance, her face wet.
'Oh, I'm sorry.'
'Is something the matter?'
People close by were switching focus from their screens to Tabatha. She felt clammy and confined—almost claustrophobic, though she had no idea what that would feel like.
'Yes. Fine. I'm so sorry.'
She attempted to laugh while wiping at the rims of her eyes, frantically thinking of anything to say.
'I used to have a dog just like yours. And it, errr, passed away. So, you know ...'
She stood up and wandered to the end of the carriage, feeling eyes in her back. Thankfully, the train was on the outskirts of the city, and it wouldn't be long before she arrived.
Tabatha stood by the exit and waited, grateful for the temporary extra space. As much as she tried to be rational, she knew this thing was going to completely consume her until she acted.

*

'You've been crying, Tabs. What's the matter?'

'Can we get a drink first? And thanks for meeting me like this—hope I haven't screwed up your plans.'

'Actually, you've cheered me up by being here. London's great for a while when you're on your own, but then it suddenly goes from fun to lonely quite sharpish. I'm glad to see you—really glad.'

He hugged her, and though it could have been wishful thinking, it felt like the best hug they'd ever shared.

'Hey, you're crying again. Seriously, what's up?'

'Drink? Please?'

Which was available almost precisely where they'd been standing, except ten metres directly above.

It was one of those noisy, impossibly transient bars, that can only ever exist in international airports and the major travel hubs of large cities.

As boisterous noise levels went, train stations had the edge over airports. The perceived fun of air travel was less apparent on imminent train journeys, as if the passengers had to make up for that with over-exuberance. In these places, alcohol was the very life-blood of society.

'I may be wrong, but I don't think I've ever seen you drink a pint before. And Guinness of all things—I thought you hated beer?'

'I'm not mad on it.'

'Hmmm. This is definitely not a celebration, eh?'

She took a large gulp of the black liquid and winced, surfacing with a cream-coloured foam moustache. Rick wiped a finger gently above her top lip like a windscreen wiper, glanced at the catch, then popped it in his mouth.

Self-consciously, she looked down at the table for a napkin. There was nothing but two sodden beer mats sitting amongst the dried rings of a dozen Olympic logos; their table needed a wipe.

'No, this is not a celebration. I don't even know where or how to begin.'

'Hey, this is me. You start where you want—you *know* you can tell me or ask me anything. How about starting at the beginning?'

She snorted bitterly.

'If only that were possible, though God knows when the beginning was. God and Mum, I guess; she might know as well.'

Another large gulp, but this time she used the sleeve of her jacket.

'So, what does Tracey think about this problem. Surely she's had something to say about it?'

'She's done exactly the opposite—*that's* the problem. Mum never said anything about it.'

'Right—which is why you needed to talk with me? But I still don't know what the prob ...'

'She's dying. My mum is dying.'

The blood drained from his face. He looked around the bar before resting his eyes on her face.

'How? When? Why?'

'Cancer. She has cancer, Rick. As for when, she won't and didn't tell me. Maybe years ago, maybe sooner? And as for why?'

She shook her head slowly and stared back at him—this time she wouldn't cry.   'Ultimately, you'll have to ask God, I guess. More recently? Well, that'll be down to my grandmother, then my great-grandmother; I don't know how far it goes back before that.'

The background noise filled their silence, as Rick tried to make some sense of things.

'So, you're saying it's hereditary?'

The question had arrived slightly ahead of his comprehension.

'But … but that means …'

She had to look away—what was there to say, other than '*Yes*'?

'What type of can … illness is it?'

'Breast illness? I think you have to use the *C* word?'

It came out harshly—not what she'd meant. She put a hand on his.

'I'm sorry, that was unnecessary. It's breast cancer.'

The light in his eyes re-ignited as he straightened up in the chair.

'But lots of people get over that, right? Like prostate cancer in men? Or testicular cancer? Tracey can go to hospit …'

'She's chosen not to. Like I said, she's had it for some time. I've spent a while researching online, and I think it's spread to her lungs. You can't cure that, Rick—it's too late.'

He slumped back in the plastic seat.

'Why the hell would she do that? *Why?*'

'She hasn't said it in so many words, but I think it's the horror of seeing her grandmother, then her mother, go through horrible deaths. Maybe her mum tried everything, but it still didn't work—I have no idea. What I do know, for certain, is that she doesn't want to fight it.'

'Oh my God, that's just awful—terrible. Why did you come all the way here to tell me? Why didn't you ask me to come back to Cambridge? Surely you knew I'd have been on the first train back?'

She spent some time draining her glass, looking around at all the other drinkers, wishing she was one of them. Anyone would do.

'Mum's on a journey, and I'm powerless. Whatever I say or do, I'll have no effect upon the outcome. I also feel like the most selfish cow on earth.'

'Don't be ridiculous; you're the least selfish person I know.'

'I know I have this gene in me—I just *know* it.'

'That's crazy. How can you know that?'

'Because I've looked at enough stats to realise it's very unlikely that I don't have it. And, however stupid it sounds, I can sense it; I can *feel* it in me.'

She put both hands on her breasts and challenged him with her eyes—defied him to tell her otherwise.

'You don't know that, Tabby. Whatever you say, you can't know that—not for certain.'

The fear in his face was contradicting his words, and he couldn't think what else to say.

'Another drink? Maybe a glass of wine or something stronger?'

'Guinness'll be fine—thanks.'

As hard as it had been to break the news to him, it wasn't what was making her most nervous.

She *needed*, more than *wanted*, another drink.

'I have to come with you when you go to, you know, find out. If that's OK—of course?'

There was a tumbler in front of him with more than a double whiskey and a lot less water. It was a drink he used to consume in abundance in *the old days*, but which he'd made a Herculean (and ultimately successful) attempt to cease after they began dating.

She had no idea, nor would she—ever.

Tabatha felt bloated from the first pint but still managed a large mouthful before speaking.

'What do you think of my shape?'

'Your what?'

'My shape? You know—my figure?'

'What's that supposed to mean? A trick question or you're fishing for compliments?'

Is that what you think I'm doing? *Really?*'

'No, I don't, which is why I'm confused and a little defensive. I don't know what to say, or what you want me to say. Surely you know what I think of your figure, for Christ's sake?'

This was every bit as embarrassing as she'd feared. Worse, she seemed to be getting nowhere.

She raised her glass.

'To Mum.'

'To Tracey. I'm coming back with you now, obviously; I just need to grab my stuff from the hotel.'

'What about your meeting? You can't miss that; isn't that why you're down here?'

'Partly, but the meeting is irrelevant compared to getting back to see your mum.'

'You don't need to do that. She's not on her deathbed, not yet, at any rate. Please, just humour me and tell me what I look like … you know … to others?'

'You look great—fantastic! What else can I say?'

It was his turn to take solace from the glass in front of him.

She took a deep breath.

'You know the way I'm skinny?'

'You mean slim?'

'Same thing.'

Hardly—one's derogatory and one's complimentary. In my humble opinion, of course.'

'What about *up here.*'

Tabatha, somewhat unnecessarily, put her hands on her chest once again.

'What's a man's opinion of a woman's breasts?'

'Oh, come onnnn ...'

'Sorry, I was being ambiguous; I meant, sort of specifically, what your opinion was of *my* breasts?'

'This is ridicule ...'

'They're hardly anything to write home about, are they? Really?'

She pulled the front of her shirt more firmly against her body as if this might help him remember. It had, after all, been a while.

'Err, tell you what—how about another round?'

'*Rick*! It's taken me a lot to ask this question; can you at least *try* and give me an answer?'

'Okay, I think your, you know, upper half ... chest ... I mean breast ... *breasts* are perfect. There—satisfied? Now how about a glas ...'

His core temperature had risen alarmingly.

'No, not satisfied. I wasn't seeking a compliment, or '*fishing*', as you put it; I wanted a genuine assessment. For instance, my breasts are smaller than average. Quite a lot smaller, I reckon.'

She looked down and appraised herself again, then released the taut shirt. Before Rick could object, she held a hand up to silence him and continued.

'So, the question is, have you been out with a woman who has smaller breasts? Or would you be prepared to go out with someone who was, let's say, *nearly* flat-chested? Or *totally* flat-chested, say?'

Tabatha couldn't hide the relief on her face, which only served to further confuse him. It had taken her most of two pints to get this far down the line.

'If you must know, the answer is *no*; I haven't been out with a woman who has small breasts. And as for part two, if you made it very clear to me that we will never have a future together, then the answer is *yes*—the size of breasts would neither encourage or put me off when considering a new partner. It would bear no relevance to my decision if the woman were flat-chested. Now shall we have one for the road before I get my gear from the hotel?'

As if contagious, the relief had now transferred to Rick's face. Tabatha started to smile.

'I'll have one more if you'll stay in London and go to your meeting tomorrow.'

'So I got it wrong? You'd have let me come back home with you if I'd said something different?'

'No, not at all. All I wanted from you was the truth, and that's what you gave me. But whatever you'd said, I'd still insist you stay on for your meeting. However …'

'Here we go again—what have I done wrong now?'

She put a finger to her lips.

'However, if you tell me what time you can be back tomorrow, I'll cook you a meal at my place. If you don't have anything planned, of course?'

'Nope, nothing planned—thanks very much. Will Tracey be there as well? I'd really like to see her.'

'It'll be a family affair—I'll ask Dad if he'll eat with us too. Now what are you going to have—it's my round.'

'Okay, if you're one hundred percent sure you're not going to let me travel back with you, then you've got a train from platform eleven in fourteen minutes—it's the quick one too. One question first, though?'

'Go on then, the Fifth Amendment notwithstanding.'

'You told me that your mum and gran and great-grandmother all had this in their fifties, but that means you have maybe twenty-five years before you, you know, if you're right?'

'Uh-huh.'

'So you don't need to confront this for a couple of decades?'

'That's the individual's choice. And there are different ways of dealing with it, obviously.'

'Obviously, yeah. But what did you have? After you've found out if you have this gene thing, obviously.'

'Obviously.'

'I have to tell you, Tabs, I don't think you have it. I mean, as much as you really sense that you carry this gene, I don't think you do. Honestly and truly, I don't think you do.'

'I'd better get my skates on, or I'll miss the train.'

'I'll come down with you.'

'Stay put; finish your drink and then finish mine—I've had plenty. I'll see you tomorrow at my place—let's say seven o'clock if you're back by then?'

'Perfect—I'll be there.'

He stood up, and they hugged again, then she put her hands on his face.

'Thank you, Rick. I really mean it.'

She kissed him on the lips for a lingering second, then turned and walked down the stairs.

He had a bird's-eye view of her as she strode purposefully through the throng of travellers, nearly all craning their necks up to the enormous Departures board.

Her image melted into the crowd, and he took a sip from the half-finished glass of what he knew would be Prosecco. He actually hated the overly-sweet taste, always had done, but it was another way for his lips to make contact with hers, albeit a sad replacement for the reality of a moment ago.

She was not ill, did not carry the lethal genes she spoke of, and would not have her life cut short by the cancer which was killing her mother.

He would not allow this. Whatever it took, he would protect her and love her and grow old with her. This was their destiny, together, and he would make it happen.

When she kept her eyes on a specific point, the landscape on the other side of the carriage window was blurred. As the train rushed through provincial stations on its non-stop journey to Cambridge, she would catch a name board and follow it with her head, to see if it was readable.

Of course, she knew all of the station names from a myriad of journeys to and from the city on slower trains. But that was cheating.

The game was to clearly read one of the signs, and it was difficult—very difficult.

She tried moving her head at what she thought was the same speed as the train. Easier, but then one had to pinpoint and immediately focus on the sign when it came into the field of vision.

Nope, still no good, and only three stations to go; Meldreth, Shepreth, Foxton. Tabatha decided that if she couldn't read a sign clearly between here and home, then she carried the gene.

She caught the *ETH* at the first two, and the *FOX* on the last. She could have cheated—could have convinced herself she'd read one of the signs in full.

CAMBRIDGE was easy. Every sign on the platform was crystal clear, from the very first to the one that sat, static, in front of her now.

Except, of course, this one didn't count.

She had BRCA—1 or 2—one or t'other—made no difference. Tabatha knew it, for one million, billion, trillion, per cent certain.

Coming out of her self-imposed trance, she saw passengers taking their seats around her, and knew the doors were about to shut.

She ran out just as the whistle blew, and the doors began to slide together, instantly greeted by a blanket of rain. Her natural inclination was to run for the shelter of the station, but she no longer felt natural. She felt anything *but* natural.

It was this feeling of grubbiness again—something dirty, lying deep within. The rain was a relief, cleansing her, washing away the poison which was going to kill her— slowly, agonisingly, and with no mercy.

The train had departed some moments before, but she still stood close to the edge of the platform.

The sky was very dark—God had a hold of the dimmer switch and had wound it all the way down. But the rain was good—cold, rhythmic, consistent. It felt right.

With a certain amount of alcohol, looking up to the heavens can be beautifully relaxing.

Floating sensations—bobbly—like those little toy figures with a ball-bearing in the round base. However far they lean over, they always come bobbing back up.

Turning in a circle—tiny steps—enhances this wonderful floatiness.

Gravity takes a step back, leaving a sense of detachment from the earth—a mystical sense of freedom.

Her arms moved wide apart, her fingers splaying, each free and independent. She marvelled at the whole sensation—this moving away from the confines of the body.

Was this what it felt like in the very beginning of life, before the violent introduction to the world, and all its lethal germs? Suspended entirely in amniotic fluid, no negative or positive buoyancy. Ensconced in a temperature so perfect, that the very concept of heat was unfathomable.

Free from everything.

No pain, no anxiety, no sadness, no misery, no more.

Just free from every …

'*Ma'am*! *MA'AM*? I think you'd better step away from there—let's get you inside the station, eh? You'll catch your death out here.'

12

'I'D HAVE picked you up from the station, sweetheart. Look at the state of you—you'll catch your d ...'

'Yeah, I know—I'm sorry, Mum. There was a massive queue for taxis, and I was already soaked through by then, so walking seemed like a good option.'

Tabatha shrugged and deposited more water on the wooden hall floor.

'You've missed dinner, but I can rummage something up. Did you have a good time with Rick? How's it going with him? Oh, you didn't tell him, did you? I really don't want ...'

'Mum, how could I *not* tell him? *Why* would I not tell him?'

Tracey sighed.

'I do wish you hadn't. You know I want as little fuss as possible.'

'*FUSS?!*'

'*Ssshhh*, you'll wake your father up—he's dozing in the lounge. This has taken him harder than I'd feared. You're going to have to keep a careful watch on him. I can't be sure, but I sense something's not right.'

'For God's sake, he's just learned his wife's dying!'

'*SSSHHH*! Don't talk like that, Tabatha.'

'You're right, of course—I should stick to first-person singular.'

'What?'

'Never mind. Can you bung a frozen meal in the oven while I grab a shower? Then, if you're up to it, maybe we can have a chat?'

'As long as it's not about …'

The cough interrupted what she was going to say.

Tabatha wondered if the cancer realised its imminent public exposure and, preferring to wallow in darkened pockets of secrecy, quickly silenced any possible discussion.

She'd never hated anything so much in her life.

'Go and sit with Dad—I'll get you a glass of water.'

But Tracey was going nowhere.

She put a hand out for the main bannister rail whilst the other covered her mouth. Pivoting sharply, she sank heavily onto the carpeted stairs, bumping into the edge of one and sliding down to the next step. She barely managed words between guttural gasps.

'Couple of tissues, dear? Please?'

Tabatha's face had turned white with fear. Stuck between crouching with an arm around her mother and running to the kitchen to get tissues, she opened the cloakroom door with her foot and stretched to grab hold of the toilet roll.

'Take this for now. Let me get Dad while I call the doctor.'

Tracey grabbed her daughter's shoulder.

'*No*! No doctor.'

Another violent coughing spasm stopped all further communication. She held the toilet paper to her mouth, as Tabatha watched in horror at the evolving crimson stain.

'*DAD! Quickly—come here—NOW!*'

David Mercer had the foresight to circumnavigate their family doctor, opting directly for the emergency services instead. For the second time in a month, he found himself listening to the sound of an ambulance siren from within the speeding vehicle.

There had been few emergencies in their lives, and for this, he was eternally grateful. However, watching his stricken wife now, he realised that balance was being redressed.

He'd been asked to sit as far away as he could, kindly but firmly, from what he knew to be life-preserving care. His hope of holding Tracey's hand was thwarted, by tubes, wires, and a paramedic.

Not that comforting would have been easy; he realised that. Should she pull through this intact, she'd give him living hell.

They'd had '*The Discussion*'. He was left in no uncertain terms about her wishes, and rushing around in an ambulance was absolutely *not* on the bucket list.

Seeing her daughter engaged again *was* on that list, but she'd not mentioned marriage. Not that she wouldn't have dearly loved that, but she was ever the realist. It was now agonisingly apparent that Tracey knew much more about her health than she'd let on, and ultimately, how long they'd have left together.

When was the last time I told you I loved you?
  Was there ever a day when you didn't tell me you loved me?

David Mercer did the maths quickly—one of his few talents.
  Twelve thousand, one hundred, and ninety days.

The bank manager had factored in the leap years, of course.

We were married in a leap year.

I was going to propose on Valentine's Day, but you guessed—asked me to hold off for a while.

I was devastated.

On the twenty-ninth of February, you came to the bank and went down on one knee, in front of everyone.

And you asked me to marry you.

'Not long to go now, Mr. Mercer.'

'I know. I know there's not long to go.'

He locked eyes with the young paramedic. They were eyes that had seen everything—more than anyone should have to witness. Those eyes gave him no false hope.

'I love you, David, will you marry me?'
  'Yes.' T
  The bank erupts in cheers.
  But even then, I never said,
  'I love you.'

'Mr. Mercer? Sir? We need to get by; right away, if you don't mind.'

He hadn't heard the doors open and found himself in the middle of the two paramedics, plus a nurse and white-coated doctor, standing outside in a squally gale.

'Just wait inside, and we'll be with you in a jiffy, sir. Alright, Tom, we have a Mrs Tracey Mercer, aged 53, suspected ...'

The bright lights made him flinch.

The vast, white room of organised chaos was reminiscent of soaps Tracey followed on television. The initial reflex was to look around for familiar faces.

The shrill noise of his ancient phone broke the spell—a text from Tabatha—the taxi was stuck in traffic, but she wasn't far away—how was Mum?

Default human behaviour was unable to help him type '*She's fine*'. He stared at the screen and could think of nothing to send in reply—just nothing.

*

Many hours later, the family and a doctor sat in a private room, the legacy of generous medical insurance provided by the bank, to its valued past and hoi polloi present employees.

Tabatha had pinched the blinds open. This high up, the view would have been pleasant under normal circumstances. Now, it served only to gain distance from normal life, but that was no bad thing.

A doctor had already explained the severity of the condition, questioning why there had been no earlier medical records of this '*situation*', as he so carefully and succinctly put it.

The x-rays he held were '*not optimum*', and Mrs Mercer (why not '*Mum*' or '*Tracey*'?) had been '*lucky on this occasion*'.

She imagined her mother hearing this news, making enough of a recovery to punch him in the face.

He was too young, and she hated him for being what Mum might describe as '*dashing*'—what she was loath to admit she could think of, in a different lifetime, as '*hot*'.

Tabatha would so much have preferred an elderly doctor for her mother, with grey hair, a faded gold wedding ring, and crinkles around his glass-wearing eyes.

He'd have the expression of a St Bernard dog and touch a hand when he spoke, which would be quietly and gently at

179

all times. There'd be no clichéd metaphors, not an acronym in sight, and he'd be concerned if tea had been offered to everyone. This man would have been an owl in a previous life and would hold the healing powers of Christ.

This was the doctor Mum needed.

'She's comfortable now, though. I expect her to sleep until the morning, and we'll make another assessment then. In the meantime, I'm sure it's fine for you both to go home and get some rest.'

'Is she happy?'

'Excuse me?'

'My mum—is she happy?'

'Well that's obviously a very difficult question to ans …'

'No. No, it's not very difficult at all. It's actually very *fucking* simple—she'll only be happy when she's *dead*.'

'*TABATHA!*'

Her father sat bolt-upright, horrified.

'I'd say your Hippocratic Oath leaves you with a conflict of interest, wouldn't you.'

'*Tabatha, please!*'

The eyes burned with fury as she considered saving her mother the effort, going for the face-punching option herself. Balling her fists she backed away, glaring at the doctor, daring him to return her stare.

He didn't, seeking solace instead with her father.

Storming out of the door, she heard herself being described as *'a child'*, and maybe that was exactly the point.

'It's a lot for a child to take in.'

She sat in the taxi and pondered this. It resonated on a level that left her puzzled. The intense seething was evaporating, replaced by confusion.

'Where exactly in Brookside, love?'

'Sorry? Oh, can I change my mind? Make it Mill Road, please.'

Rick wasn't back until tomorrow, and she was willing to bet he still left a spare front door key in the same place, buried in a tiny old Tupperware container full of ground and moss.

She couldn't bear the thought of staying in her home tonight.

The bed smelled of him. She'd thought of using the little spare bedroom, but there were no bed sheets.

It was a relief that she was able to do this on her own. Some time ago, she'd accepted that she would sleep with Rick again, in his bed—their bed. But she'd dreaded the first awkward moments—this was, by far, the easier route.

Should she leave before he returned tomorrow, removing all trace of her presence? It wasn't that he'd mind or object to her doing this, but Tabatha wondered if she was making it all too easy for him.

She was being childish, of course.

And there it was again, but this time it hit home with a searing clarity.

She pulled the duvet over her body and curled into a foetal-like ball.

There would be no children.

There couldn't be—she must never bring anyone else into the world to suffer this.

*

Everything in the kitchen was exactly as she'd left it.

So many months ago, and still the same amount of decaffeinated teabags in an airtight jar. And still a label sellotaped to the side—a skull-and-crossbones and the words *'Danger - Tab's scummy non-tea bags.'*

It seemed a strange object to make her smile.

There was even some in-date milk in the fridge—impressive for a single guy.

She left a note leaning against the kettle—*'Someone's been sleeping in your bed. Sincerely, Goldilocks. ps Mum very ill and at Addenbrooke's so no dinner tonight, sorry. Call me later. X'*

'Any news, Dad?'

'Mum's comfortable—she had some breakfast earlier, and the specialist is seeing her later this morning. Are you coming back here soon? Sorry I didn't get home last night, but I just wanted to be near to hand—with her.'

'It's fine. I'm going to walk there—I need the exercise. See you within the hour.'

'Okay. I may go home while you're here and get a change of clothes.'

'Sure. Dad? How is she—really?'

'She's ... she's doing alright. Actually, she's a bit cross. It'll be good for you to talk with her. Hey, that doctor last night—he was only trying to ....'

'Yeah, I know. Look, I'll see you soon—bye for now.'

Tabatha didn't need that type of chat with her dad right now. She'd been in the wrong, and she knew that, but the guy had asked for it. Or maybe he hadn't; she didn't know or care. Her mind was consumed with problems she could hardly bear to comprehend.

*

'You'll need to keep a close eye on Dad, sweetie—I'm worried about him.'

'Did you really just say what I thought you did?'

'There's no need to be like that, dear. I'm tired enough as it is, without having to worry about him, as well.'

'Mum, if you were truly worried about Dad, then why wouldn't you have fought this … this *thing*, when it first started? You could have beaten it and then looked after him yourself.'

'You don't *'beat'* this *'thing'*, as you put it. I've watched people I loved with all my heart, and it's taken them away from me; *torn* them away from me. Lingering on and on, doctor after doctor, never-ending hospitals, watching them slowly die in front of me—watching them die, in agony.'

'So you're scared?'

'So help me God, I'm scared. I'm so damn scared.'

Tracey wiped away tears, wincing as the cannula in the back of her hand tugged spitefully.

'So am I, Mum.'

She clambered up on the narrow bed, careful to avoid vital tubes, pressing the side of her face gently into her mother's shoulder.

She felt a kiss on the top of her head, then her hair being slowly stroked, over and over again, with metronomic rhythm.

The memory felt older than her whole life. It was the most comforting sensation in the world. Her mother was dying, yet Tabatha could feel no safer than here, now.

Her voice was no more than a whisper.

'I can beat it, Mum. I'm going to beat it. It's not going to destroy me—I don't want to die.'

Tracey stopped stroking and attempted to sit up to see her daughter's face more clearly. She couldn't mute the sigh of pain.

'What are you talking about?'

'I'm not going to lie down and take it. Oh, I'm sorry—I didn't mean that you were doing that. I just meant that ...'

'What do you mean, Tabatha? You're not going to *get* breast cancer.'

'Mum, I've done the research. I've seen the figures—I know the odds. Every specialist would tell me I probably have the gene—if they didn't, they'd be lying.'

'But ...'

'It's not going to happen—it's *not* going to happen. Maybe it wasn't available to you at my age, but it sure is now. I'm going to sort this out for good.'

'You don't understand. You can't ...'

'Prophylactic Mastectomy, Mum. It's not that unusual anymore. Have you even heard of it? They also call it Preventative or Elective Mas ...'

But Tracey had grabbed her daughter with both hands— painfully hard.

'*NO!*'

She was breathing hard, high-pitched intermittent tones howling from a machine. Her eyes wide open, she gripped her daughter's arms.

'*NO!*'

'Hey, it's okay. There's next to no cases of death following the procedure, and the younger you are, the bet ...'

'*NO!*'

She started to cough and choke, her face blossoming;

'*NO, NO, N ...*'

'Alright, Mrs Mercer, it's alright.'

Two nurses had appeared from nowhere, simultaneously hyper-speed and total calmness. One of them tended to their patient whilst the other gently helped the baffled girl off the bed.

'Everything's fine, but we just need you to wait outside for a few minutes. Can you do that, please? It's all good.'

Unlike the doctor of last night, Tabatha was immediately in awe of the two women; how she'd love to be under the care of these angels when she came to do what she had to do. She walked out of the room in a daze.

A few minutes drifted, and she pondered knocking on the door, but then a doctor, this one pleasingly ancient and exuding wisdom, entered her mum's room.

Feeling helpless, stuck between a month-old copy of *Hello* magazine and potential WhatsApp messages, she sat down on a plastic hospital-orange chair and took the iPhone out of her jeans pocket.

She'd expected a message from Rick—there were three, spaced evenly apart at approximate hourly intervals. He was clearly worried about her mum, about her and, perhaps more touchingly, even her dad.

She looked at her watch; he'd be back in Cambridge in a few hours—'immediately' if she needed him.

She needed him alright, and in more ways than she'd care to admit, but there was nothing he could do—she just needed to be with her mother now.

'Thanks but don't worry - just come to Addenbrooke's when you get home. Message me when you're on your way and I'll tell you where we are. Safe journey x'.

Two porters walked past her and into the room.

Oh God, please God, not that. It can't be—they'd have called me in already. Surely?

She stood up and walked towards the door. As she was plucking up the courage to knock, the door opened, and a porter walked out, pulling the grey bars at the foot of the bed. There was a mask over her mother's mouth and nose, her face drained of all but an ashen hue.

Tabatha looked at the elderly doctor, but his focus was solely on the patient. One of the nurses was pushing two trollies holding liquids high in the air. The other held the door wide open as the second porter pushed the top of the bed past her. It was the woman who'd ushered her out of the room, and she was looking directly at Tabatha.

It was a different expression—less efficient determination, more sympathetic resignation. The very embodiment of clichéd Britishness—the stiff upper lip.

As Tabatha felt her legs weaken, threatening to buckle from under her, she wondered how many millennia that expression had been inextricably linked with sadness; with death.

'We're going straight to Intensive Care—we need to monitor your mother carefully for now.'

The angel's voice was subtly different, the previous confidence and authority replaced by a quieter gentleness. The urgency reserved for emergencies seemed to be missing.

As the seven of them travelled down three stories in the lift, the daughter looked at her sleeping (or was it unconscious?) mother—was there a difference anymore?

Doctor looked at patient—nurse at nurse. The porters, sentries symmetrically opposed and divided by their precious goods, stoically stared at their shoes.

It was this observation, more than anything else, which confirmed her dread. Hospital porters were cheerful and cheeky. They were jesters and jokers and flirters and lads. Perhaps singlehandedly, they lifted the atmosphere—the stark severity and seriousness of a hospital.

This time, they didn't.

They couldn't, and they didn't, and they *knew*.

A wretched gasp of dismay escaped from Tabatha. She now had the undivided attention of all Addenbrooke's employees within the confines of the shiny aluminium box.

More significantly, she had the attention of Tracey.

Spanned above the misty plastic mask, her eyes were pooled with liquid. The vibrant pearl-blue irises, such a feature of her being and in such stark contrast to her husband and daughter's mundane brown, now void of their deep lustre. The surrounding sclera, bloodshot, the left, pooled red on one side.

Tracey lifted one hand and waved at Tabatha.

With horror, she thought her mother was saying goodbye, but misinterpreted the movement. She tried to speak from within the oxygen-mask, but her words were incoherent. The distress she immediately displayed, causing the doctor to lift the cup away from her face.

It was not a voice. Rather, an escape of noise from somewhere within the ruined chest, but the words were understandable. Tabatha's head throbbed with a pain she thought must be audible.

I'll swap places with you, Mum—right here, right now—let's do it, let's make it happen—now.

'Darling, don't do it. Don't do it. Don't. Promise me. Don't do …'

The doctor replaced the mask as he saw the distress this effort was causing his patient. An angel stroked her hair, damp and matted.

An intrusive tone and a piped announcement of arrival at the *Second Floor.*

Relieved porters with work to do—escape from the atmospheric tension as the lift-doors part.

'Do you understand the message?'

It was an angel speaking, her surprisingly cold hand on Tabatha's wrist.

'Yes. And no. The words, yes—the meaning, no. Look, how long does Mum have? Please?'

'Sweetheart, you'll have to direct that one at Doctor Bayliss—he's the expert. Right now, the only important thing is your Mum's comfort.'

'And not her health?'

Tabatha looked away, ashamed of herself.

'I'm sorry, that wasn't fair.'

Another wrist squeeze, and there was that expression again.

Tabatha had nothing left.

'You're an angel. How do you deal with all this? How? You're a fucking angel.'

The floodgates opened, and she sunk to her knees on the hard floor, face buried in her hands. Only then did she become aware of the others patiently waiting outside the lift, staring at her.

*

At the nurse's suggestion, Tabatha had gone back to her mother's room with a porter to collect personal belongings and clothing, which seemed hopelessly frivolous and frighteningly ominous.

The hospital box she'd been handed seemed almost mockingly large.

'Thanks for coming with me, but I'm okay now—can I just do this on my own, please?'

The porter looked sympathetic but unsure; he'd been tasked with keeping an eye on the emotional woman until they returned to the IC Unit.

'Maybe I'll just wait outside the door for you, madam? You won't know which unit your mum's been put in and, you know, probably easier if I …'

'Okay, sure—I'll just be a couple of minutes. Hey, and thanks.'

It was a very soft cashmere jumper she'd bought recently. Tabatha had been with her, and remembered how close a match it was to her mum's nail varnish—'*claret by floodlight*'.

Would it ever be worn again? She bundled the garment in her hands, brought it to her face and inhaled deeply; too new to have the essence of her mother, but the daytime perfume she often used, '*Chance*' by Chanel, lingered.

'*Why do you never try any others, Mum?*'

'*Because any woman who can create 'Number Five' deserves absolute brand loyalty.*'

'*But I've just Googled it, and Number Five perfume was created by Ernest Beaux.*'

'*And was it called Beaux Number Five?*'

'*No, but …*'

'*Exactly. It was called 'Chanel Number Five'. Coco Chanel—Number Five.*'

Her daydream was interrupted by the door opening; the porter obviously thought she was unstable or deranged—probably both.

'Just one more minute, please? Oh—Dad.'

'Where's Mum? Oh my God—*where is she?*'

'They've taken her to Intensive Care. I was just collecting everything to take to her.'

'What happened?'

The porter saved Tabatha from further grief.

'I'll take the box for you. Why don't you both follow me, and we'll go and see her now.'

It was the nature of a hospital that some of the longer-term patients jokingly imagined themselves as inmates. And, just as in prison, an initial common bond and rank were created by establishing the duration of one's stay; both time served and time left, though the latter was obviously less apparent in a hospital.

They shared a lift down the building with two more porters, an impossibly-young doctor, and a middle-aged man sporting a large ball of cotton-wool over his left eye. His bare arms were resting outside the bedsheets, both covered in so many tattoos, as to render the colour of his skin pure guesswork.

'Escaping? Or done your time, eh?'

He chuckled then winced, putting a hand against the cotton wool patch.

Neither David nor Tabatha could immediately come up with an answer, which turned out to be fine, as the question proved rhetorical.

'Been trying to get parole for a while now, but can't get any straight answers from anyone, can I Doc?'

The patient looked at the doctor with his right eye, and Tabatha followed his stare. It was a mean thought but valid nonetheless; could patients trust their health to a medical professional yet to recover from the inconvenience of teenage acne?

'As we discussed earlier, Mr. Fletc ...'

The youngster was not so much a doctor as a fully-qualified ophthalmic surgeon. Given the requirements of a doctorate degree in medicine and a further four years of ophthalmology residency training, this was no mean feat for a person who Tabatha had guessed was yet to officially receive his key to the door.

In the confines of the UK, the man was already somewhat of a legend in his profession. In later decades, he would go on to become one of the pre-eminent eye surgeons in the world (though no one in the world yet knew this, obviously).

For now—the present, he joined a list of the many who'd misinterpreted his patient's rhetorical language.

'He says that once I've had the eye out, I can scarper. I'll have to come back, 'course. Just to check the cancer hasn't spread and all that malarkey, right Doc?'

Once more, the doctor grammatically tripped up.

'You see, I've got eye cancer. Well, that is, unless Apple has a patent on those words, then we'll have to think of something else to call it, eh Doc?'

The future surgical-god seized his moment.

'It's an ocular melanoma, Mr. Fletcher. You have every chance of a ful ...'

'Here we go then—this is me—Ground Zero. Well, Level Three, anyways, as the lady robot says. You have a good time guys—off you go to the Land of Freedom, and sink a few pints for me, too. Ta Ta, my lovelies.'

The little menagerie departed, and the doors slid shut, a thunderous stillness enveloping the lift.

A porter, a father, and a daughter looked at each other in silence, then all three shrugged. It's recently fashionable to accept that *'it is what it is'* and, clearly, this was an exceptionally accurate example of this deep philosophy.

'What happened, Doctor? She was fine a couple of hours ago—I don't understand?'

'I'm afraid this is the nature of the problem your wife faces, Mr. Mercer. She's in no pain now, and we've issued a little sedation—just to help her rest.'

'Will she go back to her room when she's stable? We've had to clear all her things out—I don't understand?'

'It's just a process due to the never-ending shortage of beds. If and when we can move Mrs. Mercer out of IC, we can find another room at that time.'

'So ... So, there's a chance she ... she might not move out of ... *here*?'

'Mr. Mercer, it's a very grave situation your wife is facing; I cannot over-emphasise that fact. The x-rays of her lungs show a very advanced state of ...'

'She'll wake up, though, won't she? You don't expect my daughter and I to just sit here and ... and watch her ... I mean, we can talk to her when she comes around, surely?'

Her colour was different now, and it was as if her eyes had sunken.

David Mercer couldn't comprehend how this could have happened in such a short space of time. He put a hand on his wife's, now much colder—somehow drier.

He watched her eyes dance behind the lids and wondered what she was dreaming. And the mask—that *damn* mask covering her beautiful face.

'How vital is that mask?'

'It's vital, Mr. Mercer.'

'But what if she wants to talk?'

'It's highly probable that removal of the oxygen mask, plus the additional stress of talking, could produce very distressing symptoms for your wife.'

'When will she wake up from this sedation?'

'At the moment, the most comfortable scenario for her is sleep. We can reassess the situation after she's had a peaceful night's sleep.'

'But what if ...'

As he faltered, Tabatha put a hand on his shoulder. A simple gesture of unconditional love and comfort, it produced instant heart-ache and forlorn helplessness in the broken man.

'I'm very sorry, Mr. Mercer. The nurses will be with your wife at all times. She really is receiving the very best possible care. And, of course, you and your daughter are welcome to stay here. If she wakes during the night, I'm sure it would be a great relief for Mrs. Mercer to see you both.'

The elderly doctor put his hand on David's other shoulder;

'Sir? Once again, I'm very sorry—I truly am.'

He looked from the distraught man to Tabatha, and there it was again for her to observe—that most disguised, juxtaposed and contradictory of all human expressions—the thin smile of mortality.

'Let me get two chairs, and how about a cuppa for you both, eh?' said an angel.

*

The beeps and pings of the baffling array of machinery, initially intrusive and irritating, were now inaudible. Similarly, the seemingly impossible task of sleeping in a hard chair was now proving, if not comfortable, then certainly possible in short bursts.

There were three other beds in this Intensive Care ward, but currently only two patients.

David Mercer had watched as an almost impossibly-frail old man was tended to by first one, then two nurses. A doctor had appeared soon afterwards, the plastic curtains drawn around the bed.

Would they have bothered to draw those curtains had his little family not been present? Perhaps it was a habit, or a regulation, or best practice?

He looked up and studied the curtain tracks running around their own area, attached to the suspended ceiling by thin metal rods.

David shut his eyes, dreading the moment when the creamy beige plastic started its cable car-like journey around their lives.

At least his daughter was asleep, immune to these most personal and profound moments of an old man's life.

Beneath her blanket, Tabatha watched the drama unfold.

She strained her ears to hear any words after the curtains had been drawn, but the staff were talking so quietly.

Occasionally, she'd see bumps moving along the plastic like a magician's trick, as the staff moved around the bed.

Where was the poor man's family? To live that long and have nobody there when it was time—how appallingly unfair and unimaginably sad.

A braver woman would have walked over and offered her hand to the poor man.

She didn't feel brave, though; never had, if truth be known. A coward to the bitter end, more concerned with her own health, even as her mum lay dying next to her, hiding away the pain so as not to cause distress for her precious daughter.

Why am I so completely unable to think of anyone but myself? How did I become like this?

Lights inside the room-within-a-room were dimmed. The curtains made their way back, much slower on the return journey.

Around the patient, the life-giving bank of machines had been put to sleep. The only illumination came from an overhead angle-poise lamp above the bed, set to its dimmest mode.

The white top-sheet now extended from the foot to the head of the bed, the gentleman within so slight, as to hardly cause a bump or crease in the starched cotton.

The four of them (or was it now three?) slithered silently past the Mercer family, eyes firmly and grimly ahead. There was no disguising the fact that this was a procession.

At least her father was asleep, immune to these most personal and profound moments of an old man's death.

When Tracey woke, it was not yet dawn.

She was drowsy, but aware of being more comfortable than she could remember in months—perhaps years. No pain—nothing—freedom of a sort.

David and Tabatha were either side of her, asleep. They mirrored each other, sitting awkwardly in chairs, covered with a blanket, their heads resting on her bed.

They held her hands in their sleep.

She rested her back against the stacked pillows and breathed as deeply as her shattered lungs could manage, feeling slightly claustrophobic from the ever-present oxygen mask, pressed firmly against her face.

All the time she'd spent since goodness knows when, thinking ahead to now—to this very moment. Answers were appearing to questions she'd never dared ask but had wondered for eternity.

Yes, I know the time is near—I sense it though, thank God, I don't feel it.

And it's not frightening—it truly isn't—not any more. Without the pain, there's space for clarity.

There's a peace that can't be comprehended. It just exists all around, present like a parent, or a guardian, or a saviour.

But with the growing clarity came the dawning realisation.

She gently pulled her hand out of her daughter's and placed it on the girl's head. When Tabatha was young, stroking her hair would often induce sleep, where a bedtime story had failed. Now she hoped for the opposite effect.

'Mum? You okay?'

She lifted her head and looked at her mother, who was lifting the mask from her mouth and nose.

'Ssshhh—don't wake your father. Come closer so I can whisper; it's easier for me.'

'I should call a nurse.'

'No! In a minute; just listen to me first. Understand that this is me talking and not the drugs, though I thank the Lord for them.'

'Mum, I love you so ...'

Tracey put a hand on the girl's cheek and smiled.

'I know you do, and I you. But just listen to me—it is *so* important.'

Her breath became ragged, and she let the mask seek its place again.

'Let me call a nurse.'

Tabatha put her hand towards the red cord hanging by the pillows.

Tracey's expression changed to one of fear as she pulled the mask away again.

'No! Just listen ... to me.'

She took more small breaths of the oxygen and continued.

'That operation ... please don't ... you mustn't.'

As Tracey's anxiety grew with the laboured breathing, a machine was finding its own voice. Although the skin was cold, sweat beaded and trickled down her forehead.

'Mum, please stop—put the mask back on.'

David was lifting his head off the mattress as a nurse rushed into the room.

'Just give me some space, guys. Alright, Tracey, let's keep that mask on you; that's it.'

She scanned the monitors and hit a reset button to stop the unnerving, high-pitched tone.

Tabatha backed further away to make space for another nurse, but David was still holding onto his wife's hand.

'Is she okay? Will she be okay?'

His expression of fear and devastation made Tabatha want to wail in anguish. She needed a few precious moments to get herself back together; then she'd be okay—be strong again.

She could see her mother's face between the tending nurses, signalling that she was going outside for a moment. She knew the expression this would provoke, and there it was, once more.

'*Five minutes, Mum—just give me five minutes.*' Silently mouthed sign language.

She passed a doctor at the door; a new one she hadn't seen before. The woman was of similar age to her mother. It made no sense to Tabatha, but the presence of this woman made things a little easier.

'You'll feel more comfortable now, Tracey; may I call you Tracey? Just relax and keep with the oxygen; it'll help, love.'

There was an empathy and connection between the two middle-aged women, but Tracey would never know that this doctor had suffered breast cancer in the recent past.

Lifting the mask slightly, she put her hand on the woman's arm and gripped as hard as her body would allow.

'Just a moment with my husband alone, please? Then I'll do everything you say.'

The doctor glanced at the senior staff nurse, and with no words, nothing and everything was spoken. Had Tabatha witnessed this, she could not have held herself together any longer.

'Of course. We'll be right outside.'

Her eyes flicked to the door, and the nurses retreated, followed by the doctor.

I'm so tired. So very, very, tired. Give me one last moment.

This time she pulled the mask right off her face and let it lay, quietly hissing, on the pillow.

He looked at his dying wife through a film of tears, mute and hardly daring to breathe. Wishing himself dead, anything and everything ready to be sacrificed, in order to remove them both from this point in time. His helplessness was threatening to swallow him.

'Kiss ... me ... David. Please?'

And he did. So tenderly, as if she was a bubble about to burst and evaporate into the atmosphere, disappearing forever, before his eyes.

Sooo tired.

'Don't let her ... don't.'

She could find breath from nowhere, the machines screeching their concern.

The door opened, and three women moved towards her. Tracey held out a hand in their direction, momentarily holding them back.

Can't breathe, can't breathe. Breathe, damn you—BREATHE.

'Do anything to stop her, David.'

She grabbed his head and pulled his face as tight to hers as she could manage.

'*Anything.*'

Amidst the flurry of medical activity, Tabatha walked back into the unit.

Her father was holding his face, silently and openly sobbing as he witnessed the nurses doing all they could, within the confines of Tracey's wishes for no resuscitation.

She ran to her father and held him tightly, burying her face in his chest, then looking at her mother.

When she could look no longer, she sought his chest again.

Neither knew the exact moment when Tracey died, but when the doctor turned and approached them, they knew it was over.

She put an arm around them both, and their three heads bowed and touched.

13

One month later.

'YOU SHOULD do that exercise stuff you used to do, Dad. You can't just stay at home all the time.'

'I was actually thinking the same thing about you. I'll never be able to tell you how grateful I am—you've literally looked after me like … well … like Mum would have. And I had no idea you could cook; how long had you been hiding that?'

'The power of Google. Look it up, go get the ingredients, chop them up, and throw them in the oven—voila. And maybe a little bit from when living with Rick, though we were both take-away connoisseurs. I've actually enjoyed cooking every day—given me something to do.'

'I've been waiting for you to bring up the subject of Rick.'

'Oh, oh—here we go.'

'No. No, not at all. I meant, I wondered why you hadn't been to see him, or maybe him come here for dinner— something like that? I really appreciated the way he came up to me and shook my hand at Mum's funeral. He was very kind … kind words.'

'He's a kind guy, Dad. And before you raise your eyebrows, there are things you don't know about … about things that happened in the past—a specific thing.'

'It's none of my business. It wasn't then, and it isn't now. All I've ever been concerned with is your happiness. You knew that, of course?'

'I always knew that, and I'm not going to sit here and make excuses for him. What he did was unacceptable on all levels and at all times. I'm just saying that there were … there were mitigating circumstances.'

'It's okay—no explanations needed. Whatever works for you is fine by me—really.'

'I'd like to tell you one day. I never told Mum, but I think I was going to at the right moment. If it's okay, I think I'd like you to know at some point—just not quite yet. Is that cool with you?'

'It's cool with me. As long as it's cool with you for me to say *'cool'*, that is?'

'It is *totally* cool. Mum would have said that. Anything you do that reminds me of Mum is …'

Tabatha looked down at her plate and tears fell from her eyes; tears from a seemingly endless supply, that was never going to stop.

There were so many things that triggered the crying. When she thought she'd found them all, another would overwhelm her, yet again.

David had learnt not to comfort his daughter when she broke down. If anything, his contact seemed to make matters worse.

He'd been putting the subject off, waiting for the right time to raise it. Now certainly wasn't the occasion, but as the days went past, he was becoming more anxious.

But for him to be too late wasn't an option—it didn't bear thinking about. Time was absolutely of the essence.

He quietly prayed for strength and guidance. He knew he was many thousands of prayers behind—let him get through this, and he'd make it all up.

'Tabatha?'

His voice was an inaudible whisper and stuck in his throat.

'Tabatha?'

She looked up at him and sniffed, taking a tissue from her pocket—she was never without them nowadays.

'Your mother said something to me. Just before the end, she spoke to me—pleaded with me. There was nothing the doctors or nurses could have done to save her, but it felt as if the effort to talk brought forward ... I sense, however fractionally, it brought forward the end. In a way, passing on the message to me was more important to Mum than her own life.'

He looked at a photograph of Tracey, which he'd hung on the kitchen wall a couple of weeks ago, with Tabatha's approval. It showed the three of them in the garden, standing beneath a bizarrely tall sunflower. He hadn't planted it, though he'd certainly nurtured the flower when it started to approach his own height.

With the help of a stepladder, he'd measured it at nearly four metres. He was in the process of recording it for posterity on an old Canon camera he still used when Tracey and Tabatha had come outside.

Tracey wanted to take one of David and their daughter, but Tabatha insisted they all be in the photo.

After a series of failures on Tracey's phone (it slid off the stepladder twice, then when it behaved, the shot was either of the enormous flower-head only, or the three of them and a thick green stalk), she had them all stand on garden chairs, arms around each other.

It was a technically hopeless and delightfully natural picture.

At this moment, the image cheered him and gave him the strength he'd asked for, and for that, he was eternally grateful.

'Mum told me what you're intending to do.'

'I don't understand.'

'You do understand, sweetheart.'

It was the first time he'd ever called his daughter that—may probably have been the first time he'd ever even used the word.

He was subconsciously speaking as Tracey would have done, and he sensed his blasphemous attempt at a prayer was being answered.

'Mum told me because she trusted me to talk you out of it.'

'But she promised! I *knew* what you'd be like. God, she was bad enough about it.' Tabatha put her hand to her mouth.

'I didn't mean that. I'm sorry, Dad—I didn't mean that about Mum.'

She put a soggy tissue to her eyes.

'Whatever you say is alright—nobody could question the love you had, the love you *have*, for Mum.'

He stretched a hand across the table, and she took it.

'You needed to listen to her, and now you need to listen to me.'

He squeezed her hand and looked at her intently.

'You don't, I repeat, you do *not* have that gene your mother carried. I've done a little research of my own, and I see they've now turned the letters into a word; I believe *BRCA* is now pronounced *Bracker*—is that right?'

Tabatha nodded. She wanted to run upstairs or out of the house, but she couldn't move.

'So, what I'm saying ... what *Mum* is ... was saying, damn it, what we're *both* saying, as your parents, is ... you don't need to ... to take *drastic action*. Do you understand? Do you?'

She couldn't hold his stare any longer and looked down at her lap. There was a silence that David took as a positive; his precious daughter had understood.

The relief was short-lived, however, as something catastrophic began to gnaw at his mind.

It made no sense and was impossible—Tabatha had been with him for virtually the whole of this last dreadful month.

Before then? No—it was absolutely impossible.

He was unaware of his grip tightening around her hand.

'What? Ow, you're hurting my hand. Yes, I understand, alright? I understand.'

'You haven't ... you haven't *done* anything, you know ... *have* you? *Tabatha*?'

Her coy expression left him crushed. He heard his heart hammering in his ears, and clamminess gripped his body. He swallowed painfully.

'Tabatha? Look at me? Please tell me that you ...'

'Tuesday—after this weekend. They said I can be there on Monday evening. The procedure's scheduled for early on Tuesday.'

He felt light-headed, drunk with relief—like he'd surfaced from a deep dark ocean into the blessed light.

'Thank God.'

He wanted to hug his daughter but was worried it would start her crying again. It was all he could do, not to break down with relief himself.

'Dad, my mind is made up. I hear what you and Mum say, but everything says you're wrong. Study the facts, and you'll know why I'm doing this. And Christ knows, I don't want to go through what she went through. You surely can't wish that on me?'

He took another look at the photo. It was taken last summer, maybe fifteen months ago. Tracey would have known by then, of course. She'd never told him when the symptoms had started, and in some stupid way that felt like a betrayal—as if he couldn't be trusted with something of such enormity.

They'd had endless discussions over the years, particularly early on in the marriage. It was unbearable for him at first, but he came to accept his wife's decision—and her will. Christ, that single-minded, cast iron will.

So there she was, in the middle of the photo, holding her family together. She'd insisted Tabatha be in the middle, but that didn't work with the three-second sprint from the phone to being in the shot, so she'd begrudgingly backed down.

Tracey looked at him from the photograph.

Do anything to stop her, David.'

Those were the last words he ever heard on her lips.

The clamminess was coming back—what else could he do? Was there a way around this?   And it wasn't her last words.

She'd said one final thing.

'Anything.'

206

'All I wish for you is health and happiness and a long life. And children as well, if you want them. Have you thought about children?'

'Of course I have; that's the most painful part of all. I'm not judging Mum at all—or you—but I couldn't bear the thought of passing this thing on to anyone else. I'm sorry, Dad, I'm truly not passing judgement, but if you look at the tragedy of Mum's family, you can hardly blame me.'

'I *don't* blame you—I'll never blame you. Can I hold your hand again if I promise not to squeeze too hard? I know I've never been an overly demonstrative person, but I feel it's what Mum would do. Do you mind?'

She put both hands palm up across the table, and he took them in his.

'I'll listen to you. I love you and know you hate the thought of me going through with this, but it'll save my life. You want me to have a long and healthy life, and this is the only way I can make that happen. You need to understand that there is nothing, absolutely nothing, you can say that will talk me out of this.'

He took a deep breath and had one last look at the photo of his family. Tracey was looking directly at him—right into the very depth of his soul.

'Do Anything. ANYTHING.'

'You're not going to have that operation, darling.'

'Daaad, I've told you, I'm go ...'

He couldn't take an interruption—not now.

'You're not, Tabatha, because what I have to tell you will make you realise it's unnecessary—it needn't happen—it's *not* going to happen.'

She wanted to pull her hands away, but he held onto them.

'Please? I need contact with you now. Just one minute? Hear me out—please?'

She relaxed, but there was a hint of exasperation in her expression.

'There's a reason that Mum and I knew you didn't carry this gene. I can't emphasise that word enough—we *knew*, I *know*, you don't have this hereditary disease.'

Even as he knew he had to continue, he looked for the slightest hint of realisation in her face—something to make his task easier. There was nothing, and why should there be—not a spark of recognition.

He fought for the words—a way of explaining to her in the very gentlest possible way.

'Mum felt exactly the same way as you do. About having children, I mean. After watching her gran and then her mother go through this nightmare, she knew that having children would never be an option. And I agreed, of course. But we so wanted to bring up our own child. She said I'd be a good father, which may have been just her kind words, but by God, I knew she'd be a wonderful mother. And she was.'

'So I was an accident, you mean? I don't understand—is that meant to make me feel better? Hereditary genes don't just disappear because of unintentional accidents. You think that gives you and Mum the right to stop me having an operation to save my life? You're a clever man, Dad—I'm surprised at ...'

'You *weren't* an accident. I didn't say you were an accident, sweetheart. You were the most planned, and wonderful, and beautiful, thing that ever happened to Mum and I. You were, and are, our … my, life.'

'This is ridiculous—you're making no sense at all. You and Mum said you decided not to have kids because of the huge risk of BRCA, then you say I'm not an accident, but you know I don't have the gene. You *'know'*. What gives you the divine right to go against all the medical studies carried out over the years, and tell me I don …'

Her mouth froze, though her eyes were now moving all over the place, focusing on just about anything but her father's face.

David could almost hear the gears meshing inside her head. God knew how much he needed Tracey by his side now—what would she say now—what would she do?

He felt his daughter's hands pull away from his. He opened his palms but left them where they were. There was still contact.

Now her eyes rested upon his, searching for denial of what was dawning on her.

Time staggered as she willed him to say, *'Don't be ridiculous'*, or *'What?'*, or *'Are you mad?'*

Anything but this silent, almost apologetic scrutiny.

When his eyes lowered, it was as good as an answer.

A slow-motion shock took hold of her—at least, that's what she thought it was. That, and a staggeringly overpowering loneliness.

It felt like she didn't know another soul on the planet. If she were to approach anyone about anything, they'd lie to her.

Ultimately, she could trust nobody, alive or dead.

As of this moment, she felt an unbearable loneliness that few could know existed.

He was talking to her. She could see his mouth moving and hear the words, but the noise was void of any meaning.

Her mouth had now closed, the lips forming a thin line. It was impossible to talk like this, and that was for the best. Never talking again felt like a very appealing idea—a genuine solution.

'Tabatha? Tabby?'

She pulled her hands back across the table, and they fell into her lap.

'Tabby?'

'Yes?'

'Would you like to … ummm … say anything? Or ask anything, of course. *'Anything.'*

She stared at him. There was no inquisitiveness or aggression in her expression. If anything, her face felt singularly unable to convey any form of emotion.

'A glass of water, perhaps? Or some wine? Yes, how about some wine? Let's share a bottle of wine. No—a *really* special bottle. You choose—anything.'

His offer was so stunningly inappropriate, as to make him openly wince.

He silently thanked the God that who recently been so helpful, that he hadn't thought to suggest some champagne as an alternative to the wine offer.

He was also bewildered that he'd called her *'Tabby'*— could only assume it was some sort of hopeless effort to emulate Tracey. Christ, he couldn't miss that woman more than he did now; dying would have been much easier and less painful.

'What do I call you?'

The sound of her voice made him jump—he'd resigned himself to a one-way conversation.

'Eh?'

'You've started calling me *Tabby*. Will you be progressing to *Tabs*? Just so I know.'

'What? I don't understand.'

'I thought it was a bit strange, but of course, it now makes perfect sense. Stupid of me, really—do I call you '*David*' from now?'

'Oh Tabatha, don't be ridiculous. I'd have given anything in my life not to have to break this … this news to you … like this.'

'I'm sure. It's quite some '*news*', right?'

'Look, Mum and I couldn't let you go through with this … this *mutilation*. If she'd been here, she'd have explained it so much better than I have.'

'What, so it turns out to be good news, you mean?'

'You know I didn't mean it like that. I'm just trying to apologise for …'

'For turning my world inside out and upside down? Oh, hey, no probs, Dad. Sorry, I mean *David*. I'll put the kettle on, and we'll have a nice cup of tea—I'm sure that'll sort everything out.'

'Please don't get up yet, Tabatha.'

He was more lost than he'd ever been in his life. Whatever reaction he'd expected, it wasn't this.

He knew his daughter had vast experience of turning sadness into bitterness—it was her natural defence mechanism to breaking down in front of someone. There was nothing wrong with that, and he sometimes begrudgingly admired it, but Christ was it tough to be on the end of.

'How long?'

She was standing behind the chair with hands planted firmly on her hips, legs slightly apart. The posture exuded defiance and even downright hostility. It screamed *confrontation*.

'How long?'

He intended no flippancy—he simply had no idea what she was asking.

'Errrr … How long does it take the kettle to boil? Oh … No, hold on, that wasn't the question. Now what was it? Oh yes, that's right, how long have you been pretending to be my father?'

He felt scratchy tears at the back of his eyes.

Hello God, me again. Can we hold the tears just now? Please?

'Mum and I have been your …'

'You mean *Tracey and I*, surely?'

And also, please God, don't let me lose my temper—ANYTHING but that. Even tears before that, thank you. Oh, and 'Amen'.

But there was no longer a chance of tears—they'd miraculously evaporated as quickly as they'd appeared. She'd hurt him—really, *really*, hurt him. A physical punch to the stomach would have left him less winded.

'Mum and I love you dearly. Truthfully, I suspect we both love you more than we loved each other. *That's* how much she loved you, and *that's* how much I love you. You were, and are, and always will be, our world, and our daughter. That will n*ever* change.'

He'd never uttered words like this before in his life. He was momentarily exhausted—emotionally shattered, his heart and soul laid bare.

If that didn't get through to the most important person in his life, then he feared he had nothing left to give.

Tabatha turned away and made two mugs of tea. It bought her the time she needed, to realise what an awful person she'd become.

One thing was certain; she didn't get this vile side of her personality from her parents—the two people who'd given a large portion of their lives to bring her up as best they could.

'I'm sorry ... Dad.'
She handed him his mug and leaned her head on his shoulder.

'Forgive me for that, but it's just the biggest shock of my life.'

'I know, and I'm so sorry I had to tell you. I hope you'll forgive me too—maybe in time?'

'Hey, I should be grateful—you've just given me a clean bill of health. Maybe we should have that bottle of wine after all.'

'Sure, what would you like—red or white?'

'I'm only joking—tea is just fine, but ...'

She guessed this was probably the wrong time, but maybe there'd never be a right time.

'But?'

'But can I ask you something? I guess you know what I'm going to ask?'

David moved to a sideboard and pulled an envelope out of the top drawer, handing it to her.

'I came prepared—it's been in my upstairs safe for a long, long, time. It's not much; all we were given, actually. And there were very precise instructions; you were to be shown this only if, for one reason or another, you became aware that we weren't your birth parents.'

She took it from him, sat down, and opened the blank envelope. The postcard-sized photo came out upside-down, with nothing written on the back. She left it face down and sipped her tea.

'Is it my parents? Sorry, my biological … you know?'

'It's of your mother. The colour's a little faded, but you'll be surprised—you're very alike. Needless to say, she's very beautiful.'

Compliments made Tabatha feel awkward—more so when they came from her parents.

'Well, you're biased.'

She turned the picture over.

'Oh.'

Her head rotated slightly as she studied the image.

'*Oh*', indeed.'

'She's very …'

Tabatha couldn't take her eyes off the image.

'Pretty? Stunning? It's an extraordinary likeness, isn't it?'

'But she's so young. Was this taken before I was …'

'After. Your mum asked for a photo. She was seventeen.'

Tabatha was touching the outline of the girl's face. So often, the similarity of one person to another was a personal judgement, not necessarily shared by others. This was not the case now; it was a startling resemblance which anyone and everyone could witness.

'What were you going to ask me?'

'Oh, I wondered how old I was when you and Mum started to …?'

214

'Adopted you?'

'Don't say that. It sounds so cold—clinical. I didn't mean it that way.'

David couldn't help it—he chuckled.

'It's a word I subconsciously banished from our lives. It feels rather strange now it's out in the open. But it doesn't diminish our relationship in any way whatsoever. In fact, I think it makes you even more special. And to answer your question, you came into our lives when you were three months and one week old.'

'I'm glad it was so young.'

'So were we.'

'What was her name? Oh God, she's not dead, is she? I don't know why I asked that way.'

'Because you were thinking of Mum, sweetheart. I can't answer your question for certain, but the chances are that she should certainly still be alive—she'd only be, what, late forties?'

'What was her name?'

'Well her last name was 'X'. She had the right to remain anonymous and chose that path. We absolutely understood her position—Mum said she'd have done the same thing herself if the roles had been reversed.'

'What about her first name? Were you allowed to ask that?'

'Yes, and she chose to give us her real names, once she knew why we wanted that information.'

'And?'

'Her name was—sorry, *is*—Lily.'

'But that's my middle name.'

'Indeed, and she has a middle name too.'

'Which is?'

David smiled.

'Which is Tabatha.'

She gasped and looked at the photo again.

'She looks … nice.'

'We met her twice. At the first meeting, the adoption agency was present the whole time, but the second time, we had a little time to ourselves at the end.'

'What was she like?'

'Let me think about this and get it just right.'

He composed his thoughts and looked at his daughter again.

'Lily was a young girl, mature way beyond her years. I hope to God she was able to be a mother to some lucky girl or boy—your sister or brother, I guess—now there's a thought.'

Tabatha was hanging on his every word.

'She'd had a tough life. In many ways, she was the most remarkable person. Well, that's what your mum and I thought, at any rate.'

'What happened to her? And what about my father?'

'We never knew why, but she'd been in a foster home for many years. She told us she'd met your father when she'd moved out at sixteen. She left the home and went to north London—Kilburn. Lily managed to get a job working at a photographic laboratory, printing photos—she almost certainly printed the one you're holding now.'

Tabatha had put the picture down on the table, not wishing to get her fingerprints on it—she already treasured the photograph like a priceless gem.

'She met a lad there. I don't know his age, but she said he was '*much older*'. Anyhow, this turned out to be your dad— your biological father—only he didn't hang around for long. He apparently left a few months before you were born.'

Tabatha was instantly piecing it all together.

'Rick.'

'Sorry?'

'It's why you always had a problem with him.'

'That's not really fair, Tabby.'

'But it's *true*, Dad. You had a problem with Rick right from when I first started seeing him. You saw something in him that made you think of Lily's boyfriend, and then you could never get over that. When Rick did, well, what he did, then everything you'd always thought about him was justified in your mind.'

'Let's not talk about that now, hmmm? Let's just leave it that there are parallels to be drawn. I don't know what his name was, and we didn't ask, but I'd be very surprised if Lily ever heard from him again. I'm really sorry, sweetheart. If it makes it any easier, I think she'd love the thought that you now have her photograph.'

'Where was Lily from?'

'From here. You were born at Addenbrooke's Hospital, just as we said you were. You're as local, as local can be.'

'I'm glad. I've always felt linked to Cambridge, however odd that sounds.'

'Not odd at all. Everything we ever told you about your life was true, from the moment you were born until you came to us fourteen weeks later.'

'Except who my parents were. I'm sorry—I didn't mean it like that.'

'Hey, it's fine. I spent years talking to Mum about the situation. I think I had a huge guilt complex about the whole thing. She even got me to go and see a psychologist at one point.'

'What? *You*? Seeing a *psychologist*. But you're the most *normal* person in the world!'

'Well, there you go; your dad's a man of mystery.'

He was going to smile, but the unfortunate irony dampened his spirits.

'Sorry—bad choice of words. I'll just say I'm incredibly relieved that I no longer have to keep this interminable secret. Much more important, I hope you don't think of the news as a disaster? You understand why we … I mean, *I* had to tell you? There honestly was no other way.'

'I know. And there's a part of me that's so grateful—it was a massive burden. I don't know how Mum coped.'

'She was a very strong woman; a wonderful, strong, woman. Actually, you're a lucky girl—*both* your mums were very special people.'

This time he allowed himself a small smile, though the memory was still desperately raw.

Tabatha was gazing into the middle distance as she smiled back.

'Penny for them?'

She came back to the present with a start, those seemingly innocent words still haunting her.

David observed his daughter absently turning a silver ring on her thumb. He could hear his wife telling him that this was a sign she wanted something but was afraid to ask.

He was hopeless with loaded questions, but now there was nowhere else to turn, and no one else to turn to.

'It's okay. Whatever it is, we can work it out. What are you thinking—you look as if you're miles away?'

She tried to anticipate how her dad would take this. He wouldn't be angry, but she was desperate not to hurt him.

'I'd really like to try and find Lily. Does that upset you? I so don't want to hurt you in any way.'

'No, it's fine. I'd always thought you'd want to find her, if and when you knew about this. I went through years of torment thinking about this moment, but it feels different now. I think I may have been terrified of you meeting her at one point. I played out scenarios where you'd just bump into her in the street, and everything would come tumbling out.'

'But why?'

'I don't know—I never got that far. I guess I wondered if we'd lose you, or that you'd hate us? Can we tuck this away under the banner of unconditional love?'

'Dad?'

'Yes?'

'Is a hug out of the question? I mean, quite a big one— really quite big.'

And it wasn't out of the question.

*

The time since Tracey's death had seen daily messages from Rick.

They'd shared a coffee at a nearby café after the wake, but it was very brief. There were relatives staying at the house who'd travelled from around the country, and it was only right she be at home.

It occurred to her that none of them would be blood relatives. Did it matter? No, of course not. Did any of them know? She'd have to ask her dad, though she guessed not.

Rick had been everything that she could ask of him.

He knew to give her the space to come to terms with everything—but made it clear that all she had to do was call—he'd be there '*in a heartbeat*'.

She'd seriously thought about telling him of her life revelation, but there was plenty of time for that if they ever ended up together again.

For now, she just wanted to be close to her father, supporting him in any way she could.

When she lay awake into the depths of the night, thinking how her life had shifted on its axis, Tabatha realised she was never closer to her dad than now.

Why had it taken the loss of her mum and the news she was adopted, for this to happen?

Life had always been a mystery—now it was impossibly unfathomable.

In many cities throughout the UK, bonfire night was a big occasion. With 25,000 students, nearly all in permanent party mode, Cambridge was no exception.

It was a major evening in the social calendar of the town, and people came from far and wide to be a part of the evening.

Few, however, would be travelling quite as far as one particular person.

A familiar pinging informed Tabatha of an incoming WhatsApp message. They were rare of late, except for the daily one from Rick. His was normally in the evening, though—not the morning.

She looked at her phone.

'Hello stranger! S'been a while – how you been keeping, Tabby?'

'Hey! Long time! Nice to hear from you. Yeah, I'm ok I guess. You too? If you're going to boast about the weather, I'm not listening.'

'Nope, no boasting here – weather is crap actually!'

'Hmmm, well it would be I suppose, in the middle of your evening. Dropped all the way down to a balmy 35c now, has it?'

'No chance. Pouring with rain, windy, and about 3c. Brrrr and yuk!'

It was strange; she hadn't been in contact with Grant in an age, yet his messages felt instantly familiar. It was good to hear from him again.

'I see... Been looking up the weather in Cambridge on Google, have we?'

'Me? No, of course not. Good job it's meant to dry up by this evening, though they're saying it'll be below freezing for the fireworks. As I said – BRRRR!'

'Are you at the display now? I've seen the fireworks at Sydney Harbour online. Well impressive!'

'Ah, that's new year's eve you're thinking of – we don't have bonfire night. Anyway, I'm a long way from there - long LONNNGGG way! 10,519.814 miles away from there actually (and yeah, I did use Google for that one)'

'Errr, that IS a long way. Soooo, you're in Europe - somewhere like that?'

'You're not wrong. Bingo! I AM in Europe!'

'OMG! You're not in the UK?!?!

'Hold tight, I'll just go look outside. Yup, you're right again - I AM in the UK ☺

'Bloody hell, Grant - are you in London??? OH MY GOD!'

There was no denying—it was an exciting thought. If Grant was in England, she'd definitely have to meet up with him one day soon.

A little shiver of nerves went through her.

'Nah, not London. Not far away though…'

'How far away?'

'Hold on again. Google says 49 miles.'

'Let me take a wild guess - that'll be 49 miles NORTH of London, will it?

She was grinning, and there was a definite tightness in her stomach.

'You know me – I'm hopeless with directions. Not a clue - sorry.'

'Grrrrrr… GRANT?!'

'Ummm, well maybe - yeah – kind of north-ish? Perhaps?'

'Kind of Cambridge-ish? Perhaps?'

'Now you come to mention it…'

'GRANT!!!!!! ARE YOU MAD???!!!'

'Guilty as charged. Are YOU mad? At me, I mean? ☹'

'I'm... hmmmm *thinking*'

'*gulp*'

Tabatha laughed out loud—very loud.

It seemed an age since she'd done that. God, it felt good, though—so good.

'I'm absolutely NOT mad - anything but. You however? You are TOTALLY mad! Where are you staying?!'

'I got a serviced apartment – wasn't sure how long I'd be here so it seemed like the best idea. I've taken a week for now – it's quite close to the train station.'

'Cool! You there now? ☺'

'Not now - no. ☹'

'Oh. Where are you? In a pub, right? Figures—typical Aussie!'

'Not exactly.'

'So where? EXACTLY?!'

'Exactly? Well not to be creepy or spooky but.............'

'But.............'

'Well if you were to... say...'

'*Say…*'

'*Say… look out of your bedroom window… *gulp 2**'

As it happens, she was downstairs in the kitchen. She went to the front door and, not really knowing why, pushed the letter-box open and peered outside.

There were a couple of cars in the extortionist pay-parking spaces, but nobody on the far side of the road. On the pavement beside her home, a small, elderly lady scurried along, huddled below a beige umbrella. The rain was moving from heavy to torrential.

Tabatha opened the front door and stood under the alcove, rain splashing up onto her feet and shins. She looked at her phone and went to peck out another message—was this some sort of a joke? If so, it was a crap one.

'*Where ar …*'

The *parp* of an old car horn momentarily stopped her.

She looked across the road; A big black 4x4, absolutely *de rigueur* for the Cambridge private-school run—probably without a payslip on the dash, and she wickedly hoped for a lurking traffic warden. Mean-spirited, maybe, but a surprisingly common emotion towards off-roader owners throughout the UK.

Next to it, a tradesman's white van. Two spaces further up, a tiny little sports car in the same colour.

But no Grant.

She went to finish her message, disappointment building. Another *parp-parp*.

Tabatha looked up again—definitely coming from the little white car.

Oh—the little white Triumph Spitfire car …

'You're mad!'

'Thanks, I'm an Aussie. Are you getting in?'

'I'm soaked—I'll ruin the leather.'

'It's Ambla—you won't ruin it.'

'What's *Ambla*?'

'I'll tell you when you get in the car.'

Tabatha attempted a cool entry into the cabin, but this proved difficult when she sank into the passenger seat, placed at least a foot lower than she'd anticipated.

True to her word, she was, by now, soaked.

'G'day.'

'It may well be in Sydney. As for here and now, I'm soaking your ampler. Oh, and hello.'

'It's Ambla—imitation leather. To you and me, plastic. You're fine.'

'Oh—okay then. It's very … ummmm … small in here, isn't it?'

He couldn't take his eyes off her.

'Can we settle for *cosy*, perhaps? And I meant what I just said.'

'About ampa?'

'No, not about *Ambla*—about you being *fine*.'

Her face went very hot, very quickly.

'My father warned me about smooth-talking Aussie boys. I'm Tabatha, by the way.'

She held out her hand in mock sincerity.

He took it, but not as she'd anticipated—it was a sportsman's hand-shake, thumbs inter-linked with fingers touching the wrist. This was a first for her—there was a strange intimacy about it.

He wouldn't let go, and his eyes remained unblinking.

'And I'm Grant—may I call you Tabby? You're blushing, by the way—that wouldn't have come across on WhatsApp.'

She pulled away and put both hands on her face.

'Yeah, well I'm hot.'

'I can't deny that.'

'I meant, it's hot.'

'It's *three degrees*. And dropping.'

He was just short of smiling, the merest hint of a little line or two at the sides of his eyes.

'Yeah, well I meant in here—in the car.'

'The heater doesn't work; hasn't since Gramp first had the car. It's not really critical in Sydney, you see. Looks like something I'll need to sort out, though. Know any good mechanics?'

'As it happens, I do.'

'But would he know how to work on a really old Triumph?'

'Oh, for definite—it's his specialist subject. I'm not sure you could trust him, though?'

'Would *you* trust him?'

'Wellllll, he *is* Australian, sooo …'

'I like him already.'

'You know what? Actually, so do I.'

Tabatha leaned towards him which, within the confines of the miniature car, was very little distance, closed her eyes, and kissed him briefly on the lips.

'Welcome to England, Aussie-Boy.'

Then she sat back in her seat and faced the front.

'Going to take me for a spin?'

Later in the afternoon, they found themselves back in the same place.

'You sure you're okay to meet up for the display later?'

'Wellll, since you've come ten and a half thousand miles for it.'

'I'm really looking forward to seeing your dad, too. But I'll totally understand if you guys want to go alone – really.'

'Actually, I think it'll help with you being there. It was sort of a family tradition. Even when I was living with Rick, he used to leave us to it on Bonfire Night—just me, Mum, and Dad.'

'If you have a change of heart or your dad doesn't fancy the extra company, please, just let me know?'

'He'll enjoy your company—trust me.'

'OK, I'll see you here at six.'

Tabatha wiggled out of the car and tapped the metal roof. 'I thought this was meant to be a convertible?'

'It's the original hardtop. Gramp never used it, but I thought it might be a good idea to fit it for the English winter. Once the spring arrives, off it comes. Then you just have to make sure you don't leave the soft-top down when it rains—you have no idea what a drama it is if that happens.'

Such a vivid image. How did life deal those things up; were the dice weighted?

'Oh, I have some idea.'

*

'It was good to meet you, Grant. I'm glad we were able to share that spectacle together. You'll be staying in Cambridge for a while?'

'No definite plans, Mr. Mercer, but yes, I'd like to think I'll be here for a while.'

'Please, call me David. Will you come in for a nightcap before you go back to your flat?'

'Very kind of you, David, but I need to unpack and sort all my stuff out.'

'I'm going to give him a hand, Dad. He's only on Hills Road—I'll be back in an hour or so.'

'Oh, of course. Well, goodnight you two.'

They took a short cut through the back streets.

As the weather forecast had promised, the wind and rain had died down, replaced by a crispy thinness in the air, and a temperature heading below zero. The evening was still interspersed with the pops and bangs of private firework parties, and for the students, the night was young ...

'He's a lovely guy, Tabby. I'm so terribly sorry for you both—I don't know how you're managing, really.'

'We're coping by being together. It's strange, but I've never been as close to Dad as I am now. Isn't that kind of tragic?'

'No, it isn't. Absolutely not. Your mum will be looking down and smiling.'

'Wow, you're religious? I guess we never talked about that, did we?'

She looked up at him as they walked. He was at least six inches taller than her, and a couple of inches taller than Rick. Quite why she'd made that extra comparison, she didn't know.

He had his hands deep in the pockets of a long and clearly well-used sheepskin coat. It felt right and natural to loop her hand through his arm.

228

'I can't remember the last time I went to a church, but I won't say I believe in nothing—that's way too depressing.'

'Reincarnation, perhaps?'

'Nahhh, a bit too far-fetched for me.'

'So, not kneeling in one particular camp, then?'

'I guess so. I don't like the thought that when you die, there's nothing to look forward to. I want there to be something—I'm just too lazy or dubious to want to worship it every Sunday. I've definitely asked for help on a few occasions, though. Maybe if it was a really important State table-tennis championship, and I was letting the team down.'

'Are you serious?'

He stopped walking and turned to face her.

'Yes, absolutely, though there have been a couple of more serious occasions as well.'

'I think I may be like that, and maybe my parents—well, Dad now, I mean.'

'I'd never have come here to see you if I'd known about your mum. I can't put into words how sorry I am.'

'Then I'd say it's a good thing you didn't know, then.'

She smiled up at him, and they continued walking, her arm still in his.

'So here we are—my pad for a little while.'

'Nice. Where's your car?'

'Oh, just down the lane—there's a space that comes with the apartment.'

'You got lucky.'

'I have to say, it feels a bit weird that you've walked me home, though I'm really grateful—I'll try and remember those shortcuts.'

'S'okay. I was serious about helping you unpack, by the way—I'm nosey by nature.'

'Ah, a bit late. I told your dad that because I felt I should be getting along. I'm actually … quite tidy and organised by nature.'

'Prove it. You can make me a cuppa as well if you like … before I head back.'

'Good job I was given a starter pack with the place, then—I'm not *that* organised. I think they left me a few tea bags and sachets of coffee, and a little carton of milk in the fridge.'

Tabatha was impressed—the flat was almost brand new. She'd been cheeky enough to ask how much he was paying—it was a cracking deal, particularly when a parking space was included—like hen's teeth in this town.

They sat at two stools nestling beside a breakfast-bar table, all part of a small kitchen that fit snugly into the open-plan living area.

'You must be shattered. Does your body clock tell you it's time to wake up now?'

'I'm okay at the moment. I won't plan on getting up early tomorrow, though.'

She had a strong desire to unburden herself of what she'd imagined would be a long-term secret.

'Grant, there's something I want to tell you.'

'Sounds ominous—I'm guessing it's about just turning up here unannounced? If it is, guilty on all fronts, and I'm happy to …'

'No, it's not that at all. I'm really glad you're here. It was kind of perfect timing in a way, and I love surprises anyway.'

'Phew—I'm relieved big time. You have no idea how often I questioned if I was doing the right thing. That's why I only booked this place for a week. The landlady's given me the option to extend though, and the price would come down a bit if I committed to longer.'

He felt awkward and started to wipe invisible water-mark rings off the worktop with a piece of kitchen roll.

'I'm not who you think I am. In fact, I'm not who *I* thought I was.'

'Confessions time? Let me know if I need a seatbelt—I did wonder if the drop-off in our chats had coincided with … well, a new relationship. I even wondered if Rick could be back on the scene. And when I first saw you for real, standing outside your home in that monsoon, I realised I must be mad to have thought you'd still be single.'

'I recently discovered that Mum and Dad aren't my real parents.'

'Oh … My God.'

'It's a long story, but Dad *had* to tell me—there was no other way. I couldn't believe it at first. I kind of felt betrayed—maybe even cheated? I was awful to Dad and felt terrible for that.'

She drifted back to painful memories—shameful behaviour.

'Look, I'm sorry to burden you with this, but can you imagine what it feels like?'

'I can do more than that. It seems we have something else in common.'

'*What?* You were adopted too?'

'Yup. My mother died of an overdose when I was six.' Tabatha was stunned.

'Oh my God, I can't believe it. I'm so sorry.'

'Nothing to be sorry about. My parents were druggies— we were on the road a lot. I don't remember that much of it, but my father either didn't want to or couldn't bring me up. I guess the authorities stepped in because I went to a sort of

231

care-home for kids for a while—not too long—then this amazing couple started visiting me and taking me out. I'd never met anyone as kind as them.'

'But you told me your mum died when you were thirteen—of cancer?'

'She did—my step-mum. Worst thing that ever happened in my life. A bit of a cliché, but hardly a day goes by when I don't think of my mum—still miss her so much.'

'Oh, Grant.'

'No, you're the brave one, Tabby. I couldn't handle seeing anyone for a long time after she died. Well, apart from my father and brother. That's why it meant so much that you and your dad could still put up with me being around. I'll say it again, if you need more time on your own …'

'Please stay, especially now I know just how similar our life experiences are. Can I ask you something?'

'Sure you can—anything.'

'How long does this pain last for?'

'It may not be what you want to hear. You must have had plenty of family and friends say it'll get easier in time, right?'

'Not *plenty*, no. We're a small family, and I'm not using the sympathy card, but we don't, *I* don't—have that many friends. But yes, I know what you mean.'

'Well, in my experience, I'm not sure it gets easier. It gets less frequent, that's for sure, but sometimes, when I lay awake and think about things—memories of Mum—my step-mum, that is—and the loss? Well to me, it feels just as painful at that moment, as it did when she first passed away.'

Tabatha was staring intently at him but could offer no words.

'I'm sorry. Not great news, eh? Hey, but remember, that's only *my* experience—you could be totally different.'

'Somehow, I suspect I'll be very similar to you. Thank you for sharing that.'

It was the last thing she wanted at this second, but a single tear trickled down her face—there was no prior warning.

Instinctively, he put a finger towards her face, but then stopped himself.

They both stood, and he moved nearer, wrapping his arms around her.

It was a hug that was more appropriate for a brother and sister, or a father and child, or lovers of old.

It was not what she expected, but to Tabatha, it was a moment of enormous relief and release.

He virtually demanded he walk her back, but she was unmoved—adamant.

Like a spoilt child, there was a sigh as she gave an inch, agreeing to send him a message when she was '*safely back home*'.

Grant stood outside his front door, watching her receding figure up the lane and onto the main street.

He knew she wouldn't turn around and wave—he knew so little about her, yet almost too much.

She exuded a vulnerability which was palpable, but when he sensed it, could nearly touch it, she'd parry with a change of subject, a joke, anything.

He was yet to experience it, but he suspected a fearsome temper might be in the mix as well.

He smiled as she marched out of his sight—they were almost frighteningly similar.

14

One month later.

'I'M SO grateful, Rick. I don't know what to say, or how I can thank you?'

Tabatha hugged him enthusiastically.

'Did you have to break any rules?'

'I could lie and say '*No*', or I could go into specifics. Former or latter, Tabs?'

'Oh. That bad, eh?'

She grimaced, only half-mockingly.

'Things have tightened up in the past couple of years. Data-bases are a seriously protected species, nowadays.'

'Oh God, I'm sorry. What do I owe you?'

He frowned theatrically and paused for further dramatic effect.

'Eternal gratitude and never-ending love. And if you're going to give me the same option I just gave you, then I'll take the latter.'

She grinned, but he could see there was just a hint of awkwardness in the expression.

He held his hands in the air.

'But I'll settle for you making the tea—you'll find the guest mug above the sink, and mine's here.'

He handed her a deeply tannin-stained cup, and she winced.

'It's so I can tell the difference between mine and the other one.'

His grin was still the most potent of weapons, which she knew he'd retain to his dying day. An image flashed of him as an old man; the smile was still there, in all its endearing glory.

'That's disgusting—you can't drink out of that. *You* have the guest mug, and I'll go without—I assume that one's clean?'

'You used to say *'s'gusting'.'*

'Sorry?'

His grin slipped, and he sighed, just briefly.

'Yeah, me too.'

Her awkwardness was back and would soon be replaced by embarrassment—he wouldn't allow that.

'Okay, okay—the mug gets ditched. Let's use the other one—I have two straws somewhere.'

'But you take two sugars. Yuk—no fear, thanks very much—that would be *s'gusting.'*

Her gesture pierced his chest, an overwhelming sadness nearly knocking him sideways as he tasted his heart. For once in Rick's life, the despair was beyond disguise, and he was utterly exposed.

'Sorry,' he choked, but she interrupted.

'No, *I'm* sorry. I've acted in a very unfair way.'

'Not as unfair as me.'

'That's as maybe, but I haven't been honest with you. Now may be the time to …'

'I'm not blind, Tabs.'

'What do you mean?'

'Just what I say. I'm not blind, and I live in town. And I like cars, particularly old ones, and a little white Triumph Spitfire sticks out a bit, particularly in the winter.'

Her cheeks flushed. Hopelessly, she spat out the first thing she could think of.

'It's not what it seems.'

Silence reigned as the five words sucked the air from his office.

'You don't understand, Rick—please?'

'Look, I don't just have the ability to hack into old adoption files. I can manage car registration numbers too.'

'I don't understand?'

'It doesn't matter. Let's drop it, eh?'

'No. What registration numbers?'

He sighed and wished he could have spooled back a bit. Maybe nine months back; that would have been perfection.

'The Spitfire? It used to be registered on Australian plates until it was imported here a few weeks ago. Sydney, to be precise.'

'But how do you ...'

'From your mum. Tracey told me about it, months back—an Aussie guy chatting with you online every evening. That's why she didn't want me to hang about—she could see things, *'developing'*, as she put it. She wanted us to get back together.'

He smiled at her. This was a whole new agony, and he wasn't sure he was going to get through it.

'His name's Grant. We're ... He and I—we're just friends; just good friends.'

This time the silence screamed—Rick was being deafened by the crushing pulse in his temple and heart. Defensive measures were all he had left to give.

'Well, I like him already. It seems we have plenty in common. I mean, we both like classic cars and we're both *'just good friends'* with you.'

Self-loathing smothered him.

She looked down at the piece of paper he'd handed her.

His awful writing—barely legible scrawl but oh so familiar—a part of him—traced it with her finger.

She felt a segment of her heart shatter, crumbling into a deep abyss of nothingness.

It was an address, in the Channel Islands, of a *Ms Lily Tabatha Barnes, formerly of Cambridge.*

'Thank you for this—you could never have given me anything more precious.'

She moved close and kissed him on the side of his face, close to the corner of his mouth.

Hugging him tightly, she held on to his back and pressed her face against his.

His arms moved around her in a way that only years of familiarity with a lover can allow.

And they both knew, instinctively, what this embrace represented.

'Goodbye, Posh Girl.'

It was an expression of deep intimacy, and Tabatha was sure she'd never heard it outside of their bed. She was certain of this.

'Au revoir?' she ventured, but there was nothing in her voice or body language that suggested this might be a possibility.

'I don't think so—not this time.'

He picked up his grimy mug and moved to the sink.

By the time he'd poured the boiling water on a tea bag and turned to the little fridge for milk, she was gone.

*

Tabatha stood in the window of her bedroom and stared out at yet another depressingly miserable winter day. The middle of the afternoon and dusk was approaching like a rolling sea mist.

The temptation to call Rick was so great that, for once, she'd actually turned her phone off. But she knew there was no chance of missing a call or message from him—he would never contact her again.

Are you mad at me, Mum? This wasn't what you wanted at all, was it?

She pulled the scrap of paper from her jeans pocket and looked at it again. The writing tore at her again, and she vowed to type it out on her phone—throw the last remnants of her old life away.

Did you know I'd go looking for Lily? Did you guess it would all come down to this?

Help Dad understand why I have to do this—don't let him think I'm betraying him.

Please Mum, don't let him feel that.

*

'Are you sure that's the best way to handle it? Don't you think she'd want some time to process it first, perhaps?'

They were sitting in a coffee-shop directly opposite one of the city's most imposing Colleges. The tourists mingling outside in an orderly chaos, mostly of Asian descent, seemed impervious to the bitterly cold temperatures.

A girl started playing a violin on the walkway, accompanied by exquisite sampled backing-music. A golden saxophone stood on its stand next to the small speaker. She was wrapped in layers of clothes that covered everything but lips to eyes, her nose glowing moist pink.

The music was a type of smooth jazz-funk fusion, and Tabatha became utterly transfixed. The girl was almost certainly a music student attempting to busk some extra drinking money.   She was the most talented musician Tabatha had ever heard, and there was an overwhelming desire to change lives with her, right now, this instant.

Had a button been on the table in front of her to enable this unlikely transposition, then push it, she would.

'Tabby?'

'Sorry? Oh yes. Right. And no, I'm not sure of anything—I think I'm just scared Lily won't want to see me.'

'I don't think that'll be the case, but she may need some prior warning to prepare herself. Wouldn't you, if you were her?'

'I'd like to be her.'

'What, Lily?'

'No—her.'

She pointed at the musician.

Grant looked out of the condensation-coated window.

'Oh, right. Yeah, decent sound. She's an Aussie, too.'

Tabatha was astonished.

'You can tell from the way she plays?'

'No, from the koala-bear backpack on the ground with '*Wish I was back home*' written on his or her vest.'

She peered out to where he was pointing.

'Oh.'

The exotic mystery of the girl had slightly faded.

'You don't like Aussies?'

'Hmmm. Well, I have limited experience of them.'

'Well, what are the ones like that you *do* know?'

'I'd say they were …'

She looked to the overly-ornate ceiling for inspiration.

'If that girl out there is anything to go by, I'd say they were a very talented nation.'

'Right. '*Talented*.''

Grant was doing his best to hide any disappointment.

'If you go fishing, you have to accept the possibility you'll come back empty-handed.'

'And that's my point entirely—if you go and see Lily unannounced, you'd better be prepared for … well … maybe a similar scenario?'

'Thank you.'

'Aww, don't take it like …'

'No, I really mean it—thank you—I'm so grateful for you being here these past few weeks. You know my dad thinks you're a remarkable guy?'

'Yay. So, Dad likes me, and I've inspired gratefulness? I can work with this.'

She leaned towards him and kissed him briefly on the lips.

'And I agree with Dad—remarkable.'

'Is that a fish I feel at the end of my line?'

'It very well could be.'

Tabatha placed a five-pound-note in the violin case as they headed back to her home.

'Thank you—you're remarkable.'

The girl beamed and mouthed her thanks. It was only as they walked away from the music that Tabatha identified the song—a track which Rick had played in his old Mercedes.

She buried her hands in the Parka pockets and huddled her face into the fake-fur hood.

*

'I think you should listen to Grant. You've been through enough lately—I couldn't bear to see you upset anymore. Can't you see we're only thinking of you, Tabatha?'

'I know, Dad, but can't you understand it from my side as well? It may be that seeing me in the flesh for the first time will make a difference. Isn't it easier to say *no* to someone in a letter, than face-to-face?'

'It's also easier to be hurt much more in person than it is in a letter, sweetheart.'

She was getting exasperated, trying to hold it together for her father's sake.

'You've met Lily—does she seem like the type of person who would just turn her back on someone—especially when that someone is her own daughter?'

'That was such a long time ago, and it's not as if your mum or I knew her well—the two meetings were so brief.'

'But you said she was a wonderful person?'

'And she was … is. I don't know, Tabby—people can change a lot in thirty years. I can't see the harm in a letter to start with. Maybe she'll be over the moon to hear from you? Insist you get together as soon as possible?'

'In which case, she'd surely react in the same way if I suddenly appeared from nowhere?'

'But if she acts differently, you have to admit it would be easier to bear in a letter. Nobody likes an awkward confrontation—especially when you're in a foreign island, a long way from home.'

'Shame on you, Dad.'

'What do you mean?'

'You were a banker your working life. You, of all people, know full-well that Jersey is part of the UK and a well-known finance centre. As for '*a long way*', if you headed in the opposite direction from here, you wouldn't even reach Scotland.'

He had to concede that she had a point.

'What about if I came with you—for moral support?'

'Daaad, we've already gone through this. It's something I have to do on my own.'

David Mercer had chosen to live his life flanked by two very strong-willed women. He was a past master of accepting defeat graciously.

'Can I at least pay for your flights? And drive you to and from Gatwick?'

Like her mother, Tabatha was a past master of acknowledging victory graciously.

'The flights would be wonderful, but don't worry about the lift—it's only an hour-and-a-half on the train to the airport.'

'A hotel, perhaps? I guess you'll be staying overnight?'

'A couple of nights, but it's fine—I've already booked a little guesthouse very close to where Lily lives.'

'Oh. All planned already, then?'

'Pretty much. I've also checked where she lives on Google Earth. I assume she lives on her own, as the address gave just her name, and she was a '*Ms.*', but I suppose that may mean nothing. There must be a few apartments within the farm—it looks very upmarket.'

'In what way?'

'Oh, you know, big gates and a long drive, then a tennis court and swimming pool close to the main building—a big main building.'

'Golly—it sounds like luxury apartments to me. Good for her, but maybe she works there and lives in staff quarters?'

'Maybe ...'

She was determined to keep her ideas to herself. They were fanciful and romantic, and she felt a little foolish.

'So, when were you thinking of going? I'm guessing you'll have something planned for your birthday next week with err ... would it be Grant? Or Rick?'

She couldn't face explaining the situation to her father, even though he was bound to consider the outcome in her best interests.

'I was thinking of going next weekend. I reckoned Lily probably worked during the week, so the weekend may be the best time to catch her.'

She tightened inside—it would be the first birthday without seeing her dad.

'Oh. Right.'

He was doing everything he could to hide his disappointment.

'Will you give me the flight times you want, and I'll sort it out for you.'

She hugged him and pecked his cheek.

'Thanks, Daddy—call it my birthday present.'

'Oh—I've already got you ... well ... not to worry about that for now.'

'Dad?'

'Yes?'

'You're my only dad—there will never be any other.'

She hugged him again.

*

The problem was slowly creeping up on Grant. He'd been fully aware of it before he came over and even had a file with accurate spreadsheet calculations.

He'd made level-headed assumptions and looked on the worst side, just to be safe. It was a genuine coincidence that Tabatha's 31st birthday coincided with what he'd come to think of as D-Day.

There was a special treat in store for her birthday—something he'd been excited about for months. It really was true; the giving was more exciting than the receiving.

A couple of times he'd made the mistake of visualising the big day when he was with her and his gleeful expressions had caused confusion. So far, he'd got away with it, but with only a few days to go, he had to be extra careful.

He'd never been so excited about giving a present.

It was tempting to shove his head in the sand when it came to D-Day. At that point, he'd have six weeks left in which to add substantial funds to his finances—a month's salary, for instance—or he was on his way back to Heathrow for the long journey home.

With her birthday falling on a Saturday, Grant had already booked a meal at a plush hotel on Friday, and one of their better rooms.

They hadn't consummated their relationship as yet, but he was determined not to rush Tabatha. And, if he was honest with himself, it was still a relationship in the very loosest of terms.

Yes, they'd become close—very close, in fact—but their hugs and the occasional kiss were anything but of a sexual nature.

It was a mystery to him why things hadn't blossomed much earlier, but he sensed this was one of two things; the terrible trauma she'd gone through with her mother's death, or the continued existence of what he'd always assumed was very much her *ex*-boyfriend.

Grant had twice heard mention of Rick's name when at Tabatha's home—on each occasion, her father passing on a message that he'd called. Whether that was a telephone call or if Rick had actually come to the house, he didn't know, and perhaps it wasn't his business, anyway.

He'd also been with her when she'd been sending messages to Rick.

In some ways, this hurt more—reminding him of how their own relationship had started. Ironically, he'd taken solace from Tabatha's complete openness—she'd never attempted to conceal her actions. On one occasion, she'd even apologised for needing to send a reply.

At that moment, he was sorely tempted to raise the question of Rick's status in her life, but by questioning her, he'd be displaying a type of jealousy.

Worse, he'd be insinuating that his curiosity was derived from fearing she was still in a relationship. In short, it would not be cool, and he knew *cool* was required, however tough and frustrating that indefinable course of action proved to be.

'It's my fault. I should have mentioned it a while back—I guess that's the problem with a surprise.'

'I'm so sorry, Grant. If it was anything but this, I'd postpone it. It's just that, you know, I've booked a place to stay, and Dad's done the flights, so ...'

'I totally understand—honestly.'

He put on a smile, attempting to appear considerably more cheerful than he felt.

'Is it possible to shift it to the following weekend? I've got nothing on then?'

Yeah, great, maybe you can advance your birth date by seven days at the same time.

'I'm sure that'd be fine. I'll give the hotel a call later and change the booking.'

'Oooo, '*hotel*'—sounds very nice.'

And it would have been, but now I've blown part of the surprise, like an idiot.

'Oh, it was nothing special. Just a meal that sort of led into your actual birthday, that's all—no sweat.'

'It sounds lovely—you're a real sweetie. Dad was really disappointed as well—it'll be my first birthday when I haven't seen him. I just hope it's worth it.'

Jesus, that's what my ex called me the day before I found out what she'd been up to forever, behind my back—'Sweetie'—'SWEETIE'. Jesus H Christ. 'SWEETIE!'

'Grant? Sweetie?'

'Sorry—you've never called me that before.'

'Well … you are being sweet to me. Nobody's been this kind to me for ages.'

'Oh … right … Hey, here's an idea. When you first told me about Jersey, I had a look online at the ways to get there. Did you know there's a car ferry from Poole—only a four-hour crossing. If you like, I'm more than happy to take the Spit …'

'Dad's already booked a flight, remember?'

'Oh yeah. Of course.'

Well, if I didn't know exactly what 'cool' was, I sure know what it isn't, and that was a class example. What a dick I am.

'You sure you're okay?'

'Yes, fine—sorry. Hey, I think I'll get an early night. I'll walk past the hotel and change the reservation, too.'

'Ah, a hotel near here? Bet I can guess which one.'

Shit.

'As I said, nothing special. I'll see you before you go, will I?'

'Yes, of course, you will. Let's grab a drink on Thursday evening—I'll message you during the day.'

'Yeah, sure. See you then—bye to your dad.'

He was as low as he'd been since arriving in Cambridge.

*

'And you're absolutely sure you don't want me to add some extra luggage onto the ticket? It'll only take a minute—it really doesn't look like much to take on a trip, to me.'

'I'm sure I'll be fine. Isn't it meant to be women who fuss over that sort of thing?'

'Possibly, but your mother was always having a go at me for packing too much. She'd say, *'David, we're flying to Paris for the weekend, not permanently emigrating to New Zealand.'* I always liked to be on the safe side, though. You never know wh ...'

'Sorry, Dad, but I really should be heading for the station. Can we make a move if that's okay?'

'Yes, of course. Car's outside and all ready.'

'Full tank of petrol, warning-triangle and spare bulbs?'

'Oh, but I thought we were only driving down the road to the station?'

She smiled and touched his slightly spikey face—it was so early that he hadn't managed to shave—an almost unheard-of situation.

'You'll let me know when you arrive?'

'Sure, will do. Remember to check your text messages.'

'And ... ummm ... if you see Lily?'

'Yes?'

'Well ... send our love. I mean *my* love—sorry.'

He tilted his head downwards, and at that moment, she'd never felt closer to him or loved him more. For the first time ever, he looked old—old and vulnerable.

She slung the small back-pack over her shoulder and headed for the station entrance. Tabatha knew he was watching her and knew she was his world. Looking back wasn't going to happen, though—she didn't want him to see the tears.

*

It had been a while since she'd been to an airport, but it didn't take her long to remember when that was; the aborted Santorini holiday with Mum.

The memory wasn't quite so bitter now. Was that because more time had passed, or was it due to some kind of balance being redressed?

Perhaps she was kidding herself. How could it ever be all-square with Rick, however many years passed?

In the departures lounge of a genuinely international airport, it was difficult to remain miserable or morosely reflective for long. There were simply too many happy people, many set free from their daily drudgery.

She sat close to a brand-new convertible Aston Martin, glinting in the spotlights and shiny tiling—definitely the most convenient parking place in the whole of Gatwick Airport.

The car was a raffle prize, and the tickets were only £25. Had it been a 50-year-old Triumph Spitfire and the tickets were a pound, she'd have bought one.

The idle daydream led her to thoughts of Grant. He, of all people, could surely understand the motivation to meet her birth mother, yet he'd acted strangely and in a way she hadn't seen before.

Guilt crept in as she realised they hadn't met yesterday as planned, and she made a mental note to call him from her guesthouse. She'd be back in Cambridge by Sunday evening, and perhaps he could come around for dinner—Dad had promised to celebrate her return with an attempt at a roast meal.

Walking down the gangway to her plane, dawn was making a feeble impact on the moody sky, almost begrudging of the feeble intruder. The high winds rocked the metal walkway under her feet, the squally rain blasting the flimsy metal tube.

At least she was heading south to the relative warmth of the Channel Islands, a full five degrees warmer than here, at a positively balmy eight Celsius above freezing.

A member of the cabin-crew welcomed her on-board with a perfunctory greeting delivered through a rigid grin, but his face lit up upon sight of a blonde-haired, twenty-something surfer-dude directly behind her.

Like Grant, this boy was still tanned bronze (she couldn't deny she'd noticed him at the Gate), and probably of very similar age to Grant. There was an entirely illogical and statistically ridiculous urge to ask him if he knew a Grant Davis from Sydney, but it fortunately passed. Just as well when she heard his reply to the steward—he was probably Swedish and certainly Nordic.

Tabatha wrapped herself tightly in the Parka and strapped herself in, glad for the luck of a window seat. The flight was less than half-full, and there was an empty seat between her and an elegant-looking lady in her sixties.

She had a lovely smile, and Tabatha warmed to her instantly.

'Mind if I put my bag on the spare seat, dear? Bloody thing's always getting in the way—I'll grab it before the steward walks past, then put it back there again if that's alright? They're a bit strict and sniffy about that sort of thing.'

She sniggered in a conspiratorial way.

If Tabatha was correct, the bag was a genuine Hermes. In an unassuming shade of greyish blue, it had a certain patina about it, like the woman had cherished it for decades.

From online dream-shopping with her mum, she was able to identify it as a Birkin model and probably the '30'. It matched the owner's skirt and top perfectly, as one would hope for a bag worth the thick end of £15,000 to £20,000, and maybe an awful lot more.

'That's a beautiful bag—I've never seen one in the flesh before.'

'Why, thank you, my dear. It's a sad fact of life that I'm not able to use it that often nowadays. It's stayed out of sight for most of the last week in London.'

'Is it safe in Jersey?'

'Oh, of course—everything's safe in Jersey.'

She chuckled again, and it was infectious.

'Have you not been there before?'

'No, never. My mum and dad threatened to take me there on a family holiday a couple of times, but it never came off.'

'And now you're going on your own—well you're in for a treat. Are you meeting anyone there?'

'Well, hopefully, my mum.'

The woman looked confused.

'It's quite a long story.'

Tabatha shrugged and smiled.

'Now I hope you won't think me funny or anything like that, but I'm liable to stretch over the seat and look for a hand to grasp when we're about to land. I'm not a very good flyer, and the landings in Jersey can be quite bumpy and abrupt. Oh, and noisy follows abrupt—*very* noisy.'

'I don't think I'll be much help—I'm not so good in planes either.'

'In that case, we'll help each other. I'm Philippa, by the way, but everyone calls me Filly—because I'm horsey-mad.'

She extended a hand over the spare seat, and they shook. It occurred to Tabatha that she was in contact with the biggest diamond she'd ever seen.

'You know, I met three of my very closest friends this way, holding their hands while landing in Jersey.'

Tabatha was still looking down at the diamond under her thumb.

'And that was one of the three—Gerald. Dear Gerald.'

She sighed, and the girl pulled her hand away, embarrassed that her fixation with the ring had been noticed.

'Your husband?'

'Yes, though sadly no longer here.'

'Oh, I'm so sorry.'

'Yes, no longer here—he's gone back to Lichtenstein. Well, he was limited to tax-havens, of course.'

'Ah.'

The captain's voice saved Tabatha from any other faux pas.

Filly hadn't been exaggerating—the landing had been exciting enough that the passengers burst out in spontaneous applause, though this was drowned out by the deafening reverse-thrust of the two jet engines.

During the 40-minute flight, Tabatha learnt that Gerald had been Filly's fourth husband. All four were still alive, though none remained in Jersey. This was no mean achievement, as two of them had been born there, with families going back centuries.

Filly was now a self-imposed *life-bachelor*—she detested the word *spinster*—thought it '*demeaning and foul-smelling*', at which point Tabatha succumbed to a laughing fit.

She'd insisted on giving Tabatha a lift from the airport—the woman would listen to no other suggestion, despite pleas that a taxi would be fine.

'My dear, with a tip that will come to twenty pounds. *TWENTY POUNDS!*'

This from a woman who, with jewellery, handbag, and watch combined (an elderly and very complicated man's Patek Philippe which Tabatha found delightfully eccentric), was walking around with a hefty six-figure sum of accessories.

It therefore came as no surprise when an attractive, middle-aged man of Mediterranean descent, wearing a dark suit with a black chauffeur's cap held discreetly behind his back, met them at the arrivals hall.

'My dear, this is Juan. It's spelt with a *'J'* but should be pronounced as the past tense of *'win'*, or the number before two, isn't that right, Juan?'

The driver's reply was inaudible beneath his employer's voice.

'In fact, if one were to be pedantic, one needs to form a small circle with one's lips and blow, before *Juan.*'

As the man simultaneously put his cap on and swept the matching suitcases up from the trolley, Filly put a hand to her mouth in simulated horror, closely followed by the giggling, which Tabatha was by now getting used to.

It was clearly a rehearsed and oft-used gag. Nonetheless, it was extremely funny to witness, though perhaps less so for Juan.

'Hook your bag over his shoulder.'

'Oh no, really, that's fine—he's got plenty to carry.'

'Juan is very strong, my dear—plenty of stamina.'

She looked over the top of her glasses and winked at the girl.

Just for a second, Tabatha had the sensation of gate-crashing an elite and exclusive club for which she had no entitlement, nor any desire to be associated with.

'I'm good, thanks—how far do we have to go … Oh.'

As they approached the black Bentley, its boot began to open. She'd seen them wafting around London and occasionally in Cambridge, but this appeared to be much longer.

Juan swiftly deposited the cases in the boot and scurried around to the back door, opening it and lowering his gaze.

'Hop in; there's plenty of room—sit where you want, dear.'

The rear of the car was cavernous, with four lounge-style chairs facing each other in pairs. As she sat down and looked out of the heavily-tinted window, Tabatha saw queues for both the bus and the taxi-rank. Some people were blatantly ogling the vehicle, but most were talking to colleagues or glued to their phone screens.

'The ones looking our way are the visitors, sweetie. Locals are immune to anything and everything—they've seen it all, darling.'

'I see.'

She'd been in Jersey for ten minutes and been as far as the airport car park, yet already she was slightly in shock.

'This car? It seems very big in here—are they all this spacious?'

'Oh, good Lord, no. Gerald owns a coachbuilding company in the north of England—York, maybe? Anyhow, they are stretch cars—chop them in half and stretch them—voilà, a homemade limousine—cool, huh?

'Um, yes. Very. Err … didn't Gerald want his car?'

Filly's blank expression suggested the question may never have crossed her mind, then Tabatha realised this was because it hadn't.

'I suppose he might have. Good Lord, do you think so? Quentin, that's my lawyer, he sorts all that sort of stuff out for me.'

'And what about Juan, sorry, *Wwwwwwon*?'

'What about him?'

'Well, was he employed by Gerald? Sorry, I shouldn't be asking such personal questions.'

'Not at all, dear—not at all. Juan came with Tristan. Hold tight.'

She pressed a button on her armrest, and a glass divider slid silently between the driver's compartment and their leather-clad cavern.

'As I was saying, Juan originally worked for my previous husband. Oh, no, hold on, not previous, the one before— Tristan was number two.'

A Spanish-sounding voice came through some speakers in the doors and rear parcel-shelf—it seemed to surround the space.

'We go to where now, Lady P?'

She pressed another button, this one on a centre console, and gave her chauffeur the name of the guesthouse.

'I've never heard of that one. You know, if you wanted a little more comfort, you're more than welcome to stay at my estate.

Tabatha was taken aback and didn't know what to say.

'No. No, really—you've been more than generous already. The place is close to where I'd like to go. I've kind of got it planned out in my head.'

'So, where's this place?'

Tabatha gave her the name of the farm.

'It's in the town—St. Helier. You probably know it, I guess?'

'My dear, all of the nicer properties are converted farms—it's the only way to snare a decent piece of land to wrap around oneself. Privacy, you understand? Over a hundred thousand people and only forty-five square miles to jostle around in. One needs one's space. There are probably at least a dozen farms in each of the twelve parishes.'

'Oh, I see. So, I'm guessing you live on a farm, then?'

'No dear, I live in a manor.'

Had anyone else delivered this line, it would have sounded arrogant and obnoxious. Coming from Filly's mouth, it just made Tabatha chuckle.

'A bit like a green house or red hotel on a Monopoly board, then?'

'That's a very quick-witted analogy, my dear. I hope it's not too forward of me to say I like you and enjoy your company? Best of all, you take me back, oh, fifty years, so a big thank you for that.'

'I don't know what to say—thank you so much for befriending me. This is, well, a rather unexpected and amazing way to get to my guesthouse. Oh, and I hardly think *fifty* years!'

'So sweet of you to say so, sweetie, but it's probably more than that. Fifty years ago, I'd have been thirty-one, and I'm guessing you're in your mid-to-late twenties?'

Tabatha couldn't hide her shock. She turned and stared at the woman's face. Filly looked back at her and smiled.

'The wonders of modern science, eh? Oh, and Tristan, of course.'

'Tristan was a plastic surgeon?'

'No, silly, Tristan didn't have a profession—just more money than God.'

Tabatha was struggling to process all the information.

'Riiight. Umm … Juan called you '*Lady P*'—is that a nickname?'

'Yes, dear; it's short for Philippa, or Filly to you and all my friends.'

'Er, no, I meant the first bit—the '*Lady*' bit?'

'Oh *that*. That's from Duncan, my first husband. I could have chosen Countess—he was an Earl, you see, and one has a choice, my dear. However, I thought it sounded oh, I don't know, perhaps a bit foreign and ostentatious?'

She put a hand to her mouth and grabbed the girl's forearm.

'Oh, am I allowed to say that? '*Foreign*'? Is it, oh, what's that acronym?'

'PC?'

'Yes, that's it. Am I allowed to say something like that? I suppose I'm not, am I?'

Filly looked a little crestfallen, and Tabatha noticed the slightest of signs that this octogenarian could conceivably have been in her early seventies.

'I'm no expert, Filly, but I'm fairly confident you could say just whatever you like.'

The woman beamed and shed fifteen years.

'What a sweetheart you are. Duncan would have loved you—probably still would, given half a chance. Mind you, he's ninety-six—lives in a retirement home he owns outside Dublin—a retirement castle, really. I shouldn't say this, but my *God*, that man couldn't keep it in his trousers—never known anyone like him.'

She laughed out loud at a decades-old memory and started to cough. Tabatha was instantly reminded of her mother, the air suddenly taken from her lungs.

Juan had glanced in the rear-view mirror and powered down the glass division. He was holding a small brown bottle of tablets in his hand, reaching into the back.

'Give please, one to Lady P.'

Tabatha took the bottle, and the dividing glass went back up.

She held Filly's wrist just below the light blue jacket sleeve, in order to place a tablet in her palm. The sleeve moved up as the woman turned, and Tabatha involuntarily gasped. Just above the wrist, faded and blurred, were five illegible, dark blue, numbers.

'Three-one-oh-three-two.'

She put the oval red tablet on her tongue and tilted her head back.

'Sorry about this. Apparently, I have the heart of an eighty-one-year-old.'

She opened a dark-faced cabinet and took two small bottles of water out of a fridge, passing one to Tabatha, who was still in a state of awe.

'I know—from camps to castles—who'd have thought, eh?'

Tabatha's jaw still hadn't made it all the way back, so her new friend continued.

'I remember almost nothing of it, thank the Lord. I entered as a toddler with my parents and left as a six-year-old orphan, in the arms of a saviour, in the guise of a tall, dark, British officer. So, you could say that history repeats itself. Again, and again, in my case.'

She'd disregarded the unimaginable horrors of her earliest years in the space of a moment, shrouding it in light-hearted irony, painting it as some sort of little adventure.

'The destination has been achieved, Lady P.'

'Here we go, darling. Oh … it looks quite small—are you sure you won't take up my offer? I'd be so grateful of the company.'

'I'm fine thanks, Filly. It's all paid for, so I'd better go and check in.'

'I fear you won't be able to move into your room until the afternoon. Perhaps a coffee—maybe a spot of lunch?'

She was a persuasive and determined lady. Tabatha could understand how this woman's life would have panned out in precisely the way she desired.

'I'm ever so grateful for your kindness, but I need to do this myself. I promised myself that.'

'It's a big deal, isn't it? I didn't enquire why you were here because I sensed it was, how shall I put it … *delicate*?'

'It's not even a drop in the ocean compared to what you must have had to endure, but yes, it's a big deal for me.'

Tabatha moved to get out of the car, Juan already holding the door open patiently, her backpack in hand.

'Wait, one last thing; if I give you my number, will you promise to call me if you need anything?'

The woman nodded at Juan, and he pulled a card out of his inside pocket.

She walked around the car to the little hotel entrance—it was a little grander than a guesthouse in her opinion—and Tilly's window came down.

'Tabatha?'

'Yes?'

'Anything.'

The darkened-window closed, and the huge car dropped gently off the pavement, wafting swiftly up the hill in virtual silence. Gerald had obviously had electric motors fitted to save on fuel bills.

15

FILLY HAD been right—Tabatha was unable to move into her room until mid-afternoon.

It was still blustery, but the rain was holding off for now. In every way, it was a typically British, late-November, winter day, but just a little warmer.

With time to kill, she chose a circuitous route taking in the whole of the town, then a walk up the hill adjacent to the guesthouse and to the farm, where Lily lived and very probably worked. This deduction was made after checking how high the rents were in Jersey; she sensed that Lily could only have afforded an apartment at the farm by working there, getting some sort of generous staff discount.

There were banks—lots of them. There were beautiful old buildings made entirely of local pink or grey granite, and there were both attractive and awful examples of moderately-sized office and apartment blocks. Overall, there was an underlying sense of prosperity, but it was more than that.

At first, she couldn't put her finger on it; the pace was a little slower than Cambridge and incomparable to the frantic tumult of London. The locals were either polite or openly friendly, and the few visitors she encountered were French or lost, or both.

Walking away from the town, past the hospital, and into the suburbs, it came to her; there was an overwhelming sense of privacy. Did this come hand-in-hand with the atmosphere of wealth—the lack of obvious poverty?

Here was a world-renowned finance centre with a clean bill of health, and that sort of reputation wasn't gained overnight. A lot of the locals were probably very protective of that reputation.

Although she had Google maps up on her phone, Tabatha had already acclimatised herself with the geography when back home. Every time she'd followed the little road to the farm online, it gave her goose-bumps. Now she was here, physically walking up that very same *green lane*, as local signposts pointed out. The lane was *'bicycle-friendly'*, carried a *'15mph speed-limit'*, and she idly wondered whether this applied to reasonably fit runners as well as cyclists.

There was no point in getting nervous at this stage. She was just doing a quick recce to get the lie of the land—maybe have a quick peep down the drive while standing in the road.

She still didn't have any precise plans, despite visualising these moments in a never-ending cycle, day and night, ever since she'd had that piece of paper in her hand.

When she came back tomorrow morning, perhaps then was the time to allow the nerves to creep in. For now, there was nothing at all to get wound-up about.

Tabatha knew she was trying to psyche herself up.

Ultimately, it was what everyone, everywhere, feared. When you were meeting someone new (and she was under no illusions—it may be her mother, but this was someone '*new*'), you feared rejection. That's all it was—straightforward rejection.

She pulled the photo out of her Parka and looked at it again.

My mum. Lily Tabatha Barnes. 'Mum'. What do I mean to you now?
 Do you ever think of me—wonder how or where I am?
 What have you done with your life since we parted?
 What will you say when you see me again, Lily?
 How will you feel?

She stopped in the middle of the road. It was a sleepy lane, and no car had passed either way so far. There were speed bumps—lots of them—larger, then smaller—a nod to that speed limit.

It was quiet. Very quiet and very private.

She looked at the two low walls slowly curving from the road and ending by the large wooden and stainless-steel entrance. Cobbles led to the gates, matching the pink granite stonework she'd seen on many buildings already.

There was no security camera, but it would have been irrelevant; fields ran either side of a long-paved driveway, giving access to anyone who wished to wander down to the property. The home itself was not in view, save for the very top of a pinkish roof in the distance.

A rustling noise behind a grass bank made her jump, but it was just an inquisitive cow who'd wandered away from the main herd. All of them appeared to be roaming free with direct access to the road, but closer inspection revealed a thin line of cable running between wood posts. It seemed woefully inadequate to keep these beautiful-looking cows in place, but then she noticed a car battery nestling in the grass, the cable running to it. Twelve volts didn't seem much to keep a huge animal in its place, but what did she know?

'So that keeps you safe from the road, does it? You're very pretty, you know. Aren't you cold?'

The animal clearly wasn't, happily munching fresh tufts of grass on the bank. Tabatha reached and stroked the big, wet nose, and the cow looked up at her.

'What are the people like who live here? Oh, and do you know Lily? She works here—you must know her?'

There was a deep snuffle, and Tabatha's hand and sleeve were licked by a very warm, large tongue, then it was back to the infinitely more appealing clump of grass.

More of the herd was moving lazily over towards the new visitor, and soon she was standing within touching distance of at least a dozen of them—all gentle, all calm, and all seemingly very happy. It was rumoured that Jersey had the best milk in the world—maybe now she knew why.

It was too good an opportunity to miss. Tabatha took a couple of photos on her phone. It was a nice way of telling her dad that she'd arrived safely and that all was well. She added a little message and sent him the photo on WhatsApp, hoping he'd think to open it.

She was writing a longer note to Grant with the same picture attached when the noise of a car made her turn around.

The gleaming silvery-blue 4x4 towered over her, and as its front wheels met the start of the cobbled paving, the two front gates began to open. She peered through the window at the driver—dark hair but greying at the sides; she guessed he was in his fifties.

Though she was well clear of his car, he was making absolutely sure his tyres were nowhere near her feet. As he peered out of the passenger window, their eyes met, and he smiled, then waved.

Taken aback, she did the same, then the gates had parted enough for him to creep through and slowly burble down the long drive.

The light was drawing in as dusk threatened. She watched the tank-sized vehicle retreat, lights on either side of the drive coming on to show the way ahead, the massive trees in the distance suddenly illuminated by more spotlights.

The man was probably driving back from the office. She looked at her watch—a few minutes to five o'clock on a Friday afternoon—Tabatha wondered how many other cars would be heading back to the farm, as people made their way back from work. And if Lily didn't work at the farm, perhaps she might be driving home at this moment.

It was getting cold now she was no longer walking, the chilly air starting to make her shiver.

Sitting on the roadside wall of the property was a bit cheeky, so she leant against the granite wall of an old farmhouse on the other side of the narrow lane.

She made her mind up to hang around for another half-an-hour unless it became too uncomfortable, in which case she'd be back first thing in the morning.

Tabatha pulled the Parka tightly around her body, the furry-rimmed hood pulling down comfortingly around her face.

*

She rose stiffly from a tiny grass verge she'd been half-sitting on. The temperature was now uncomfortably cold.

There'd been a smattering of cars go past as darkness fell, but none turned into the electric gates of the farm. The only thing of note had been a large muscular cat, presumably on sentry duty around the perimeter of his or her land.

Having no knowledge of Jersey wildlife, she'd initially worried it was some type of wild cat or even an ocelot, so defined were the dark stripes and spots on the off-white fur. Luckily and delightfully, it was instantly friendly towards her, even allowing Tabatha to gather it up in her arms and cuddle it.

'You're gorgeous. I guess there aren't many mice around here anymore, huh?'

The cat replied with a loud and continuous purr.

'Do you live in that big farm? I bet you do. You'd fit in well there—you look very expensive.'

She put the exotic-looking animal back down on the tarmac, and it jogged nonchalantly across the road and through the bars of the electric gates. Triggered by the movement, the lights came on again all the way down the drive, and Tabatha briefly pondered the concept of a cat having the luxury of flood-lit hunting.

As she was about to set off back to the guesthouse, outside lights came on in the opposite property, and a farmer walked out of the gate and across the lane to the field entrance. There was absolutely no question he was a farmer, right the way down to flat cap, dusty green overalls and similar colour wellington boots, the entire ensemble caked in mud. In the illumination, she even spotted a straw in his mouth.

He placed two ropes across the road, signs hanging from them. '*Slow Cows Crossing*'—Tabatha smiled at the ambiguity.

Walking into the field, the small, curly-grey-haired man started making guttural, vaguely musical sounds, the cows immediately moving towards the noise.

Like a doorman, he stood by one of the two huge pieces of granite, which acted as field entrance pillars, the cows dutifully walking past him in an orderly single file. A car's headlights further illuminated the scene as it stopped near to the warning sign, the driver and farmer exchanging waves and a brief greeting.

The last cow crossed the lane, the dozens of hooves having smothered the area in mud, and the farmer took his rope barriers down. She took a deep breath and moved towards him.

'Hello, I'm sorry to trouble you, but do you know how many people live on that farm?' She pointed to the ornate granite name-plate imbedded into the curved wall, though it was patently unnecessary—there wasn't another property for some considerable distance.

'Reckon I do. Who wants to know?'

It was obviously the local accent, though it sounded vaguely South African to her. It was also the first time today that she'd encountered anything but a polite or friendly attitude.

'Oh, forgive me—I'm just a tourist. I've taken a wrong turning and wondered which way it was back to the main road.'

'So why do you want to know how many people live at the farm?'

Tabatha had to concede that this was a fair point—her nerves had let her logic down.

'I guess I should be going—thanks anyway.'

'And why have you been hanging around here for the past hour?'

She was getting uncomfortable. It was dark, and there were no cars in sight.

As she took one last look down the drive, car lights appeared under the trees near the house. By the height of the headlamps, it was the same 4x4 again.

It approached, and the gates opened obediently, the farmer and Tabatha both shading their eyes from the beam of the powerful headlights. As the car came through the gates and paused on the cobbles, she could see there were two people inside.

It was the same man again in the driver's seat, but this time he was in a black jacket and bowtie. There was dim lighting coming from the passenger seat, and Tabatha could see a woman leaning forward. Her face was close to the sun-visor, which obviously held a mirror, carefully applying lipstick.

She wore a dark overcoat which appeared to cover a slender black dress. She was unquestionably beautiful and possessed that certain look, which only women in privileged circumstances can hope to achieve and maintain.

She was also Lily.

Five things happened then, in as many seconds.

The man waved to the farmer, the farmer grunting in reply.

The man turned his attention to Tabatha, initial confusion turning to recognition. He smiled, and her face flushed as she smiled back, unable to restrain a small wave.

The man turned to Lily and said something.

She stopped tending her lipstick and looked out of the window, first at Tabatha and then the farmer, a polite smile for them both.

Finally, as the car moved slowly past, Lily's head swivelled back, and she stared at Tabatha in undisguised horror.

In dismay, she watched the car recede, then the brake lights came on, and her heart went straight to her mouth.

Equal amounts of terror and excitement filled her veins as she wondered if the car was stopping, but then it turned left onto another lane and was gone.

'Best you leave folks like that alone, missy.'

It took a moment for Tabatha to regain her wits.

'Excuse me?'

'People like you—you shouldn't go bothering proper people like that.'

She could feel anger rising, and it had rarely helped any situation she'd ever found herself in.

'Does anyone else live in that property? Other families, in other apartments?'

'*What?* Are you stupid in the head, girl? You'd best be off before I call the police; taxes from the likes of those folks make this Island a very nice place to live, and we don't need them getting bothered—by *anyone*. Now be off with you and go back to wherever you came from.'

A red mist was now cascading over her vision.

'How come you have such sweet, clever, cows, yet you're a nasty, ignorant, pig?'

'Right Missy, you're coming with me—let's see what the authorities have to say.'

He grabbed her sleeve.

Lightness of frame was rarely of use in a fight, particularly one against a man, albeit a small, middle-aged one. However, what she lacked in strength she made up for in speed.

Tabatha pulled the back-pack off her shoulder and, leaning back, swung it across her body, all in one very swift, blurred, movement.

The corner of the little canvas bag caught the farmer squarely in the face.

Unfortunately for the man, this particular corner contained the small amount of make-up Tabatha had elected to bring with her, plus obligatory mobile charge-plug.

He staggered to the ground, a hand covering his temple and eye.

'You little cow!'

'I'd have thought you, more than most, could correctly identify a cow.'

She started to run, then slowed to a jog—the farmer wouldn't be chasing her anytime soon.

By the time she'd reached the main road to her guesthouse, the adrenalin had completed its primary task, and she was shaking.

The farmer had really frightened her, but far worse, was the expression on Lily's face.

It wasn't the expression she'd dreamed of—a mother setting eyes on her daughter for the first time in 30 years.

Laying on the bed in her little room, she couldn't hold back the tears. Tabatha had never felt more alone than the moment she'd learnt of the adoption, but somehow, this was even worse.

*

'Hey Tabs, good to hear your voice—I expected radio silence and maybe a message if you had a chance. How's Britain's South Sea island?'

'Good to hear you, too. I needn't have bothered to pack sunscreen.'

'You sound a bit down—everything alright? Oh, or not so good?'

'Bit of both, I suppose.'

She told him of the high of realising she was looking at her mother, then the lows of the expression she couldn't shift from her mind, and the mad farmer.

'It was probably just the shock of seeing you. Oops, you know what I mean—that didn't sound very kind, did it?'

'I know what you mean. I guess I'll know for certain tomorrow.'

'Are you definitely going to see her? I mean, what if she isn't at the house or leaves early and doesn't get back until late? Will you go and ring the doorbell?'

'Is that what you'd do?'

'I reckon I would—you've gone to a lot of trouble and expense to see her—why not? Yeah … I think I definitely would, Tabby.'

'Thanks for that, it really helps. I'm also a little bit nervous about that farmer, actually.'

Grant laughed.

'From what you describe, I'd imagine it might be the other way around. It sounds like you gave him a good twatting!'

'I'm being serious. It was a really scary situation, especially at night.'

'I'm sorry—you're right. Hey, the offer still stands—I'll fly over first thing. I can be with you when you go to see her—it's no problem.'

If he was honest, it *was* a slight problem, and would probably knock a week off the time he had left to find a job. Tabby didn't need to know that, though.

'Thanks for that, I really mean it, but I have to do this on my own. But maybe I can ask you one small favour?'

'Sure, go ahead.'

'I've sent Dad a fairly long message, but he can sometimes go for days without reading them. I don't know why, but I'd prefer to speak with him *after* I've met—or failed to meet—Lily. I know it's stupid, but I can't explain it. Anyhow, if you could give him a call and tell him to check his phone, that would be great.'

'Leave it with me—no problem.'

'Thanks. Oh, and don't say I called you, please? It might upset Dad that I spoke with you but not him.'

'Will do. Hey, and remember to call me if things get a bit lively—there's probably a law against farmer-bashing in Jersey.'

It was one of the things she really liked about Grant.

'Never make a drama out of a crisis', the advert said, but adding a bit of humour didn't do any harm either.

She knew he was genuinely worried, but he'd held back from burdening her with that.

Fair play, Aussie Boy.

*

'Tabatha! How simply *wonderful* to hear from you, and such an unexpected surprise.'

'I feel really guilty phoning you this late.'

'Late? *Late?* My dear, in the great cities, a Friday night doesn't start for at least another hour. This is the champagne segment of the evening. Don't you youngsters call it *pre-drinks* or something like that?'

She couldn't help smiling.

'You're absolutely right, Filly, but I'm sure there's a *very* big difference between the type of drinks involved.'

'Oh, nonsense. At the end of the day, alcohol is alcohol. Now here's a thought—where are you now, dearie?'

'In my room.'

'Good Lord, I thought you'd be out gallivanting with this mysterious man I've invented in my mind for you. But seriously, it *is* an assignation, surely?'

Now she had to stifle a giggle.

'Only in the very loosest sense of the word. It's a secret meeting, agreed, but the other person doesn't know I'm meeting them.'

'Oh, how exciting! So, you're a stalker?'

And now she laughed.

'No. At least I don't think so. And I was about to say that this person is not a potential lover either, so it really isn't anywhere near as exciting as you imagine.'

'Oh.'

The lady sounded deflated and a little disappointed.

'But … and this is why I think I called you, there *is* someone who thinks I'm stalking, and they've made my life a little awkward.'

Filly was instantly filled with indignation.

'Right, well we'll get that sorted this very minute, sweetie. *'Juan! Pen and paper, please—soon as poss.'*

Tabatha was temporarily deafened—her new friend had omitted to hold the phone away as she called her chauffeur, or butler, or whatever positions he may hold.

She related the afternoon's *'entertainment'*, careful to include as much information and detail as she could.

'Oh, my poor darling—but that's outrageous. We'll come and collect you and go to the police station immediately. Are you hurt, my dear? Goodness, this is a dreadful business.'

'No! I mean, no—no, I'm not hurt, and no thank you to the police. If anything, I suspect the farmer is injured and may already have gone to the police.'

She heard Filly talking with Juan. There were some '*uhuh*'s', then a pause, then a confident '*AHAH!*'

'He won't have gone to the police, Tabatha; not this side of the next millennium, at any rate.'

'I don't understand—how do you know that?'

'Because I know the family. Well, me and just about everyone else on the Island. You've come up against one of the Jegoutin clan—Martin, by the sound of your description. As pure a breed as you'll ever find.'

'Oh God. Pure-bred and famous—am I in the crap?'

'*Pure-bred* as in, there hasn't been a marriage involving anyone but family members for the past twelve hundred years. And *famous* for having managed to avoid paying all but a pittance in tax for a similar period of time. He tried to corner the entire global supply of Jersey new potatoes a few years ago, and I won't even hint at what a lot of the locals think his cows have to put up with ...'

Had Filly sent this information to her via a WhatsApp message (admittedly unlikely), there was an emoji which Tabatha could have replied with, literally created for this very situation.

As it was, the elderly lady had to put up with a modicum of silence; the girl really wasn't sure how to respond.

'Tabatha, are you still on the line? Oh, really, Juan, these blasted phones—was there ever a problem when we all had a *normal* telephone? Tabatha?'

'Yes, I'm here.'

She could here Juan in the background, confirming that, yes, indeed, Lady P was unquestionably correct—the advent of mobile communications had unquestionably caused a drastic and detrimental effect upon the landline telecommunication system. Or, more specifically, '*Lady P correct yes—mobby-phones they poorly hopeful.*'

'If he has a large family, won't they be furious with me and cause big problems?'

'You think Martin's going to tell his many kids that a slim young woman gave him a black eye?'

'I don't know. From what you're saying, I guess not?'

'Sweetheart, why were you there? Forgive me for asking, and you don't have to answer, but I'm curious.'

Tabatha told her. It was a relief for someone else to know, and it somehow seemed right that Filly should know. So out it tumbled—Rick, Grant, Dad, Mum, cancer, Lily.

'Dear sweet girl. I knew you were special when we were on the plane. Juan and I are at your disposal—just say the word. Oh, and Tabatha?'

'Yes'

'Do you want to know his name? I know the man who owns Anabel Tomb Farm. I'm afraid that's just about all I know, though. Most people who come over here as wealthy residents eventually open up, even if they're initially shy. The basic rule of thumb is that there's always someone richer than you, so drop the airs and graces. However, there are a few—not many—who really *do* keep themselves to themselves.'

'Who is he?'

'His name's William Levington. I'm told by a friend of a friend who plays an occasional game of squash with him, that he started off with a chemist's shop in a small town somewhere on the outskirts of London. Several years later, he sells a huge chain of chemists to Boots for a nine-figure sum, then retires to the much kinder tax-status of Jersey.'

'Oh. Tens of millions of pounds—wow!'

'Hundreds, dear—*hundreds* of millions of pounds.'

'Fuck. Oh, excuse me—I just meant, like, wow.'

'My husband always said that when remarking on personal wealth beyond a certain level, an occasional expletive was acceptable. I can't remember the exact amount, but I'm sure you're in the clear.'

Tabatha wondered which husband she meant, but let it slide.

'So, Anabel Farm isn't a collection of apartments, then?'

'Anabel *Tomb* Farm—good heavens, no. It was owned for many years by the former Deputy-Bailiff of the Island, but by the time he died, it was in need of major work. Levington bought it from the estate and spent a couple of years and probably a fortune on the restoration. Nobody I know has been there, and it's impossible to see from the road, so we can only assume it's fabulous. I have no doubt that it is.'

'And no one knows if he's single or married? How's that possible in such a tiny place like this?'

'Discretion. A communal acceptance to honour privacy.'

'You mean secrecy?'

'No, I mean privacy. If it were secrecy, we wouldn't have the highest divorce rate in the world.'

'Really?'

'Yes dear, *really*. Public records will show it's the Maldives, but there are no officially separate records for Jersey—the figures are lumped in with the rest of the UK.'

'But I don't understand—what's the difference between privacy and secrecy?'

'Now there's a sixty-four-thousand-dollar question. Tristan, my accountant husband, was constantly having to explain the difference between tax *avoidance* and tax *evasion*, to his clients'

'Which is?'

'Well, the first one is legal, and the second one isn't.'

'So secrecy is against the law and privacy isn't?'

'Not quite, sweetie; secrecy is sleazy, distasteful and repugnant, and privacy is an acceptable and, quite honestly, *vital* part of Island life.'

'So how come you have so many divorces over here?'

'My dear, without a continual respect for privacy by every islander, there'd be *twice* as many divorces. I'd probably have been married more times than Henry the Eighth.'

She burst into a cackle of laughter, which developed into a barking cough.

'But I'm digressing; we have private detectives over here who could find out the official relationship, if any, between William and Lily. I'd be more than happy to call one up and get them on the case.'

William and Lily.

  Is it possible?

  Are you living a life of luxury with a multi-millionaire, Mum?

  I thought you'd be a poor, rejected waif, living a sad and lonely life on the breadline.

  Tell me, Mum.

  Tell me your secrets.

'I'd cover the cost, of course—insist upon it—they'll charge treble-rate for a non-local. Shall I call one up now, dear?'

'Eh? Oh … no, absolutely not. But thank you, Filly, really—I feel like you're some sort of angel to me.'

There was another cackle.

'Well, I've been called a lot of things in my long and varied life, but '*angel*' is a first. If you're not going to let me do that, how else can I help?'

She didn't want to ask anything of Filly, but it would be so much easier with her help, especially with the close proximity of the black-eyed farmer, and where her mother lived.

'The one thing I hadn't planned on was meeting my mum when someone else was there—especially if it was someone she was involved with. I just never gave it a thought that she'd have a partner or a husband. I could end up ruining her relationship if she hasn't … you know … told him of my existence?'

'So how can I help with that?'

'I'd like to be near the farm entrance in the morning, but if I'm on my own standing in the lane, I'm concerned the farmer will confront me again. More importantly, though, if I see Lily leaving the farm in a car on her own, I want to be able to follow her. If Mr Levington leaves on his own, then that's fine—I'll go and see her at the house.'

'And what happens if neither leaves the property all day or if they both go out together in a car, like tonight?'

Tabatha sighed.

'Then I guess that's a bit of a problem—I can't work that one out.'

'Get some sleep, sweetie. Juan and I will pick you up in the morning. I'll have him make some breakfast for us, and we'll have a picnic in the car while we wait. Eight o'clock okay for you?'

'If you're sure that's alright?'

'More than alright—the most excitement I've had in ages! See you in the morning—sleep well.'

The line was dead before Tabatha had a chance to reply.

*

'How dare you come here? How *dare* you!'

'But I ...'

'Never mind your pathetic excuses—you think I don't know who you are? You think I didn't recognise you? Didn't you see the horror etched all over my face last night?'

'But ...'

'And, what, this pathetic old photograph gives you a right to come and see me, does it? To stalk me, because that's what you've done—you've *stalked* me. I'm going to call the police.'

'No, I ...'

'Don't you realise I had to *pay* David and Tracey to take you off my hands? God, you were a nightmare. You know the worst news of my life?—when we discovered I was pregnant. It was *you* that ruined my life; you *ruined* it, do you hear? He left me—the love of my life, and he left me—all because of *you*.'

A cursory glance at the postcard-sized photo. A snort of derision and the picture is torn in half, revolved 90 degrees, torn in half again.

Revolved ~torn ~revolved—torn.

Tabatha watches transfixed, as sixteen jaggedly-rectangular pieces of photographic paper fall towards the multiple shades of bespoke paving.

The misery takes place in agonising slow-motion. The dissected image is about to land when a savage blast of icy wind lifts the debris high into the air, snaking over the roof of Anabel Tomb Farm.

She stares through tear-blind eyes until there's nothing to see but blurred midnight-blue sky.

278

But it's not over.

'That's what you did to my life. You ruined everything—the whole fucking lot. The only person I ever loved, and you took him from me. All you had to do was exist, and that was enough—he left me.

You're a nightmare, Tabatha. A spoilt, snivelling, child—an obnoxious, precious, teenager—a selfish, useless adult.

And who could blame Rick? You deserved everything you witnessed, and it'll happen again, and again. Over, and over, and over, again. It'll *never* stop happening. Every man you find will do the same thing for the rest of your life. And all because you ruined *my* life.

You're a *nightmare.*'

It was five a.m., and she was drenched in sweat, no comprehension of her surroundings.

In the dark, Tabatha bumped painfully into the doorframe of her bathroom and staggered to the basin. She pulled the mirror-light cord, and a nicotine-coloured glow illuminated the room, enough to stare, bleary-eyed, at the reflection.

A dull sickness washed over her. Not quite nausea, but the type of flatness in the stomach that always seemed to be triggered by a lack of sleep. A feeling that breakfast was needed but couldn't be faced. A hangover of sorts, but without the alcohol to blame it on.

She looked from the hot tap to the cold tap—the first decision of what could be a momentous day in her life.

The warmth on her face, and she may have the chance of some more sleep; the cold, and her levels of consciousness would rise dramatically.

She peered into the bedroom, and red digits below the tiny television glowed '*05:03*'—a couple of hours before light started to pierce the thin curtains. But how quickly would she get to sleep after what she'd been dreaming, still so vivid in her mind?

And, God knows, she didn't fancy a sequel to the last episode.

Tabatha gasped as the water hit her face and splashed over her bare shoulders.

She grabbed the towel and looked again in the mirror, her reflection now distorted by rivulets of water—a blessing of sorts.

Making her way back to the bed, she flicked the bedside light on and pulled the charge lead out of her phone.

One WhatsApp message sent at 00.01 from Grant:

'*Hope I'm first to wish you a Happy Birthday! Big kiss and good luck today Tabs. Thinking of you. X*'

The first and only, for sure. To imagine Lily remembering her birthday was almost laughable.

The thought of meeting her brought the feeling of sickness back to Tabatha's tummy. When was the last time she'd felt this nervous? She had no idea—maybe never. She began to peck a reply.

'*Thank you—the first and maybe the only one—we'll see. x*'

About to hit the *Send* button, the nightmare wafted back into her mind; those words—those images.

Her fingers moved back to the little keyboard.

'Missing you, Grant. Big kiss and thanks — Thinking of you too. X'

*

It was the smell that hit her first, any hint of sickness instantaneously evaporating, replaced by a yearning hunger.

'I've never smelt bacon like it.'

'It's one of Juan's many talents. Guests have commented on his breakfasts before; he has a secret recipe he brushes on the bacon before grilling. Oh, and he sprinkles white truffle shavings on the scrambled eggs.'

Filly pressed a rocker switch, and her voice went through to the driver's compartment; 'You're being complimented on your breakfast again, Juan. Top marks as always.'

The two women saw his flashing teeth in the rear-view mirror.

'I've never eaten in a limousine before. I'm really nervous I'll make a mess all over the leather and carpet, especially with this coffee. It's amazing—what is it?'

'That's Blue Mountain coffee, dear, from Jamaica—I'm so glad you're enjoying it. Did you sleep well?'

'Okay, I guess. I woke up a little earlier than planned.'

'That'll be the nerves, perhaps?'

'Yes. Well that, and the nightmare.'

'Oh dear—I won't ask. So, the plan is that we'll stop where the lane widens and park up; Juan tells me there's perfect visual access from there to the main entrance, so we'll see everyone that comes and goes.'

'How can he be sure?'

'He went off on his motorbike before dawn and carried out a little advanced-surveillance.'

'Oh. Wow, that's so kind of him—I feel dreadful putting you guys to all this trouble.'

'Not a bit, it gives us something to do, and this is all jolly exciting. Now my only concern is that they may be off-Island. They could have driven straight to the airport last night.'

'In black tie and evening dress? And wouldn't it be a bit late to catch a flight?'

'Not when you have your own private jet, darling. It's a little easier, then.'

Tabatha looked down at her empty breakfast plate sitting on the mahogany picnic table. It was a massive mental leap to picture her mother travelling everywhere by private jet.

She still couldn't really process any of it.

Filly seemed to read her mind.

'Never be scared of wealth, dear. You hold something far more precious than money—than anything. You can't buy youth, Tabatha—you hold all the aces.'

The women looked at each other intently for a long moment.

'How old are you—twenty-five? Twenty-six?'

'Thirty. No wait, thirty-one.'

'You're not sure?'

'No, it's just that it's my ...'

'Your ... ? You mean it's your birthday? Today?!'

The silence confirmed the answer. She leaned over and hugged the girl.

'Something special is going to happen today, sweetheart. Trust a wise old owl.'

And if not *special*, then something significant did happen a short while later, just after the rain started in earnest.

Juan switched the wipers on as they watched a light-coloured Range Rover pull out of the entrance.

'Will it drive past us?'

'Unlikely—town and the airport are the other way. If someone wanted to go east, they'd still turn away from us and take the nearest lane to get onto the main road, especially in a car that size.'

She knew the lane; the one she'd gone down the previous evening after hitting the farmer.

'He's on his own.'

Tabatha couldn't hide the excitement from her voice.

'Your first birthday present. Apart from staff, your mother is almost certainly on her own.'

A shot of adrenalin coursed through her body, the excitement and nerves making her tingle. She pulled the photo out of her inside pocket and looked at it.

The nightmare came flooding back and jolted her.

'Lily? May I?'

Tabatha passed the picture almost reverently, noticing Filly's rings were entirely different—all of them—diamonds replaced by emeralds of even larger size.

'She looks so much like you. What a beautiful woman and her face is vaguely familiar. I've seen her or met her before, obviously here in Jersey, but goodness knows when or on which occasion. You certainly wouldn't need a DNA test to prove who your mother was.'

She passed the photo back.

'I think it's time you went and became reacquainted, dear. Would you like us to drive you to the house? You'll get soaked if you walk.'

But Tabatha already had her hand on the door handle, pulling the jacket hood up over her head.

She saw Filly's car waft past the entrance. Tabatha turned to wave and saw the old lady blow a kiss; then they were gone. She was on her own.

She'd assumed the gates would open when she walked up to them, but they remained closed. She looked for an intercom, but there was nothing on either pillar.

As Tabatha contemplated a clamber up the grass bank and onto the field running alongside the drive, she noticed a large grey switch mounted to the side of the right pillar, almost hidden from view by foliage.

She pushed the greenery away and pressed the button, watching as just the right gate swung open with an almost inaudible whirr. The aperture wasn't big enough to allow a car access, clearly for the benefit of those on bikes or foot.

Walking gingerly onto the paving, she turned back—it would have been just her luck to see the farmer standing in the lane, now that she was on her own again.

There was nobody—even the herd had moved to some oak trees on the other side of the field, huddling together out of the rain. They were all turned her way, seemingly intrigued by the intruder. Who'd be stupid enough to be out in this weather? Who'd be mad enough to trespass on Anabel Tomb Farm?

It was tempting to sprint through the rain and seek shelter, but the further she ventured down the drive, the slower she walked.

There were stainless-steel blocks set into the side of the interlocked pink, grey, and yellow paving, with little windows in the sides—the lights she'd seen last night.

Nearer the house, she noticed much larger black lamps set into the flower beds, pointed at one vast tree. As the paving sloped down and to the right, a large white garage door came into view. She had the choice of a path to the right of that, which led to formal gardens, a palm tree, and what was clearly the front entrance, or continue down the drive to the left, running along the side of the granite property.

She felt much more of a tradesman than a guest, so opted to stay on the paving to the side of the house.

Tradesman? I wish. I'm an uninvited visitor—a trespasser.

She looked back again. This time, the desire to run straight back where she'd come from and out of the place was powerful.

Isn't it enough to know where Mum lives? Know that she's well? Believe that she'd like me if we ever met?

Isn't that far better than discovering she never wanted to see me again?—that the expression on her face last night told me everything I needed to know?

It was the weather which prompted her to move—bitterly cold and monsoon-like—almost more uninviting than her fears.

She turned around and walked down the side of the house, going past a vast conservatory which attached the garage to the main house.

Another large field with yet more cows under the umbrella-like canopy of trees. A winding pathway made of tiny granite chippings appeared, leading to some white rails and then what appeared to be a forest in the distance.

Directly in front of her, a burgundy-coloured tennis court surrounded by high green fencing; next to it, a swimming pool surrounded by tinted glass panels. Looking to her right, a large granite arch extending the length of a couple of cars, suggesting the promise of a back-door under the porch.

Again, Tabatha could not comprehend how Lily could even live here, much less be the partner or wife of the owner. It was all so surreal.

She walked towards an alcove through the arch, desperate to get out of the rain. Her faithful old Parka had initially offered some resistance, but she was now completely drenched.

There was a doorbell by the side of the rear entrance. She thought to try it, then shivered from the cold and her own nervousness.

There were no signs of life through any of the windows, and a glance back through the alcove showed only an orchard in the distance, a building close by with one darkened window and a garage door at the far end, but no human presence—anywhere.

She looked at the bell again. There was no white card underneath to divulge the occupier's name, and why would there be? People who managed to get this far from the public road had no excuse for being lost—there could be no excuse for not knowing who the owner was.

Unless they were up to no good.

Tabatha looked again at the doorbell.

Why is this so frightening?
Because you did it all the wrong way.
Because you were scared of rejection.

She pressed the button and heard chiming in the distance.

'Mrs Levington isn't here at the moment.'
    'Oh, but I thought …'

'If you'd care to step inside, I don't think she'll be long—she's somewhere on the estate. May I ask who wishes to see her?'

'So ... she's married to ... to Mr Levington?'

'Yes, that's correct—Mrs Levington is indeed married to Mr Levington. Can I ask your name, please?'

'I'm sorry, my name's Tabatha—Tabatha Mercer.'

The tall woman stepped aside and invited her in.

She was efficient but in a friendly way. In her forties, with dark hair loosely piled up and wearing a pink apron, worn over a white button-down shirt and jeans. The apron stated boldly that the wearer was the *'Prosecco Princess of Jersey'*, and Tabatha decided it was this detail which made her feel a little less nervous.

'Right, well if you'd like to give me your jacket, I can hang it up in the drying room.'

There was a quick appraisal.

'And perhaps I can exchange your shoes for some house slippers?'

It was definitely a rhetorical question but delivered pleasantly enough.

She was shown through an open-plan kitchen where the woman had clearly been working on a black marble island in the middle of the huge room. There was a lot of flour and what appeared to be small balls of fish, surrounded by various types of greenery and herbs.

'Local scallops—in the sea until an hour ago. Can you pick up that controller and press it, please?'

She pointed to a chunky key fob, sitting in an array of black pigeon holes attached to the wall.

Tabatha did as requested, and two large glass-dividers parted swiftly, giving access to the conservatory she'd walked past earlier.

'Make yourself comfortable. I'm sure Mrs Levington won't be too long. I'll give her a call and let her know you're here. She's expecting you?'

'No. I can't lie—she's definitely not expecting me. Is that still alright?'

'Oh, I assumed you had a meeting. Let me call her—sit tight for now.'

The woman picked up a cordless-phone and left the kitchen.

Tabatha sat on the edge of a small sofa for what seemed like an age. With nothing to do but ponder this momentous occasion in her life, she looked around the glass construction for more clues to Lily's life.

There was opulence everywhere, from the two large modern chandeliers, one of which hung precariously over her head, to four gigantic fern-type plants in each corner of the conservatory, standing in two metre-high iridescent-cyan vases.

A thin, black, monitor sunk into the far wall was surrounded by two square-framed paintings. They were clearly by the same artist and depicted coastal views, probably local beaches, neither in traditional nor abstract form. She'd never seen a style like it.

Tabatha was admiring them when someone sat down next to her.

She jumped and inhaled sharply, turning to be confronted by the cat she'd seen on the road yesterday.

'God, cat, you frightened me to death! So you *do* live here, hmmm?'

The animal was even bigger and more striking in daylight. It studied her silently, then tilted its head sideways and upwards, pressing an ear against her shoulder.

'You're the biggest cat I've ever seen, but you're very soppy. What's your name?'

'It's Benji.'

This time she left contact with the sofa as she jumped, the cat leaping to the floor and trying, but initially failing, to gain traction on the pale cream marble.

Tabatha stood and swivelled around, now staring directly into the eyes of her mother.

16

LILY WAS taller than Tabatha had imagined, both the photo and her appearance in the car disguising this feature. She stared at herself in the future, wondering if her mother was doing the same, but in reverse.

Mrs Levington was very much the relaxed lady of the manor—dark trainers, soiled jeans, and a well-used Barbour anorak. As Tabatha noted the two rings on her wedding finger—subtle but quite beautiful—small diamonds and both platinum—so very different from Filly's—it was hard to imagine her formative years had been spent in a care home.

She was also holding a colourful collection of flowers that dripped onto the floor as she walked up to her daughter, passing them to her.

'I'm afraid I didn't have time to get a birthday card.'

She leant forward and put her hand on Tabatha's shoulder, kissing her on the cheek.

'Happy Birthday—Dawn tells me your name is Tabatha?'

The woman's eyes pooled with tears, but she made no attempt to cover it up.

As Tabatha's gaze moved from one eye to the other, tears fell simultaneously from both.

She extended her arms to the girl, and there was not a moment of hesitation—Tabatha fell into her mother's embrace, the garden flowers falling from her hand.

'There's rarely a day goes by when I don't think of you, Tabatha. I can hardly believe I even know your name, never mind look at you with my own eyes.'

She hugged the girl tightly and didn't want to let go.

'I made a promise with myself that I'd never contact Tracey or David—I mean your mother and father—after I let you go.

They're wonderful people. I was never concerned that you'd be brought up in a loving way; I just felt it wasn't fair on them if I made contact again. Do you understand that?'

Tabatha gathered the flowers up off the glass table.

'Yes, of course. Well … I think so. This is so strange that I'll need a long while to let everything sink in.'

'I know, and for me too. I'll be in a state of shock for days, and I can't really afford that.'

'I'm not sure I understand?'

'Oh, it's nothing, just ignore me, I'm talking gibberish—put it down to nerves.'

'*You're* nervous? Now that's something I hadn't thought about, if and when we met.'

'Don't worry about it. By the way, how did you find me?'

Tabatha felt her cheeks redden.

'Would it be okay if I said the same thing?—*don't worry about it?*'

'Sure. Let's go into the kitchen and have a coffee, yes? I'll get Dawn to wrap those flowers up for you; I'm afraid there's not much in the gardens at this time of year.'

'They're lovely—Dad would be very impressed. He's a bit of a gardener himself, especially now he's retired.'

'He was in banking, wasn't he?'

'Yes, though not in the type of banking that would allow him a place like this, of course.'

As soon as she said it, she wanted to bite her tongue. It was perhaps the one and only plan she'd conjured up in the last few minutes—not to mention or be overcome by this obvious display of wealth. Tabatha immediately wanted to change the subject.

'I have a photo of you. Oh, it's in my jacket—the lady took it away to dry.'

'I think I know the one you mean. Tracey asked me for it, actually. She said that one day it would be nice for you to have a look at. When did she show you?'

'Not so long ago. I ... I didn't know they weren't my real parents until ...'

'Until recently?'

'No. Well ... yes and no.'

'What made Tracey want to tell you about me?'

Tabatha tried to inhale fully, but it was a ragged breath, her lower lip quivering.

'Dad told me—showed me your photo. It was after Mum died a couple of months ago.'

They talked for over two hours, mostly about Tabatha, to her disappointment, and the time flew.

She still knew next to nothing about Lily. It was surely her imagination, but it felt as if every time the subject veered away from her own life, Lily was able to skilfully deflect any skirting around her own circumstances.

'How long are you here for? I'm asking because I need to go now, but we must meet up again soon.'

'Oh, of course—I'm sorry for going on. I had loads of questions for you, too. I go back to Cambridge tomorrow.'

'Maybe I can come and visit you there? As long as David is okay with it, obviously.'

Tabatha felt a little hollow. She couldn't be certain, but it was as if something was missing.

The thought of meeting Lily had been so all-consuming of late, almost to the exclusion of anything else. Perhaps the reality could never have quite lived up to the expectation?

But it was more than that.

'Maybe we could meet for dinner tonight? If you're not doing anything, that is? I only came over here to see you, so I have nothing else planned until I fly back.'

'It's a lovely idea, but that would be ... difficult, I think.'

Lily looked out of the window, and Tabatha could tell her mind was miles away.

'I have some commitments I can't put off; otherwise, it would have been perfect.'

'With Mr. Levington?'

'Sorry? Oh, yes, with Bill. I'm afraid it would be absolutely impossible for us to meet tonight.'

Tabatha thought it a strange choice of words. *'Absolutely impossible.'* Not *tricky,* or *difficult,* or *not possible.*

It was probably just the stress of seeing her only child for the first time in 30 years.

And then something struck her.

'I don't have any brothers or sisters, do I?'

Lily laughed.

'Good grief, *no*! Now that really would be ridiculous, right?'

She laughed again and looked at her watch.

'I hate to appear rude, Tabatha, but I'm really going to have to get my skates on. I need to join Bill at the restaurant—I should be there already. God, the time's flown, hasn't it?'

'Of course. Oh, and I'm really sorry for turning up unannounced. Somewhere nice for lunch, I expect?'

Lily looked at her blankly.

'With Mr Levington—for lunch?'

'Yes, absolutely. Somewhere really nice. Anyhow, can I get Dawn to give you a lift to your hotel?'

'No, that's fine, thanks. It's stopped raining, and I'd like a walk.'

Lily glanced at her watch again.

'Okay then, well, you've given me your number, so I'll call you before you go. We'll arrange to meet up soon, okay?'

She was gently ushering Tabatha to the front door as she spoke.

'That sounds lovely. I just need to get my coat. And, umm … shoes.'

They both stared down at the pair of slippers.

'Good point—silly me.'

She called out for Dawn, who was already on her way with a dried coat and warm shoes.

'Thanks for the coffee and flowers. I'll look forward to your call. Oh, I don't have your number, do I?'

'Don't worry; you'll have it on your phone when I call. I'll see you very soon. Sorry to dash.'

Lily hugged her daughter briefly, then ran up a wide, curved stairway, glimpsing at her watch again.

*

She reached the main gates, pressed the switch again, looking both ways before crossing the lane.

The limousine flashed its lights and was next to her seconds later.

'Hop in, dear.'

294

'You've been here all this time?'

'Not exactly. I've been doing a little homework while you were gone. Now tell me all about it—did you have a wonderful time?'

Tabatha gave Filly a brief rundown, omitting the nagging doubt in her mind.

'Shall we go and have a spot of lunch and a chat? Juan …'

'Is it okay if we stay here for a few minutes? Maybe where we parked earlier? I just want to see where she goes. Do you think there'd be any chance we could follow her?'

Filly rubbed her hands together and grinned.

'Splendid idea, sweetie, I like the sound of that. Of course, we'll have to hang back a fair way—this isn't exactly the most inconspicuous vehicle in Jersey.'

Juan reversed the car, and they tucked into the natural layby again.

Twenty minutes later, and there was still no sign of Lily.

'I don't understand. It was all such a rush—she was meant to be at the restaurant before I left.'

'All will become apparent, dear, I'm sure.'

Ten minutes later, and things became even less clear.

The familiar Range Rover turned into the farm, with William Levington at the wheel of his car.

'I don't get it. She said he was at the restaurant already, waiting for her.'

'A change of plan, obviously. Did Lily tell you how long she'd been married?'

'Not in so many words. I asked her but don't remember her being specific. I think she said something like, '*a few years*', or something like that. Why do you ask?'

'But did she intimate an approximate time they'd been married?'

'I don't think so. I guess I sensed a few years. I didn't really think about it.'

'More than a decade?'

'No, not really. Why?'

'More than twenty years?'

'God, no! What's this about?'

'I got a local investigator on the case yesterday, burning the midnight oil. He found out when your mum changed from being Miss Barnes to Mrs Levington. They were married at Camden Registry Office in London.'

'Okay, makes sense. I think that's pretty close to where she worked in Kilburn. Dad told me she used to work there in a photo lab. I don't think that's too signific ...'

'Thirty years ago. They've been married over thirty years, Tabby. You were three months old when she became Lily Levington.'

'Could you do with something to eat, dear? You must be hungry by now?'

It was after two o'clock, and they'd been sitting in the car for what seemed an age, mostly in silence.

Tabatha had been trying to process Filly's news and the implications. She would have welcomed being on her own at the moment but was desperate to see what might happen next at the farm.

Nothing seemed right, and the longer there was no sign of Lily and William, the more hurt she felt. The first time she'd ever consciously met her mother, and she'd been lied to—sent on her way—history repeating itself.

'How about we leave it until three, then go and get a late lunch? I just want to see if they go out.'

Try as she might, she couldn't hide the sadness in her voice.

'Don't think the worst, child. You told me she hugged you hard enough to almost make up for all those lost years. People can't do that unless they mean it, Tabatha—there's bound to be a simple explanation. My guess is they're having lunch at home. Maybe they were going out with friends who cancelled at the last minute, or they simply had a change of mind. I've cancelled meal bookings dozens of times, sweetie—don't read anything into it.'

'Maybe you're right; I don't know. What would you do if you were me?'

Filly pondered for a moment.

'Juan, call a taxi, please.'

'For where to come, Lady P?'

'Well here, of course. And we'll be going back to the manor, thank you.'

She looked at Tabatha.

'We'll leave Juan here to keep an eye on our friends— sorry—your mother and her husband, I mean—and we'll grab a sandwich at home. Oh, if that's alright with you, dear? I'm sorry—I'm being very presumptuous, aren't I? My husbands, all of them to be precise, said I was always over-organising things.'

*

She'd gone from never having been in a privately-owned manor in 31 years, to visiting two in a matter of hours. Admittedly, one was a farm but, if anything, that was even grander than Filly's home.

Which was not to say that Lady P's place was sub-standard. As the covert-baroness was keen to point out, there were seven spare bedroom-suites available to Tabatha. If she had a change of heart, she could spend her last night in Jersey at Gorey Manor.

'But what about my stuff at the guesthouse?'

'Juan can easily pick it up for you, but I suspect you'll want to do that yourself?'

An image loomed of her few possessions strewn all over the room.

'I think that might be best.'

'Good, then I'll call Madge and get us some food; smoked salmon sandwiches and salad okay for you?'

A woman mystically appeared. She wore a black-and-white waitress uniform straight out of a Fifties movie of the same colours, her neat, permed, grey hair the precise mid-shade of the outfit. Madge also looked much older than Filly. In fact, she looked Filly's age.

Introductions were made, Tabatha was persuaded to share a half-bottle of champagne to toast her most-bizarre-ever birthday, and Madge made a slightly-stooped exit.

'Eighty-two.'

'Excuse me?'

'Madge—she's a year older than me.'

'Oh, well I wasn't ...'

'Yes, you *were*, dear. Bridge cards on table, I'm at the time of my life when I get a little satisfaction from letting slip to guests that I'm not the oldest biddy in the room.'

'I didn't know I was so transparent.'

'You aren't—I cheated. It's basically the first question *everyone* asks me about Madge. And now I'll answer the second one; she had a dalliance with Duncan in the Sixties— that's the decade—not her age at the time.'

'I'm lost.'

'You remember Duncan—the Earl?—my first husband?'

'Oh yes, of course. Sorry.'

'Don't be; I'll probably be asking you to remind me of them at some point today, no doubt. Anyhow, Madge worked for us, and Duncan took a fancy to her. You remember me telling you he was the one who couldn't keep it in his trous ...'

'Yes. Yes, I remember now.'

'It's pure speculation, of course, but I do wonder if she was wearing the same uniform, you know, when he ...'

Tabatha had lost control of her lower jaw again.

'So that's why she's still here. It's a lesson it took me a lifetime to learn, and sometimes it still hurts—I'm still learning. Just a twinge now and then, you understand. I had to accept that it was nothing—absolutely *nothing* to do with Madge. So, by continuing to let her work for me, it cleanses my soul and makes me feel a better person than I really am.'

The door opened in a timely fashion, and Madge appeared with a bottle of champagne and two glasses.

The instant silence from both women was obvious and deafening.

'Thank you, Madge.'

Tabatha watched in awe as taut smiles were exchanged, and heads were deftly tilted. It was like being on a period-drama film set, and she was mesmerised.

'No, I'm almost certain she doesn't. *Almost* certain.'

Tabatha looked from the door to her host, lost for words yet again.

'And to your third and final question on Madge—*does she know that I know?*'

She poured them both a glass from a bottle which Tabatha had never seen before, though she was no champagne connoisseur.

'I hope you'll forgive an old lady her coupe glasses—I really have no time whatsoever for those lanky, modern flutes. I hear the arguments about containment of effervescence for longer, but quite frankly, who wants to spend too much time consuming a bottle of fizz, eh?'

'Ummm … Did you say a half-bottle?'

'You're right—good girl and well observed. I suspect there were no halves of Krug in the cellar, and Madge used her initiative.'

'I'm not sure I can drink half a bottle on my own. Could she have found another type, perhaps?

Filly looked incredulous.

'For a birthday celebration? I don't think so, my dear.'

*

The bedroom was about five times the size and at least ten times as comfortable. It was so perfect, that she felt guilty about sitting on the bed or drawing the curtains.

Her meagre weekend clothes looked woefully out of place in such surroundings. Though not contemporary, the tasteful furnishing and ornaments dripped with wealth. It was what she imagined a suite at The Ritz would be like.

The news from Juan that only a courier van had been into and out of the farm throughout the afternoon was a bitter disappointment. Not only because Tabatha had no idea what to do next, but she couldn't rid herself of the upset of Lily's deception.

What was the point? Why was it so important that she leave the place so urgently?

It was almost certainly something which would always remain a mystery, but similarly, it would always nag away at her.

Would it have been worse if Lily had said, '*Look kid, I'd like you to go now—I'll be in touch.*' When she thought of it that way, it was a little easier to accept. There were lies, and there were white lies.

There was still the question of the phone number, as well. Nowadays, people didn't give their number; they exchanged numbers. Yet when Lily had taken down Tabatha's number, she hadn't offered hers in return.

There was no way to justify this. It was as if Lily didn't want to give away her number—didn't want her daughter to be able to call.

'I don't know how I can pay you back. This is the third meal I've had with you, and now you're putting me up in your home.'

'It's honestly no problem at all—the very least I can do on your birthday. I was actually going to suggest you stay here a bit longer—maybe change your flight? My chap will probably dig up some more information in a day or two, and we can continue to monitor your mother's movements. It's ever so exciting, isn't it?'

Filly was beaming, and it occurred to Tabatha that for all the trappings of wealth, here was a lady who had probably become a little bored with her single life, whatever public façade she displayed.

'I'm not sure if Dad bought me a changeable ticket— probably not. I'd also have to get him to book me into a hotel or guesthouse somewhere—I'm a bit short for cash at the moment.'

'Well, flights are cheap as chips from here to Gatwick— probably cheaper than changing your existing flight. As for accommodation, I was rather assuming you might want to stay here for the duration. If, of course, you're quite comfortable in your room?'

'Oh, it's nothing to do with here—it's the nicest room I've ever stayed in. I just meant that I should probably go back home as planned.'

'Do you have any urgent appointments next week, or anyone who'll miss you? If not, you're more than welcome, dear—really; for as long as you like.'

Tabatha gazed out of the huge, arched window, one of three in this dark-panelled dining-room. It was a dark night, and there was nothing to see. She was amazed at the lack of outside lights and security in general, but Filly seemed immune to the need for security.

Is there anyone waiting for me—anyone who will miss me?
There's Dad, but we live together—that's not liable to change in the next …

She tried to project the future into the now.

In the next few years.
At least …

An image of Grant came into focus.

You are way too good for me—can't you see that, Aussie Boy?
I can't even have a relationship with my own mother—how could I possibly manage one with you?
You'd end up finding someone else, and I can't face that.
I can't face that again …
I can't …

'No, I don't have anything on next week—I guess I could stay for a couple more days. If it means I can see my mum again, it'll be worth everything to me.'

'Excellent. I'll give that investigator a call in the morning—see if he's dug anything else out of the woodwork.'

'I hope you don't mind, but I think I'm going to get some sleep. I don't know what I was expecting, but it feels a little more overwhelming than I'd anticipated. I need to give my dad a call too—let him know my plans.'

'Of course. Sleep well, darling. Oh, and don't worry about any noises you hear—all part and parcel of a house that's four-hundred years old.'

Upstairs, Tabatha went to her Parka and searched the pockets for her phone. She'd decided a quick call to her father was much more reliable than a text, and then maybe a quick WhatsApp message to Grant.

With growing concern, she went through the jacket again. Nothing. She searched her backpack but knew it couldn't be there—she'd had the phone earlier today, while the bag was left back in her room.

She went through the day in her mind, trying to remember when she could definitely remember seeing it last. It didn't take long.

She could hear Lily asking for the number. Like many people, she wasn't certain of her own mobile number and had to look. Nobody needed to remember those sorts of things nowadays. Even filling out forms which required that detail, she'd simply flick the phone to its number display and copy it out.

And then Dawn had passed her the toast-warm coat and dried shoes. She'd put the phone on a semi-circular glass-topped table as the woman held the coat open for her to snuggle into.

It was the urgency with which Lily was trying to get rid of her—her brain was temporarily scrambled—the phone forgotten.

Well, at least I have an excuse to go back there.

Making a mental note to call her dad in the morning, she slid into bed and turned the lights out.

I can't message Grant.
I hope he'll understand—I'm sure he will.

*

He knew it wasn't what she'd wanted or requested, and there was every chance she might be put out or even a little upset.

He'd given careful consideration to this, but his heart had still ruled his head. After all, what was the worst that could happen? At least he'd sent her messages announcing his intentions and his movements, so it wouldn't be a shock.

'I'm afraid she checked out of here earlier today, sir.'

'But she'd booked to stay until tomorrow. Are you sure?'

'Very sure, sir—I've been on duty all day and took her room key back. I was at pains to point out that there would unfortunately be no refund for the vacant room. It's company policy, you see—it would be next to impossible to …'

'How long ago was this?'

'Not that long ago, sir—no more than a couple of hours.'

'And she left no forward address? No indication of where she might be heading?'

'No sir, and I wouldn't be at liberty to divulge that information, even if she had. But no, I can confirm she gave no indication.'

'Christ, so she just upped and left on her own, then?'

'Errrr, that type of information would fall into the same category I'm afraid, sir.'

'Soooo, what … you're telling me she didn't leave on her own?'

Grant was getting a little agitated.

'I didn't say that, sir.'

The duty manager's face was beginning to redden a little.

'Look, it may not have escaped your notice that I have an Australian accent. I've come all the way from Sydney to Cambridge to see my sister for the first time in five years, only to find she's gone to Jersey for the weekend, for a work-colleague's thirtieth birthday. Rather than wait at our dad's house in Cambridge for her to come back tomorrow, I thought I'd give her a little surprise. Are you saying you can't tell me if she left on her own or not?'

Grant was rarely, if ever, impressed with himself—it wasn't in his make-up. However, lying didn't come naturally to him—he had to admit he felt quite chuffed with his spontaneous effort.

The man put both hands on his thin black tie and tightened it. This only served to deepen his glowing complexion.

'I sympathise with your situation, sir, I really do, but …'

Grant clenched and unclenched his right fist, then put it in his jeans pocket. Two twenty-pound notes appeared on the desk in front of the man.

'There *was* a man waiting at reception for Ms Mercer. He took a bag from her as they walked down the steps to the car. That's all I can tell you, sir.'

The money was scooped up and put in the man's inside jacket pocket.

Grant could feel sweat seeping—forehead, neck, armpits. He was going to hold this together.

'They got in a taxi?'

'I'd hardly call it a taxi, sir. More like the biggest Bentley I've ever seen. I'm not a motor trader, but I'd say it was a good half-a-million pounds worth of motor, sir.'

Grant couldn't be certain, but he sensed the man had taken pleasure in divulging the last snippet of information. Perhaps the sister-story wasn't quite as convincing as he'd hoped.

Both fists were now clenching, so he made a swift exit.

Had he stayed a moment longer, all would have been revealed, for Grant had understandably misinterpreted the situation.

The duty manager would have happily revealed that after letting the young lady into the back of the vehicle, the guy had jumped into the driver's seat and donned his chauffeur's cap. It was the least the duty manager could have conveyed, for what amounted to more than half-a-day's wages for a brief chat.

No wonder she hasn't been responding to my messages—what a total fuckwit I am.

Christ, I bet her mum isn't even in Jersey—it's probably all just a bloody con so she can have a weekend with her millionaire boyfriend.

Grant even briefly wondered if it was Rick.

He'd felt guilty at the time but needed to know more about the guy, so had innocently started a discussion with David about him. It helped that the man clearly still bore a grudge, and it wasn't long before he'd heard where Rick worked.

He'd studied him from a distance for most of an afternoon, trying not to dislike someone he neither knew nor was ever liable to meet, but it was tough. It was like looking at an older and better-looking version of himself, and he begrudgingly realised why Tabatha had been attracted, hair or no hair.

But if he didn't like Rick, boy-oh-boy, he absolutely *loathed* his shit-brown Merc convertible.

Thankfully, the day-dream was popped in seconds. Rick Harrison might be running a successful little business and enjoying a tidy earner, but he certainly didn't have the wherewithal to drive around Jersey in half-a-million quid's worth of customised limo.

No, thank God, Tabby was not in Jersey with Rick.

Which was blessed relief for all of three, deep, calming breaths.

Then who the hell is Tabby with?

God, he loved her so much that it felt like she'd died.

Was it really true that the cooler heart always won?

Did it have to be like that? Hadn't he played it cool enough for long enough? For Christ's sake, he'd been as cool as a Melbourne winter for months and months and bloody months!

307

But, of course, Tabby had always been that couple of degrees cooler …

He was also certain she didn't have to deal with the constant struggle of keeping her emotions in check. No—not as he had to—for just about every waking moment.

He walked down the hill towards town, wheeling his small overnight bag behind him, one hand flicking through the messages he'd sent her on his phone. He almost laughed at himself as he read them.

You're such a drongo, Grant Davis. What are you doing on the other side of the world, chasing someone who doesn't even give you a thought?

There were six messages in total. They broke the news of his hair-brained idea, then his imminent arrival, then his landing in Jersey, each one a little more pleading than the last.

He remembered spending much time deciding if an 'X' was in order at the end of the message and, if so, a capital or a lowercase kiss. Or maybe even two if he was feeling brave?

How much time have you spent thinking about an X at the end of a message to me, Tabby?
Be honest—tell me.
And if you deemed me worthy of an 'X' or even an 'x', what did that mean to you?
Tell me?

Because he'd kept every message, Grant had the ability, if he so desired, to check every one of the many hundreds they'd exchanged, to see how many kisses he'd been *awarded*.

Perhaps he'd discover something about her which would give him enlightenment—tell him what he wanted to know?

Instead, he backed-up to her name and pressed the delete option.

Even his phone was taking the piss out of him now, asking if he was absolutely sure he wanted to go through with this somewhat drastic action.

Hell YES, that's just what I want to do.

Click.

There were so many that it took more than the regular nano-second. Maybe up to a whole second, even, for the many months his heart had literally bled onto the little screen.

And as for his special birthday surprise, what on earth was that all about? Was he completely mad?

Grant was boiling into a fury.

If he thought his best friend cheating behind his back with Kimberley was painful, well this, now, was middle-ages, torture-until-death, agony.

He composed one final text and then deleted her from his list, just in case he ever felt the desire to call her again.

Even as he did this, he knew he'd feel that desire forever.

'Goodbye. Oh sorry - G'DAY!
XXXXXXXXXXXXXXXXXXXXXXXXXXXXXXXX'

He went into his WhatsApp system and blocked Tabatha from contacting him, then clicked on her name in his main contacts, staring mist-eyed at the letters and numbers.

How long had it taken him to get these precious ten digits next to her name? How many all-nighters and lost sleep? And how did he feel when she finally imparted the information to him; the trust she extended with those innocuous yet vital digits?

He'd been ecstatic; punched the air with sheer joy.

His finger hovered over the red letters:

Delete Contact

He touched the space in between the two words lightly, reverently, with his middle finger, his breath caught, his throat dry, his eyes wet.

Click

But no, it hadn't gone. He'd never deleted a contact before— had no knowledge of the process.

Two options now appeared, taunting him:

Delete Contact
Cancel

He hadn't the faintest idea of her number—not a clue— wasn't even sure of the four-digit prefix. Nobody had any clue of numbers nowadays—why would they need to remember—thank you, Bill Gates—thank you, Steve Jobs.

Consequently, this was it. The action, the fractional finger movement—it should be identical to a moment ago when he assumed her number would be lost to the ether.

Why wasn't it?

Press it, for fuck's sake, just press it! Be gone with her.
    Why? What if she …
'If she' what?! She's screwed you over, pal. Delete her—now.

But if ...

Oblivious to the fact his gradually slowing steps had come to a halt, he now stood at the exit to a hotel car park. A guest, tired of waiting for the young guy to move out of the way, had attempted as short a honk of the horn as was politely possible. Even so, the close proximity was always going to win his attention.

Grant jumped, and the phone screen pushed against his finger.

Click

*

At the airport a £20 taxi fare later, he discovered just how much one can pay, if one tries really, *really,* hard, for a forty-minute flight from Jersey to London Gatwick.

Surprise, surprise, there were only business-class seats left on the last flight. He noted with an almost self-schadenfreude pleasure, that the cost for this 160-mile journey—a full 10,400 miles shorter than his flight back to Sydney—was over half the price of his return leg Down Under.

Still, with the smallest of mercies in mind, the fare-class had allowed him access to the airport business-lounge. It was there that he discovered his country's most popular beer—*Foster's*—available in a non-depletable fridge.

It was rumoured that Aussies believed Foster's to be their biggest export-beer because none of the locals would touch it with a bargepole.

For Grant, this was not to be the case tonight.

He pulled his phone out and took a selfie, toasting with one of the famous blue cans, then sent it to his father with a brief message.

'I'm coming home, Dad — see you very soon. Love, Grant X.'

17

TABATHA WOKE with a sense of loss, and it was much more than her phone.

That was a nuisance, admittedly, but the optimism she'd carried was now gone, replaced by a growing depression.

Although the phone gave her a legitimate opportunity to go back to the farm, this time there was more than nervousness at the thought.

Through most of another sleepless night, she'd replayed her precious time with Lily. The way her mother's mood had shifted as their time together grew to a close. The affection and what felt like genuine love evaporating, replaced by barely-disguised anxiety and coldness.

How different your life is now, from when we were together.
Two very different worlds.
Why did you want me to go, Lily?

'Well, if you don't want to confront her, then there are only two options available; either Juan can collect your phone, or we can wait in our normal spot until we see them leave the property, then you retrieve it yourself. At least you get it back whatever happens—I know how precious these phones are to your generation.'

'It's not as bad as it used to be. At least everything's in the cloud now.'

'Why do I suspect that's not a profound biblical statement?'

'Sorry, it's not important. I don't want Juan picking the phone up, so if we could wait for Lily to go out again? I'm sorry to be such an imposition.'

'You're not being an imposition at all, Tabatha. But you are being stubborn—you're very single-minded and independent, aren't you?'

It was an observation rather than a question.

'Oh, it's not a criticism. You just remind me of someone.'

Filly smiled, and Tabatha took another sip of her breakfast coffee, to diffuse the embarrassment of what could have been a compliment. It was Blue Mountain once more, and she realised that coffee would never quite taste the same again.

*

There were no post-vans or couriers delivering to the farm, but then it was a Sunday. In Jersey, Sunday was very much a day of rest, Filly had explained.

Mid-morning, a small, brightly-coloured Fiat 500 left the property with Dawn at the wheel, probably having finished breakfast duties for the Levingtons, and finally with a little time for herself.

A day of rest for everyone, save for those servicing the constant needs of the rich, Tabatha wondered.

She idly glanced into the rear-view mirror, and the chauffeur returned her stare. Lowering her eyes swiftly to the opulent Wilton carpets, Tabatha pondered the powers of telepathy.

They didn't have long to wait until another car appeared, its red, low-slung nose easing onto the lane; a stark contrast to the enormous Range Rover they'd been expecting.

Lily was driving and on her own.

'That's an old Ferrari, but you probably knew that, sweetie? Juan, which model?'

The car pulled out, and they watched it disappear down the road, accompanied by a high-pitched growl.

'Dino 246 GTS, Lady P, from nineteen-seventy-two to seventy-four. Molto Bellissima.'

It was the most animated Tabatha had seen Juan, both hands pressing on his cheeks in a style of open worship.

'Lily was born in nineteen-seventy-two. You don't think . . .'

'I absolutely *do* think, my dear. A Ferrari born in the same year as his wife, and almost certainly a birthday present— William wins ten brownie points.'

'William's also still at home. I hadn't thought about that scenario.'

'Is that a problem? You said he looked friendly in his car.'

'It's not that.'

'Well, what is it? He's been married to your mother for thirty years—no offence to Lily, but for a man to stay married for that duration suggests sturdy moral fibre. Not to mention the classic Ferrari, of course.'

Filly grinned, and Tabatha knew she was being teased.

'And you have a formidable back-up army, of course. Juan, pass Tabatha the car phone.'

She inspected the chunky Nokia with bewilderment and a little apprehension.

315

'Tell you what—thank you, Juan, but I'll be fine. It's my mum's husband, not Jack the Ripper. I need to *man-up*, so to speak.'

She leaned over and opened the back door before Juan was able to sprint around the car and carry out the duty for her—it was a battle which, in different circumstances, could have lasted forever.

'Hang around if you can. If not, I'll call you from my phone—at least I'll be able to do that.'

Jogging the short distance to the gates, Tabatha realised she hadn't been strictly honest with Filly. Something wasn't quite right, but she had no clue what it could be.

Tabatha just wanted this over and done with as soon as possible.

She chose the front door this time. It symbolised the formality of the occasion in her mind.

Good morning—collect phone—thank you so much—goodbye.

Tabatha could hear the electronic rendition of the eight notes before Big Ben struck the hour, but apparently Mr. Levington could not.

She pressed again. And waited—less patiently.

There was little point in knocking—the chimes were louder than her knuckles would be, unless she was to be very rude.

Formality. Decorum.

The background music was the culprit—coming from a floor above—jazz on a piano, no other instruments.

316

Third time lucky—come on, come on.

Silence. Patience evaporating.

Christ, now what …

Big Ben faded, but the piano continued. She looked at the bell she'd been pressing, then at two sculpted knobs in the centres of the twin doors. They were shiny brass in the shape of symmetrical scallop shells. At least, she thought they were brass; they surely couldn't be made of gold, could they.

She put her hand on the right doorknob. It was freezing, literally. It was also immovable, with no rotation either way.

The next track started. Similar laid-back jazz—the sort of thing she imagined one might hear in a jazz club in Manhattan, deep into the middle of the night. Her mind was working overtime, clearly, as she'd never been to the States, let alone New York, and neither had she ever been in a jazz club.

The left doorknob twisted with surprising ease, given its imposing size, With the slightest of pushes it broke from its twin, exposing the ornate hall. The narrow field of vision gave her sight of the glass half-table, but her phone was no longer sitting on the top.

The piano was also instantly louder, the doors having done a sterling job of insulating the sound. No wonder he couldn't hear the bell.

She looked up the sweeping staircase, towards the source of the music. No concerns about disturbing the neighbours for the Levingtons; whatever else William was wearing or, God forbid, *not* wearing, he sure as hell wasn't donning earphones.

'Hello?'

The word stuck in her dry throat, so she tried again.

'Hello? Mr Levington? Hello?'

Nothing.

Tabatha considered raising her voice further, but it felt so rude. As rude as unlawful entry? She shuddered and tucked the thought away.

There was another problem. Pathetic though it felt to acknowledge, she was at odds to know whether she should remove her shoes as before. She looked up the gleaming white and black chequered-marble steps.

Get a grip, woman, this is your mother's fucking home!

She closed the door quietly and pulled her trainers off.

Thank God. It wasn't a bedroom. Thank you, God.

The room looked almost empty of furniture and ornaments, in stark contrast to downstairs. The doors, two again, were both wide open, exposing a floor-to-ceiling window that stretched the full length of the back wall. At either end was a black cube on top of a steel tripod, a black leather recliner forming a triangle of the three objects.

The piano was loud but not deafening, and the music wasn't emanating from the state-of-the-art speakers, but to the left, out of her line of sight.

She took a further step into the room, and there it was, a glossy-black grand piano, its top cover pivoted 45-degrees upwards.

Though the sound had the quality of a recording, the music was being produced solely by William Levington's fingers.

He was dressed the polar-opposite from the last time she'd glimpsed him, now in scruffy, light-blue jeans and a baggy, ill-fitting, black sweat-shirt.

As shocked as she was, she took a sliver of solace from observing his bare feet, her shoe-removal vindicated.

She was also aware of the warmth of the marble under her socks—floor-heated bliss.

The man was clearly in a world of his own.

Tabatha was no expert on either jazz or the piano, but the sound was sensational enough for her to question if she could interrupt him, or simply go back out of the house and wait until he'd finished playing, then have another prod of the doorbell.

'Hello?'

Both hands were touching her mouth when he responded.

'*JESUS!*'

He span around as the second syllable was echoing off the walls.

'Sorry, sorry, sorry. I knocked, I mean rang …'

'You're Tabatha. Not a bit—entirely my fault—come on in. Well … in further, so to speak.'

He stood, his smile both charming and disarming as he moved to shake her hand.

'It's a pleasure to meet you, Tabatha—I'm William. Lily told me a little about you—how exciting!'

She shook his hand—firm enough to be just short of painful—returning the smile.

Much to her irritation, she was flustered. Flustered was bad enough—lost for words was worse.

'Hi.'

He left it a second to see if anything further was forthcoming.

'So … what a lovely and unexpected surprise.'

Still silence—sweaty silence.

'And after such a long time—incredible!'

'Yes.'

'Oh. Oh, sorry, she's not here at the moment—she went to the gym.'

He lifted his head and eyes conspiratorially, as if likening the act of a workout to chain- smoking or the inability to ski on black-runs. It flashed through her head that he may even be attempting to create a tiny bond of camaraderie.

She'd experienced awkward and embarrassing moments in her short lifetime, one of which always headed the list, obviously. She wasn't going to compare the two for a single moment, but this was up there with major lost-for-words moments in Tabatha Mercer's existence.

'Yes, I know—I saw her go.'

Unwittingly, this reversed the silence stakes, the man of the house now a little taken aback.

'So, you … you haven't come to see Lily?'

The atmosphere was thickening to a point where no anti-perspirant deodorant yet created could have coped.

'No. Well, yes … but not specifically. I didn't come *only* to see her.'

'Oh, you came to see me as well?'

'*NO!* I mean, *no* … not as such. When I saw Lily drive away, I realised you'd probably be here on your own—that there was a good chance of that—because I'd seen Dawn go a little earlier. So yes, I reckoned you'd probably be on your own.'

Was it possible for someone to hear your thoughts if they were *really* loud?

For instance, could William hear '*Oh. My. God.* and/or '*For. Fuck's. Sake. You. Moron.*'?

'I'm probably having a senior moment, but I'm not entirely sure what you're trying to say?'

'Okay. Right, okay … so I came here to collect my phone, but …

'*Ah.* Of course. Sorry, go on.'

'But I noticed Lily driving off as I was walking towards your entrance gates.'

'And Dawn? You noticed Dawn leave too, you mentioned?'

'Yes, that's right.'

'Who left about half an hour before Lily.'

'Yes.'

'While you were walking up the lane? The really quite *short* lane?'

'Yes.'

'For half an hour … About …'

'Ye … Well, that's the thing.'

'Let me guess; you thought a couple of hours every half a lifetime was enough with Lily?'

'I'm sorry – this is very difficult for me.'

Tears weren't far off, and his face seemed to change.

'I'm sorry, too—that was facetious of me. I'm making no allowances for what must have been an extraordinary meeting with our dear Lily. She said you were a lovely person, by the way. May I ask—how did it feel to meet up with her after all this time?'

'It was amazing!'

Was that true? How much should I tell him?

'When I found out where Lily lived, I could think of nothing else but coming to see her. I was frightened and excited, I guess?'

'Cool—and how did you find out?'

Why don't I just shut up and go?

'Find out what?'

'Where we live—where Lily lives.'

'Oh, just a weird series of coincidences—you wouldn't believe me if I told you.'

'No, perhaps not. Well anyway, she said it was lovely catching up. I can definitely see the likeness between the two of you—strong family genes, eh? And you even blush like her.'

Is he laughing with me or at me? What a dumbass question ~where's that hole in the ground.

'Oh, but it's a compliment, Tabatha! You really do look similar—extraordinary. So you're … what did Lily say … thirty-one yesterday? Well, very happy belated birthday to you.'

He leant forward and kissed the side of her burning cheek. As she moved back, he gently pulled her forward to kiss the other side.

'Jersey rules. We're much nearer to France than England, and they go for three kisses, so two it is over here—a happy medium.'

He let go, and she put her hands down by her sides, a schoolgirl in front of the headmaster.

'Anyhow, I hear you're going back today? Such a short visit, but at least I understand the two of you will be meeting up again in England soon?'

Really?

'Oh, yes, but only if she has the time, of course.'

'Nonsense, there's nothing more important than family. Always remember that.'

He broke eye contact and looked out of the vast window—William's mind was suddenly far away.

Don't break the silence. Do NOT break it, woman.

He drifted back. It was the clipped-smile expression she'd come to fear so deeply.

'Was the bond still there, even after twenty years?'

Tabatha was stunned at the question. She was also confused.

'Yes, of *course* it was—how could it *not* be? And it's thirty years—over thirty years, actually.'

'But … hold on … it can't be that long—you'd have been one—less than one?'

'And?'

'Well, Lily said you were ten the last time she saw you.'

'Excuse me?'

'Well, I can't imagine a baby being much use on a punt in the middle of the River Cam. Or swinging on a tree rope and falling into the river—now that would be *some* achievement!'

He laughed, and her confusion was drifting to annoyance.

'Lily said she got soaked rescuing you, and Auntie went mad when she saw the state of your dress. You remember it, right? I assumed that must be one of the things you reminisced over yesterday?'

It was absurd enough that Tabatha wondered if she was somehow dreaming.

'My '*auntie went mad*'?'

'No, not *your* auntie—*Lily's* auntie—your mum. Is it Tracy, or something like that?'

Get out of here now. RIGHT now, before you faint.

'Can I have my phone, please.'

'Oh, Lily has it with her. She was going to drop it off to your guesthouse on the way back from Pilates. She reckoned she'd bump into you before you left for the airport.'

'Thanks for meeting me, Mr. Levington, and sorry for intruding like this. I'll be going now—I know the way out.'

She shook his hand as hard as she could, glaring into his eyes.

'I can give you a lift down the hill?'

'No thanks.'

'*Not this lifetime*,' she muttered under her breath.

Tabatha was crying as she reached the main gates.

*

'Oh dear, has he upset you, sweetie?'

Normal service had been resumed as Juan managed to open the door for her this time, passing a silver tissue-box before closing it again.

Tabatha could think of few things less cool than public sobbing, but there was nothing she could do about it. She buried her face in a wad of Kleenex.

'I don't exist. Not in her eyes.'

Filly slid across the bench seat, and the girl felt the frail arms of her newest and oldest friend around her.

Why does this singular act of kindness make the tears flow harder? Why is that so often the case?

She cried until she could hardly breathe.

'Why does my mum have to die all over again?'

'Sshhh, it's okay. It's going to be okay.'

She was whispering to Tabatha. Juan had made the immensely stylish decision to vacate the car and gently kick a non-existent pebble on the lane.

Lady Philippa Matchan née Schultz caught his eye and imperceptibly nodded. How very right she was to be giving this special man a very substantial part of her fortune, whatever that may be—only Quentin, her lawyer, truly knew.

Juan would find a partner when freed from her employ, a life-partner she hoped, another man, naturally. His devotion to her prevented a private life—his choice, she knew—it was how he wanted it.

He was Portuguese, from the island of Madeira, going back there twice a year to be with his large family. At her insistence, of course. She'd peeped at one or two holiday snaps—perhaps twenty people from very young to impossibly ancient—sitting on a long table under orange grove trees, all toasting the camera.

She'd only been able to look for a moment, or she'd have been in exactly the emotional state her poor girl was in now.

Whilst glimpsing those photos, she had made the decision. Juan would have the ability to house his whole family in a vast home, pinned to a cliff above the sparkling, iridescent sea. At least, that was her vision—she hoped it was his.

And Madge, dear Madge, would live just where she was now. Again, it was what Filly believed the old lady would most want. No change in the lifestyle she'd known forever. Except, of course, the manor would belong to Madge.

If there was a heaven, and she'd always maintained there would be, then God willing, she'd be able to look down and see someone looking after Madge, in the manner she'd looked after the current owner.

All pure conjecture, but one thing was certain—strictly private and strictly certain—neither Juan nor Madge would have long to wait.

It was a blessing from the-Man-upstairs that she'd met Tabatha.

Harley Street had done their best, they really had, but the occupants of that famous street had enjoyed their last excessive contribution from her.

How mysterious a lifetime could be.

'Tabatha? Listen to your wise old owl, sweetheart.'

The girl surfaced from the shredded wad of damp tissue.

'It's not as it seems. A whole lot of life experience tells me that something is awry.'

'Lily's got my phone. He said she was going to drop it back to my guesthouse.'

'Enough said, child. Juan?'

'Oh, hello again.'

It was the receptionist who'd initially checked her in.

'Have you forgotten something?'

'I'm just waiting for someone—is it okay if I sit in the bar?'

'Sure, of course. I'll get a waiter to take your order.'

'I'm not sure I can eat anything at the moment. Would it be alright to just have a glass of water?'

And her wait began. She was facing the bar, a large wall-mounted clock to one side. A few moments later, she turned the other way—the minutes were going by way too slowly.

'Anything else I can get you?'

'Maybe a glass of white?'

'We've got a promotion on one at the moment.'

The waitress consulted her notes.

'It's called *'The Dreamer,'* produced by Philip Shaw. It's a 2013 and then a word I can't pronounce—*'Viognier,'* or something like that? A large glass for the price of a small.'

'It sounds expensive—where's it from?'

'Not at all—only six-pounds-fifty. And it's from Australia—New South Wales it says here.'

Tabatha smiled ironically.

'Well, of course it is.'

'You know it, then?'

'No, not at all, but it just made me think of someone. Yes, one of those sounds great, thanks.'

'Sure, coming right up. Sandra said you were waiting for someone—shall I leave a menu for him?'

'No, that's okay, ta. And it's not a *'he.'* It's …'

She thought for a second.

'It's my mum.'

She sipped and wondered, staring at the liquid.

How far away were you made from where Grant lives?
  Where Grant should have stayed—he must realise that by now.

Another mouthful.

Why am I like I am?
   Isn't he the nicest guy I've ever met? What am I afraid of?
   I wonder if he's tried to call or message me?
   Maybe, maybe not. I'll know soon enough …

'Hello.'

Tabatha jumped back into the real world. Her mother stood in front of her—dark, figure-hugging, gym gear—spotless trainers.

'Oh! Hi Lily.'

She stood up, and they hugged.

'Can I have one too? But first, *dah-dah.*'

She fiddled in a shoulder-mounted designer bag and produced the missing phone.

'I know how insane it can be when you lose it. I'm just so relieved I could get it back to you before you left. I mean, how would I have managed to contact you if you'd already gone?'

'True. Or I you.'

The comment sank home almost immediately.

'Thanks anyway.'

'Don't mention it—I was concerned you wouldn't remember where you'd left it and traipse around everywhere looking. Nightmare.'

She ordered a glass of the same wine, and they sat down.

'I actually remembered exactly where it was—on that glass table in your hall.'

'Impressive. You have a much better memory than I do, but then you're a lot younger.'

'Yes—sixteen years younger, I'm told.'

'Indeed, it was.'

Lily fiddled with her reddish-brown bobbed hair. It was a pointless exercise as she'd already made sure it was perfect after her workout.

Tabatha took her time on the last drop of wine, putting the glass down and nodding to their waitress.

She couldn't remember at what point in her life stress had equalled alcohol. Nevertheless, it had, and now wasn't the time to break that cycle.

Breathe.
Fuck's sake—breathe.

'I didn't know you were going to bring my phone to me, so I went up to the farm to collect it.'

Lily took a sip from her glass, noticeably larger than previous ones.

'You did? Was Dawn there?'

The colour was draining from her complexion, the foundation not quite able to fully disguise such a rapid change of shade.

'No, she'd already left.'

'So … was the house empty?'

'It was quite frustrating—I tried the doorbell three times.'

'Damn, I'm sorry you wasted your …'

'But there was piano music coming from somewhere—jazz, I believe.'

'Was there now?'

Lily's glass was empty. Tabatha signalled for another.

'I have to be honest. You know how it is when you have to be honest, right?'

Nod—a slow one—no words—Tabatha took it as a request to continue.

329

'I tried the front door, and it was unlocked. My phone wasn't on the table, and the music was coming from upstairs, so I just assumed you'd be up there, listening to a CD or whatever.'

'So ... you went upstairs?'

The waitress deftly placed the refill in Lily's floating hand, though the woman seemed oblivious.

Again, no words. A replenishment gulp.

'Well, I figured it would have been rude not to. In for a penny, in for a pound, right? Oh, and I took my shoes off.'

'You what?'

Lily seemed hypnotically mesmerised.

'Shoes? Off? I took them off—before going up the stairs?'

'Right.'

Gulp.

'Talking of feet, William's were bare. Oh, or should I say '*Mr Levington*?''

Silence again, though louder—fairly deafening.

'And my choice had therefore been vindicated, so to speak. You know—about taking my shoes off?'

Tabatha took a sip. This was going swimmingly—so much better recalling than live.

'I'm afraid I made him jump. I felt bad, actually—he's a very accomplished pianist. I have to admit I was really impressed. Mr Levington, William, your husband, whichever you prefer—he was excellent. Oh yes, and then we talked.'

'*Talked.*'

Delivered robotically.

It didn't sound like a question, but Tabatha continued regardless.

'Yes, I think that's a fair description of what took place. *Social intercourse* if you prefer?'

330

Gulp.

'I'll confess, our little chat was about as one-sided as this one. It's likely to end at the same stage as well.'

'Stage?'

'Uhuh, '*stage*'. The *stage* of make-believe and fantasy, where you and I find ourselves on the River Cam, I believe? Oh, and big thanks, by the way—I was probably a bit too young to be grateful at the time, but cheers for the rescue from inevitable drowning.'

She gave a sarcastic thumbs-up, the waitress mistaking it as the signal for another round—not a disaster under the circumstances.

'So, we're *cousins*? Sweet. And you're cool about us sharing an '*Auntie Tracey*,' even though the '*auntie*,' as such, doesn't exist? And even though Tracey no longer exists, either?'

And at that moment, Tabatha loathed the expensively-beautiful woman in front of her; really and truly hated her.

'I can explain.'

'Oh, I hope so. I *SOOO* hope so, *Mrs Levington*.'

She leant forward and tried to put her hand on Tabatha's, but the girl was an ocean away from reconciliation, never mind the River Cam.

'Please don't call me '*Mrs Levington*,' Tabatha. Don't do that to me—*please*?'

'*Miss Barnes*? I guess that's who you were the last time we met. Well, apart from when you threw me out of your oh-so-very-posh home yesterday, when you'd morphed into Mrs Gazillionaire Levington.'

'Please, darling, let me ex …'

'Don't you fucking *DARE* call me that! Only my parents get to call me that, and you are *NOT* one of those.'

She stood up abruptly, and the two empty wine glasses tipped onto the table. The waitress had two more full ones in her hand, exchanging them as unobtrusively as she could manage.

Lily stood and attempted to put her hand on Tabatha's shoulder, but she shrugged it off.

'Give me just five minutes, then go. At least you'll know everything, then. One for the road, then you can forget about me forever.'

She picked up both wines and passed one to Tabatha, offering to chink glasses.

There's that brave smile—that brave fucking smile—haunting me, taunting me.
I hate you.
Run away—NOW!

She watched a single tear fall from her birth-mother's face. It brushed Lily's cheekbone and was gone. The eyes showed no brimming of tears and no pinkness. Just one tear.

Tabatha sat back down, theatrically looking at her watch, the irony not wasted on Lily.

'When you were born, I was still sixteen. My boyfriend was much older than me—twenty-four by then. Maybe it's not such a big deal nowadays, but it was then. My parents nearly disowned me when I moved in with him a few months earlier, then completely cut me adrift when I told them I was pregnant. I've never seen them again. It hurts me to this day, but that's how it is. I *do* know how you feel, okay?'

'So why be so affectionate—loving—to me, then throw me out of your home? Why no phone number? Do you know what that felt like? Feels like?'

332

'I know, and I'll never be able to say how sorry I am, but listen to me, I'm begging you. Four months pregnant and all I had was you and my boyfriend, and suddenly no parents to fall back on in an emergency.

'And then you went to London to work—I know that.'

'I made a big mistake. No, I made *two* big mistakes. The first was that I hadn't told my partner I was pregnant. The second was a much bigger mistake.'

She took a small sip of her wine and continued.

'We were at a bar one Friday night, and he was pressing me to have more to drink. He didn't understand why I used to drink plenty and have a laugh, and now I was making half a pint last me for ages. I told him why—I told him about you.'

'And he left you.'

'The very next day. I'd gone into town to window shop—we had very little to spend, so I hardly ever came back with anything.'

'Excuse the lack of sympathy—you seem to have turned things around a little bit.'

Lily held a hand up.

'Just hear me out, darl … Just listen another minute.'

When did I start to be so cold?
Why did I start to be so cold?
Have I been frozen forever?

Then the cyclic, never-ending image of the girl's back—Rick's face peering over a bobbing, slender shoulder, rapidly turning ashen.

Where it had been cold and soothing, the wine now tasted warm and acrid.

'I looked in the shops for baby clothes, but I didn't know which colour—pink or blue. So, I made a decision, there and then—I remember it so clearly even now—*especially* now, actually.

'I was due a scan the following week, and I'd ask them to tell me what sex you were. Your dad would be there as well, and we could share the news. He'd given me absolutely no indication at the pub that he wouldn't be happy with that. In fact, he'd bought a bottle of sparkling wine to celebrate.'

'And?'

'I got back to our crappy little flat, and he'd gone. No message, nothing. He'd cleared out everything—there was no trace that I lived with anyone—he'd evaporated off the face of the earth.'

'But you phoned him?'

'For the rest of the day, and into the evening and the night. I couldn't sleep, so I just carried on straight through and into Sunday, hitting the redial button every few minutes. And then it was midnight—I was shattered—physically and mentally. Then life interrupted, and I realised I had to work the next morning—bills to pay which I couldn't manage on my own. And I had nobody.'

'You had me.'

Layers of bitterness were gradually falling from Tabatha's body armour.

'Yes, I had you. Eventually, I fell asleep, but the light woke me—it was late June, and the days were long. I thought about your life beginning in a few short months, and what it would be like for you. Then I *knew* what I had to do. I walked out onto the street and up the road to Kilburn Underground Station.'

She looked away, and Tabatha thought it might be the end of the story.

Lily was uttering words before she turned back to look into her daughter's eyes.

'I'm so sorry—so *terribly* sorry for what you're going to hear. I walked down the steps to the train. I sat down on a bench—it was still very early, and there weren't many people about. I felt the warmth of the air in the tunnel as the train approached the station. I remember how comforting the heat felt, and that was something I was craving—*comfort*'

Tabatha's scalp was starting to prickle.

'I stood up and walked to the waiting-line near the end of the platform. As I saw the lights of the train, I stepped to the edge and put my foot out into the air.'

Tabatha closed her eyes and shook her head, slowly and repeatedly, in denial.

'I thought it was for the best. For both of us.'

The two women looked at each other again—the connectivity only a child and mother can share, crackle-sparking invisibly across the table—synapses and neurons fusing indelibly.

'A guard grabbed me—us—at the point of no return. They'd seen me walk in the station and go through the barrier without paying, so he was sent to sort me out …'

'I don't know what to say.'

And the girl didn't. There was every chance it would never sink in.

'And the rest you know. I was taken into care, gave birth to you, and the parents you deserved came along. Two people who mean as much to me as they do to you.'

She leaned forward again, and this time Tabatha accepted her hand and squeezed it.

'And then you met your husband. So ultimately, it worked out for both of us.'

'Except that's not quite the end of the story. I couldn't get your father out of my mind. I'd still call him or send text messages. Not as frequently, of course, but I never let go of him. I couldn't let go of him. Have you ever known someone like that?'

The saliva evaporated from Tabatha's mouth as she took a deep breath.

'Oh, well sort of, yeah … I guess.'

Vivid images of her dream floated back. Two tanned men squeezed up close in a tiny car, driving towards her—bright teeth, big smiles.

'Perhaps it's the other way around with you? I suspect it is.'

Lily smiled, and there was pride in her eyes.

'I couldn't say. Perhaps one—sort of?'

'The man has good taste. Perhaps you should make his day, one day?'

'Perhaps. So, did you ever hear from him again?'

'I tried calling him from a different number, but still he didn't pick up, so I just resorted to texts in the end, pretending to myself that even though he never replied, he was still reading them. Isn't that hopelessly pathetic? He was my first love. Do you remember your first love? Do you know what it's like when your first love lets you down?'

The surreal image of Rick and Grant faded, replaced by the girl's back.

Why Rick?—

Why?—
WHY?!
Loved you so much. Loved you so much.

'Tabatha?'

'I'm sorry, it's nothing. Please go on—you never heard from him again?'

'When you'd gone to David and Tracey, I started to think about what I could say in my texts that would get him to reply. By that time, I'd have written anything, just to get him back. I knew he'd left me because he'd made me pregnant, and I suspected he was going to stay away forever because I had a child. I assumed he couldn't come to terms with that— couldn't handle it. I know this sounds terrible—I don't mean it to—can you understand how I felt?'

The image was fading as she removed Rick from her heart for the umpteenth time. It would never stop—she knew it would *never* stop.

'I think so, yes.'

'It's just that I'd tried to kill you and failed, but now I knew I had to succeed, or I'd just die. I couldn't live without him anymore.'

Pop—the final vestiges of her unending nightmare melted to blackness.

'I told him you'd died. I sent him a text and said I'd lost you during the birth.'

Tabatha felt the weight of the words crushing her chest.

'You told my father I was dead?'

'I had to—don't you see? And because I thought he was still terrified of having children if we got back together, I told him I'd been so damaged in your birth that I couldn't bear any more children. You have to understand, Tabatha? You do, don't you?'

Lily's superficial beauty was still visible for all to see.

Tabatha felt ashamed at the self-indulgent vanity, but there was no doubting their similarity of appearance—it was an unquestionably startling resemblance.

Flawless skin, high cheekbones, darkest brown eyes oozing with an air of confidence and authority. Slim and, in her mother's case, pristinely gym-toned.

And then there was the posture—exuding sexuality yet at the same time, a *don't-fuck-with-me* stance. A minefield for a man, and only the very strongest would survive.

But just beneath that sophisticated veneer there was something menacing, and this was what Tabatha was seeing, *feeling*, now. This presumably rare feeling of exposed vulnerability was being replaced by something ugly in defence.

Tabatha loathed to admit it, but she was beginning to find her mother disturbing. She'd never know what her father was like, much less meet him, but she felt a growing sympathy for the man.

Still, it could have been worse—a *lot* worse—he could have ended up back with Lily.

'But it didn't work, did it? He never contacted you again. Perhaps that was for the best.'

The woman scoffed and downed her drink, banging the base onto the table.

'Tabatha, come on, girl—of *course* it worked! Actually, it was rather tragic, because I'd got it wrong all along—can you believe that?'

It made no sense, and she wasn't sure she wanted to hear any more.

'Turns out he'd left me because he couldn't bear the thought of not being able to give his child a proper upbringing because he wasn't earning enough. Turns out he assumed I was devastated at the thought of bringing up a child. He thought I never wanted one in the first place and would certainly never want any more.'

Her voice was rising in volume, and Tabatha was thankful it was only the waitress within earshot.

'So, turns out he's been spending every waking hour trying to make enough money to get a mortgage on a house, eventually planning to come back and present me with the keys. A kind of special surprise. Oh, and he gets a non-reversible vasectomy to prove to me he means what he says—if I don't want any more kids, then neither does he. It'll just be the three of us—happy families forever. Sweet, eh?'

She lunged for her glass and took a dry gulp.

'Shit, two more please—quick as you like.'

Tabatha turned around and signalled that just one was required—none if the waitress was sensible.

'Where was I? Oh yeah, so he's so devastated about the news of your death—I mean, he's totally bloody *distraught*. And it's a mad irony, of course, because we'd both like kids, but he's going to be firing blanks forever, and I've already been a naughty fibber and told him I can't have any more. Madness, right? But ten-out-of-ten for a Top Trumps sympathy card, eh?'

 Lily cackled, and Tabatha was beginning to see a very sick woman emerge from the glamourous façade.

'But it never happened, and then you met your husband?'

'What? You've lost me.'

'You've been married to Mr Levington for thirty years.'

Tabatha realised, a little too late, that this wasn't news she should have been privy too. By the looks of Lily, however, it was likely to slip well under the radar.

'Yes. And? Where the hell's my wine? Waitress?? Fuck's sake.'

Her body was swaying, her eyes glassy and unfocussed, hardly built to consume large amounts of alcohol. Tabatha was bad enough, but she'd fortunately had the benefit of more drinking time, and she'd shied away from finishing more than a sip of the last glass.

'Well my father obviously didn't end up with you, or you wouldn't be married to your husband.'

'Darling, what part of, '*MY HUSBAND'S YOUR DAD,*' don't you get?'

Tabatha's little world stood rock-still as her ears rang painfully, her jaw fixed rigidly, half-open.

Then the world wobbled precariously.

I can't breathe.

I don't want to breathe.

Finally, it came crashing down around her, in a smoke-filled heap of rubble.

'So now you know why he can't *ever* meet you—can't *ever* know who you are—can't know you even *exist*. And finally— *FINALLY*—you know why I had to hustle you out of our

340

home. *Phew*! So, no hard feelings, right darling? *WAITRESS?!*

Tabatha was numb—there were just no feelings left, physically or emotionally. Just a sickening void of emptiness.

She slowly stood and picked her phone up, not daring to look at Lily. Distance was needed from this woman—needed now—even sooner. Tabatha headed for the sanctuary of reception.

Lily had swivelled around in her seat, shouting at her daughter's departing back.

'Oh darling, no silliness please? You know—no covertly contacting Daddy and blubbing. We still adore each other, and I know you wouldn't want to mess things up between your *real* mummy and daddy. And you'd be doubly hurting your father—Jersey is *more* than favourable to us ladies in divorce courts nowadays. I'm sure neither of us would want to see Daddy back to square one again, would we? That would be such a lonnng way down. *Waitress!* Geez, what does a lady have to do to get a drink in this fucking hole?!'

18

'GOOD AFTERNOON, Madam. Nice to see you again—how are you?'

She didn't recognise him at first, immersed in a stream of messages from Grant.

'Oh, hello. Yes, I guess—I'm okay, thanks.'

The man who'd checked her out on Saturday.

'Coming to stay with us again?'

'Umm … no—not this time.'

It was difficult to be adequately sociable while trying to take on board what she was reading.

He was thinking of coming to Jersey—Christ.

He was coming to Jersey—bloody hell.

He'd landed in Jersey—Oh my God!

There were many tasks to carry out for the duty manager of a small hotel (he liked to think of it as that. Irritatingly, and by law, the word '*Guesthouse*' appeared above the main entrance). In a similar vein, although a group-director had confirmed a tie unnecessary, he still maintained this smarter style of appearance.

Of all his myriad duties there was, above everything, just three golden rules:

1: Friendly and courteous to guests at all times. *And smile!*
2: Helpful to guests at all times. *And smile!*
3: Absolute discretion at all times. *And smile!*
Of this Holy Trinity, there was one be-all and end-all.
Discretion. *'Discretion, discretion, discretion.'*

Without this unwritten backbone law of tourism, well …
Jersey would have an even higher divorce rate (though it
could technically never overtake its own world number one
position, of course).

Which was why he couldn't believe what he was about to
do. It made no sense and could certainly cost him his job,
probably never to work in this industry again.

But, despite all that, there was something nagging him—
something he'd done wrong, *very* wrong.

He wanted to make it right—that was all.

'Madam?'

'Goodbye. Oh sorry, G'DAY.'
'Oh no. Oh noooooo.'

'Errr, Madam?'
'Excuse me? I'm sorry—I'm just reading a message. Yes?'
She didn't mean to be short, but the man happened to be
in the epicentre of her disintegrating life. Slap bang dead
centre.

Who's left?
There's nobody left.
I should have died—Lily was right—I'm better off dead.

A text message flashed:

'Tabatha, I hope you're alright. I've tried to call you many times. Let me know when you arrive. I will pick you up from the station. Love from Dad.'

The guilt wrapped around the pain, and Tabatha felt herself go light-headed.

'Madam, are you alright? Can I get you a glass of water? Sit yourself down here.'

She passed out on a sofa beside the reception desk.

The man was holding a pint glass with water in it, the waitress hovering behind him. A couple stared at her on their way to the lift.

'How long have I been …?'

'Not long at all. You just went pale and fainted, Madam. You've only been out a few minutes, not even that. Here— sip some water.'

As she drank, the noise of a screaming engine encroached, the gearbox crunching in sympathetic tandem.

Tabatha peered out of the window to the road beyond. A red sports car was snaking its way up the road, closely avoiding the kerb before crossing the white line in the middle.

'*Bloody maniac*. Do excuse my language, Madam. She staggers out of here, and now she's driving—I should phone the police before that woman kills someone.'

The waitress whispered something in his ear.

'Oh, forgive me, do you know her, Madam? I'm most dreadfully sorry.'

Tabatha was still staring out of the window. Dusk was beginning to settle, a drizzle now smearing the view.

'No … no, I don't know her.'

'Well, in that case …'

He turned to the waitress.

'Best report it to the police, Elaine. The registration number's in the car-park book.'

'Madam, before you took a turn, I was going to inform you of something. It's none of my business, and please stop me if I'm encroaching in any way, but a man was here yesterday. He was asking of your whereabouts, purporting to be your brother.'

She sat up, and the back of her head thumped in objection.

'My brother? I don't have a brother. What did he look like?'

Her world had toppled off its axis today, so anything was possible now.

'Well Madam, my belief is that it wasn't your brother. He was a young person like yourself, perhaps mid-twenties, and an Australian accent. He told me he came from Sydney.'

'When? When was this?!'

'As I say, yesterday—late afternoon.'

'Where is he? Did he say where he was going?'

There was desperation in her voice—a yearning to make contact with him at any cost.

'My belief is that he went back to the airport. He'd come straight from there, assuming you'd be here. He'd have had plenty of time to get the nine-p.m. flight back to Gatwick if that's where he was indeed headed.'

'Fuck! *No! FUCK!*

She scrambled for her phone.

As the manager watched, she pecked the keyboard, getting more and more agitated.

'He's blocked me—blocked everything.'

The man hung his head in shame.

'Madam, I have a woeful confession to make. I fear that in giving him limited answers to

the questions he was pressing me for, I may have given him the impression that ...'

He faltered, trying to think how best to impart the information he was struggling to deliver.

'What? What impression? *What did you tell him?!*'

'Well, he asked me why you'd checked out and where you'd gone. I didn't know, of course, but he pushed me to a point where I had to divulge a couple of details to ... oh dear, how do I put this ... to *placate* him.'

Ice was clawing at the tattered remains of her heart.

'He asked how you'd left and who you'd left with, and I may have inadvertently mentioned that you left in a very large and expensive Bentley, with another man.'

'*WHAT?!*'

'I was just about to point out to him that the man was, in fact, the chauffeur, but ...'

And for the second time that weekend, someone stormed out of the hotel while he was talking to them.

*

'You sound terribly out of breath, dear—are you alright?'

'Yes. No. Maybe. I'm not sure.'

She was crying as she spoke, tears of desolation mixed with tears of frustration.

'I need your help again. I'm so sor ...'

'Shut-up, Tabatha.'

It was like an oral slap across her face.

'Am I right in thinking time is of the essence?'

'Yes, but ...'

'Where are you—we can be there in ten minutes. *JUAN—BENTLEY.*'

Filly had forgotten to take the phone away from her mouth when summoning her chauffeur-cum-everything, temporarily rendering Tabatha deaf in the left ear.

She gave her location.

'And there's something else—I'm really sorry, but is there any way you can grab all my stuff and bring it with you?'

'Already done.'

'But how did ...'

'Ten minutes, probably eight—don't move.'

The phone clicked before the girl was able to say another word.

Tabatha sat on the brick-topped granite wall of another hotel. Across the road, she watched the activities going on in a local Fire Station. No emergencies, but what looked like a very slick dry-run of a rescue, from a purpose-built four-storey concrete construction.

Other people's business was cathartic. In some strange way, it soothed an exhausted soul.

As it was in Cambridge—it was here. It was everywhere, of course. Life.

She breathed in and out, slowly and deeply. Calm—take control.

She had the time to phone her dad, and his voice was the most calming influence of all. How could he have escaped her mind when all around her, everything was poisoned—ruined? Her pillar, her rock, her dad.

He understood—he'd been worried, but he was okay—was she? He'd been looking up things on the computer—he thought he'd worked out how to cook a pizza. He'd bought

all the ingredients, and they could wait—tonight or
tomorrow—even Tuesday, but there was disappointment in
his voice which he couldn't hide.

And no, he hadn't seen or heard from Grant—should he
have?

I love you so much, Dad.

'I love you, Dad.'
   'Oh … yes, me too. Absolutely. Hold on a minute.'
   She thought she could almost hear him mentally prepare.
   'And I love you, too. Tabatha. Tabby.'
   The words went straight as an arrow, right the way
through her heart. It was piercingly painful joy, and she cut
the call only a fraction before she cried out in the drizzle that
had now permeated its way through all her clothing yet again.

She ran around the back of the car as Juan opened the door
for her. She still hadn't seen him look directly into her eyes
once during this whole insane weekend, his head now
stooped, the top of the black chauffeur's cap facing her.
   She took the hat off and kissed him on the cheek,
remembering the two-for-Jersey rule another dad had taught
her.
   'Thank you, Juan. You are one, exceptional, guy.'
   She stepped into the limousine, and the owner looked at
her.
   'Where to, sweetie, or am I allowed to guess?'
   Tabatha nodded.
   'Anabel Tomb Farm, please Juan.'

The gates were mysteriously open, but brief further investigation revealed the answer—the lower stainless-steel bars and wooden frame on both sides were damaged.

'Oh dear. Why do I have a feeling you know the cause of this?'

'I can't be certain, but I'd probably place a small bet on it, yeah. Can we drive down this time?'

'Can we just! I've been looking forward to this all weekend—thought you'd never ask. How exciting—I get to see the fabled Levington residence at last. Juan?'

They pulled up beside a police car and the Ferrari Dino. They could only see the left side of the little red masterpiece of automotive beauty, but the front had been crumpled in, deep gouges running down its feline-like bodywork for the entire length of the car. From the state of the gates, it was reasonable to assume the other side had suffered a similar fate.

'Meu Deus, meu deus.'

Juan was visibly horrified. Tabatha watched as he performed the sign of the cross on himself.

'He's very keen on religion,' Filly whispered.

'And Ferraris?'

'It would appear so. Very nice place, dear. Nouveau, you know, but nice in its own way.'

The lights in the kitchen allowed sight of William Levington, peering at the unknown vehicle outside. She could see him, but his vision couldn't possibly penetrate through the darkness and deeply-tinted glass.

Looks are and will always be, subjective. But his eyes and maybe his mouth—certainly the way he squinted—gave every appearance of confusion.

You are my dad.
You really are my dad.

She touched the car window with her fingers, framing his face, burning the image in her mind.

'As long as you like, dearie—we have all the time in the world,' and only Filly knew how very untrue those words were.

'Oh, I'll not be long at all—just a few minutes.'

A few minutes …
   Or a lifetime …

The back door was already open as she walked under the alcove.

'I wondered who that was. Tabatha, how lovely to see you again. I thought you'd already flown back?'

'I'm on the last flight out tonight—just popped in on my way to the airport.'

He leant down to kiss both her cheeks, and this time it felt so very right.

'Come on in. I'm afraid Lily might be a few minutes—a bit of a bump, and the police are just taking down details. Purely routine—I'm sure it won't take long.'

She followed him to the kitchen, taking in the way he walked—trying to observe everything.

'That's some car outside—a private-hire taxi of sorts?'

'Something like that.'

They entered the kitchen to the sound of voices. Some thirty metres away, Lily and a policeman stood by the far wall of the conservatory. Her voice was slurred and raised, the officer attempting to calm the situation down.

Tabatha watched William pick up the controller she'd operated herself yesterday, and the glass dividing walls cut the kitchen off from the conservatory.

The operation was silent, but bright downlighters were reflecting off the movement and caught Lily's attention.

Their eyes met, and the expression was a replica of Friday evening's glimpse from her husband's car—abject horror.

'Can I get you a drink while we wait for Lily?'

'Oh no, no really, that's fine. I'm late for my flight already.'

'Right, of course. Sooo …?'

So, you're my dad—my real dad—and I love you.
If you knew who I was, I think you'd get to love me too.
And then we'd all live happily ever after.
In another lifetime. .

'So, I simply came around to give Lily a hug goodbye.'

'Oh, but you'll be seeing her again soon, she said—over in England?'

'Well, that's the thing, you see—I've decided to emigrate.'

Surprise on his face.

That's how I look when I'm surprised!

'A sudden decision?'

'Yes, very sudden.'

Lily's face was moving from the policeman's notebook to her daughter's face, then back again. They caught each other's eyes, and Tabatha winked at her from just above William's shoulder.

Pure and unadulterated hate. And there it was …

351

Flash—Bedroom.
   Flash—Girl's back.
   Flash—Rick's face—but now you see my face.
   Flash—And there it is—that's my face—but now it's yours.

Tabatha now had Lily's full and undivided attention, much to the officer's irritation.

'I really must be going, Mr Levington. Perhaps I can ask you to pass something on to Lily for me?'

'Please, it's William—and of course, what is it?'

'It's this.'

She moved close and went up on her toes, put her hands around his back and rested her chin on his shoulder, their cheeks touching.

Her eyes closed, and she loved purely, deeply, unconditionally.

It was a forever moment—*her* forever moment.

Her eyes opened directly into Lily's through the glass door, and the hatred was breathtaking.

So she closed them again.

Tabatha moved quickly to the back door before he could say anything or keep up with her.

She turned in her seat and watched him, studied him, standing in front of the police car.

He waved, but his hand and arm were motionless, and God knows why, but she knew that would be how he waved.

Then the hand went to his lips, and just before they turned the corner, he blew her a kiss.

Bye-bye, Tabatha Levington.

Bye-bye.

*

'Better now?'

She turned to her companion. For the first time, the woman looked tired, though the sparkle was still there in her eyes.

Lady Philippa seemed to have aged, even in the complimentary ambient light of the Bentley's interior.

'Yes. Thank you.'

'Feel like you've turned a corner?'

'Yes, I do—I truly do.'

'The future's more important than the past, young lady.'

'I don't under …'

'Yes, you *do* understand. Let me ask you a question—do you know how many times a heart can be broken?'

'I … Well no, I don't know.'

'Nor does anyone, and until the scientists have irrevocable proof of that number, life teaches us that it's best to continually risk breaking our hearts in search of happiness, rather than protecting it for fear of eternal sadness. Phew, now that's philosophical for an old woman, isn't it?'

'You're not old, Filly.'

'And *you* can't lie, dear girl.'

She tapped the back of Tabatha's hand, then rested it there as they both stared ahead.

'Don't let him go, Tabatha—not this time. Go to him, wherever he is.'

She turned to the woman with a mix of bewilderment and awe. Filly was still looking ahead, towards the flare of white xenon beams cutting through the dark lanes.

353

Tabatha studied the elegant side profile—even now, the Lady of the Manor was beautiful. The light created a silhouette around her head, giving the appearance of something magical and other-worldly.

'Are we going to the airport?'

Tabatha had no clue where they were, nor any idea of the time. She looked at her watch.

'Oh. I've missed my flight, haven't I?'

'Yes and no. You'd be hard pushed to make the nine-o'clock. Besides, Juan had already discovered it was full anyway.'

The girl sighed quietly, and her head dropped. She felt Filly squeeze her hand gently.

'Which is why one has to make exceptions for scheduled airlines.'

Tabatha saw the airport sign straight across the roundabout, but they took the first exit left instead.

'Where are we going?'

'To the private aviation port. There's a little jet waiting for you. They're in no rush—when you turn up, they go.'

Tabatha turned to Filly with mouth wide open, unable to comprehend her words.

'I … I don't understand.'

'There's nothing to understand, young lady. Time is of the essence—you think I don't know that? In any case, this speeds things up considerably—they'll take you directly to Cambridge Airport.'

'But that'll cost a *fortune!* I'll never be able to repay you.'

'Correct. You'll never be able to repay me because I'll never allow you to.'

Tabatha was about to object, but Filly steered her focus away.

'Look, isn't that a coincidence? There's your father's aircraft sitting next to your one. It's a bit vast, isn't it?'

The car was approaching an impeccably-dressed man standing on the pavement in front of the reception area, a black umbrella held open in expectation. Juan had locked eyes with him, and it was clearly going to be a race for Tabatha's door, which the driver couldn't hope to win.

'How did you know? How *could* you know?'

'Look at the registration on the fuselage—'G-BILL'—I think it's a safe bet, dear.'

'No, I meant, how did you know he was ...'

The door opened even before Juan had left the driver's seat. His spoils would be reduced to her bag in the boot—access to which only he had, having remotely locked it three seconds ago.

'Well, this is it, my special and dearest girl. It's time for us to say goodbye, and you to jump on that plane. Give me a hug—I won't get out if you don't mind.'

They embraced as if mother and daughter, or perhaps grandmother and granddaughter.

'I'll never forget you, Filly. I'll come and see you again very soon, I promise.'

'Of course you will. Now be gone and get that man of yours.'

The woman turned away. Not since the camps, had anyone seen her cry.

Juan passed her the backpack as an umbrella was held over her head. She whispered, for fear of Filly hearing.

'How does she know everything, Juan? How is that possible?'

His reply was a barely perceptible smile, and then his face turned to the drizzly night sky.

No words followed—he turned and got back in the car, exiting the private car park in silence.

She held up her arm, her hand still. The last time she'd felt this sad, her mother had just died.

'The Manor, Lady P?'

'Not this time, Juan—Plan B, I think.'

*

'I'm afraid I don't have a ticket.'

The man smiled as they walked through what looked to be the reception of a 5-star boutique hotel.

'Oh, and my passport's in my bag—just hold on a minute.'

'That won't be necessary, Miss Mercer—we already have a copy from when the flight was booked. Besides, you're a guest of Lady Philippa.'

He held the air-side door open for her, and they walked across the tarmac to the jet.

'Welcome to our Cessna Citation M2, Madam.'

There were two pilots standing either side of the aircraft's steps, one boasting one more gold stripe on his sleeves than the other. Except for that, they appeared identical in appearance.

I'll leave you in the capable hands of Richard and James—they're fully aware of the urgency of your trip.

'Pedal to the metal, chaps.'

The man with one less stripe followed her into the plane, the umbrella coming down at the last possible moment.

The co-pilot had seen Tabatha covertly trying to use her phone to send a message before take-off and courteously suggested she use the phone in her armrest at any point she wanted.

Before calling her dad, she'd enquired about a taxi from the airport, but been informed there was a driver waiting to take her to the destination of her choice.

'Hi Dad, just a quick call—I'll be home later this evening—we're just about to leave now.'

She put a hand over the mouthpiece and asked the pilot how long it would take to Cambridge, then added the three-mile drive from the airport to home. What she was about to say didn't really seem possible.

'About an hour.'

'Splendid. You're in London now, about to get a train?'

'Something like that, yes.'

'I'll wait outside the station. It feels like you've been gone for ages.'

'Don't worry; I'm being dropped back. Love you—gotta go now, Dad.'

If ever she'd doubted there really was an '*other half*' which lived and roamed the globe, she doubted no longer.

She knew this would never happen again in her life, so tried to seize the moment and enjoy the ride.

Tabatha looked again at the messages from Grant, and the misery overwhelmed her. With no way of contact any longer, all she could do was go to his apartment.

Desperate to compose a message even if she had no way of getting it to him, she went to her Notes app. If nothing else, writing something would perhaps be therapeutic.

'G'day – that's a hello, not a goodbye. Your Aussie language is weird. A few moments ago I did something I thought I'd never do – I turned down a glass of champagne – VINTAGE champagne! And not just a glass either – I could have had the whole fricking bottle – FOR FREE! Now I'd tell you where I was offered it, but you wouldn't believe me. But actually, you're indirectly responsible for the whole thing. No, I tell a lie, you're DIRECTLY responsible, Grant Davis.

Back to that shampoo… I'll never turn down that opportunity again – you'd better believe it – you'd be mad not to.

So here's the deal, and perhaps you'll never ever see or hear these words, but if I liken you to a bottle of vintage champagne, then I guess I've done the same thing, haven't I? I've turned you down, right?

Well if that opportunity were ever to arise again, I wouldn't turn it down this time.

NEVER EVER NEVER.'

As she was contemplating the amount of 'X's to put, a tear hit her phone, directly in the middle of the illuminated screen.

'Everything alright back there?'

'Yeah, guess so. Oh, pedal to the metal, please?'

'Roger that. You heard the lady, James.'

*

'Five or so minutes to Cambridge—seatbelts on, please.'

Tabatha opened the backpack on the seat next to her and rummaged for the passport. Not recognising an unfamiliar object between her fingers, she pulled out a small, padded, bubble envelope.

'For a special girl on your special occasion. Leave this ring with him until the time is right. When he gives it back, you'll KNOW the time is right. God Bless & Happy Life, Your new old friend.'

As Tabatha had exited the car to hold her dad for the first and last time, she'd noticed the ring on Filly's finger. It was impossible to miss—rectangular, emerald-cut, blindingly brilliant, with lustre so deep as to raise doubt if it could be from this planet.

And enormous.

It took her breath away, and it took her back to the only time she'd ever heard her mother swear.

They were in London, in New Bond Street, staring into the window of *Asprey*. Both of them were nearly salivating. She was eighteen.

There was one diamond-ring holding centre stage, given a wide berth and deference by every other ring in the window.

'Now that, Tabby, is what is technically known as a *'Fuck-Off Diamond.'*

She revolved it between two fingers. This could have been that ring. But no—this was actually bigger—grander—maybe way beyond Mum's *'Fuck-Off'* scale.

In her mind's eye, she saw the buff envelope sitting on the car's picnic table in front of Filly, a pen next to it.

All seeing. All knowing. All planned.

19

'TELL ME all about it. Was it as special as you'd hoped, Tabby? I'm so proud of you.'

'There's so much to tell you. I honestly don't know where to start.'

'Why don't we sit down in the lounge. Have you eaten? My pizza-cooking plan might take a while—let's order a takeaway, eh? I'll get the menus—you go put your feet up and switch the telly on.'

She felt dreadful and guilt-ridden.

'Dad, have you seen Grant?'

She tried to keep the desperation out of her voice but found it impossible.

'Not since before you went. I bet he's looking forward to seeing you as much as I was.'

I'd swap my ring for that to be true.

'So, Chinese, Indian, or pizza? Or nip down the road for sushi?'

God, I love you, Dad—please don't ever change a single atom of yourself.

'Can I just do something first? It's really important—I need to run down to Grant's place—I won't be long.'

If he was put out, she couldn't tell.

'A lift? If it helps?'

'It's fine, Dad—I won't be long.'

She kissed his cheek and was gone, running down the road.

At the top of the road, she composed herself—caught her breath.

Jesus, I must look like shit.
How can I have forgotten my make-up bag—not even any lipstick. Christ!

Grateful for the tiniest of mercies, she popped the last two mints from a small plastic box of *'Berry Mints,'* bought as an afterthought at Gatwick airport. It felt like a lifetime ago.

It was cold, and she shoved her hands deep in the parka pockets, feeling the ring against her right hand.

Two mints and a diamond that's probably worth the value of a large house.
And a man who's fifty metres away—my man.
If he still wants me.
If he'll still have me.

Ringing the doorbell again, then again, then again, had its own bitter-tasting *déjà vu*. This time, however, she couldn't kid herself that any person at home may not have heard her.

She rapped on the door with her knuckles, loud enough that nobody within, asleep or otherwise, could fail to hear.

Nothing.

There was a window looking out onto the road—the curtains were drawn, but there were lights on behind them. This meant little—most people left lights on when out, as a form of security, or to help a potential burglar realise they were out, and the coast was clear ...

Despondent, she wandered further down the lane to the private car-parking area, straddling the locked access-barrier.

And there it was.

Her heart leapt with joy—*his* car—his little white Triumph Spitfire—glinting in the reflection of the yellow sodium street lamp above.

Tabatha tried the driver's door handle, and it opened, but then he never locked it. He said it was pointless with a soft top—he said a thief would cut his way into the car in seconds with a Stanley knife.

His voice lifted her—she could hear his voice.

I hear you, Grant.
  I sense you.
  I feel you.

And there it was—her second mystery envelope of the day—sitting, so ominously, on the shiny-black, plastic *'Ambla'* passenger seat.

I miss you and your silly 'Ambla' seats—so very, terribly, fucking much.
  I can see and hear and smell and feel you here now.

It was different to Filly's surprise.

There was instant curiosity with that, free from lurking anxiety, fear, perpetual misery. Curiosity in its purist, childlike form, filled with safe joy.

This was a whole different world.

The clinic-white, self-seal envelope—so flimsy and thin—so formal—promising just one piece of paper within—his thoughts—his decision.

The guilty pen discarded on the carpet—blue ink handwriting from an estate-agent logoed biro, included in the welcome pack of his apartment, no doubt where the envelope was from as well. And the twice-folded piece of A4-sized paper he'd used to tell her his thoughts.

His thoughts. Her fate.

Two words to signify it was her letter.

'*Posh Girl*'

She traced the writing with her finger—the precise swirls— the rhythmic zigs and zags—entirely foreign and unknown to her. Of course they were—how could they not be? All the notes from him, and not one in his handwriting.

Filly's envelope had changed her life, of this she was certain. Tabatha would have it valued, but she already guessed the enormity of the gift.

Life-changing.

Yet the words she still had to read would be more than that, and it was a cold dread that seeped through her body as her finger eased the seal. At that moment, she'd have traded the ring, her world, her life, to see the right words inside.

Life defining.

Hello You,

I wonder what day it is when you read this? IF you read this?

Well, I hope it's still your birthday week, Tabby, and I hope it's still alright to call you that?

First things first. You need to do me a favour – I posted something to your address – the car keys. I've paid for a week's extra parking, so if you could get the old girl out of there before then, I'd be grateful. And in case you want to move her before that arrives, there's a spare key hanging from a string inside my apartment letterbox.

Oh, and in that package there's also a couple of docs and old invoices and stuff from when I restored her. Even some photos while the work was going on (none of me – you're safe – I took those out) and car manuals, old service history etc. – all that crap. And registration papers and insurance stuff – you're fully covered to drive the car.

Stupid Aussie tosser that I am, I'd brought all that stuff with me to Jersey, to give to you on Saturday. (you may notice the car is now registered in your name as well – just send the doc off to the authorities). So yeah - your birthday... THAT Saturday... HAPPY BIRTHDAY! ☺

So the surprise is out and a real bummer that I don't get to see your expression. Mind you, a shitty old Triumph is hardly in the same league as a half-million quid Bentley, I admit. Maybe it'll just be a hassle, but fear not, you can bung it in a classic car auction – maybe you'll get five thousand for her if you're lucky? All yours, Tabby – keep it.

They say it's the thought that counts, right?

Last things last…

PTO

She put her hand on the steering wheel of the car as if it was a small, delicate, pet.

'*No.*'
Whispered.

'*No*!'
Much louder.

'*NO!*'
With every ounce of power in her lungs.

Her head dropped, and she sobbed, wracked with frustration and grief.

I couldn't believe it when you brought your car halfway around the world. I thought you were a bit mad, actually.
And now I know why.
You'd planned everything, hadn't you?
HADN'T YOU?!
Beautiful, special, wonderful, man.

She pinched the bridge of her nose hard. There was pressure building at the base of her neck, and it was crawling upwards.
Tabatha turned the now-crumpled letter over, staring at the blurred words through tears. This was going to kill her.

I thought I was going to explode with anger, but anger at who? How could I direct my fury at you?

It was ALL my fault – EVERYTHING WAS MY FAULT! I wanted so much for us, but I only thought of me. Now I realise what a huge mistake I made.

Even when I knew I was fooling myself - when I was honest with myself about your feelings for me - even then - I still thought I had enough love for both of us.

She couldn't read on.

Please stop.
You don't understand, Grant.
Please come back—I'm begging you.

And then when you decided to go to Jersey on your birthday, I thought that was a disaster at first, but convinced myself it was all fate— everything shifting and realigning to make it all perfect. This is where it was going to happen—where you and I were going to finally come together.

As I said, what a tosser I was and what an idiot I truly am. It was never going to happen for us – it's just that you always knew that – YOU ALWAYS KNEW THAT – but I didn't.

But now I do, Tabby.

The pain was moving right through her skull, pushing towards the forehead in waves of red.

No.

No, no, no.
Please Grant—please God—no.
No more.

You can't contact me—maybe you already found that out, maybe you didn't, maybe it doesn't matter to you. Anyhow, I can't bear the thought of being near you and not with you, so the plan is easy for me. At last, something easy and straightforward for me to understand.

Finally, I get it, Tabby.

gone

forever

Grant x

20

SHE'D NEVER run so fast in her life.

Thoughts flashed through her mind as she sprinted down narrow lanes, laced with the memories of casual strolls, arm through arm, with him.

Myriad random thoughts tumbling through her racing mind, wildly diverse, yet all inextricably linked to and through her heart. To him.

At any and at all costs.

To *him*.

*

Gasping, she was about to barge the front door open when common sense prevailed. Her father would be inside, waiting for her. What would she do; what could she say?

She eased into the house and down the hall, her backpack still unopened, laying against the bottom of the stairs. She'd need it and much more besides, but ultimately, what did she *really* need?

Think. Quickly, just think!

The lights were on in the kitchen, but he wasn't there. Easing the lounge door gently open, she spied him in his armchair, snoozing peacefully in front of the ten o'clock news on television.

A lump in her throat as she knew what she was going to do—*had* to do. He'd understand. Please, let him understand.

Mum? Please help him understand. I know you do, so help him too.

She scribbled a hopelessly inadequate note and left it on the kitchen table, promising to call him and explain everything soon—very soon. As soon as she could.

A week ago, dreading the credit card bill that sat on the hall floor, she'd stifled a cry as she read the bottom line. '*Balance Due ~ £0.00.*'

Tabatha was fully prepared for the worst of news—she knew she'd exceeded her £2,500 limit—not by much, but she'd exceeded it.

Dad had told her it was a present from Mum. There'd be more, quite a lot more, but this was for now. A fresh start.

Thank you. Thank you both so sooooo much. Love you both so much.

She took the stairs two at a time, but as quietly as she could. The small amount of cash in her pocket, nestling next to the freshly replenished credit card, would now be joined by the last of some emergency funds stuffed into a pottery piggy-bank, ironically (and pathetically) sporting the slogan, '*Next Million!*'

She twisted the diamond on her finger and swivelled it inwards so only the platinum band showed, tightening her hand into a fist around the gem. Perhaps no longer ironic or pathetic, she reflected.

Just over twenty pounds if one discarded the shrapnel, all in one and two-pound coins. She opened both hands and stared at the contents of each—the ring—the coins. Yes, perhaps the irony was still there …

Tabatha turned full-circle in her room.

What else? Money, ring, what?
    Passport. Still in backpack, so just take backpack.
    Anything else?

Despite the cold, she was sticky and hot from her exertions. It would probably be some time before she had another opportunity, so she took the quickest of showers and applied the most rudimentary of make-up—there simply was no time for anything else.

Picking up her backpack, she tiptoed into the lounge and looked at her father one last time.

Sorry, Daddy. Love you for all time. Please understand.

She blew him a kiss, took one last look around the hall for any final inspiration as to what she was bound to have forgotten, then pulled the front door quietly shut, leaving in almost identical fashion to the way she'd arrived an hour before.

*

Even the act of pushing her hand through the letterbox and fumbling for the string sent tingling sensations through her.

370

She felt his presence, sharing the space he'd occupied so recently. She allowed herself a moment of fantasy.

Surprise me, Grant. Take my hand. Take it now.
  Be here for me now.

She pulled the string up and brought the decades-worn key through the letterbox, the hope of an attached note abruptly severed.

It was actually some time since she'd driven, and that was only in the automatic family Volvo. Of driving classic cars in general and this Spitfire in particular, she had zero experience, save for watching Grant whilst in the passenger seat.

The engine turned over but didn't fire into life. She tried again with the same result.

It was cold, and she shivered. There was something teasing her mind as condensation escaped her and began to mist the screen. She scoured the sparse dials and buttons with her eyes, and there it was.

She couldn't remember what he'd called it, but when the car was cold, he pulled this lever out before starting the car, gradually pressing it back in as they drove through the first mile or so—when the engine began to warm up.

And bingo. With the engine running, she tried the other switches until the headlights came on. Finally, a fan that blew warm air into the cabin and could be directed at the screen to clear it. The air was initially icy cold on her feet and face, but that would change.

She gingerly exited the car park and took a left at the end of the lane, out onto the main road. After eleven o'clock on a Sunday night and the traffic was almost non-existent.

It was a journey that would take less than 90 minutes, even in this ancient and slow little car.

*

Tabatha pulled onto the hard shoulder of the M25 motorway, just short of Heathrow Airport. An illegal manoeuvre unless it was an emergency, she knew, but it was only for a few moments. Besides, in her mind, this *was* a genuine emergency.

With the knowledge that Grant would be using the return leg of his Emirates ticket to get back home to Sydney, she used her phone to discover she needed to get to Terminal 3, then booked and paid for a week in a long-term airport car park with her credit card.

A vision of her father driving the Triumph home made her briefly smile, then a curtain of guilt spread over that image.

Finally, she checked on flights. Grant couldn't have already flown—surely not? He'd have had to pack his entire life up for the last few months and sort out a lot of loose ends. She thought of his final letter to her again, now pushed deep into her bag. Wracked with self-doubt, she forced the memory and the words from her mind.

No, he'd definitely be on a flight today. Definitely …

Please God?

Hoping to discover Emirates only offered one flight a day to Sydney, she discovered how wrong she could be. The odds of her being on the same plane as the man she feared she'd lost forever had suddenly grown by a factor of five.

An early flight, at 09.10, then one at lunchtime, and no less than three in the evening.

Best-guessing was all she was left with. If he'd taken a coach down to Heathrow earlier this evening, he was almost certainly holed-up in an economy airport hotel—he'd never have made the last flight with a minimum two-hour check-in time before departure.

The evening flights were unnecessary—why would he hang about all day at an airport, having spent the previous night there? He wouldn't have chosen that. Unless the two daytime flights were either full, or his ticket was restricted in some way.

Tabatha checked all five; spaces still available on every one of them.

It was too much to factor into an already complicated puzzle. She *had* to make assumptions and stick with them. Grant would have gone for the morning or lunchtime flight, and sleeping close to the airport meant making the earlier one would not have been an issue.

She brought up the first flight again and clicked to the next stage, where the price was shown for a one-way ticket.

It had to be a mistake. She'd definitely requested economy, definitely one-way only, definitely the cheapest available fare.

She stared at the price, and her jaw sagged.

'*£3,787*'.

And then she saw the Alert Notice.

'*No Economy Class left – Quoted Price is for a Business Class fare*'

She rubbed the diamond sub-consciously. Even if she was prepared to pay for the ticket, her credit card wasn't. The booking wouldn't go through.

Then the final nail in the coffin—a pop-up menu asking if she was in possession of the relevant visa to travel to Australia. Online applications were welcomed, and Tourist Visas were normally approved within 24 hours.

Even well past midnight, a constant barrage of cars was buffeting the Spitfire. Like New York, Europe's busiest motorway, the M25, never went to sleep.

As the freezing sleet started and she searched for the windscreen wiper switch using her phone's light, Tabatha was aware of how precarious her current position was. With visibility closing in, her flimsy car and any occupant would be wiped off the face of the earth instantly upon impact with any vehicle travelling at motorway speeds.

She pulled out and headed for the car park, not knowing what she would do. At least she was welcome there, a fully-paid up member for the next week.

Safely parked and with the engine silent, the car gently ticked and clacked its way to slumber. There was still welcome heat inside, but this would soon dissipate in these temperatures.

A sign showed her the way to walk for a shuttle bus, and twenty minutes later she was sitting in the vast land-side departure hall of Terminal 3, along with a handful of other individuals and families, presumably keen enough on saving money to ditch a hotel in favour of pulling an airport all-nighter.

Tabatha went back to the Emirates website on her phone and tapped in her requirements again, just in case the fare had miraculously halved or more in price. The visa was something that was so soul-destroying and insurmountable, that she swept it to one side for now.

It was illogical behaviour, and she knew it, but she was desperately tired and was running out of ideas, much as her phone was running out of battery. She pictured the portable battery booster on her bedside table and wanted to weep.

Waking up with a searing pain in her lower back, she stifled a yelp as she attempted to sit upright, glancing at her watch.

03:56.

Fighting a mounting headache to rival the pain in her back, depression was close to enveloping her thoughts. Nearly 4 a.m., the most common hour to die …

She woke her phone to be greeted by the warning, '*Low Battery Power*', the little red battery icon, ominously ungreen-like.

4%.

Knowing she should wander around to find a plug socket and fish the charger out of her backpack, she risked one final check.

The price hadn't changed—of course it hadn't—why would it—to suit her life, perhaps?

'£3,787'.

She stared at the flight details below the impossible price:

LHR 09.10 ~ DURATION 23HRS 30MINS ~ SYD 19.40 (+1 day)
1 connection
flight info here
*advance visa required for Australia'

3% battery remaining.

Why was she delaying the inevitable? Forget the flight—just try and spot him walking through one of a couple of hundred metres of doors, in amongst thousands of fellow travellers. Wasn't that easier, though just as pointless?

She looked at the flight details one last time before moving to somewhere that could allow her to charge the phone.

'*flight info here*'. She pressed her finger on the words:

'*LHR 09.10 ~ DURATION 7HRS 5MINS ~ DXB 19.15*
Connection in Dubai
DXB 22.15 ~ DURATION 13HRS 50MINS ~ SYD 18.05
(+1 day)'

She sat bolt upright.

2% battery remaining.

Her fingers flashed across the screen. New search—same date—same time—same flight—same plane —but … this time, destination *Dubai*.

'£647 ~ one seat left in Economy Class'.

She gasped as her fingers flicked a new page up, and she asked Google if a visa was required for Dubai.

'*An advance visa is not required for travel from the UK to the United Arab Emirates.*'

Scrolling back to the airline website, Tabatha accepted the booking and began the process of giving her details and paying.

She was switching to her email to view the booking confirmation when the phone died. But her luck had turned.

As she wandered the empty hall in search of a socket, Tabatha knew her flight was secure; she could only pray that Grant would be on the same plane.

21

HER SCRATCHY, sleep-deprived eyes had been on stalks when going through security, but the crowds made it impossible. Unless she'd been within a few metres of him, she had little or no chance of seeing Grant.

She wandered through the vast array of duty-free shops, half-wondering if she needed to buy anything, her mind still filled with the anticipation of bumping into him, and the clammy fear of missing him.

And the knowledge that he may very probably be on a later flight.

Why had she bought a one-way ticket? She had to come back, and it would have saved money to buy a return. But it felt like a betrayal—an acceptance that she wasn't going to see him or worse, far worse, that she *would* see him, and he'd reject her.

Realistically, there was little chance of him being in any of the shops—he probably had even less money than her, and every penny would count.

There was a selection of restaurants and bars, but he was in none of them. In near despair, she sat in the main concourse, watching an already attractive and heavily made-up woman receiving even more facial products from an equally glamorous, white-coated attendant.

Perhaps this was what she needed? She dug around in the scruffy bag on her lap, eventually producing a vague excuse for a make-up bag, smeared in places with years-old potions and powders.

Producing a small mirror, Tabatha assessed her face and sighed. With painful honesty, she concluded that here was a desperate woman in her thirties, bags under her eyes from a lack of sleep and a whole lot more besides, and she was dreaming if any very good-looking, single guy, in his mid-twenties, would give her a second look. Even a first glimpse seemed unlikely …

Without contemplating the matter any further, she wandered over to the beauty-stand and sat down in one of the achingly comfortable, leather chairs.

'What'll it be this morning then, darling? A quick once-over or the full monty?'

'How much will it cost to make me look ten years younger, please?'

*

With a few minutes before the flight was due to be called, Tabatha wandered back to her favourite of the many clothes shops, the parka in one arm, unable to be stuffed into her backpack.

Floating around the displays, letting her hand run over the skirts and tops, she realised the perfect companion now—her mother.

In another lifetime, that's who would have been with her now.

Mum? What do I do now? Help—please?

It was the first non-Goth clothes she'd bought in an age.

Mum would have called the floral-themed skirt *'pretty'*, and the colour-coordinated top and jean-jacket *'perfect—just right—just so.'* As for the rather flamboyant, bright pink, Irregular Choice shoes, she wasn't so sure.

Without further thought, she left the parka on a chair in the shop and walked out, catching her reflection in a mirror.

You're right, Mum—better. Thank you.

And then the flight was called again—a final call, this time …

*

Cursing her luck, then realising it was her hopelessness and not the vagaries of chance, she ran to the Gate, unsteadily at first, her feet acclimatising to the new shoes.

Her plan had been to get there before anyone else, then stand by the entrance until Grant walked through, *if* he walked through, then … Well, she wasn't quite sure about the *'then'* part, but she'd think of something.

As it was, there were close to five hundred people ahead of her—a seething mass of passengers waiting to be checked one final time before boarding the biggest flying metal tube the world had so far come up with—the Airbus A380. Peering out of the Gate windows, she wondered why they hadn't called it the Double-Decker A380; she couldn't believe the enormity of the plane. Like most confronted with this sight in the flesh for the first time, she genuinely wondered how it could get off the ground.

'Just your ticket and passport please, Madam.'

For one soul-destroying moment, Tabatha thought she'd left them in her parka, then pulled both out of the top pocket of her new jacket.

'Can you check and tell me if there's a Grant Davis on this flight?'

'I'm afraid that's not possible—unless you can prove to me that it's an emergency, of course.'

'It *is* an emergency, I promise you.'

'And that would involve what, exactly?'

'He's my boyfriend. *Was* my boyfriend … Was *going* to be, I mean. And still is!'

'I'm afraid that can't quite be defined as an emergency. I'm sorry, but I have to get you and the passengers behind you on board as quickly and safely as …'

'*Please.* You don't understand—I'm not explaining myself clearly. I …'

'Madam? If you'd be so kind? We really have a schedule to keep. Perhaps you'll see him on the flight?'

Tabatha sighed.

'Straight through this galley, madam, turn right, and just a few rows down on your left—yours is the aisle seat. Have a lovely flight.'

It was like being in a large auditorium. She sat at the end of a row of three, to her left a bank of four seats in the middle, then another set of three on the far side—ten to each row.

She put her hands on the arms of the seat to lean up and count the number of rows, but her right hand pushed against a hairy, thick, warm, bare arm.

'Oh, I'm sorry.'

She turned and was confronted by a large, middle-aged man, in a type of lumberjack shirt, brown greasy hair combed in classic I'm-not-bald style, and a thick and unruly beard, presumably to make up for the lack of hair above. He was gnawing away at a raised bump of dried, wart-like, skin, on the edge of his palm.

'My fault—seats are a wee bit small for me. I'd have gone biz-class but, you know …'

It was a heavy Australian accent. Looks could always be deceiving, but she didn't see the man forking out £3,787 for a ticket to take him back home.

'Yes. Right. Sorry.'

She narrowed her shoulders and right arm, tucking it as far away from their communal arm-rest as possible. Staring directly into her infotainment screen seemed like the best option.

'Nice ring. Imagine if that was the real thing, eh?'

He chuckled, and Tabatha caught the scent of his breath. It would be a long flight.

'Indeed.'

She swivelled the jewel, so it tucked back into her hand again.

With the seatbelt signs off and the cabin crew beginning the first meal preparations, she took a wander up and down the aisle. If Grant was on this flight, she would find him—she had to, surely?

Tabatha was used to the roving eyes of the occasional man, but something wasn't quite right. She'd had a good fifteen years to get used to this type of attention, and it never really changed. But this was different. Seemingly every male on the plane was openly staring at her, and even a few women too, not all in a friendly way.

It was proving uncomfortable, and she was beginning to feel more than a little self-conscious. A trip to the bathroom and the reflection reminded her of the earlier expenses at the airport. Perhaps this might be more acceptable in Business Class—or First Class?

She chastised herself and returned swiftly to her seat next to the lumberjack.

'The fish please.'

'Certainly, and some wine, Madam?'

Did she want wine? Possibly, yes. Did she *need* wine? Oh, so very absolutely—she really *did* need wine.

'Lovely, thanks—white? The driest you have, please. Can I just ask you something?'

Tabatha was intently aware of the proximity of her near neighbour.

'Could we just go up there—it's ummm ... it's a bit personal.'

'If it's urgent, of course. But if it can wait a little while, I just need to serve everyone lunch—is that okay with you? Then I'll be all yours.'

It was a genuinely lovely smile, and she didn't have the heart to plead with the woman.

'Yes, of course. That's fine.'

After all, what's the rush? It's not as if you can get off the plane. If you're on it ...

She planned what she'd say as she picked at the '*Filet of Lemon Sole bonne femme with capers, shallots, and button mushrooms.*' Okaaay then.

It was probably just her taste buds—they said taste buds suffered at altitude, didn't they? Or perhaps it was because she'd been inhaling entirely through her mouth since the earlier aromatic nostril-assault from her travelling partner.

The very beautiful and increasingly very nervous girl requested a pen and paper when asking for another glass of wine. She knew the answer would be the same when she begged for information about Grant. How could it not be?

But, perhaps, just perhaps, human nature could trump the rules? Just this once?

Can I really write this? Even if I can, will I pass it on? And if I do, will it work?

Of course it won't—I'm mad.

It won't work—no chance.

So what's the harm in trying?

At least try. Or maybe not …

'Do you know how many times a heart can be broken?'

'Nor does anyone, Tabatha.'

'Nor does anyone.'

'Look into my diamond—your diamond—right into the epicentre—right into the heart.'

'Your heart.'

22

'LADIES AND gentlemen, this is your captain speaking. I trust you're all having a pleasant journey and our brilliant cabin crew are taking care of you.

'Just a little mid-flight information for you all. We're travelling at a height of forty-one-thousand feet, and at a ground speed of six-hundred-and-fifty miles-per-hour. Time to our destination of Dubai, in the United Arab Emirates, is approximately four hours and twenty-five minutes, so we're scheduled to arrive at nineteen-hundred hours—a little ahead of schedule. The weather there is a very pleasant twenty-six degrees Celsius.

'If there's anything you require, please press the call button above your seats, and our crew will do everything they can to make your trip as enjoyable as possible.

'I'll be speaking to you again with an update as we near our destination, but for now, I'd just like you to sit back, relax, and enjoy the flight.

'And there is just one other thing I'd like to bring to your attention …

'In an attempt at multi-tasking, I'm very briefly going to become a postman as well as your captain. To that end, I'd like to deliver a message, and this special message is for a Mr Grant Davis.

'If you're in your seat, Grant, can you stand up and make yourself known to everyone around you—give them a little wave. If not, please get back to your seat pronto!'

*

Grant was in his seat—towards the back in the main Economy section, next to the window on the left-hand side of the plane.

He was in the middle of some deep contemplation about the complete disaster his life had become, in the space of the last couple of days. It may be that he would never really get over this. The worst thing? The fact he'd never again see the love of his life—his soul mate.

Even seeing her with another man would be better than *this*. Just to physically see her, even from afar, had to be better than *this*.

She was dead to him, and he was dead to her.

It was the end.

He knew it was a standard waffle by the captain, but he listened nonetheless—it was extraordinary to imagine travelling in this metal bullet high above the earth, at a speed it was difficult to comprehend.

And, even better, it briefly took his mind off the deep depression smothering his mind—and his heart.

*

She couldn't believe it was happening. He was on the plane! Not only that, but the announcement … her face went crimson with a mixture of joy and terror.

The cabin crew girl had seemed optimist about the chances but admitted she'd never personally witnessed it before. There was certainly no harm in trying, though—she'd deliver the note up to the nose of the plane straight away.

And, in some ways, if it wasn't '*an emergency*', it was definitely '*extremely important.*'

Oh, and would Tabatha mind if she retold the whole story to her colleagues because it was '*awesome*' and '*right out there?*'

*

'So, Mr Davis, or Grant, if I may. There are four things for you to take on board if you'll forgive the pun.

'The first two, well, they're a little obscure but I'm sure they'll mean plenty to you. As for the other two, well, I think nearly everyone on this flight will be able to relate.

'So here we go …'

*

Was this some sort of dream? The captain giving him a personal message—for everyone to hear—what the hell? It *was* a dream, though he felt wide awake as he stood, many people turning to look at him, much to his embarrassment. Grant was right at the back of the queue when it came to seeking attention.

*

She was half-sitting, half standing, frantically attempting to scan a couple of hundred seats, ahead, in-line, behind her.

Nothing.

A couple of people returning to their seats and none leaving them—the announcement had everyone intrigued.

He was obviously in another section of the plane, probably ahead of the entrance where she came in. She was about to release her seatbelt and walk up the aisle when something made her turn back. Right on the other side of the plane—much further back than her.

Someone slowly standing; even from this distance, bewilderment etched over his face.

His sweet face.

She stood up.

*

'Grant, this message comes from Tabatha Mercer.'

*

He gasped.

'Oh my God.'

*

She shuddered.

'Oh my God.'

*

Way ahead and the other side of the plane. It couldn't be her.
   It couldn't be.
   Not possible.

*

'First of all, Tabatha lost her phone. She could neither call
you nor see your messages.
   'She is desperately sorry, Grant.'

Half-a-thousand people were riveted in their seats, hanging
on every word.

'Secondly, that huge, expensive, Bentley? Well, that belongs
to Lady Philippa. And the guy driving it and picking Tabatha
up? That'll be her chauffeur, Juan, taking Tabatha back to be
with Philippa.
   'Ladies and gentlemen, intriguing or what? Right?
   'Okay, now here's where everyone gets to join in, I
suspect …'

*

The two people standing up in their seats were holding their
breath. They were, by no means, the only ones.
   Over a distance of ten metres their eyes met and locked,
unblinking.

*

'Number three: Grant, she's loved you since before she first met you for real, and never stopped loving you, though you may not have realised this.

'And for that, Tabatha is really and truly sorry—again.

'And she can prove it, because …'

*

The noise of the gigantic aircraft piercing the sky, and a captain's voice.

A thousand ears tuned.

*

A woman leaves her seat and walks down an aisle. Her eyes never leave the man.

Two people next to the man pull their legs in, and he moves past them to the aisle. His eyes never leave the woman.

They walk to each other, entirely on their own, at last.

*

'Grant Davis, Tabatha knows it isn't February the twenty-ninth or even a Leap Year, but she's wondering if you'd like to marry her.'

*

Oblivious to the instant eruption of noise, they hold each other, properly, for the first time.